Gray Matter Splatter

A Deckard Novel

Jack Murphy

Also by Jack Murphy

The Deckard novels:

Reflexive Fire
Target Deck
Direct Action
Gray Matter Splatter

The PROMIS Series:

PROMIS: Vietnam
PROMIS: Rhodesia
PROMIS: South Africa

Non-Fiction

The Benghazi Report
The ISIS Solution
US Special Forces Weapons Report Card

Printed in the United States of America

http://reflexivefire.com

First Edition

For Benni

Chapter 1
The Russian Arctic

"I'll tell you boys what," the mercenary said with a knowing grin, "it smelled so bad that I almost didn't eat it."

The room exploded with laughter as his fellow mercenaries roared in approval.

"Anyway," he continued, "that's how I got pink eye for the second time."

Spinning turbines hummed outside, the buzz growing louder as the engines flared. It was one of two C-27J transport aircraft owned by Samruk International, a Kazakhstan-based private military company the mercenaries worked for. Outside, the C-27J screamed down the airstrip and lifted off, its passengers successfully delivered to the remote outpost in northern Russia.

The door swung open with a gust of arctic wind that sent playing cards flying off an overturned cardboard box that served as a poker table. In filed a dozen new recruits, big European and American dudes looking to secure their slots on Samruk International's oil security contract with American gas and oil companies in the Arctic.

The mercenaries looked at the new guys with a mixture of curiosity and skepticism. Samruk was a multinational company, split down the middle between Kazakhs and Westerners. Over the last couple of years they had seen action in Afghanistan, Burma, Mexico, and Syria. Killing was their business, and a batch of new guys could prove to be a valuable asset to the team—a team that had taken plenty of casualties over the last few missions. The newcomers could also prove to be incompetent idiots who got their teammates killed.

"Lookit these new jacks," the mercenary with a sense of humor commented. The men shuffled by to their boss's office carrying rucksacks, black roller bags full of tactical gear, and OD green aviator kit bags.

"Welcome to the Thunderdome, assholes."

* * *

"Send the first one in!" Chuck Rochenoire yelled. The former Navy SEAL sat on a folding chair next to the door. Also sitting with their backs to the wall were other leaders within the private military company. Pat, Aghassi, Frank, Nikita, Kurt, and Sergeant Major Korgan sat in on the informal board that would be the final interview for the new recruits. New hires would begin training, and rejects would be sent packing.

The first recruit came through the door and set his bags down. He was tall, with dark hair and a two-day beard.

"It says here you served in Italy's counterterrorism unit?" Pat, a Delta Force veteran, asked.

"Colonel Moschin," the Italian responded with the nickname for his unit. "The 9th."

"You were a member of Task Force 45," Pat said, looking down at the resume in his hands. "Maurizio?"

"Yes. Also deployed to Libya and Sudan."

"You also list military free fall and sniper operations among your qualifications."

Pat grilled him on technical and tactical data for a few more minutes before looking across the room at the CEO of Samruk International. He sat behind a desk with a mug of coffee in one hand and a lit cigarette in the other. He nodded his head.

"Arctic, mountain, or winter warfare training?"

"High-angle sniper courses and mountain warfare courses my unit did with the French."

6

"Welcome to the team," Pat said, shaking Maurizio's hand. "You're on probation for three months, meaning your contract can be cancelled at any time if you fail to perform."

"I won't," the Italian soldier said, clearly happy with their decision.

The next recruit strode in as the Italian departed, and stood in front of the desk.

"Name?" Pat asked.

"Jacob."

The former soldier had the physique of a bull, but his muscle mass was the type built through long, hard endurance exercise and training. His hair was salt and pepper and his hands the size of catchers' mitts.

"Former unit?"

"Jaeger Corps."

"Danish special operations," Aghassi commented. "Were you on Operation Anaconda?"

"Ja, calling in airstrikes for U.S. forces."

"I appreciate that."

"You were there too?" the big Dane turned to look at the former Army intelligence operative.

"I don't remember," Aghassi replied with a smile.

"Six rotations to Afghanistan," Pat said interrupting Aghassi's stroll down memory lane. "It says here you did clandestine intelligence work out of the Danish embassy in what country exactly?

The questions came hard and fast.

"We are specifically interested in your Arctic warfare training," Aghassi announced toward the end of the interview.

"We did plenty," Jacob said. "Cross-training in Greenland with Danish forces and other exercises in Switzerland, Sweden, and Norway."

Pat probed for another few minutes until the CEO waved him away. Another new mercenary to add to the company rolls.

The next recruit walked in wearing a North Face jacket and Danner mountain boots.

"Nate," Pat began. "Served in Force Recon until you guys got absorbed into MARSOC, huh? How did that go?"

"It was a total nut roll," Nate answered. "But we eventually got our shit straightened out."

"Did you go through Derna Bridge?"

"Later, yeah."

"And MTSC?"

"Yeah, to learn the spooky shit."

"How many deployments?"

"Nine, including the Indonesia deal."

"What about Arctic warfare training?"

"I did some of the mountain warfare and cold-weather training at the Mountain Warfare Training Center in California."

The Samruk boss took a sip of his coffee and nodded before stubbing out his cigarette in an ashtray.

"Next!" Rochenoire yelled.

In walked another towering European.

"You served with Norway's FSK?"

"Yeah," the Norwegian guffed.

"Dag, is it? It says here you worked in an intelligence cell for your unit for several years. Tell me about that."

Pat grilled him before asking about his Arctic warfare experience.

Dag laughed. "We get plenty of that. A third of our country is inside the Arctic Circle."

8

The CEO nodded and Dag was sent out to sign his contract with the others.

"Bring in the next—" Chuck's words were cut off as the next recruit floated into the room. He had shed his cold-weather gear once inside, opting for something more comfortable. He wore capri pants and Vibram FiveFingers so that his little toes could stretch out. His shirt had some ironic pop-culture reference on it that the other men were too old to even understand.

"Please tell me you are not American," Pat pleaded.

"Whah-ut? Of course I am," the new guy replied.

"Jesus. Throw me a bone and tell me you were one of those West Coast SEALs or something."

Rocheniore's eyes narrowed.

"I was Special Forces, man."

Pat rested his face in his palm.

"Why are you guys so aggro?"

The boss slammed his coffee mug down on his desk.

"Get the fuck out of my office."

* * *

Washington D.C.

Third time.
Third time.
One more time.

Harold wrung his hands as a smile crossed his face. His eyes lit up, stars dancing around in them as he looked at the white building behind the black iron fence. The path was clear and nothing would stop him this time.

Not like the last two attempts. This time he was going all the way.

Jump!

Harold sprang into action, launching himself at the fence. Filled with excitement, he bounded over the fence with little difficulty and hit the immaculately manicured green grass on the other side.

Success!

On the last two tries he was stopped on the lawn, brought down and tackled to the ground by the bad men. But not this time. This time he was going all the way, all the way to the big white house where the important man lived.

His legs pumped, propelling him across the open lawn like a gazelle. He hadn't been this excited in a long time. All the lawyers and all the judges scolding him like a child, calling him crazy, saying mean things about him. This time he would prove them all wrong.

And he did.

Harold sprinted across the lawn like an Olympic athlete. He had even surprised himself with his speed, struggling to slow down before he plowed right into the side of the white house. His hand wrapped around the brass door knob. He twisted and the door opened.

Finally!

Harold stepped inside. This was the farthest he had ever made it. Now he just had to go and find the important man. Harold had big ideas about economics and social issues to share with him. This was about the future of America! Looking around, he found himself inside an empty room filled with chairs. It looked like it might have been set up for press conferences, with a big podium standing on a stage at the end of the room.

But where was he?

Harold walked out into the hall. Pictures and paintings hung on the white walls. Fresh flowers leaned out of a glass vase sitting on an oak table.

Boring!

Harold went down the hall, opening doors, finding little of interest until he stepped into what looked like a living room. Overstuffed leather chairs were arranged around a table. More paintings hung on the walls. This was where the important man did important things.

A staircase!

Harold smiled. The important man must be upstairs. He walked toward the stairs, his hand caressing the wooden railing as the sole of his shoe landed on the first step. That was when the doors burst open and the bad men in black suits rushed him.

Not again!

Harold screamed as the bad men slammed him to the floor.

* * *

"Hey," Pat said as he stood in the doorway, "what do you think of the new guys?"

"They're good," Deckard said. "Except for that one guy."

"We need all the help we can get with this Arctic warfare business. This is a different ballgame than we're used to."

"I think we ran a pretty good winter warfare course for our guys," Deckard added. "But two weeks isn't enough to understand how to fight in this kind of terrain. The cold and the long distances involved add up to serious issues when it comes to maneuverability." Deckard finished his coffee and looked inside his mug as he set it down.

"You want the boys to brew some more coffee?" Pat asked.

"Good idea."

"How do you like it?"

"The way I like my women."

"Black and strong?" Pat joked.

"Ground up and in the freezer."

"Holy shit," Pat laughed. "It's good to hear you joking again. You've been in the dumps for weeks."

"Fuck you talking about?"

"Come on man, it's obvious to everyone that something is bothering you."

"Shit," Deckard trailed off. "I guess I've been wondering what the hell I've been doing here."

"This oil security contract?"

"No, the whole thing. Our entire careers."

"I know that last one was rough," Pat said, making a statement rather than asking a question.

"If even our own guys are sinking to these depths, then yeah, it makes you wonder what the hell all of this is for," Deckard said, referring to his last mission.

Deckard had gotten on the trail of a very dangerous group of former SEAL Team Six operators known as Liquid Sky. They were cold-blooded killers. Samruk International put them out of business once and for all in the killing fields of Syria six months before. Deckard had recovered from that mission—physically at least.

"You know just as well as I do that those guys were outliers," Pat warned. "Crazies who should have been put out to pasture a long time ago. That's not who we are."

"Then who are we, Pat? We're the guys who spent the last fifteen years landing helicopters on rooftops and

12

shooting dirt farmers in the face, as if that's even that difficult. What the fuck for? It hasn't gotten us anywhere. We haven't made any progress and there is no victory."

"That's bullshit, Deckard, especially in this company. We've gone toe to toe with some evil motherfuckers and walked away from it. Even our own kind when they stepped out of line. I know you didn't expect a ticker tape parade."

"Of course not, but...." Deckard trailed off.

"You of all people should know better, Deckard. With Samruk International, we took no shit. We got right down in the mud with the nastiest people out there and gave them the business. Stop this self-loathing bullshit. You're not a pussy, so don't act like one."

"I'm not throwing in the towel, Pat, it's just that..."

"What?"

"I just don't know."

* * *

Highway 70, Missouri

Jake Reynolds leaned back in his seat, thinking that it was going to be a long night. These types of trips didn't happen too often, but they were the entire purpose for which the 25-year-old former Ranger had been employed. Another nine contractors sat with him in the back of the truck's cargo compartment. They had served in various special operations units. A few of them were still in 19th or 20th Group, the Special Forces National Guard components.

Highway 70 was long and lonely at three in the morning, which was exactly why the convoy was traveling on it. Five blacked-out SUVs surrounded a tractor trailer truck that cruised along just over the speed limit. The Department of Energy vehicles only traveled in the dead of night when transporting highly sensitive cargo. Just behind the convoy, and several hundred feet up in the air, a Little Bird helicopter provided overwatch.

The contractors were locked in the back of the truck with the cargo; the final line of defense. They wore OD green flight suits, body armor, and had HK416 rifles slung around their necks. The reality of their job was that it was boring as hell. For the most part, they spent their days qualifying out on the range until getting the occasional long-distance transport job. Despite the mundane nature of the work, the cargo was so sensitive that the U.S. government hired the best to ensure its safety.

The highway they were on cut straight through the state of Missouri as they drove from one secure DOE facility to the next. The ex-Ranger chugged some more water and sat patiently. It was during times like this he missed the excitement of rolling out on midnight raids with 2nd Ranger Battalion.

There was no way he could have known that tonight would be hairiest mission of his career.

Jake was rocked back in his seat as the entire vehicle shook, his rifle swinging up and smacking him in the face, opening a ragged cut above his eyebrow.

Outside, the entire highway split into pieces and rose up into the air. The two SUVs in the lead floated into the night like Matchbox cars, turning sideways and then upside down before gravity could inevitably bring them back down to the ground. The tractor trailer driver slammed on the brakes, then jerked the wheel in a desperate attempt to prevent the truck from jackknifing.

Several more improvised explosive devices were detonated, taking out two more SUVs. The remaining escort vehicle slid to a stop as the first two, which had been propelled into the air, crashed back down in a rain of debris. The doors on the surviving SUV were flung open, and more contractors in OD flight suits jumped out just as a linear ambush along the side of the road initiated with fully automatic fire.

The pilot of the Little Bird pulled hard on the stick, bringing the agile little helicopter back around on the convoy. The two contractors riding on the external pods attached to the side of the Little Bird spotted the muzzle flashes coming from the treeline, but they could not identify any white-hot thermal signatures on their forward-looking infrared systems.

The pilot clicked his mic to transmit over their secure communications net.

"Prairie Fire! I say again, Prairie Fire!"

The distress code was the final word the pilot was able to get out before a SA-7 surface-to-air missile slammed into the side of the helicopter. The Little Bird was knocked out of the air and crashed into the forest on the opposite side of the highway in a brilliant ball of red and yellow fire.

In the back of the tractor trailer, Jake wiped at his forehead and tried to blink blood out of his eyes. As he reached down and undid his seat belt, he realized that he couldn't hear anything. His ears were ringing, but he wasn't sure why.

The other contractors were coughing and struggling with their seat belts. A few of them fell out of their seats as they tried to stand. Jake struggled to his feet and jacked a round into the chamber of his HK rifle.

Over the ringing in his ears, he could now make out the staccato bursts of gunfire from outside. Rounds were thudding into the side of the truck. Thankfully, the armored cargo compartment kept them safe, at least for the time being.

Their team leader, a retired sergeant major, was already barking orders as the other contractors racked rounds into the chambers of their rifles. He was pointing to the door at the end of the compartment.

Even though he couldn't hear him, the message was clear to Jake.

They were the last line of defense.

* * *

Deckard set down his second cup of coffee and opened a laptop computer. The reality of running a private military company was that there was a lot of boring logistics planning to be done. Samruk International had expended a lot of human and financial capital lately. He had been reduced to selling off two of the company's mammoth An-125 cargo jets. Now they only had the one An-125 and two C-27Js left in their aviation wing. At least the C-27s had been bought dirt cheap. The U.S. Air Force decided they didn't want them anymore after wasting millions of taxpayer dollars to build the aircraft.

They had taken the oil security contract in the Arctic to keep the revenue coming in. Maintaining a small private army wasn't cheap, and this wasn't the way most companies did business; usually they just hired independent contractors from job to job. Deckard was instead running a de facto military unit, and he wanted to keep his team intact.

However, as it turned out, there could be many interesting tasks rolled up under an oil security contract. Not only could those tasks include static security around offshore oil rigs, they could also involve training other security personnel, and maybe even killing off those who would threaten the business interests of said oil companies —threats like the Russian mafia, who had recently been acting like Arctic pirates.

Deckard's office door swung open again. Rochenoire looked at him with a grin.

"We got the green light," the former SEAL announced.

"No shit?"

"No shit."

"Everything is prepped and pre-staged, correct?"

"You know it."

Now it was Deckard's turn to smile.

"Spin the boys up."

The giant black man turned around in the doorway.

"Drop cocks, grab socks. It's a go!"

Deckard flung open his gear bag and began donning his kit. The first layer was thermal clothing, over which went a cold-weather shirt, followed by a bare plate carrier, and then his parka. Over his clothes he wore the new Samruk uniform for their Arctic contract: a winter camouflage pattern made by PenCott called SnowDrift. Finally, a chest rig loaded with ammunition and grenades went over his chest. Picking up his AK-103 rifle, Deckard walked out into the the warehouse.

About 80 mercenaries were going through the same routine, kitting up for combat. The mission had been planned and re-planned for weeks. They were just waiting on approval from the Russian government. Mob ties ran deep in the halls of power, and getting the political ducks in a row took some time. At the end of the day it was all about business, and the pirates were costing both the government and private industry millions of dollars in extortion fees. Someone had finally gotten fed up.

Using a private military company that had a Kazakh face rather than an American one made the job more politically acceptable, and kept the Russian military out of the firing line when things went pear-shaped, which, of course, they always did.

"What about the new guys?" Kurt Jager asked as he spotted Deckard walking out of the office. The former GSG-9 commando spoke perfect English, leaving no hint of his German nationality.

"Take them along. It will be on-the-job training. Keep them with the security elements so they can observe how we do things without getting them overly involved on their first op."

"Got it."

Deckard slung his rifle and pulled a white watch cap over his head. Pushing open the door, he pulled his hood up as well. The sunlight stung his eyes. As outlined in the stipulations of their contract, Samruk International was based out of an unused warehouse leased to house oil-drilling equipment, and the occasional private army.

The wind swept snow across the desolate coastline, the cold already stinging Deckard's cheeks. By the end of this deployment he knew they would all be sporting lumberjack beards just to try to keep themselves a little bit warmer.

A few hundred meters away was their new ride. It was a monstrosity of a ship, a chimera that never should have existed, but did thanks to a failed U.S. Navy and Marine Corps experiment gone awry. But just like the C-27J airplane, Deckard saw an opportunity to purchase some hardware that fit his needs at bargain basement prices.

Renamed the Carrickfergus, the ship was one of a kind. Sharing the characteristics of both a barge and a catamaran, the ship rested on two massive pontoons, with the bridge of the ship, housing the captain's control center, joining the double-hulled design. On top of each hull were two passenger compartments.

It was big, it was blue, it was ugly, and it wasn't even that fast.

But it was an icebreaker with a cargo deck that lowered from the center and accommodated beach landings. During travel, the deck would be raised, then lowered again along with a ramp when the vehicles onboard were ready to drive up onto the shore. Currently, the deck was lowered and waiting to take on the passengers. Under tarps were eight Iveco assault vehicles, six snowmobiles, a few kayaks, two Zodiac boats, and a small Conex container filled with ammunition.

"Let's go!" Frank yelled, ushering the mercenaries out the door. The former Ranger was about as wide as he was tall and had been with the company since the beginning.

The Kazakh mercenaries were led out in an orderly fashion by one of the two platoon sergeants, a man named Fedorchenko. He had started with Samruk as a corporal after being recruited from a Kazakh special police unit. Since that time he had more than proved his mettle. He had been leading a platoon since Mexico and had done an outstanding job.

Integrated into the platoons of Kazakhs were Westerners from units as diverse as the Polish GROM and the French Foreign Legion. Initially, they had been the trainers and mentors, but now they were assaulters fighting alongside their former students who were every bit as good as they were.

The mercenaries boarded the Carrickfergus and began climbing up to the passenger compartments. Inside, the seats had been torn out and the space converted for military purposes. Gear and weapons were everywhere; white boards with task lists scribbled on them were hung on the walls; and the soldiers' individual equipment, bags, and boxes of military rations were neatly stacked on plywood shelves they had constructed. The ship was set up not just as a means of transportation, but also to act as a mobile staging ground.

The Carrickfergus was designed to accommodate 130 passengers. There was enough room for two platoons of mercenaries, plus Samruk's intelligence, mortar, recce, and headquarters sections, but it was still cramped inside. Deckard walked up the ramp and climbed up the ladder to the bridge as the captain began raising the deck, preparing to get underway.

The ship was a hulking beast at 59 meters long, and looked like it had been cobbled together from the leftover parts of other ships. As Deckard reached the bridge, the twin motors that powered the hydraulic system for lifting the deck switched off as it was locked into place. Walking inside the bridge, he was confronted by a dizzying array of dials and instruments on several consoles.

The old salt who captained the Carrickfergus stood behind the helm. He wore a battered old sweater, out from which his beer belly swelled, revealing a stained white T-shirt underneath. His beard was almost fully gray and his shoes were a beat-up pair of loafers.

"Hey Deck!" he exclaimed. "Glad you could make it."

"Thanks Otter."

They had been calling the captain by his sea name long enough that no one really remembered what the real name on his file was anymore.

"Time to go kill some commies, huh?"

"Organized criminals," Deckard carefully corrected.

"Same difference," Otter said as he grabbed the wheel with one hand. In the other was a coffee mug that looked like it hadn't been washed in years. Unlike Deckard's coffee, Otter's was always spiked with something a little more fun.

"Can you get us to the beach landing zone without killing us?"

"We'll find out," the captain chuckled.

The four diesel-fueled engines churned and the Carrickfergus began reversing out into the icy waters. This close to shore, there wasn't much ice to cut through, but they would still be traveling relatively slowly. The ship's top speed was only 20 knots. By comparison, most commercial shipping vessels traveled at 25 knots, although many of them deliberately slowed to 20 to keep fuel consumption down.

Deckard swept his gaze across the ocean and was greeted with a sight that would have been impossible just a few years ago. A half dozen commercial cargo ships, loaded with Conex containers or sitting low in the water because they were filled with oil, could be seen in the Arctic with the naked eye.

With polar ice melting, a new trans-Arctic sea route had been opened. The opening of the northeast passage in the spring and summer months in Russia was already saving European companies billions of dollars and cutting days off their shipping times to Asia. Ice cutters were now sailed through the northeast passage all year long to keep the routes open.

The opening of the northwest passage in northern Canada was having a similar effect on commercial shipping. More than that, the melting ice was also opening up the region to other commercial ventures. From oil drilling to the mining of rare earth minerals, the Arctic Circle was now ripe for the taking.

But with that came Arctic sovereignty disputes, and the further militarization of the Arctic as great powers like Russia and the United States eyed each other from across their frozen shores. Of course, with the advent of commercial interests in the Arctic, along came crime. That was what brought Samruk International to the Arctic in the first place.

Oddly enough, what really shifted commercial maritime traffic up into the Arctic was ISIS. Once the jihadis had launched terrorist operations around the Suez Canal, sinking several ships, the insurance premiums for ships traveling through the canal skyrocketed. A few months before, terrorists had detonated a SMVIED—a suicide merchant vessel improvised explosive device, an entire commercial ship packed with explosives—in the canal. Churning through the Arctic was cheaper in more ways than one. The result was a push of maritime traffic between Europe, Asia, Africa, and Australia up into the Arctic in order to avoid the turbulent Middle East.

Looking through the window to the deck below, Deckard could already see the mercenaries throwing the tarps off their vehicles and mounting PKM machine guns in swing-arm mounts.

"How long?"

Otter snorted. "I'll get you there by EENT," he said, referring to end of evening nautical twilight.

He could have just said at dusk, but the U.S. Navy has a way of institutionalizing sailors.

Deckard ran the numbers in his head.

"It's almost too good to be true."

* * *

Croatia

Seventy Special Forces commandos assembled at the tarmac, kitted up for war.

A C-17 waited for them in the distance, bathed in the airfield's blue lights. The turbine engines hummed as the pilots went through their pre-flight check list as quickly as possible.

"Gather around," Major Thomas shouted. "We'll do this right here."

The C/1/10 CIF commander had gotten the orders just an hour before, but the Commanders In-extremis Force was designed for no-notice deployments. The Green Berets belonged to a specialized direct-action company within 10th Special Forces Group. While Special Forces soldiers specialized in training foreign troops and conducting unconventional warfare, the CIF's sole purpose was counterterrorism.

"You've probably figured out by now that our mission, training the Croatian counterterrorism unit, is on hold until further notice. The latest reports out of Nairobi indicate the U.S. embassy is under siege. At least half of the compound is now in enemy hands. Intel is shit, but what else is new? No one knows if it is al-Shabaab, al-Hijra, or someone new to the game. The Kenyan government has already cleared the way for us to drive straight to the embassy grounds after we hit the ground. We'll clear the exterior of the embassy and secure the area. Flight time is seven hours, and the boys from Bragg should be just an hour behind us."

The MultiCam-clad Special Forces soldiers understood the mission immediately. They had trained for It countless times, but had never gotten the call.

Until now.

Once they secured the perimeter of the embassy, Delta Force would breach the buildings and conduct the hostage rescue mission.

"Size, strength, and disposition of enemy forces?" one of the cell leaders asked.

"We're expecting close to a hundred crows," the major said, using their internal code word for enemy combatants. "Expect them to be armed with AK-47s, RPGs, and PKMs. Remember that the bad guys in this AO have a history of using suicide vests. The IED threat is assessed as high. Diplomatic Security Services and the contractors pulling static security were quickly overwhelmed, so that should tell you something. CNN is reporting small arms fire and several explosions."

"CNN is reporting?" one of the weapons sergeants asked.

"You know the deal," the CIF commander replied. "We're going in blind to act as the eyes and ears for the main effort."

"Roger that."

The major looked down at his watch.

"We're wheels-up in fifteen. You know what to do."

The CIF team members turned around and jogged over to the aircraft. Their plate carriers bounced slightly with each step. Getting closer, they pulled on their Peltor headsets and snapped OpsCore helmets over their heads. They had already received their basic load of ammunition and explosives. The gun trucks were tied down inside the plane with ratchet straps, ready to roll off the ramp the second they hit the ground in Africa.

As the CIF team sat down in the red fabric seats lining the inner fuselage of the C-17, Major Thomas went over to the loadie. The flight crew member wore a khaki flight suit and helmet with a long, black wire linking his headset to the aircraft's comms system.

"We're up!" the commander yelled over the whining engines.

The loadie nodded and clicked on his mic, saying a few words to the pilots. The flight crew then walked down the ramp and began flipping up the two flaps that reached down from the ramp to the tarmac.

Major Thomas took an empty seat next to the rear of the aircraft and buckled himself in. His executive officer was sitting next to him and immediately started asking more questions about the mission.

"Hey, what the fuck?" the the loadie yelled, his voice drowned out by the engines.

A black-clad man suddenly scrambled up the ramp of the aircraft and into the interior.

Major Thomas looked up at the interloper with a frown. He held something in his hand.

"ALLLAAAAHHUU AKBAAAR!"

* * *

The president looked away from the screen as a half dozen Secret Service agents burst into the war room and slammed the door shut behind them.

"We have a situation, Mr. President," one of them announced.

"What the hell is going on?"

25

"Sir," one of his aides said, trying to get his attention. "We need—"

"Perimeter breach," one of the agents said.

"Where is—"

"Sir!" the aide screamed. "We need your authorization!"

The president swung around angrily to face the aide.

"Sir, F16s are on station."

The president looked up at the black-and-white image displayed on the screen at the end of the room. It showed a tractor trailer stopped in the middle of a highway. White thermal images surrounded the truck and a bright glow came from the rear doors. Apparently, someone was trying to burn their way inside with a blowtorch.

"Do it," the president ordered. "Now someone tell me why we are on lockdown."

An officer sitting at the other end of the table, wearing a blue Air Force dress uniform, picked up a phone and relayed the president's authorization.

"The situation is still developing, Mr. President," one of the Secret Service men said. "We were told that someone breached the White House."

"Another fence jumper? Are you fucking kidding me?"

The president had deep lines around the corners of his eyes and a lot more gray hair than when he had taken office seven years prior. An administration plagued with scandals and an indecisive Congress could do that to any president.

Another phone rang, and the president's aide picked it up.

"The suspect has already been apprehended, sir, but we can't take any chances."

"This is the third time this month," the president complained. "What the hell is the problem with—"

All eyes in the room suddenly shot back toward the screen. The tractor trailer disappeared in a massive gray cloud. The 2,000-pound Joint Direct Attack Munition vaporized the truck, and everyone except the Secret Service agents knew that 10 good men had been vaporized with it. It was all part of the protocol, but that didn't make it any easier.

"It will be reported as an eighteen-car pile-up in the news tomorrow," a Department of Homeland Security representative said, breaking the silence. "We'll say a chemical spill was involved to explain the clean-up crews."

"Jesus," the president said under his breath.

"The truth is that this section of Highway 70 will be unusable for decades. The JDAM will have spread radioactive material for several kilometers. Destroying it like this creates an even bigger radioactive mess than an actual detonation," the DHS rep said ominously.

"We just got hit in Croatia," an Army general said as he slammed down his phone. "The entire CIF team got taken out on an airfield in Zagreb."

"What happened?"

"We don't know yet."

The aide sitting next to the president set down his phone softly.

"Mr. President, a situation is developing in the Arctic."

"I don't think we have time for that right now."

"I agree," the aide said, leaning on his chair closer to the president. "Sir, it is now very clear."

"What's that?" the president asked, his eyes still fixated on the smoking hole in the middle of Highway 70.

"Someone just declared war on America."

"Who?"
"We don't know."

Chapter 2
Russian Arctic

The Carrickfergus reversed its engines, churning up a froth of freezing water as the icebreaker ship inched up to the coastline. The deck was already lowered down to sea level and the ramp dropped down to the beach. Eight Iveco assault trucks rolled off the ship in four-wheel drive and sped up the beach, scattering a trio of walruses. The creatures wiggled off like giant, obese inchworms and slipped into the ocean.

Two snowmobiles rolled off the ship behind the trucks and took off on their own infiltration route. The sniper section had to get into place prior to the assault force, both to provide eyes on the objective as well as to conduct precision fire once the shooting began.

Twilight bathed the surrounding snowy landscape in hues of blue, only interrupted by crags of rocks poking up through the surface like the scaly back of a lizard. This time of year the Arctic Circle got about 12 hours of daylight followed by 12 hours of night.

Deckard stood on the back of one of the assault trucks, watching the others struggle on the snow and ice, slipping and sliding, before they reached an unimproved road a hundred meters from the shore. The Samruk assault vehicles were built on Iveco LMV chassis, but from there had been modified to the company's specifications. Behind the armored compartment where the driver and passenger sat was a gun ring, a rotating turret where a PKM machine gunner was located. In the back of the truck were eight seats facing back to back, four on each side. There were also swing arms that mounted two additional PKM machine guns for the assaulters to use in transit.

Despite winterizing the engines and buying all-terrain tires for the assault trucks, it was evident that the vehicles simply were not designed for arctic conditions. They had to make do with what they had. It may have worked like a charm when they were in Burma, but the assaulters would be freezing in the back as they were exposed to the elements. Once they were on the road, it wasn't long before everyone started tucking their turtle head into their shell, pulling up hoods and drawing them tight.

"We're en route," Deckard said, clicking his hand mic and talking over the command net on his radio. "See you at the exfil point."

"Have fun," Otter radioed back from the helm.

The Carrickfergus shoved off and began turning around as the assault trucks moved toward their objective. Deckard hunkered down in his seat with the other mercenaries. He wiggled his toes and fingers, trying to keep them warm. The Arctic itself was their biggest obstacle, not the enemy forces. If they were all frozen half to death by the time they got to the pirates, they would be useless.

The trucks were still slipping on the ice, and it was only a few minutes before one slid right off the road and into a snowdrift.

Sergeant Major Korgan began barking orders over the assault net, and another vehicle pulled up alongside the one trapped in the snow. Mercenaries leapt off the back of the two trucks and quickly began unrolling tow cables that were tied to the front and rear bumpers of each truck. They secured one cable from the front of the disabled vehicle to the other and quickly towed it out of the snow. The entire drill had been rehearsed hundreds of times. The training paid off, and they were back on the road in a few minutes.

Then it happened again. This time it was Deckard's truck. The driver lost control and the vehicle began sliding sideways on the ice. All four tires rested on a large patch of ice and couldn't find any traction. They spun out until the smell of burning rubber wafted through the air.

"Stop, stop," Deckard yelled at the driver.

Jumping off the truck, he immediately slipped and busted his ass, his AK clanking on the ice under him. The other mercenaries were holding on to the side of the truck as they slipped around, trying to free the tow cable. Eventually they got it attached to the next vehicle, which towed them off the ice. Then the towing vehicle got stuck and had to be towed out itself.

Chuck Rochenoire shook his head as the truck's wheels spun on the ice.

"At this rate we might as well just daisy chain every vehicle together with tow cables."

Deckard keyed his radio. "Shooter-One, this is Six," he said, radioing Nikita, who led their sniper team.

"This is Shooter-One."

"I think this is going to take a while."

"We should have eyes on in five mikes."

Deckard looked at the horizon as the last hints of sunlight disappeared. The wind howled across the road, carrying gusts of snow with it.

"Shit."

* * *

The Samruk International assault element arrived three hours late. The batteries in two of the trucks had actually died due to the freezing conditions, and the vehicles had to be towed the rest of the way. The remaining vehicles switched from running on gasoline to electric, making their final approach nearly silent. Perhaps the most disconcerting aspect of the Arctic wasn't the long periods of darkness or the desolate landscape, but how quiet it was. There wasn't much human presence to be found on the tundra.

The delay had provided the sniper element with extra time, which they spent building a proper sniper hide. At this point they were willing to do anything to keep moving and keep warm. The snowmobiles were stashed a few hundred meters back under white camouflage nets. From there, the four snipers split up into two teams to cover different angles of the objective.

Nikita shivered next to his sniper partner as he tried to pull his watch cap down farther on his head. Finding a small ridge at the outskirts of the village, Nikita and his Kazakh sniper partner had tunneled through the top layer of snow, hollowing out a small belly hide. Then they had carefully poked two small holes through the layer of snow facing the village, giving them a loophole to shoot through.

Nikita's radio crackled in the earpiece he wore.

"GPS says we are a few minutes out," Deckard reported.

"Minimal movement here. One guard on the roof of building three and a few people passing between buildings three and two." During the planning sessions, each building in the village had been designated with a number. Like everyone else on this mission, Nikita wore a clear plastic sleeve on his wrist showing an overhead map of the village with the corresponding numbers over each structure. "Correction," Nikita transmitted back to Deckard as he watched through the 10-power Nightforce scope on his HK417 rifle. "Another guard just came up on the roof."

"Standby."

The two guards stood on top of the only three-story building in the village, which had once been used to house oil workers during the Soviet era. In the barren no-man's land that was the Russian Arctic, the structures had been occupied by the mafia. They ran a refueling station a half kilometer away at the coast where passing ships would fill up. They also charged exuberant "taxes," which had only become more costly as the oil industry began drilling in the Arctic. It was a typical extortion racket, one backed up by coercion, and on a few occasions, physical violence. The Russians lit up their cigarettes but said few words to each other. Like the mercenaries, the Russian gangsters were primarily concerned with staying warm.

Nikita ranged them at 300 meters away and checked the windage and elevation settings on his scope again. The harsh environmental conditions even impacted the trajectory of a sniper's bullet. Nikita was lucky to have been able to re-zero his HK417 out behind their compound once they had arrived in the Arctic. In warmer climates, a bullet would travel faster, but the freezing cold air in the Arctic was denser, meaning that his rounds would travel slower and drop faster.

At 300 meters, the conditions would only throw his shot off about an inch, but the effect would only become more exaggerated when he had to fire at targets farther out.

"We're in position," Deckard announced over the radio. "Shooter-One, do you see that dead guy standing up on the roof, puffing on a cigarette?"

"Roger."

"Kill him and the other dead guy standing next to him. We'll initiate on you."

"Copy," Nikita said as he settled into position. "Ready?"

"Da," Aslan, his sniper partner, responded.

Nikita lined the crosshairs of his reticle on the guard as he stubbed out his cigarette. Slowly exhaling, the sniper squeezed the trigger. The suppressed shot still let out an audible *crack*. Aslan was a fraction of a second behind him, their shots almost sounding as one.

Nikita watched through his scope and saw the guard crumple and fall as the shot impacted his chest. The second guard also disappeared from view.

It was on.

* * *

Nikita's team dropping the guards on the roof signaled the assault.

Sixty-four Samruk mercenaries advanced across the snow, their PenCott camouflage almost unnecessary due to the pitch-black night sky. The snow slowed the advance somewhat, but each team member wore assault snowshoes. They were small plastic snowshoes that allowed greater mobility and gave them some much-needed extra traction where the snow grew deep. The attack angle had been chosen deliberately so that they were assaulting down a slight decline in the terrain, speeding up their movement as the mercs closed on the pirate enclave.

Hearing the muffled crack of gunshots, several more Russian mobsters emerged from building three. Through the PVS-14 night vision goggles he wore,

Deckard could see that they were wearing thick winter parkas and carrying AK-47 rifles.

The second sniper team made short work of them. The first shot took one of the Russians down immediately. The second shot left the sniper's target limping, but then he keeled over and expired on the frozen ground.

Deckard could now see the steam from his breath fogging up the PVS-14 night-vision tube. He wiped it off with a finger as they closed within 25 meters of the nearest structure. Most of them were just old wooden shanties, and not expected to be occupied. It was only building three that had any electricity, as proven by the lights in the windows.

As they reached the first wooden building, a five-man assault element entered the open door and cleared it. Now they could hear shouts from Russian voices in the distance. The enemy knew that something was going down.

When the first of the Russian pirates stepped out of building three, the base of fire opened up. PKM machine guns roared with a cyclic rate of fire that slung angry hornets through their front door. Belts of 7.62x54 ammunition were eaten up by the guns, which had been dismounted from the assault trucks and laid down where they could overwatch the objective area. Green tracers streaked through the night like something out of a *Star Wars* movie, keeping the enemy fixed inside the building while the assaulters cleared their way through the village.

Flashbangs were tossed into the other wooden buildings as the Samruk mercenaries entered and cleared the structures. Deckard jumped into the stack and gave the last man lined up outside the door a squeeze on the shoulder, letting him know they were ready. The six men flowed inside the building, their AK muzzles sweeping for targets. Empty.

Back outside, muzzle flashes were coming from inside building three, the automatic fire sending shards of glass glittering to the ground, captured in the green tint of Samruk's night vision goggles.

A two-man team from the anti-tank section loaded up an 84mm high-explosive dual-purpose round into their Carl Gustav recoilless rifle. The blast interrupted the flow of the entire firefight, shaking the ground under Deckard's feet. The shot rocketed into a window where muzzle flashes had been spotted and detonated inside with enough force to shake the foundation of the building.

The sniper teams were engaging targets of opportunity, but by now the sounds of their gunshots were drowned out by all of the other shooting in the village.

"Hit building three," Fedorchenko ordered his men over the radio. "Get in there!"

Deckard reached down and clicked his mic. As commander, it was his job to hold his guys back when they got too aggressive. He had to make sure he set the conditions for success before his men blindly charged into something they didn't know how to get out of.

"Negative," he said, stopping their assault. "Wait a second. Have AT prep the target for another minute."

The Gustav gunner went to work, hosing down the building with five more rounds, the blasts echoing through the night. Yellow explosions flashed from inside the building when the rounds made it through a window.

"Winchester on rounds, boss," the AT section leader reported. He was a 1st Ranger Battalion veteran named Marty and had trained his Kazakh Goose gunner damn well.

"Hit it," Deckard ordered.

The assaulters sprinted from building five over to building three and immediately charged through the door.

Within seconds, over 30 assaulters had made it through the breach. They had been trained to conduct free-flow close-quarter battle, a method of room clearing that emphasized speed without fixating on team integrity as they moved from room to room.

"Objectives secured," Fedorchenko radioed in over the assault net. "Back-clearing now."

"Shooter-One," Deckard called to Nikita, "collapse down to our position."

"Roger."

Deckard walked into building three, finding expended shell casings all over the floor. As he walked from room to room he counted 20 bodies. They had been living in makeshift conditions, sleeping on cots with space heaters and lots of blankets. These guys were just the Russian mob's foot soldiers. Petty enforcers who pulled Sheriff of Nottingham shit on passing commercial vessels.

The job was done.

There was no need to search through pockets and look for documents that could provide intelligence value. They had been assigned to wipe this target off the Sputnik map, and that is exactly what they did. Russian law enforcement would move in once morning rolled around and take credit for the operation. Yet, he saw that one member of the team couldn't help himself.

"What do you got there?" Deckard asked Aghassi as he was walking out with a black trash bag loaded down with something.

"Found a few laptops."

"You need something to play Minecraft on?"

"You never know," he said with a shrug.

Aghassi was one of the best in the business when it came to tactical and targeting intelligence. He had previously served in JSOC's ultra-secretive Intelligence

Support Activity, conducting operations all over the world that would remain classified for the rest of their lives.

"Have Cody look at it when we gets back to the ship and let me know If there is anything interesting on the hard drives," Deckard said, referring to the hacker whom Samruk employed.

"I will," Aghassi said before disappearing out into the night.

The assault element began a controlled withdrawal from the objective and started moving back to the assault trucks, leaving nothing behind except dead bodies and expended brass.

Deckard followed closely behind. He cursed as his night vision goggles blinked off. Despite turning the on/off switch back and forth, the PVS-14 refused to fire back up. Its AA batteries had frozen in the cold. He made a note for the after-action review; they would have to keep spare sets of batteries inside pockets near their skin to keep them warm so they would always be ready to swap out.

As he walked, Deckard realized he hadn't fired a single shot during the entire mission. Maybe he was finally taking Pat's advice and becoming a leader instead of just another trigger-puller. It felt like things were finally coming together, but in his experience, that was usually when he got the rug pulled out from under his feet.

The special operations veteran let out a sigh as the trucks came into view. It was going to be a long ride back to the Carrickfergus.

Chapter 3

"Deckard."

"Huh?"

Deckard rubbed crust out of his eyes as he sat up on his cot. After getting back on the Carrickfergus, he had slept like a rock, the ship's purring engines putting him out for hours.

"We've got a problem," Frank said. "Come up to the bridge."

"Shit, what is it now?" Deckard rolled off the cot and slid into his Merrill combat boots.

"You're not going to believe this shit. C'mon."

Deckard followed Frank out of the passenger compartment where the rest of the mercenaries were sleeping. Only a few remained awake, playing video games or watching movies on portable DVD players. The post-mission hot wash had been just as ugly as the actions on the objective. They were a soup sandwich out there and they knew. The entire team was embarrassed by their vehicle issues and now realized just how dramatically they would have to adapt to the environment. Now they were sleeping it off. Tomorrow was another day.

Climbing a few flights of metal stairs, they arrived at the bridge. Otter looked at them with a worried expression Deckard had never seen before.

"They burned it," the captain said.

Deckard was about to ask what the hell he was talking about when he looked out the window. Orange flames raged in the distance, illuminating the ocean and sparkling off floating ice bobbing up and down in the sea.

"Is that—"

"Yeah," Otter replied. "That's our joint."

Samruk's ad hoc operations center lent to them by the oil company had been set on fire. Thankfully, most of their combat equipment and supplies were on the Carrickfergus, as Deckard intended for the ship to act as a floating forward operating base more or less independent of any other logistical support structure.

"I think this is far enough," Otter said as he eased down the throttle.

"You're right," Deckard said. "Whoever it was might have mined the waters around the building."

"What did we leave behind in there?" Frank asked.

"Four assault trucks that we brought with us as spares since there wasn't room on the ship," Deckard answered.

"Not that they are worth a fuck out here anyway," someone said.

Deckard turned toward the voice. Kurt Jager leaned against the back wall with his arms crossed.

"I'm going to have to call our paymasters and find out what is going on. This is a hell of a way to cancel our contract."

The Iridium satellite phone Velcroed to the console started to ring. Deckard saw that the number belonged to the head of security for Xyphon Industries, the American oil company that had hired them to protect their personnel and assets in the Russian Arctic. Apparently, they had the same idea. He picked up on the third ring.

"Hey Eliot, this is Deckard."

"Got a minute?" the security executive asked.

"I'm watching the building you lent us burn to the ground right now."

"You're what? What the fuck is going on out there? I thought you guys were doing that job that I asked you never to speak to me about."

"Yeah, we did that job that we aren't going to talk about just fine but now we're arriving back in time for hot sandwiches and we've discovered that we are homeless vagabonds. I just hope that we're not unemployed homeless vagabonds, because I'm trying to run a jobs-for-vets program over here."

"No, no, no. Listen, I was going to call you and bring you up to date. Things are blowing up over here at corporate."

"Yeah, here too it seems."

"I don't know what the hell is going on but the Russians are going apeshit."

Deckard appreciated the vernacular, Eliot being a former Marine who had heard of Deckard through the old-boy network, but he wasn't feeling any more illuminated about their current situation.

"Talk to me."

"My contacts in the Russian government are saying that they got hit. They are telling me that it was Site 17 in the Ural Mountains. Supposedly a highly secure facility. We were thinking it was separatists from Chechnya or Dagestan, but something is going on. The Russians are scrambling forces into the Arctic."

"Who the hell tries to make a getaway into the Arctic Circle?"

"Think of all the commercial shipping lanes opening in the Arctic. That's the whole reason why we sent you guys up there. No one is really telling us what is happening and I'm beginning to think that not many people in the Russian government know in the first place."

"And they burned my place on their way out? What for?"

"Maybe they were expecting you guys to be there."

Deckard let that sink in for a moment.

"Listen," Eliot continued. "Just lay low for a few hours until I can sort things out on my end. We'll divert you to another one of our company's stations up there once we figure out what is going on. You should know that the Russians have Navy icebreakers and fighter jets sweeping the entire region, presumably looking for whoever hit their base in the Urals."

Otter looked down at the computer screen, which displayed the ship's Automatic Identification System, or AIS. AIS was a VHS responder and transmitter that displayed the call sign, heading, and speed of commercial vessels in the area. After seeing which commercial vessels were in the area, Otter then turned his attention to the radar display.

"Yup, look at that," he said. "AIS is showing a dozen commercial ships just within a few miles, and radar is picking up a few more ships not displaying any AIS information. That must be the Russian Navy."

"Any idea who they are after?" Deckard asked.

"It looks like they are trying to intercept a couple of these call signs," Otter said, pointing to the AIS screen.

Deckard picked up a set of binoculars, knowing that he was going to have a hard time spotting anything at night.

"Deckard," Eliot's voice came from the Iridium phone. "You still there?"

"Hold on. I think—"

Suddenly, a burst of yellow flashed on the horizon.

"Oh shit," Otter grunted.

A second flash came a few kilometers away from the first, and a little farther out. Then a third. Otter reached over and grabbed the binoculars from Deckard.

"Fire boat," he said after examining the burning fires in the distance. "They go back all the way to ancient Greece."

"Loading a ship with explosives and then using deception to lure in an enemy vessel," Deckard thought aloud.

"And then they both go *kablooey*," Otter finished. "They just used decoys to take out the Russian Navy."

Otter was right about the fire boats, even if the modern term used was SMVIED.

"Deckard," Frank whispered. "This isn't some half-assed Chechen terrorist action. This is an act of war."

"Eliot," Deckard said, picking up the phone. "I think we're in deep shit."

"Tell me about it. Turn on the television. Any channel will do."

Kurt reached up and turned on the satellite television mounted in the corner of the helm. The sound was muted, but they didn't need to hear. One of the major news networks was reporting on a series of terrorist attacks against Americans at home and abroad.

Deckard looked back out at the sea, seeing several more flashes across the ocean and a few more in the sky as Russian aircraft were shot down.

"Welcome to the Thunderdome," Frank mumbled.

* * *

Tampa, Florida

Outside a nondescript building, a man in a black trench coat lit up a cigarette. Flicking the lighter closed with one hand, he quickly looked down at the insignia etched into the side and remembered another time.

Another place.

"Hey," someone shouted from behind him, "it's done, Will. You're all set."

Taking a deep drag on his cancer stick, Will dropped it on the sidewalk and stubbed it out with the sole of one of his cheap dress shoes before turning to face the man holding open a glass door. Exhaling a cloud of smoke, he walked over to the door.

"I've never heard of a security clearance being reinstated that fast," Will said sarcastically. "It reeks of desperation."

"Don't start. I had to pull some serious strings to bring you back in."

"I'm sure World War Three cooking off helped, Gary."

At the front desk, a bored-looking kid in an Army uniform checked Will's ID card and then issued him a visitor's pass. Both men were then waved through a security checkpoint. As they walked, Will looked around, seeing that not much had changed since he had left. He still had a lot of bitter memories about the place. He never expected to be allowed back inside.

At an unmarked door, Gary swiped his security pass against a scanner, and a light above the doorknob turned green. Stepping inside, he walked around a table where several other men were already seated. Will stood in the corner, eyeballing the group. They were drilling holes in him as well.

Craig wore old-man glasses with a cord that ran behind them so they could hang around his neck when he wasn't reading something. Joshua wore a pink polo shirt and sported a perfect military buzz cut. In Will's eyes they were a bunch of geriatric spies, despite his being just as old as they were.

"Let's welcome Will back to the team, gents," Gary said, his words ringing hollow with the other three men.

Joshua nodded toward Will. Craig sat motionless. The second hand on a wall-mounted clock ticked slowly.

"We'll get Will read back onto the project in a more formal manner, but right now we have more pressing concerns."

Will took a deep breath.

"What are we looking at?"

"We've been tasked with assessing a situation developing in the Arctic Circle. The Russians got hit at one of their Ural facilities, and we are now receiving reports that they are losing naval ships and fighter aircraft in the Arctic Ocean."

"So we're in agreement that today's attacks, including in Russia, are not merely a coincidence?" Will asked patiently.

Craig and Joshua looked at each other before turning back to Will.

"We are," Craig answered.

"But we are not just to assess," Gary elaborated. "As of 0300 this morning, SCOPE has been operationalized. NORTHCOM has the lead for anything in the Arctic, but domestic terrorist attacks and cyber-war penetrations are keeping them tied down. Resources are being diverted everywhere but to our area of concern."

"Operationalized? SCOPE is just a think tank for JSOC," Will said. "I guess someone finally found their balls."

"The White House signed another exemption letter in order for us to support Arctic operations," Gary informed him. "I don't think I need to tell you that they are desperate."

"Desperate and scared," Will said.

"And apparently someone felt that you were needed here," Joshua said bitterly.

"Don't be such a sourpuss, Joshua. How many times did I try to warn you about this? Instead, you railroaded me right out of SCOPE and threw me out on my ass after stripping me of my clearance."

"You only have yourself to blame for that," Craig said. "For the record, I was completely against bringing you back. I regard you as an unbalanced lunatic at best, and a national security disaster at worst."

"Thanks for the endorsement. Maybe I can put that on my resume."

"You should be pitching old ladies Amway products in a supermarket somewhere."

"I thought ponzi schemes were your forte, Craig. Think I forgot about your little foray with discretionary funds in Algeria?"

"You know what Will," Craig countered. "This reminds me of the time you tried to brief the director of Central Intelligence on 9/11 conspiracy theories."

"This reminds me of the time I fucked your wife at 29 Palms, but you don't hear me bragging about it."

"Motherfucker—" Craig's chair shot out from behind him as he stood up.

"Sit the fuck down!" Gary ordered. "You two are yakking like a couple girls in junior high. For Christ's sake, I thought this was a professional organization."

"More like a fucking high school organization," Will said under his breath.

"I told you to knock it the fuck off, Will. Now sit down so we can get to work. Last time I checked, we were hours away from a global fucking war."

Will and Craig sat down.

"Bunch of drama queens I have to work with," Gary muttered.

"Getting back on track," Joshua interrupted. "We're looking at a nuclear incident in Missouri; our embassies in Kenya, Libya, and Saudi Arabia under attack; the White House was penetrated both physically and via cyber attacks; gunmen shot up a movie theater in North Carolina; the Russian northern fleet is under attack; a Special Forces team got taken out in Croatia; and suicide bombers detonated themselves in Washington D.C. and in Austin, Texas."

"They are trying to overwhelm our ability to respond by using swarming tactics," Will said.

"Yeah, but who are *they*?" Gary asked.

All eyes went toward Will.

The disgraced intelligence operative cleared his throat.

"America's enemies are now emerging from the shadows. They have prepared the environment for decades using probing techniques, testing our defenses. They know where our stovepipes are, they know about our bureaucratic rice bowls, they have assessed our reactions to cyber attacks and know damn well that we won't respond to hacker penetrations with military force. Now they have hit three embassies and launched domestic terrorist attacks to overwhelm our counterterrorism forces. Three Delta squadrons, three embassies. Do the math."

"But we still don't know who they are," Craig said.

"Again, do the math. Make an inference."

"Stop being cryptic, Will," Gary said in frustration.

"Through our actions, America has created a coalition of countries who see themselves as adversarial to us. If we don't like what a country is doing, we call them rogue states. We sanction them. We try to strategically encircle them. We sabotage them. Sometimes we even use military force against them. It was only a matter of time before we had to face the aggregate result of our political policies."

"Here we go again," Craig said, rolling his eyes.

"The nations we've ostracized have begun working together to counter America's status as a global hegemon. We are heading toward a multi-polar world, but they don't want a multi-polar world. They want a world crafted in their own image."

"What the fuck does that even mean?" Joshua said in frustration. "I told you Gary, we're getting nowhere here."

"American power has side effects, and this is one of them," Will continued. "By isolating and casting out various nations from the global community we created after World War Two, we inadvertently created a coalition of enemy states. A shadow NATO."

"This is pure conjecture," Craig said. "You can't prove a fucking word of it. Not a single national intelligence estimate supports any of your conclusions."

"That's because people like you got comfortable. You thought things would stay the same; you had hoped they would so that your bureaucracies would remain relevant. But the old rules don't apply anymore. The players involved will soon signal their hand. Watch for Russia to invade what is left of Ukraine and for China to take over some key islands in the South China Sea. That, or they simply go for the killing blow that takes America out as a global power."

"You have got to be kidding me," Craig said as he threw his hands in the air.

"We can debate what might be true some other time," Gary said, trying to get the think tank back on track. "Let's address what is. We have HUMINT and SIGINT data coming in that the Ural facility was not just attacked, but that something was stolen. The Russians are panicking and are deploying their forces into the Arctic as fast as they can. Then they get blown up by players yet unknown."

"Players without names." Will shrugged as he tapped a cigarette out of his pack.

"This is a federal building, you can't smoke in here, Will," Gary said before continuing. "Considering what happened in Missouri and the reaction of the Russians, I think we have to assess a worst-case scenario."

"That terrorists hijacked a Russian nuclear weapon?" Joshua asked.

"Yeah," Gary sighed. "DOD thinks this conclusion is premature, but we have to consider the possibility."

"You're probably right," Will said. "Except in thinking that it was terrorists who stole it."

"So the question is, what kind of assets do we have in the Arctic that can intercept the weapon, if that is in fact what happened?" Joshua asked.

Gary swallowed.

"What?" Craig asked, seeing the frown on Gary's face.

"Next to nothing."

* * *

A castle sat atop a mountain, over which dark storm clouds gathered. The villagers at the base of the mountain knew better than to approach the castle; the reckless few who had tried in the past were never seen or heard from again. It was just as rare to see anyone emerge from the castle and travel down the treacherous path to the village. When they did, they passed through the village without a word spoken. Once, those dwelling inside had been adventurers, but today they lurked inside the dark corridors of the castle, conjuring the dark spells of necromancy.

Inside one such corridor, a single torch lit the way, casting long shadows against the cyclopean walls. The massive stones used to build the structure looked like they had been melted together. Such architecture was only possible for something old, something ancient, as such knowledge had long since been lost.

In one of the adjoining chambers, a council of three met to discuss a matter.

"The talisman has been stolen," an old mage reported. He wore long black robes, his face framed by a hood that left little to be noticed aside from his burning black eyes.

"But it is not yet in our hands," the necromancer standing next to him said.

"We are close," the third man, a druid of the Tuatha order, said.

The old mage reached toward the pedestal in the center of the room and pulled a heavy bear fur from it. The portal revealed a map with sparkling stars at various important locations.

"The plan progresses as expected," the mage stated. "The king and his men have grown vain, his kingdom ripe for the taking."

"It will do little good if the talisman cannot be extracted," the necromancer said as he rubbed a small leather bag tied around his neck.

"The kingdom is in a panic," the mage said to alleviate the necromancer's concerns. "They lack organization and structure. They are a new kingdom. An immature one."

"Others have tried," the druid said as his eyes narrowed.

"Now is not the time for doubt," the mage said as he pointed to one of the stars that was slowly moving across the portal. "Even now, our dark lords carry the talisman back to us."

"The time grows near," the necromancer confirmed with a smile.

"Yes," the mage said as he looked up at the portal with fire in his eyes. "And when it is done, we will be crowned the kings of a new world."

Chapter 4
Russian Arctic

"They want you to go after them."

"What the fuck does that mean?"

"It means the Russians are desperate," Eliot said over the satellite phone. "They are scrambling more ships from the Northern Fleet, but they will never get there in time."

"How is this supposed to work?" Deckard asked.

"You intercept the enemy vessel—"

"Assuming there is a vessel."

"And they pay the company in oil, so it is all legit. Just like that job you didn't just do for us. Deckard, they are talking about opening up the entire Pechora oil field to us. That is worth hundreds of billions of dollars—"

"Assuming the check clears."

"This is huge. Everyone at Xyphon is very excited, but frankly they need me to sell you on the idea. Suffice to say we will cut you in for a percentage. Three percent of hundreds of billions of dollars is a lot of money."

"Enough to keep my company running indefinitely."

"You're a hell of a soldier, Deckard, but unless you acquire some serious business acumen in the next year, you are going to need a steady stream of revenue."

Deckard was silent for a moment. Everyone on the bridge of the Carrickfergus was looking at him.

"Any idea how I'm supposed to track them down?"

"One lead. Our crew on the Orion gas and oil platform spotted a ship passing them an hour ago. Heading east. No AIS and the radar signature was so small that it looked like an iceberg on their displays. That ain't normal. They never would have spotted it if we didn't have so much illumination tonight."

"Get me an estimate on the heading. If we can get into the general vicinity by daybreak, we might be able to follow their wake."

"So you're in?"

"They burned our compound to the ground. I would like to know who it is that wants me dead."

"Keep me up to date."

"I will," Deckard said. "And Eliot?"

"Yeah?"

"I want paper."

"You'll have a contract sent to you within the hour stating that if Xyphon is granted oil rights to Pechora, you will receive three percent of our net profit."

"We'll see," Deckard said, hanging up.

Kurt, Chuck, Frank, Pat, and Otter stood looking at him.

"What you are waiting for? Turn this ship around and make way for the Orion platform."

"You got it, boss," Otter said as he began working the helm.

"Here we go again," Frank said.

"You think I made the wrong call?"

"No," Pat interrupted. "Someone just declared war on both Russia and America. They are seconds away from starting World War Three, and whoever they are, they are out there," Pat pointed out into the darkness.

"Besides," Chuck said, "a brother has to eat."

* * *

Tampa, Florida

"You've gotta be kidding me," Joshua said, the exasperation dripping in his voice.

"They are the only ones we've got up there," Gary stated.

"You keep using that word—we—but he isn't really one of ours," Joshua countered.

"He's a freelancer," Craig chimed in with nothing of any relevance. "A loose cannon."

"I acknowledge that there are aspects that make this...problematic," Gary said. "But beggars can't be choosers. For decades we neglected our capabilities in the Arctic. The Coast Guard only has three icebreaker ships. One is in the process of being decommissioned and the other two are in dry docks being overhauled to extend their lifespan a few years."

"This guy is a fucking mercenary for Christ's sake," Craig said. "You can't trust him."

"We talked to an officer Grant with Central Intelligence," Gary said. "He said they had a fairly good working relationship for a time."

In the corner of the room, Will's chair screeched across the white linoleum floor as he stood up. He had been huddled over a JWICS computer terminal for hours. The Joint Worldwide Intelligence Communications System was how some of America's most classified information was shared within the intelligence community.

"I like him," Will announced.

"Takes one to know one, huh, Will?" Craig said sarcastically. "Disavowed and disgraced."

"The president just took us to DEFCON 2 in case you haven't been keeping score," Will said. "That's the problem with bureaucrats, you are afraid to get your hands dirty. Well, today, we are going to do just that."

"Oh my god," Joshua said. "We're all going to jail."

"You don't have to trust him," Will said. "You don't even have to like him, but this is the guy who can get the job done, and there isn't a single other person we can call on."

"You understand your colleague's concerns though," Gary added. "He brings substantial baggage."

"Read his file," Will said. "Special operations, Ground Branch, Omega. This guy is one of ours. If the ring-knockers hadn't pissed him off he would probably still be one of ours. Instead, he took his show on the road, and by all accounts this guy has more kills than cancer."

"That's what we're afraid of," Gary said as he leaned back in his swivel chair.

"Don't concern yourself. It's the Arctic; it isn't like there is much up there for him to destroy, anyway."

Craig rubbed his forehead.

"This is illegal as fuck," Joshua said in a last-ditch effort.

"It doesn't have to be."

"How?" Gary asked.

"Letters of marque."

"What the hell is that?"

Will tapped a cigarette out of his pack and popped it between his lips.

"You can't smoke here," Craig whined.

"Go fuck yourself," Will said as he lit it up. "So here is the deal: Back in the days of Sir Francis Drake and Captain Kidd, letters of marque were issued by the king to commission and authorize privateers to attack enemy vessels. They were government-sanctioned pirates."

"I hate to break it to you, but we had this little incident in 1776, and ever since we haven't had a king," Gary said, swatting at cigarette smoke.

"But there is a historical precedent. President Madison authorized letters of marque during the Second Barbary War off the coast of Libya."

"That has got to be the most obscure legal justification I've ever heard," Craig said.

"Are you kidding me?" Will asked as he exhaled another cloud of smoke. "We break the law all the time in JSOC, we just do it legally by exploiting loopholes and bypassing the intent of the law. If anything, this is on far more solid legal ground. Letters of marque are constitutional."

"Who has the authorization to grant a letter of marque?" Gary asked.

Will arched his eyebrows.

"Shit."

"Run it up the flagpole," Will said, turning back to his terminal. "A lot has changed tonight. They will sign it."

The men sitting around the table let out a collective sigh. Will just chuckled as he scrolled through files on JWICS.

* * *

At daybreak, Otter spotted clouds of black smoke billowing in the distance. It was becoming an all-too-familiar sight. After making contact with Xyphon's oil platform, they determined a rough heading that took them straight to Kotelny Island.

Deckard stood next to Otter on the bridge, kitted up except for his heavy snow-camo parka that he held in one hand. Xyphon and the Russian government had been in touch via a cut out that Deckard probably didn't even want to know about. The Russian military lost communications with their base on the island during the night. When aircraft were scrambled, one of the MIG fighter jets was shot down. Now they were requesting that Samruk scope the situation out prior to Russian forces making an amphibious landing later that day.

All the boys were jocked up down below. They were going to execute a forced entry to the island, eliminate any enemies they encountered, attempt to rescue any remaining Russian soldiers, and report back to Xyphon with their status. If the base had been compromised, the enemy might attempt to utilize the airstrip that the Russian military had recently upgraded. Kotelny was a strategic base during the Soviet era, but had been shut down at the end of the Cold War. It was only with the opening of Arctic transit lines that the Russians renewed their focus on the region, seeking to assert their sovereignty and fossil fuel rights.

As the Carrickfergus neared the island, they could see burning vehicles. They were Russian GAZ 3351s, treaded personnel carriers made specifically for traveling across the Arctic's snow and ice.

"Somebody pushed their shit in all right," Otter said, taking a sip of spiked coffee as if it were just another day at the office.

Deckard stepped out of the bridge and climbed down a ladder onto the barge deck. His men stood assembled and waiting. This time they were not even going to dick around with the trucks. Bringing them had been a huge mistake in the first place, one he chalked up to his lack of experience in the Arctic. These weren't counterterrorism raids in Baghdad, and he should have adapted to his environment better.

The Carrickfergus cracked through the sheets of ice as they closed in on the island. The Samruk mercenaries almost looked robotic in their Arctic gear. In addition to their snow camouflage and heavy parkas, they each wore tinted SnoCross goggles, which also included a nose protector. Without them, they would suffer from both frostbite and snow blindness. Under that, they each wore a No-Fog breath deflector that would help keep them warm, but more importantly, would prevent their goggles from fogging up. That was one of those little details that, if overlooked, could get you killed in a firefight.

"Listen up!" Deckard yelled as he strode into the middle of the group. "First Platoon, you have the airfield. Second Platoon, you have the barracks a few kilometers east. Afterwards, we will consolidate and sweep up anything else we missed."

The orders were brief to say the least, but he had faith in his platoon sergeants. They were just making this shit up on the fly, anyway.

As the Carrickfergus approached the icy coast, the ramp lowered and the mercenaries flowed off the ship, already wearing their assault snowshoes. Fedorchenko took his platoon toward the airfield while Shatayeva took his platoon to the barracks. Deckard shadowed Fedorchenko while Sergeant Major Korgan trailed after Shatayeva, the senior men present to help provide command and control.

The only thing the mercenaries heard was the whistle of wind in their ears and the crunch of snow under their boots. The columns of black smoke rising into the dreary gray sky warned them that, despite the alien desolation and emptiness of the Arctic, something was very wrong on Kotelny Island.

"We have bodies," Korgan reported over the command net. "Someone tore them to ribbons. Looks like large-caliber rounds were used."

"I'm seeing them," Deckard replied as he walked past the remains of a Russian soldier. He had been wearing a heavy jacket with a fur-lined hood. His entire body was scorched black up to his neck and was nearly cut in half at his midsection.

Fedorchenko's men moved out in a wedge-shaped formation, spreading out and keeping a good distance between each mercenary so they couldn't be wiped out by a single grenade, IED, or burst of machine gun fire. Deckard trailed along behind them, his head swiveling back and forth but not seeing any enemy threats. After a few more minutes of treading through the snow, Fedorchenko ordered his men on line with each other to conduct a sweep of the airfield.

Deckard walked off to the side and crouched down next to a pile of expended shell casings. Picking up one of the shells with a gloved hand, Deckard recognized it as a 12.7mm DShK heavy machine gun cartridge casing. Dropping the brass shell, Deckard clicked his radio. "Seven, this is six. How are the barracks looking?" he asked Korgan.

"Mostly empty, but some of the compartments have been completely ripped apart by heavy machine gun fire, over."

"12.7mm?"

"Maybe, but I don't see any firing positions."

Deckard walked around the pile of expended brass. In the snow, it was easy to find and follow spoor. Taking the hint from Korgan, he immediately saw tank treads next to the pile of brass. They seemed to lead off in another direction.

Tanks? But where did they go?

"Barracks secured," Korgan reported.

"Airfield has been swept as well," Fedorchenko radioed in. "No sign of the enemy, over."

Deckard knew that something was seriously wrong. Someone just wasted a company's worth of Russian soldiers with tanks and machine guns. They didn't just disappear.

Deckard looked down the slope on the opposite end of the airfield, noticing that the Russian motor pool looked untouched, unlike the barracks and other vehicles scattered around the island. Reaching into his chest rig, he pulled out a small three-power monocular. Lifting up his snow goggles, he cupped his hand around the monocular and took a closer look at the garages a few hundred meters away.

The motor pool looked dead; clouds of snow had been blown around the parking area. Then the doors on the garage suddenly began to open. Deckard squinted, trying to get a better view of what was inside. Then he saw it.

Deckard hit the transmit button on his radio.

"We've got a problem."

Chapter 5

"To your three o'clock!" Deckard shouted over the assault net as he ran, but it was already too late.

Five treaded vehicles burst from behind the slope and rolled onto the airfield, their turrets scanning in all directions for targets. Then the slaughter began. Machine guns mounted on the tanks opened fire, yellow flashes bursting from the muzzles as anti-aircraft rounds began tearing into Fedorchenko's platoon.

Deckard hit the ground, hoping to avoid being detected by the tanks. He was out in the open in the middle of the airfield, just like Fedorchenko's men. He watched helplessly as a half dozen of his men burst into pieces as they tried to run, turning the snow red. The gray-colored tanks rolled across the airfield. The rotating turrets on top had 12.7mm DShK machine guns loaded into their cradles. Deckard noted two rectangular radar dishes sticking from the sides of the turrets like ears. There was also a sensor suite on each gun platform for thermals. Two of the tanks locked on to Samruk's second platoon over at the barracks and took off on a new trajectory.

Fedorchenko's men had beaten an embarrassing and chaotic retreat, desperate to find some low ground to take cover in. Their numbers had been thinned out as they crossed the airfield. They were still in danger of being overrun by the armored vehicles, as the tanks were not about to be slowed down by Kalashnikov fire.

Deckard panted, his body already covered in sweat from the brief run. The great irony of the Arctic was overheating inside all of your cold-weather gear. Fedorchenko's men were staring down three tanks, and no matter how badass an infantryman you were, enemy armor could steamroll right over you in the blink of an eye, reducing you to a pink, gooey paste.

That was when Deckard had a dumb idea.

He might be able to peel one of the tanks away from Fedorchenko's platoon so they would face two instead of three, maybe even giving them a fighting chance. Getting to his feet, Deckard unloaded on the closest tank, about a hundred meters away, with his AK-103. His rounds sparked off the side of the tank, drawing its attention. The treads on one side of the tank reversed while the other continued forward, making a sharp right turn toward Deckard as the gun turret sought him out.

As the tank swerved toward him, Deckard sprinted, but not in the opposite direction. He ran straight toward it.

Crazy as it sounded, Deckard knew that trying to outrun the tank was pure suicide across open terrain. His only chance was to charge it, knowing that the machine gun had limits to its elevation angle. His hood flew off his head as he ran directly at the tank, sweat running down his neck. Thick gray smoke suddenly burst all around Fedorchenko's position as his men deployed thermal smoke grenades. The tank was now facing Deckard, and he was staring right down the barrel of the Russian anti-aircraft gun.

Deckard dived forward as the DShK opened fire.

* * *

The Russian robotic tank swung toward the two new Samruk International recruits. It was only their second mission with the company and they were already being run to ground by robots with machine guns.

Maurizio and Jacob were quickly separated from the rest of their platoon as twin tanks suddenly assaulted the barracks and opened fire on the Samruk International mercenaries. So much for following the clues and unraveling the mystery of what happened to the base on Kotelny Island. The answer had became immediately clear to them.

The Italian and Danish mercs did what all the others had done, the only thing they could do: run and try to find cover. One of the tanks homed in on them, firing bursts that chewed through the snow next to them. By zigzagging a few times they had managed to avoid being cut down in the open snow drifts. The computer targeting programming the tank used clearly had a hard time leading targets, but they both knew they only had seconds before the machine gun fire walked into them.

"This way," Jacob said, grabbing Maurizio's sleeve. They cut a hard left and descended down a snow bank. Both mercenaries tripped in the knee-deep snow and rolled down the embankment. The men flopped through the snow, the tank quickly bearing down on them.

Maurizio lay on his back at the bottom, looking up at the ridge as the automated tank rolled over the edge. The turret swung toward them. The former Italian counterterrorist operator rolled the stock of his Kalashnikov into his shoulder, ready to go down in a blaze of glory. Both mercenaries fired ineffectively at the vehicle.

The turret tried to lock onto its targets as the tank platform it was attached to began to slide in the snow. The DShK opened fire, 12.7mm rounds spraying right in front of the mercenaries. Then the tank lurched again and began sliding down the embankment. The European mercenaries continued to fire, cycling through their 30-round magazines. Their bullets smacked into the tank armor, the turret, and the machine gun.

Now the robotic tank was sliding down on top of them. Maurizio struggled to his feet. Grabbing Jacob with both hands, he pulled him out of the way as the tank rolled over in the snow. It flopped down just a few feet away, crushing the turret under the tank platform. The treads spun, but with the vehicle flipped upside down. It was going nowhere fast.

The Dane and the Italian looked at each other with wide eyes.

"*Che palle*," Maurizio whispered.

What a ball-breaker.

* * *

Bullets ripped just inches above Deckard and slammed into the snow-covered runway, stitching a burst across the tarmac that kicked up ice and debris. Deckard slid forward on his forearms, the toes of his boots dragging as he attempted to gain purchase on the ice. He got halfway up, stumbled forward, fell, and the tank was on top of him. The mercenary lay as flat as possible, tightly gripping his Kalashnikov.

His ears rang as the tank rumbled over him, the clanking treads passing on either side.

Seeing daylight again as the tank passed, Deckard sprang to his feet, ran a few more paces to catch up with the tank as it searched for new targets, and jumped.

His hand seized a thick rubber cable looping down from an antenna on the back of the tank. With a sudden jerk, Deckard was lifted off his feet and dragged behind the tank. With the AK slung over his shoulder, Deckard reached out and grabbed the cable with both hands. His gloves had a good grip, but his hands still slipped around inside them. Knowing he was all out of options, Deckard ignored the pain in his shoulders, gripped the cable tighter, and climbed hand over hand.

As he gripped the antenna mast and pulled himself on top of the tank, he saw over his shoulder that Fedorchenko's employment of smoke grenades for concealment had worked, confusing the tanks while Samruk's Gustav gunners began wreaking havoc. It looked like they had already scored a mobility kill against one tank as it spun in circles on one tread. The other looked permanently decommissioned.

The tank cut a turn underneath him, nearly throwing Deckard off as he hugged the antenna mast. From the sensor array, he knew immediately what he was looking at. It was not a manned battle tank, but rather a deadly remote-controlled one. It was an unmanned vehicle, receiving signal commands from the antenna he clung to. The Russians called such a tank a Mobile Robotic Complex, and this particular model was nicknamed the Wolf-2. Good for protecting Arctic infrastructure since robots never got cold the way soldiers did.

Since it was a robot, Deckard knew he didn't have to actually destroy the tank. All he needed to do was make it blind and deaf by disabling its sensor array. Robots were a lot easier to game than human beings since they operate within such strict programmed parameters, much the same way he easily got underneath the attack angle allowed by the mechanics of the machine gun turret. A human operator would have known better.

The tank was circling around, scanning for more targets. Deckard climbed across the top of the vehicle as it sped across the runway, moving toward the radar dishes mounted on the turret. Reaching for his chest rig, he began freeing a hand grenade when the Wolf-2's radar locked onto a target. The entire gun turret swung around to fire.

Deckard hardly saw the DShK barrel coming as it slammed into his chest. Picked up off his feet, his legs dangled in the air off the side of the tank as the barrel began spitting fire.

* * *

Nikita threw himself through the doorway as automatic gunfire ripped the walls down around him. Between bursts, he could hear the *clank-clank-clank* of the tank treads, then another burst of anti-aircraft rounds that poked holes about as big around as his thumb through the walls of the barracks.

First, Fedorchenko's platoon got hit out on the airfield, and then a minute later, Sergeant Shatayeva's platoon began getting pounded at the abandoned barracks. The soldier housing complex was made up of adjoining compartmentalized containers that had been elevated on stilts to keep them above the snow and ice. The barracks had already been torn apart when they got there, the gory remains of frozen Russian soldiers decorating what was left of their living quarters.

Now the entire complex was being turned into a giant gerbil maze filled with Samruk mercenaries trying to find concealment as the tank's radar-guided machine gun sought them out from below. Nikita cursed himself as he came up on a knee. He poked his head out, thinking that his camouflage uniform would keep him from being spotted.

It was called chromacamo. Extremely expensive and only available in limited numbers, chromacamo was a type of 'smart' camouflage that changed color to match the the soldier's environment. Nikita had first experimented with it during a mission to Mexico, but now the entire sniper and recce section made use of it.

Camouflage worked great at keeping the sniper concealed from drug traffickers, terrorists, and enemy soldiers, but this was a different ball game. The thermal and radar system on the automated hunter/killer tank below skipped right past the optical illusion created by camouflage. It was designed to deceive the human eye, not a robotic one.

The radar or thermals on the mobile robotic platform must have picked up on something, because another long burst of autofire began tearing through what was left of the facade holding up the roof. Nikita rolled left with his HK417 rifle in his hands as more holes were punched through the floor. The entire barracks was disintegrating right out from under him.

Climbing through a ragged hole in the far wall, Nikita escaped out the back. A narrow catwalk led him to a metal ladder. Slinging his rifle, he began to scale it up to the roof. The tank was on a warpath, and running away would just earn him a bullet in the back. Up on the roof, he caught a gust of arctic wind to the face, snowflakes whisking over his goggles. Then he caught sight of a dozen other mercenaries up on the rooftops of the adjacent buildings. They were all lying low without adequate weapons to address the problem below.

One of the American mercenaries was on the radio, hissing into the mic to the mortar section that had been getting set up near where the Carrickfergus made its landing. Not that calling in a fire mission was even possible. They were just meters away from the tank below and mortars rounds would rain down right on top of them.

Nikita crept to the edge of the roof and risked a glance down. The tank was still clanking between the barracks buildings. It locked on to something for a second and let off a couple of rounds. They could always wait around for the tank's magazine to empty as it lit up suspected targets, but who knew how many friendlies would be killed in the process?

With 7.62mm rifles, they might be able to take out the thermal and radar targeting sensors if they focused enough coordinated fire on them. But from their vantage point, he had a better idea.

"Grenade," Nikita said to the others. They looked up at him as his uniform changed colors from white to gray, matching the metal roof of the barracks. Each of the mercenaries yanked the pin on a hand grenade.

"Now!"

A dozen hand grenades rained down on the robotic tank below. Blast after blast ripped across the tank in a shower of sparks and brown smoke. Some detonated harmlessly in the snow but others landed on top of the tank. The armored portions were unaffected, but several blasts left the radar ears on the side of the gun turret torn to shreds.

The tank drove along in short, stunted bursts, rocking to a stop, trying to lock onto targets, then driving along for a few more meters. The computer brain inside the vehicle was unable to function properly with its eyes and ears taken out.

"Let's get the hell out of here," the American mercenary yelled over the wind to Nikita. "Then mortar this place with Willy Pete," he said, referring to white phosphorus rounds that would burn everything to the ground.

Nikita paused for a moment. The veteran sniper was realizing that his old tactics and techniques were not working anymore. The environment was different. The enemy was different. The rules had been changed without anyone telling him and he wasn't adapting fast enough.

"Da," Nikita replied. "Burn it."

* * *

Deckard clung to the DShK barrel as it flung him through the air. He almost slipped off again when the gun turret lurched to an immediate stop and opened fire. Looking behind him, Deckard hopped backward and landed on the front of the tank. His chest was tight, like someone had just whacked him with a baseball bat. Actually, it had been a machine gun barrel, but he would worry about how black and blue he was some other time.

Initially, he had planned to destroy the antenna mast. Interrupting communications between the tank and whatever control mechanism it had might do the trick, but now that he was in front of the tank, he had access to an even better target. In front of the gun turret, below the barrel, was an ammunition drum loaded with the 12.7mm machine gun rounds that fed into the DShK on a metal-link belt.

Reaching into a pouch on his chest rig, Deckard produced a door charge. The segments of explosive cutting tape were designed for punching through doors so that assaulters could rush inside and clear a building. It would do a good number on the tank turret, too.

Peeling the plastic strip off the adhesive glue on the back of the charge, Deckard slapped it onto the ammo drum. The DShK ceased firing, then scanned for another target, causing Deckard to duck under the barrel before his head was taken off. Working quickly, he strung in the initiation system, a line of shock tube connected to an ignitor with a pull pin.

Looking over his shoulder, he saw that the tank he was on had locked onto Fedorchenko's position. In a few moments he would probably be lit up by his own men when the tank started shooting at them. Two burning tank hulks lay in front of the platoon already, and he had no doubt they were already shifting fire to the third one.

Deckard put his finger through the pin on the ignitor and rolled off the side of the tank.

His boots came down first, absorbing some of the shock. Then he landed on his side, bouncing painfully on the ice. Twisting and turning the pin on the ignitor, the chemical reaction in the shock tube caused it to blink neon blue for a microsecond.

The turret blew sky high.

Deckard cringed as the DShK actually separated from the turret and went spinning through the air. The tank rolled to a halt, and what was left of the machine gun landed somewhere behind him. Under his jacket, Deckard was saturated in sweat. He struggled to catch his breath as he got up and examined the damage. There were three smoking tank husks out on the airfield. The other two must have gone to hunt down his guys at the barracks. At least he didn't hear them shooting, giving him some hope that they had already been taken out.

"Both platoons," Deckard said into his radio, "ACE report."

ACE was a military acronym that stood for ammo, casualties, and equipment. It was a very brief report that small unit leaders sent up to higher to inform their leadership of how much ammo they had left, anyone who had been killed or wounded, and the state of their combat gear and weapons. As he waited for the reports to roll in from his platoon sergeants, Deckard walked toward Fedorchenko's position. They had found refuge in a small depression, in which they had masked themselves with smoke grenades and fired anti-tank weapons. Still, Deckard knew it was going to be bad. He had seen the aerosol spray of blood in the air from a distance.

"Second Platoon," Shatayeva reported in from the barracks. "Five magazines per man, two KIA, up on weapons and equipment."

Deckard took a deep breath as he neared the lifeless bodies of his men lying strewn across the airfield.

"First Platoon," Fedorchenko's voice said over the net. "Four magazines per man, seven KIA, one Gustav destroyed."

Deckard stood in front of the first body he came across. Among the newer group of guys, Marty had also been cut in half by DShK fire. He'd been a good dude who had previously served in 1st Ranger Battalion. Now he lay on his back with his arms sprawled out, bent at the elbows like claws. His mouth was left ajar, with ice clinging to his short beard. There was nothing they could have done for him.

Not far from him was another corpse. Deckard knelt down next to him. Frank had been with Samruk International since the beginning; he'd been one of Deckard's first hires to the company. He had been a special operations legend, at least among those in the know. He'd served in the Ranger Regiment's Ranger Reconnaissance Detachment and then the Intelligence Support Activity, where he had pulled off some very hairy assignments.

Only to be snuffed out in an instant on the Arctic tundra.

"Deckard."

Standing up, he looked over to see Pat approaching.

"It's Frank."

"I know. We just got our asses kicked."

Deckard looked back down at the body.

"They laid a trap for us and we walked right into it. Whoever they are, they're damn good. They hacked those robotic tanks, had them turn on their own operators, and then had them lie in wait for whoever gave chase. Listen, Deckard," Pat continued. "I know you're in a bad place right now, but you'd better reach on down and grab your balls because this shit over the last twenty-four hours just got real."

Deckard opened his mouth to say something, but Pat was already walking away, his legs from the knee down disappearing into the the swirling snow that gusted around them.

Chapter 6

"It's him."

"Are you sure?"

"Yes," the mage answered. "See for yourself."

The fur was flung off of the portal. It revealed an image of a man climbing on top of a tank. Snow-covered crags poked up behind the tank before the background gave way to broken sheets of ice out on the ocean.

"This is the one we have spoken about?" the necromancer asked.

"It is him," the mage answered, not leaving any room for further argument. "He struck down one of our conjured familiars on his own."

"It seems that everything we have heard of him is true," the druid said cautiously. "He could makes the situation...complicated."

The mage tossed the fur back over the portal, casting away the image.

"It is of no matter. The plan enacted by our dark lords bloodied his nose, and he won't be able to pick up our trail again. Even if he does, it will be too late."

The druid cast a spell and was suddenly awash in a swarm of what looked like blue fireflies. The restoration spell increased his magicka to its full level.

"This day is too important to have our focus drawn to one particular point in the overall operation," the druid said as he shot a look at the mage. "Too important to let a variable like this upset our plans."

"It is taken care of," the mage assured him.

"Let us hope," the necromancer said as he rubbed a talisman between his thumb and forefinger. "Let us hope."

* * *

Russian Arctic

The Carrickfergus chugged passed Kotelny Island, crashing through sheets of ice on its way. Deckard sat on the bridge watching the scorched island slide by. The sting of defeat overwhelmed the physical pain he felt in his chest where the machine gun barrel had slammed into him. They had lost nine men on what should have been a straightforward post-battle assessment of the island. The bodies of their dead had been bagged up and put down in the bottom of the ship with the ballast for the time being. The Samruk mercs had loaded up and quickly evacuated the island.

Knowing it was futile to hold off on making the call, Deckard picked up the satellite phone, even though talking about what just happened was the last thing he wanted to do at that moment. He dialed the number for Xyphon's head of security.

"This is Eliot."

"I lost them," Deckard said. "Whoever they were, they hacked into six automated tank systems that were left present on the island in standby mode. As near as I can tell they used the tanks to massacre everyone on the island, then sent them back to their garages to wait for anyone else to show up on the island. It was a baited trap and we walked right into it."

"Did you lose anyone?"

"Nine."

"Shit, I'm sorry, Deckard."

"We took a close look at the airfield, though. There was no sign that an aircraft had landed or taken off on that airstrip in a while. We would have seen some tracks."

74

"Which means they are still on the water. Makes sense, seeing that they don't have total control over the airspace. It seems like they are using an anti-access/area denial strategy, shooting down just enough aircraft to make the Russians squeamish about sending more."

"Whatever the case, they are long gone. I fucked up."

"There was no way you could have known, Deckard. You're not out of the game yet. Not if you still want in."

"What is it?" Deckard asked as he sat up straight in his chair.

"Can you do VTC?" Eliot said, referring to a video teleconference.

"Yeah, we can do that via satellite."

"Good. Call this number." Eliot then read off a string of numbers that Deckard wrote down on a coffee-stained yellow legal pad Otter had left lying around.

"Who is this?" Deckard asked as he finished writing down the numbers.

"Uncle Sam has been looking for you, Deckard. The chess pieces are shifting very rapidly back in the United States right now."

Deckard hung up and opened a laptop computer. Bringing up the VTC program, he dialed up the number Eliot had provided. It took a minute for the connection to kick in before the video suddenly clicked on.

On the screen, Deckard saw four men sitting around a table.

"Deckard," the man in the center of the table said. "We've been trying to get ahold of you for hours."

"This isn't exactly a Skype call from your local Starbucks," Deckard replied. "What can I do for you?"

"Mr. Deckard," the old man with the reading glasses perched on his nose began, "we represent a compartmentalized special-access program folded within the national security infrastructure of the U.S. government. We would like to discuss with you certain terms of employment and the legalese required therein. Your company would complete the terms of service on an operationalized basis pending certain approvals and exemptions—"

"OK, OK," Deckard interrupted. "I have no fucking idea what you're talking about."

"Goddammit," another old man on the teleconference muttered, "I fucking told you, Craig, shut your fat fucking face." The man wearing a black trench coat stood up and walked in front of the camera, standing in front of Deckard and blocking out the view of the other three men at the table.

"Listen," he said. "The bad guys stole something from the Russians, probably something nuclear, and we can't let it fall into the wrong hands."

"I'm following."

"What we have acquired for you are letters of marque and reprisal, signed by the president of the United States of America. You just became the first sanctioned American pirate in over two hundred years. As a privateer, you are entitled to raid enemy vessels designated by the U.S. government, for pay, and we can also provide you with whatever intelligence support we can from here."

"I've got wood."

"I was hoping you would say that. Your mission is simple, Deckard. Stop the enemy from getting away with the device they took from the Russians. That is your target. Kill everything between you and it."

"They must be heading east, but we lost their trail."

"We can help with that."

"How?"

"Ten-meter imagery captured by synthetic aperture radar from a passing satellite forty-five minutes ago. The national geospatial agency was able to track fourteen commercial shipping vessels passing Kotelny Island, plus one mystery vessel. All we can do is an analysis of the ship's wake and attempt to project a distance and heading."

"I'm starting to feel like Captain Jack Sparrow chasing a ghost ship."

"We'll exchange business cards and swap saliva under the bleachers later, Deckard," the man in the black jacket said. "Right now we need to get this operation back on track. I'm bringing some imagery up on your screen right now. Craig, get that shit up on the VTC, dammit."

The screen on Deckard's laptop showed overhead imagery of an ice-strewn sea, a patch of the seemingly endless Arctic Ocean just like any other.

"We've gotten no direct returns from searching for this particular ship, meaning it has poor radar backscatter characteristics."

"A stealth ship?"

"It almost certainly has characteristics to reduce its radar cross section. The wake we detected was faint as well, meaning there are probably measures to reduce that, too. Whoever these guys are, they are trying very hard to stay hidden, and that makes them very interesting to us. We need you to close the distance and keep the pressure on them, otherwise they might have time to offload the device to a waiting airplane or submarine. Zoom in on that picture and take a closer look at the wake."

Deckard clicked the magnifying glass icon and enlarged the image. The ship's wake was hard to spot at first, but it was definitely present.

"You can make out a stern wave and the turbulent wake leaving a trail behind wherever the vessel is off to," the man in black continued. "I crunched the numbers. By measuring distances where the transverse and divergent waves intersect with the Kelvin envelope, I was able to get you a new heading for the suspect vessel. This heading also backtracks to Kotelny Island."

"What am I up against?

"My best assessment is that it is a semi-submersible craft, which would explain why we can't find a radar cross section on it. The good news is that this means the ship is moving at relatively slow speeds, meaning you've got a shot at catching up with it."

"The bad news?"

"It probably lowers its draft by filling internal ballast tanks along the sides of its hull. It would also be able to evacuate those tanks quickly and then take off at much higher speeds. It's going to be hard to spot, even visually, but once you do and begin pursuit, you will have your hands full."

"You're an old sea dog, aren't you?"

The man in black chuckled.

"That was a long time ago."

"And now?"

"You could say that I specialize in quiet weapons for silent wars."

"Oh."

"You can call me Will, by the way."

"Will?"

"Yeah?"

"Who are they?"

Will was about to say something until Craig, the guy with the reading glasses, interrupted.

"We don't know who they are, Deckard. That's what has everyone here so scared. Russia has come under attack, America got hit hard last night, and we are seeing some really weird movements in Ukraine, Syria, and the South China Sea in recent hours. Right now it would be extremely speculative to point a finger at one actor or another because none of this is making sense," Craig finished. "We'll be in touch the moment we know more."

"I would appreciate that," Deckard said, his words left hanging in the air.

Will looked back at him.

"You remember the Moscow apartment complex bombing in 1999?" Will asked.

"It kicked off the second war in Chechnya."

"It's not a secret that the bombing was a false flag conducted by the Russian FSB intelligence service."

"What are you saying? That the Russians stole their own nuclear weapon?"

"I'm saying that all of the villains in Gotham City are teaming up on us."

"Wait, what?"

"As I said, we'll contact you when we have something solid," Craig cut in again.

The VTC went dark, and Deckard was again sitting on the bridge with only Otter to keep him company. The ship captain whistled as he began steering them on a new heading that had just been sent to them.

"Damn, son," the ship captain said as he took a swig of spiked coffee. "That's some black helicopter shit right there."

Chapter 7

Deckard climbed down the metal stairwell from the bridge and down into the passenger compartment of the ship. He stood in the middle of his men's living and work space, the mercenaries stepping around him in the cramped ship's quarters. His vision was still transfixed by the piece of paper he held in his hand. They had received it by email and Deckard had printed off a couple of copies.

In his hand he held a letter of marque signed by the president, authorizing him to attack enemy vessels at his own discretion. With the flick of a pen, the Carrickfergus had been made into a pirate ship, and Deckard the pirate captain. Some of the mercenaries looked at him strangely as they passed by. No one could recall seeing their boss with such a big smile on his face.

Snapping out of it, Deckard stepped over Mk48 machine guns and around winter parkas and trousers drying from improvised clotheslines. He was looking for the computer hacker he kept on Samruk International's payroll when he stumbled across Chuck Rochenoire's hootch. He and Nate, the new guy who had served with Marine Corps special operations, were sitting on top of MRE boxes while drinking a couple Miller High Life beers.

"You want one, Deck?" Rochenoire asked. "It's the fuckin' champagne of beers."

Deckard stepped forward, looking at the giant black flag that Chuck had strung up on the wall. The skull and crossbones were something Marines and SEALs could always appreciate.

"Something wrong?" Nate asked.

"Far from it," Deckard answered.

He handed Chuck the letter bearing the letterhead of the Oval Office. Chuck and Nate crowded around the piece of paper, trying to make sense of it.

"This can't be what I think it is," Nate said.

For once, Chuck was at a loss for words.

"Let's start flying the Jolly Roger and make it official," Deckard said with a grin.

* * *

Deckard found Cody hunched over a desk, finger-fucking some electronic gadget. At the end of the passenger compartment, Cody had set up a small work station. The desk was covered with wires, batteries, rechargers, thumb drives, and other odds and ends. He was perhaps the only non-combat personnel in the company, but he had a magic touch with electronics. From computer network operations to jury-rigging satellite dishes or isolating obscure radio frequency spectrums, Cody had an exceptional talent.

Not that it didn't come without its drawbacks.

"What do you want?" Cody asked after briefly looking up at Deckard. Then he muttered under his breath, "Fucking pussy."

Cody was in a unique position, as he had both Asperger's syndrome and apparently an undiagnosed form of Tourette syndrome on top of it.

"Get anything off those laptops?" Deckard asked, noticing the laptop computers Aghassi had taken off the Russian mafia target they had hit.

"Not much, just social media shit that can be used to link them back to the rest of the Russian mob. But we already knew that."

"The other thing I wanted to talk to you about is what happened on Kotelny."

Cody didn't look up and continued to mess around with the Pwn Pad in his hands. It was a Nexus 7 tablet that had been specially built for penetration testing of electronic networks.

"Tanks got hacked. What else you wanna know?" Cody asked. "COCK!"

"How hard is it to do something like that?"

"Very difficult. Just like our Predator drones. The signals being transmitted between the drone and the operator are unencrypted, otherwise the encryption would lead to such a lag time that it would be like trying to have a firefight with a 56k AOL dial-up connection."

"But intercepting signals doesn't allow you to take control of the drone?"

"No. FUCK. To do that you have hack the actual hardware on the drone and that is encrypted."

"Who could do something like that?"

"Military-grade encryption? Not me. Not anyone I would know. Governments only, I guess."

"So we're talking about a major power player? A country that has a massive electronic warfare infrastructure like China?"

"DICK. FACE. Yes. No. Or just a Russian military insider who sold his secrets to someone. I don't know."

"You are not filling with me confidence right now, Cody."

"Why the fuck would I want to do that?" Cody snorted. "We're all going to die up in this frozen shithole you brought us to."

"Well, that's nice to know," Deckard said as he looked up at the ceiling. "Anything else you can actually do to help me before we stumble into oblivion?"

"Take this," Cody turned around and tossed Deckard the Pwn Pad. "Turn it on next time you come in contact with these guys. It might suck up some interesting signals we can use."

Deckard looked down at the tablet and pursed his lips.

"OK, Cody," Deckard said as he turned to walk away. "OK."

"Little shit."

* * *

Deckard found his cot in the middle of the mercenary maelstrom and sat down. It was his ship and his merry band of pirates, but even he could get lost in the chaos. Having soldiers live right on top of each other in cramped quarters made for an interesting combination of fistfights and grab ass. These were no professional sailors either; they were blow-the-door-down, kill everyone inside, and be home by beer-thirty ground pounders. The few former SEALs and Marines may have been used to it, but most of the men adapted to the maritime lifestyle with great reluctance.

But none of them complained just as long as Deckard's checks cleared. For now, anyway.

The former special operations soldier picked up his AK-103 rifle, depressed the nub at the end of the carrier spring, and detached the dust cover. He then popped out the spring and pulled out the bolt carrier. Using a rag and some oil, he did a few minutes of weapons maintenance.

They were quickly learning how to put a weapon into operation effectively in the Arctic. More and more of the mercenaries were rolling out with just iron sights, as the batteries in optical sights froze after 15 minutes.

Deckard applied a very light coat of oil prior to reassembling his rifle. Any more, and he risked having the oil freeze and gum up the cycle of operation when he pulled the trigger, leading to malfunctions.

Next, he moved on to his Glock 19, the standard-issue sidearm in Samruk International. He had given up his much-loved Kimber 1911. As much as he loved God's gun, Deckard knew that 1911s were high maintenance tack drivers only carried by Luddites, iconoclasts, and connoisseurs. At the end of the day, the Glock 19 was more reliable, and reliability was something they desperately needed in the Arctic. It took three minutes to disassemble the pistol, wipe it down, and put it back together again.

Deckard slid the Glock into the Raven Concealment holster on his hip and headed back up to the bridge. Otter had actually let Kurt Jager take the helm while the ship's captain was looking over sea charts and plotting a course.

"Where do you think the enemy is heading?" Deckard asked him.

"Well," Otter said as he frowned and blew out his cheeks. "Based on the wake analysis we were given, it looks like they are heading toward the De Long Strait."

"Will we overtake them prior to getting there?"

"I have no idea. It depends on their speed relative to ours, and right now we have no idea how many knots they are moving at. We should have a better idea in five hours, when the next satellite in polar orbit goes overhead. If it is able to pick up the stealth ship's wake again, we could be able to calculate speeds."

"How long until we reach the strait if we continue at our max speed?"

"At twenty-five knots we will get there in just a little over twenty-four hours."

"Feels like we're fighting a war in slow motion."

"We're not hitting time-sensitive targets in some urban sprawl," Kurt reminded Deckard. "Even with the northeast passage opening up, there is still very little infrastructure in the Arctic."

"Maybe that won't be the case in another twenty years, after the oil companies try to suck every bit of energy reserves out of the Arctic," Otter confirmed. "But for now, we are faced with the tyranny of distance and the austerity of the environment."

"I guess the good news is that the enemy is as well," Deckard said.

"Their choice of vessel would make one believe that they chose stealth over speed, counting on the assumption they would not be found."

"But we've already got their heading."

"And we're probably gaining on them as we speak," Otter said with a rare smile.

Deckard ran his finger over the chart, tracing the projected route of the Carrickfergus, wondering what the next day would bring.

Chapter 8
Tampa, Florida

Craig rubbed his bloodshot eyes. Joshua had his head down on the table, taking a nap. Gary had stepped outside to call his wife and tell her that he wouldn't be coming home any time soon. SCOPE was a think tank, not an operations center that worked in shifts. Everyone was exhausted and needed a break while the Carrickfergus was in transit and they waited for the satellite window to open up again over northern Russia.

The JSOC think tank was dead tired. Most of them, anyway.

Will paced back and forth, his heels clicking on the floor. His lips were moving, the words coming out of his mouth barely decipherable even if someone had been listening. The only words that were really recognizable were the ones consisting of four letters. After years of warning the intelligence community, everything he'd said was coming true. It wasn't something he took pride in, but now no one could doubt that his assessment had merit. Or at least they wouldn't be able to much longer.

Suddenly, Will stopped dead in his tracks.

"I've got it!" he shouted.

"Got what?" Craig said with a yawn.

Joshua continued to snore.

"Something we can do instead of sitting around with our thumbs up our asses."

"Well, I could go rub one out I guess—"

"Yeah," Will said under his breath. "Or you could go dust your old lady's pussy off."

"What did you say?"

"Sorry, just mumbling to myself."

"Mumbling what?"

"We need to take a serious look at getting inside the enemy's communications network."

Craig put his head down on the table.

"Will, we don't even know who the enemy is, so how are we supposed to even identify how they are talking to one another?"

"I told you before, they use Infinity Blade."

"Infinity what?"

"Infinity Blade. It's an MMORPG."

"You've lost me."

"A massive multiplayer online role-playing game."

"My kids play those?" Craig asked no one in particular before turning to Joshua, who was still asleep. "Do my kids play that?"

The door swung open and Gary walked back inside, pocketing his cell phone.

"The game is based on a series of fantasy novels that became an underground hit. The game also has a cult following. It was produced by the same Norwegian guy who created Paradoxica."

"What the hell are you two talking about?" Gary demanded.

"Para what?" Craig asked.

"Paradoxica," Will said. "It's a game about a young woman traveling between three worlds...and filled with existential malaise...."

"Oh. My. God. I'm going back outside," Gary said as he reached for the door.

"Hold on, dammit!" Will yelled. "I'm getting to the good part."

"So there is a point to all of this?"

"I've been playing Infinity Blade for years, and I know something is going on inside this game."

"I should have known. You're a bigger gamer than my kids, but at least my kids don't have conspiracy theories about the games they play," Craig said as he rolled his eyes.

"Look, what is a video game?" Will asked rhetorically. "It's a communications medium, another way to talk over the internet. But in this case, it is within a massive multiplayer video game. The FBI identified an island in the game called Second Life that Hezbollah uses to talk to each other. Hezbollah members from anywhere in the world, including their handlers in Iran, can log into the game and meet up with each other to exchange information and issue orders."

"And you think this Infinity Blade game is used the same way," Gary said as he walked back and took his seat.

"I know it is. The FBI investigated, but they can't crack the cell inside Infinity Blade. Their operational security is tight. You don't get into their castle unless you've been extensively vetted."

"Assuming you are correct, what makes you think this is the same group behind our current situation?"

"When I realized that a number of countries antagonistic toward the United States were in collusion with each other, I began looking for traces of them and how they communicate. The servers for Infinity Blade are physically located in China, which doesn't mean anything in of itself, but that prevents the FBI from gaining access."

"So you identified some secretive group inside a video game operated out of China, which means this is just another wild-ass hunch of yours?" Craig asked.

"This is how the baddies communicate," Will replied. "I'm sure of it."

"*I'm sure* this is a waste of time," Craig said as he put his head back down on the table. "I'm taking a nap."

"I'm going to pound down a couple of Monster energy drinks and get back to work," Will announced. "No reason to sit around jagging off to gay porn or whatever it is you guys do when I'm not around. Time to call the CNO office upstairs and get a persona to access the game with."

CNO, or computer network operations, was a polite way of saying computer hacking.

Gary looked at the clock on his cell phone.

"Another five hours until the satellite window opens," he sighed. "Give them a call."

Will reached across the table and picked up the secure telephone before pressing the appropriate extension number.

"So now we're passing time by playing video games? When the inspector general investigates this office, the report will make one hell of a read," Craig said looking up at them.

"Hey, this is Will down at SCOPE," he said as the CNO office picked up the phone. "We need a persona." He frowned as he listened to the techie on the other end of the line. "Yeah. Yeah. No. OK. Hold on, look, what personas do you have on Infinity Blade?"

Another few seconds.

"OK, I'll take the chaotic neutral blade master. See you in a few."

"What the hell was all of that?" Craig asked.

"Borrowing a persona from CNO."

"You keep saying that. What do you mean by *borrow a persona*?"

"An online persona. Really Craig? How long have you worked here?"

"Twelve years."

"And worth every dime of taxpayer money you are. The techs here maintain digital personas in order to conduct cyber reconnaissance and infiltration. Each persona has its own laptop computer. Each computer has a name, a persona name. Every computer has a set of rules that you follow—that persona's bible. His turn-ons, turn-offs, political views, what websites he frequents, and so on."

"Building a false identity."

"A false persona," Will corrected. "You can then use that persona to infiltrate jihadi message boards or white supremacist websites, whatever you need. Every so often the techs pull out each laptop, be it named Mike, Bob, or Muhammad, and tool around on the web for a few hours, then move on to the next laptop to maintain the next persona's online presence."

"So we actually pay people to fart around on Facebook and play Farmville all day?"

"Well...." Will said as he thought about it for a moment. "Yes. But the system does work. And some of these personas have maintained a presence in online games. Since Infinity Blade is a popular game, we have three personas run out of this building with characters in it."

There was a knock at the door and Gary slid across the office on his rolling swivel chair to open it.

"Hey Jerry," Will said to the guy standing in the doorway.

He was a very unfortunate-looking man. Essentially, exactly what most people thought a computer hacker looked like. His face was drawn, his muscles atrophied, and his mustache and beard grew in so weak that it looked like he had pubic hair glued to his chin.

"So what do you need Roger for?" Jerry asked as he closed the door behind him, a laptop computer secured under one arm.

"Roger?" Gary asked.

"Roger is the name of this computer, and the persona on it," the computer hacker replied. "So what do you need him for?"

"Oh, nothing much," Will said as he interlaced his fingers behind his head and leaned back in his chair. "Just saving the world, that's all."

"This is a level 37 blade master that I've built up over five years," Jerry cautioned. "You can't just take him and throw him into Panchea, Wintersebb, and Ravendale without hurting my stats."

"Jerry," Will said as he leaned forward. "It isn't your character profile, it's JSOC's."

Jerry shook his head.

"No, you can't just take him away from me like that!"

Will jumped up out of his chair and lunged for the laptop under Jerry's arm.

"Give it to me you squirrely little shit!"

"No!" Jerry shrieked.

The two entered into a tug of war for the computer, the fate of America potentially hanging in the balance of a full-on nerd rage. Finally, Will snatched the laptop away from him.

"You still have a level 14 paladin and a level 32 battle mage you can play while billing DOD for your time," Will sneered. "Now get the fuck out!"

Jerry's lips and nose shriveled as he stepped out and slammed the door behind him.

"Goddamn short bus-riding window lickers they employ around here," Will complained. Sitting down, Will fired up the laptop and cracked his knuckles. "Time to go save democracy, boys."

Craig and Gary were still in shock, their minds trying to catch up with what they had just witnessed.

That was when Joshua finally woke up.

"What's going on, guys?"

* * *

The tension was nerve-racking.

Samruk International's leadership element met to conduct mission planning while they were still underway. Deckard, Sergeant Major Korgan, Fedorchenko, Shatayeva, Aghassi, Nikita, and their mortar section sergeant, Ivan, stood around a monitor looking at images they pulled off of Google Earth. Pat, Kurt, and Chuck were also in attendance. As senior soldiers in the company, they were always around to provide input during mission planning.

While most of them were sleeping, the second pass from a satellite in polar orbit came in. The imagery indicated a faint wake from the enemy vessel. It had only deviated slightly from their original heading, making way for a small cove along the Russian coast. The JSOC think tank provided some additional imagery and data, then Samruk leadership began planning the mission.

Concepts of the operation were cast aside just as quickly as they were dreamed up by the veteran soldiers. In the Arctic, mobility options were extremely limited. The cove was surrounded by steep cliffs covered in ice. Flanking around would take hours that they probably didn't have. The direct approach led them through icy waters where they were prone to being ambushed along the same cliffs.

At the far end of the cave was their objective, an abandoned naval port from the Soviet era. The imagery they had showed oblong objects strewn around the end of the cove. Apparently, it was a submarine graveyard. Doing some calculations, Otter estimated that the enemy must have set up a fuel depot there ahead of time to refuel their ship. Without knowing the size of the enemy ship, he made an educated guess that they would be running low on fuel at this point.

Whether or not they were still in the cove was another matter altogether. Again, all Otter could do was make an educated guess as to what the enemy ship's speed was relative to the Carrickfergus. They might catch them in the act of refueling, or they might miss them by several hours.

Deckard didn't like it at all. He'd screwed up royally by deploying with gun trucks when he should have brought more snowmobiles and Zodiac boats, but in the end, you deploy with the Army you have, not the one you want. Now they had to make the best of it.

Rochenoire was sketching something out on the whiteboard and waving his hands at Pat as they argued about some tactical detail. Deckard had reviewed their options and now he had made a decision as well. Once again, this was going to be sketchy as hell.

Chapter 9

Cody overhanded the miniature unmanned aerial vehicle into the air.

The wind caught the UAV's wings as the small electric engine buzzed, spinning the propeller. The drone itself was French in origin, while the sensor package had been bought in the U.K. and Austria. Cody had assembled the drone himself in his hackerspace several weeks prior. Turning away from the deck of the ship, the computer hacker quickly ducked back inside and handled the small control unit.

Using two joysticks retrofitted to a tablet, Cody could look through the drone's cameras and steer it where he needed it to go. On the screen, broken ice scattered throughout the sea quickly gave way as the drone climbed to a hundred feet above sea level and flew over land. Maneuvering the drone in a long, lazy arc, he flew around the cove, looking for signs of the enemy. Flipping a switch, the thermal camera kicked in. White splotches on the tablet would indicate the infrared signature given off by human body heat.

Leaning up against a bulkhead, he put the drone in a loiter route over the objective area. Everything looked clear. It would have a little under an hour of fuel before he had to return the drone back to the Carrickfergus and attempt to land it on the deck. Reaching into his pocket, he palmed a radio and held it up to his mouth.

"This is Fapper-1," Cody said into the radio, barely holding back a laugh as he gave his self-selected call sign. "The coast is clear. No signs of an ambush on the cliffs, over."

"Roger." It was Deckard's voice. "We're about to get underway. Can you give us a pass straight up the cove and see if anyone is active down there?"

"On it," Cody said.

Pocketing the radio, he went back to the control unit, glad that he wasn't going to be out there paddling in the Russian Arctic.

* * *

With the Carrickfergus's barge deck lowered, twin Zodiac FC470 boats were launched simultaneously. The black inflatable boats each carried 10 mercenaries, making for a total of a 20-man assault force. They were going in light, but it had been decided that sailing the Carrickfergus into the cove could end catastrophically if the enemy had another ambush prepared. Better to go in with the Zodiacs while their mothership cut off entry and exit from the narrow channel.

The coxswain of each Zodiac steered the gas-powered engine, taking them on a slow approach through the mouth of the cove. At the head of each boat was a PKM machine gunner, ready to lay down some cyclic fire if the need arose. The riflemen sat on the sides of the Zodiacs, their eyes darting around, looking for targets. Rocky cliffs lurched by on both sides of the mercenaries as the Zodiacs slipped into the cove. Coxswains eased them around drifting sheets of ice.

Deckard looked up as Cody's drone buzzed overhead like a giant paper airplane. As expected, the terrain was barren, devoid of life. Out this far, the only sort of person you ever saw on land was the occasional impoverished Russian searching for and digging up mammoth tusks for sale on the black market.

As the rubber boats edged around the rocks and ice, the submarine graveyard came into view. The aquamarine waters parted as the boats churned forward, revealing dozens of dark red and brown rusted submarine hulls dead ahead.

Back in Tampa, SCOPE had done some analysis and determined that most of the decaying husks were Tango-class attack submarines. Now they were just fading vestiges of the Cold War, abandoned in a forgotten corner of the globe.

The PKM gunner at the head of the Zodiac shifted, the black barrel of his weapon sweeping across the submarines as he scanned for signs of the enemy. The subs were in a state of obvious disarray, some lying on their side, half in the water and half out of it. Beyond the tangle of rusting metal was a dock and large industrial crane.

"Six, this is Fapper-1." Cody's voice came over the command net. "I just lost the drone, over."

"What does that mean?" Deckard hissed in response.

"It had plenty of loiter time left. All of a sudden the engine went down and it began to go into a spin. Then the video cut out. I don't know what went wrong. It could have been a gust of wind, over."

"Catch anything on video before it went down?"

"SHIT," Cody cursed, his Tourette's acting up again. "No, nothing."

Deckard wasn't about to abort the mission just because the drone went down. They had gotten some good situational awareness from its surveillance feed before the UAV crashed, at least. Now they had to get in there and do the grunt work.

Once they were a hundred meters away, Deckard radioed to Fedorchenko in the other Zodiac.

"Do you see any signs of the enemy ship?"

The Kazakh platoon sergeant turned and looked at him from the other boat, which was cruising 10 meters off their right flank. His dark eyes were wide as they drilled into Deckard. He shook his head in reply.

"Carrickfergus," Deckard said as he bumped up radio channels from the assault net to the command net. "This is Six. No sign of enemy activity. They were never here or we missed them. I'm taking our element deeper into the AO to look for signs. Maybe there is something we can use to pick up their trail again."

"Understood, Six," Sergeant Major Korgan replied from the bridge of their ship.

The head of the cove was a tangle of rusted, twisted steel that looked like it belonged on the set of a Mad Max film set in the ice age. Deckard directed Fedorchenko to take his boat to the dock while his team would explore the submarine graveyard. Deckard was already having a bad feeling that this would be a dry hole.

Still, as they approached the nearest submarine that had been scuttled along the shore, Deckard looked carefully through the snowflakes swirling in the wind. He couldn't get over the feeling they were being watched, even though Cody's drone didn't pick up any thermal signatures.

The nose of their Zodiac rubbed up against the submarine's deck. The PKM gunner immediately jumped off and scrambled up the hull. Deckard and seven other Samruk International mercenaries lumbered up in their cold-weather gear and jumped onto the sub. The coxswain stayed on the boat, making sure they were ready for extraction.

The mercenaries quickly found a hatch and descended into the belly of the Soviet-era submarine. Deckard pushed his goggles up onto his forehead, his eyes adjusting to the darkness. They stepped carefully, avoiding rusted-out portions of the deck as they walked through the corridor toward a light in the distance. The submarine was literally coming apart at the seams, as it had been exposed to the elements for years on end, including the water freezing and then melting each year.

Stairways with rust brown railings, leading to nowhere, made it feel like they were in a haunted house straight out of some Cold War nightmare. It was evident to Deckard that no one had been there in a very long time.

At the end of the corridor, the sub was blasted open where the torpedo tubes were located, the tear in the hull leaving a gap a few feet from the next submarine. The mercs hopped across the gap one by one onto the next submarine, this one lying on its side. The wind cut into their faces again, forcing Deckard and the others to pull down their goggles and pull up their face masks.

"Six," the earbud connected to Deckard's radio crackled. "The dock...clear."

Fedorchenko's voice was cutting in and out, his words full of static.

"Roger."

Fedorchenko had cleared the docks, but there were about a dozen abandoned submarines in the cove. He might as well search as many of them as possible just to be sure. It wasn't like they had any other leads. The mercenaries crawled down the hull as it began sloping down into the sea.

From where he stood, Deckard could see there was another submarine hull just under the surface of the water, adjacent to the one they were on. Trudging through an inch of water wasn't a big deal in boots. They could use the sub as an underwater bridge to make their way over to the next section of the submarine graveyard.

Deckard spoke to the Kazakhs in Russian, instructing them on which route to take. The PKM gunner went into a prone position behind what was left of the submarine mast while the rest of them shuffled down the side to the submarine that was just barely submerged. Deckard took the lead, slinging his AK and sliding down the edge of the hull on his ass. For a moment, he fell through the air, then his boots came down on the top of the sub with a splash.

Waving the other mercenaries after him, Deckard sloshed through the ice water as he walked along the top of the submarine. His fear was that the aging submarine would give way under his weight and he would tumble right through the fuselage and into the cold water, but even after decades of sitting in the cove, it was probably unlikely. Submarine hulls had to be extremely strong, made with hardened steel to withstand the pressures found in the depths of the ocean.

Looking over his shoulder, Deckard could see that the other mercenaries were lined up behind him. Their PKM gunner was still up above on the other submarine, ready to provide suppressive fire if they made contact with the enemy. Keeping his rifle at the low ready, Deckard scanned for targets. He could hear the low creaks and snarls of metal against metal that echoed through the cove as the elements took their toll on the Soviet subs.

Reaching the far side of the cove, Deckard put an arm out to grab onto the next submarine. There was a rust-encrusted ladder rung sticking out from the fuselage. Just as his gloved fingertips reached out and brushed against the ladder, machine gun fire seemed to blast all around him. Deckard was suddenly propelled backwards. One hand tightened around his rifle while the other reached out in vain to find something to brace himself against.

He flew through the air and came down hard on the top of the submarine, then continued, somersaulting backwards, and rolled off the side into the Arctic Ocean. Disoriented, Deckard suddenly realized why it felt like a giant iron hand was crushing his chest. He couldn't feel his arms or legs. And he was sinking.

Sinking deeper as everything began to go dark.

* * *

Fedorchenko was stunned as he watched the submarine that Deckard and his men were crossing swing around without warning and pop up out of the water. The cigar-shaped black ship didn't look like any submarine he had ever seen. The ship executed a sharp left turn that tossed the Samruk mercenaries over the side like rag dolls in a gale-force wind. Arms and legs went spinning and kicking through the air before they splashed down in the freezing water.

With its nose now pointed toward the mouth of the cove, the ship rose even farther out of the water, almost like a hydrofoil, and shot toward the Carrickfergus. Fedorchenko squeezed his radio's push-to-talk button.

"Incoming ship!" he shouted. "Tag it! Tag it!"

The black ship was just a few hundred meters from the Carrickfergus now, set on a collision course.

"Incoming! Anyone?"

Nothing but static came over the net. That was when Fedorchenko realized that they were being jammed. That was also when he realized that green tracer rounds from machine gun fire were zipping right over his shoulder.

* * *

Nikita's eyes were like saucers; he was still in disbelief at what he had just witnessed. His boss and a half dozen of their men had just been condemned to Davy Jones's Locker as they impacted the icy water. What he had thought was another partially submerged decaying submarine was now a sleek, jet-black speed boat racing straight at the Carrickfergus. It must have been a few hundred feet in length and looked like a giant spear heading right at them. Up on the deck, Nikita set down his HK417 rifle and reached for a Mk14 grenade launcher.

Looking like a giant snub-nosed .38 revolver, the Mk14 featured a cylinder that held six 40mm grenades. He knew he wasn't going to sink it with a couple of high-explosive grenades; they probably wouldn't even penetrate the hull, but it was what he had. Leaning over the railing, Nikita fired as fast as he could pull the trigger, walking his shots across the black ship as it bore down on him. Muffled explosions popped off across the ship to no visible effect.

The enemy vessel was only a few hundred meters away. He plopped out the empty HE canisters and dropped in a tracking round. Closing the cylinder, he looked up as he tucked the stock of the Mk14 into his shoulder.

Nikita's stomach fell out from under him. The ship was about to ram the Carrickfergus and take them all to watery graves at the bottom of the ocean. Nonetheless, his finger tightened around the trigger as the ship came in to ram them.

Then it was gone.

The black ship dropped down under the water, chunks of ice sloshing into the space the ship had just occupied. With the crash of waves, the ship surfaced on the other side of the Carrickfergus. The wake created by the surfacing ship rocked him as he stood on the deck, forcing Nikita to grab onto a railing to support himself.

Taking off at high speed, the demon ship disappeared as quickly as it had revealed itself.

* * *

Fedorchenko watched in horror as the coxswain below tried to navigate the waters between the submarines and rescue his drowning teammates, only to see him driven away by machine gun fire. They traced geysers of water back and forth in front of the Zodiac, the guns trying to triangulate in on him. The coxswain was forced to veer away and take cover behind one of the submarines.

Meanwhile, the Kazakh mercenary sergeant had taken a knee behind the old crane as staccato bursts from the machine guns filled the air. The shots were coming from behind the docks. The mercenary sergeant cursed. The enemy had left a stay-behind force to ambush their pursuers.

Then, an automatic grenade launcher started firing. White flashes ripped across the dock as the grenades exploded around Fedorchenko's position.

"One o'clock, fifty meters," someone yelled above the gunfire.

Finally, one of the mercs had announced the enemy position. It sounded like Nate, the former MARSOC Marine who they had just hired. Fedorchenko peeked out from behind the crane and his head was nearly taken off as the machine gunner vectored in on him instantly. Sure enough, not 50 meters away, he could see the muzzle flashes coming from inside an old fishing shack or storage shed. A frontal assault would be suicide.

"Nate, lay down a base of fire!"

The former Marine quickly got their element's PKM gunner on target, walking a 7.62mm autofire onto the abandoned structure.

"Flank left. Follow me!" Fedorchenko dashed from behind cover and leapt off the dock as more tracer fire sought him out. He hit the ground, stumbled, and quickly regained his footing. The Kazakh found himself in the middle of dozens of bright red 55-gallon drums. They were brand new, easily standing out by comparison to everything else in the cove, which was old and decrepit. Their intelligence estimate seemed to be correct; the enemy had set up a fuel depot in the cove.

With the other mercenaries following his lead, Fedorchenko stayed low and flanked around the machine gun position. Nate and his gunner were going cyclic in the meantime, drawing the enemy's fire. Hopefully they were drawing enough fire to distract the gunners from the twin Zodiacs out on the water behind them. Submerged in the Arctic water, the Samruk men had seconds rather than minutes before they froze to death.

Crawling up behind a pile of rotting railroad ties, the mercenaries formed up. Now within hand grenade range, one of the Kazakhs primed a frag and chucked it through the door. Once the grenade cooked off and detonated, a secondary explosion also blew the aluminum roof off the building. With the booby trap blown, the mercenaries ran toward the structure and through the open door. The smell of sulfate stung their nostrils as they entered and cleared the room.

Two PKM machine guns and one AGS-30 grenade launcher lay on their sides, knocked over by the grenade blast. There wasn't a person in sight. The three weapons systems had been mounted on tall tripods and oriented out the windows. Fedorchenko bent down to examine the odd configuration in which the crew-served weapons had been set up. On top of each was mounted a green metal square that was about one foot by two feet in size. Wires ran from the square to a control unit for each gun, as well as a battery pack. The charging mechanisms on the weapons were controlled by an automated solenoid.

They were normal Russian infantry weapons that had been fitted with a radar tracking and targeting system. Once again, the enemy had left drones behind to ambush their pursuers. They had also jammed their commo, further disrupting their normal standard operating procedures.

The bad guys got the drop on the mercenaries with superior technology.

Fedorchenko snarled. More than any of that, they had simply been outfoxed, outflanked, and out-planned by an opposing force that absolutely had their shit together.

He turned and ran out of the building as the Zodiacs circled the cove, looking for survivors.

* * *

Tampa, Florida

Will slammed his fists down on the table.

"Son of a bitch. I died again."

"How much more time are you going to waste playing video games?" Craig asked.

"It's not just that I'm losing, it's that they are not interested in me. I've been going head to head with suspected intelligence proxies on the PvP server."

"PvP?"

104

"Player vs. player. It's where the players in the game go to test their characters by dueling with each other."

"Yeah, great. Whatever."

"The problem is that they don't have any reason to give a shit about me. They need some...."

"Some what?"

Will was silent for a moment as his jaw hung open.

"They need some bait dangled out in front of them."

The corners of Will's mouth were slowly tugged up at the corners.

"You're scaring the squares in this office, Will."

Chapter 10

"Oh. My. God."

Nate covered his mouth with his hand.

"It's a tragedy," Pat confirmed.

They stood in the doorway of the ship's communal showers, the steam from hot water billowing above their heads.

"It looks just like a penis," Rochenoire stated bluntly, "only smaller."

"Hung like an elevator button," Nate mumbled.

Deckard looked up at them with fury in his eyes. His lips were still blue even after shivering himself half to death in the scalding hot water for half an hour. Crouched over, he hugged himself hoping that the feeling would return to his body at some point. At any rate, it was clear that he wasn't going to see descended testicles for at least a week.

"I h-h-h-hope—"

"Hope what, Deckard?" Pat asked. "Hope that I put you down and spare you the humiliation?"

"H-h-h-hope y-y-you ffffucking die."

* * *

It was only by some miracle that none of the Samruk mercenaries were killed in the cove, but they were all walking around with their tails between their legs as they paced the deck of the Carrickfergus. Their pirate ship was normally a heterotopia of guns, high explosives, and shitty attitudes. Now they were beaten; men had been shot to pieces and frozen half to death. An organization that was used to taking no shit from anyone was now having to admit that they were simply outclassed by the enemy.

With Frank dead, Pat was next in line to assume command of Samruk International since their CEO was temporarily incapacitated.

"I think we interrupted the enemy. If they had been expecting us, they never would have allowed themselves to be trapped inside the cove like that," Pat said as Samruk ran a video teleconference with SCOPE in Tampa, Florida. "They were caught by surprise and clearly didn't think we would catch up with them that quickly."

"Hmm," Pat saw the old guy with reading glasses rub his chin on the computer monitor.

"But they laid a trap for us, expecting someone to try to follow their trail at some point. You were right about the enemy vessel; I've never seen anything like it, but it was definitely semi-submersible."

"Forward us eyewitness accounts from your after-action review," Will said as Pat briefed them. "We can conduct our own analysis."

"I will. Where are we at with our eye in the sky?"

The JSOC think tank members looked down at the table in front of them. It didn't take a high-resolution feed to realize that something was wrong.

"Our satellite in polar orbit was blinded on its last pass," Will informed him.

"Blinded?"

"High-powered ground-based laser. We don't know where it originated from, exactly. Could have been Russia. Could have been China."

"So I don't have any ISR?" Pat said, referring to intelligence, surveillance, and reconnaissance platforms.

"We are working on getting Global Hawk into your AO, but it's taking time. The Russians are also not cooperating the way they were in the opening hours of this mess," Will said.

"None of us know for sure how this thing is going to play out," Craig said. "But we will keep working it."

"No," Pat said as he looked out from the bridge to the ocean in front of him, "*I'm* going to keep working it."

"What the does that mean?"

"One of my boys put a hole in the enemy ship before it got away. 40mm high-explosive grenade. We're following a plume of gasoline it's dribbling out behind it." Pat smiled, looking at the clearly visible trail of fuel left in the ocean.

"Any idea where the hell they are going?" Will asked.

"Ship's captain says they are probably heading to T6."

"T6?"

"The T6 ice floe," Otter shouted from the helm. "A giant piece a floating ice. A Coast Guard aircraft spotted it a month ago and estimated that it was five miles wide. T6 is projected to be right in the path of where that bat-boat is heading. It is going to take us about fourteen hours to get to T6. That semi-submersible can haul ass above water when it wants to. They might be making a beeline for the ice floe for an extract, compromising stealth for speed, instead of staying submersed."

"A plane equipped with ski wheels would do the trick," Gary said, speaking up for the first time on the VTC from Tampa.

"If they are leaking fuel, they might be going slow to conserve gas as well," Craig said as he turned toward Gary.

"Irrelevant," Will cut in. "Get there as fast as you can. If you see the enemy, wipe them out. In the meantime, we are on the horn with the Coast Guard and the U.S. Navy. Thankfully, we have a submarine of our own that was on a routine patrol under the Arctic that can help cut off access to the Bering Strait. A Coast Guard cutter is also on its way to this choke point. We prefer to keep this problem isolated in the Arctic. Once they make it into the open ocean, there is no telling where they will go. We will have lost them. At least this way, we know they are somewhere between the polar ice cap and the coast of Russia."

"We'll track 'em and assault 'em," Pat said.

"And Pat?"

"Yeah?"

"Can Deckard move his fingers enough to type on a keyboard yet?"

* * *

Screams echoed down the cobblestone street. Baskets full of produce were overturned and laundry thrown off the line as the townspeople scattered. Doors and windows were slammed shut. In seconds, the street was empty. A single bucket lay turned on its side in the middle of the road. The water that had been in it now seeped between the stones.

A blade master stepped out of the shadows.

He squinted in the midday light and held a hand out in front of him to shield his eyes from the sun. The blade master wore ornate black leather greaves and a similar cloak under which his abdomen was protected by dwarven dragon-scale armor. His knuckles were likewise protected by Cyridian metal built into his leather gauntlets, forged by a master blacksmith from ore mined from a falling star.

At the end of the street, a wooden cart was flung through the air. It crashed into the side of a house and disintegrated into a thousand pieces. From around the corner, an orc lord lurched into view. Standing nearly 12 feet tall, the orc was clad only in dirty rags, leaving his dark green, muscular body exposed. Spotting the blade master, the orc roared, exposing his white fangs.

The blade master drew his weapons. A katana appeared in one hand and a Akkaidian dagger in the other, the weapons specific to the blade master's particular style of fighting.

The orc charged the blade master, bum-rushing all the way down the street. The blade master stood his ground, ready for a fight. The orc lord was almost on top of him when he was suddenly yanked back into the alleyway.

"Have you lost your mind?" a voice scolded him.

The blade master was pulled farther down the alley as the orc lord tried to force himself through the narrow passage. A clawed hand swept frantically, scratching against the stone houses on either side as it sought out the blade master.

"You need at least a party of four to take on that bad boy."

The blade master looked up at his rescuer. His wore a brown hooded shawl, his midnight-colored skin giving him away as a dark elf.

"Let's go," the dark elf ordered. "I'm going to take you to a newbie dungeon to show you how it's done. This is a different world, with different rules."

"Yeah, I'm finding that," the blade master said sardonically.

Walking through the labyrinthine back alleys of the city, the pair came to a large, open graveyard. Past the tombstones stood a towering mausoleum constructed with green marble. The dark elf pushed on the heavy iron door and it swung open. A cloud of dust shook off the entrance as they walked inside.

"This way."

Down the well-worn steps, they came to a balcony. In the dark chamber below, a reanimated human skeleton paced with a short sword in one bony hand. A few burning torches mounted in the walls let off a dim light, casting shadows in every direction.

"Equip your rope dart," the dark elf instructed.

"Rope dart?"

"Really? The micro-bow mounted to the gauntlet on your wrist."

"Oh, cool."

The blade master loaded a dart affixed to a fiber cord into the six-inch bow on his gauntlet.

"Now fire it at that wooden beam on the other side of the chamber."

The blade master fired and the dart slammed into the wooden beam with an audible *thwunk*, which made the skeleton look around in confusion.

"Tie the other end of the rope around the balcony railing."

With the rope pulled taut, the line now wobbled above the skeleton below.

"A blade master fights using indirect methods, which should be right in your wheelhouse. You can also use the environment to your advantage to get the drop on the baddies."

"I'll give it a try."

The blade master leapt onto the rope and began balancing his way over the chamber, putting one foot in front of the other. The skeleton was now on alert, sensing someone else in the chamber. Once he was directly overhead, the blade master drew his katana and dropped down on top of his opponent. The four-foot blade sank right through the skeleton man's skull as the blade master landed a perfect attack. Bones cracked and scattered across the floor.

"Not bad," the dark elf said from the balcony.

Just then, a stone slab on the side of the wall began to groan. It receded back into a hidden passage. Inside, the blade master heard the distinctive clacking of bony feet scraping against stone. Metal weapons gave off a ring as they collided with each other.

"Uh oh," the dark elf said, now seemingly fresh out of sage wisdom for his protégé.

Four animated skeletons burst from the chamber door and rushed the blade master. Turning, he found a way to escape, up a ramp that led to another part of the dungeon. Sprinting up the ramp, the blade master looked back to the see the skeletons following him up. A wooden barrel sat in the corner where the ramp changed directions, wax from a long since burned-out candle decorating the top of it.

The blade master threw the barrel on its side and rolled it toward the ramp. The skeletons would be on top of him in another second. Kicking the barrel down the ramp, the blade master tapped into his magicka, casting a fireball at the barrel as it began to gain momentum. The barrel burst into flames and rolled right over the four skeletons. Their short swords went flying into the air as they crumbled and burst into bone fragments.

"OK," the dark elf said, somehow materializing back at the blade master's side. "I think you are getting the hang of this."

"Now what?"

"Now you go and get their attention."

"Whose attention?"

"The ones you are chasing halfway across the world, of course."

Chapter 11

"Keep the drone near the ship," Deckard told Cody as he prepared to launch his toy airplane. Thankfully, he had more than one. "I don't want it getting brought down by electronic countermeasures or otherwise being spotted by the enemy."

Cody hurled the drone off the deck of the ship and into the air, using his tablet to control its flight. The drone spiraled over the Carrickfergus as it gained altitude. Night had set in and everyone knew that the coming movement was going to be perilous in the dark, but on the other hand it would limit the enemy's visibility as well. It was safe to assume that an opponent this sophisticated would have access to night vision and thermals, but just like Samruk, the Arctic would severely limit their battery life.

"OK, I've got something," Cody announced. "Thermal signatures on the other side of the ice floe."

"How far out?"

"Hard to say. A couple of miles, I would guess."

"OK, get me your best guess at a distance as well as a direction. We'll initiate the movement. Keep the drone up, then bring it back to refuel, and send it back up when we are ready to make contact with the enemy."

"I will."

Deckard turned to prepare the movement across the ice.

"Hey," Cody said, stopping him. "I heard you are playing Dungeons and Dragons in your free time or something?"

"What?"

"D&D is great, man. I have some 12-sided dice and a dungeon master guide at my work station if you ever want—"

"Hey, fuck you dude. That is work-related shit."

"No, I am a big fan. My character has gone into legendary status."

"Go fuck yourself, Cody, I have shit to do."

"Fine. Fuck you then."

* * *

One by one the mercenaries scurried down a cargo net that had been hung from the side of the ship. They slipped down and landed on the ice floe before moving out and establishing a security perimeter. No one was more cautious about the landing than Deckard. He still didn't feet quite right after his accidental swim in the Arctic Ocean. Getting crushed between the Carrickfergus and the ice floe seemed like a better fate than going for another dunk in the water.

With the two platoons deployed out on the ice, the more experienced men in Arctic and winter operations took the lead to guide the others through the darkness. Ice floes were dangerous to begin with, even more so at night when you could run into a lead—an opening or crack in the ice—at any time. Also present would be pressure ridges. While leads happened where the ice was pulled apart, pressure ridges were created where the ice had been pushed together. Aside from that, new leads could appear as the ice cracked, and new fissures were created as the ice came apart.

Deckard chambered a round into the chamber of his Kalashnikov, the others quickly following suit. They were going into combat in the most inhospitable environment on earth, and this time they were all looking for some payback after a string of embarrassing defeats.

There was one thing that scared every former special operations soldier more than death, and that was failure. They had lost men, and with everything happening back in the world it was clear that the stakes didn't get any higher. Once again, Deckard and Samruk International found themselves shadowboxing an elusive enemy.

Fanning out in a series of squad-sized wedge-shaped formations, the mercenaries crept forward, their boots crunching through the snow. It was really the sound of the Arctic, or lack of sound, that drove home how far away they were from everything. Other than the wind in their ears and the snow under their feet, there was absolutely nothing. In the dark, they were isolated, each man looking back and forth every few steps to make sure he wasn't abandoned and alone.

The formation moved northeast toward the enemy position. From what little Cody had been able to surmise from the drone's imagery, the enemy had docked their boat alongside the five-foot-thick ice floe and looked to be offloading personnel and equipment. In a quick planning session, Deckard and the others gave it a high probability that the enemy would be flying out the nuclear weapon on an aircraft with ski wheels for landing on the ice. They would do it tonight, under the cover of darkness. Deckard had to make sure that didn't happen.

A clenched fist was held up by Jacob, who was leading the movement. The signal was then passed down the line by the other mercenaries. They were taking a tactical pause; something was developing up ahead. Jacob cut a hard right and led them around a lead that they had almost walked right into in the darkness. The movement wasn't especially strenuous since they were on a nearly horizontal plane with little snow, but it was nerve-racking nonetheless.

Halfway through the movement, someone broke squelch over the radio net.

"Six, there is a new thermal signature." It was Cody. "Looks like an engine block."

"Can you tell what it is?"

"I can't see shit. I'm barely keeping this thing in the air with all the wind!"

"Roger."

One day they were going to have to waterboard Cody until he learned proper radio procedures.

The mercenaries continued through the night, crossing over several pressure ridges, one of them almost six feet tall. As they got closer to where the enemy had docked, Deckard gritted his teeth. If their adversary had more operational radar-guided machine guns, they would quickly come under fire. His only hope was that the wind and snow would interfere with those systems if they had them.

Then a high-pitched whine sounded in the distance. It sounded like a massive lawnmower closing in on them as the buzzing sound got louder.

"Get down!" Jacob barked over the radio as he threw himself down on his belly. The mercenaries dove to the ground as a hovercraft emerged out of the darkness and sped right past the formation, seemingly unaware of their presence, bouncing by on its rubber skirt. Deckard reached into his jacket and pulled out a small Insight SU-232 thermal sight he wore around his neck by a lanyard to keep it warm against his chest.

He pressed the rubber protector around the lens against his eye, the thermal sight activated. The black-and-white image showed the white-hot engine block in the rear of the vehicle. It looked to be a fairly small hovercraft, maybe a two-seater with a storage compartment in the back.

"That's it," Deckard said to himself. "They are transporting the nuke to a suitable place for an aircraft to land."

"Exactly what I was thinking," Kurt Jager said as he crawled up alongside Deckard.

"Otter," Deckard said as he keyed his radio. "Make sure the snowmobile teams are ready. The enemy has the device loaded in a hovercraft. We might need an intercept."

"You got it, boss."

The Samruk mercenaries waited for another few minutes to make sure the coast was clear and that another hovercraft hadn't been offloaded from the enemy vessel, and that others were not following behind on foot. Finally, Jacob gave the all-clear as they moved out in the direction of the hovercraft. Under the moonlit sky, they had visibility for about 50 meters, but the hovercraft had quickly outpaced them. Cody provided updates to help guide them in once it appeared the hovercraft had stopped in a large open patch of ice.

It took another 20 minutes of walking before they made it to where the hovercraft sat idle. The men shook out into an assault line and crawled forward. Unfortunately, they were not lucky enough to have a pressure ridge to use as cover. They were sitting ducks out in the open. At least for now, they would have fire superiority. Just to be sure, they detailed one squad to turn around and pull rear security to make sure they didn't have any unpleasant surprises coming up behind them.

The hovercraft sat in the open, waiting.

Sergeant Major Korgan was policing the line as he crawled from position to position, making sure that everyone knew to hold fire until the airplane had landed and was within range of effective fire. Taking out the hovercraft and capturing the device that was almost certainly on board would be a coup, but taking down the aircraft would ensure that none of the enemy could be evacuated along with it, essentially stranding them in the Arctic.

From there, Deckard would be happy to let the U.S. Navy sail around and blow their ship out of the water at America's leisure while he and his men took a vacation to Fiji.

The men worked their fingers inside their gloves, trying to keep them warm. They had on enough cold-weather gear for the time being, but they would freeze if they were exposed to the elements for too long. The irony was that they ran the risk of overheating under their parkas during the movement, but then froze half to death if they were stationary for too long.

The cold was starting to make Deckard sleepy, a dangerous situation that could quickly lead to hypothermia if he actually passed out on the ice. He was grateful when the door on the hovercraft flew open and one of the passengers jumped out onto the ice. Deckard looked at him through the thermal sight, noticing an Israeli bullpup rifle slung over his back. He didn't believe for a moment that they were up against Israelis, but the state of Israel had sold those guns all over the world, making them a much more deniable weapon for black operations.

He realized that this was the first time they had actually gotten eyes on the enemy. Thus far all they had done was fight robotic proxy forces. Deckard scrutinized the image in his thermal sight as their mysterious foe walked around the hovercraft, wondering who he was and what he was thinking. Was he about to deploy some flares to guide in the aircraft?

The mercenaries nearly jumped out of their skin when they heard a massive fissure crack in the ice. A new lead opening under their position could kill them in seconds. The ice continued cracking, the sound reverberating across the empty expanse. Then, a few hundred meters from the hovercraft, Deckard saw something rising up out of the ice. Huge blocks of ice slipped and fell off the black form emerging out of the ocean beneath their feet. A black tower pushed right through the ice floe and rose into the air.

With the tower growing taller and taller, the ice in front of it and behind it was propelled upwards, cracking down the middle around the shape beneath it. The ice undulated and flexed outwards like a wave as the tower sank back down into the water for a few seconds. Then it was propelled back upwards, smashing against the ice again and forming a hill on either side of the tower before coming to a stop.

"Fuck me," Deckard said, exhaling a white cloud, his breath freezing in the air.

They were evacuating the nuclear weapon by submarine.

Sheets of ice were pushed off the top of the submarine mast, and Deckard could make out several forms through his thermal sight moving around up top. He was trying to zoom in and get a better look when the batteries froze and the screen blinked out.

Meanwhile, the hovercraft pilot jumped back inside the craft and powered it up. Skidding across the ice, the craft powered its way closer to the submarine, coming to a stop alongside where the sub was bulging out of the ice floe.

Deckard reached down and keyed his radio again.

"On my mark, give me a mad minute. Unload everything you've got on them. Only put 7.62 on the hovercraft or we risk covering ourselves in radioactive material."

Fedorchenko and Shatayeva radioed back to confirm the order.

The driver was back outside the hovercraft and opening the bay doors in the rear. It was going down now. If they got away, the next thing any of them knew, that nuclear bomb would be creating a mushroom cloud over New York City or Washington D.C.

Resting his elbows in the snow, Deckard tucked the stock of his Kalashnikov into the pocket of his shoulder. Looking down the iron sights, he took aim at the rear of the hovercraft. The creeping feeling of impending doom snuck up on him once again. Deckard had seen enough combat to know that he had to act now, not let himself be paralyzed by the fear of what could be.

Deckard milked the trigger until the stock recoiled back into his shoulder.

Then the whole world exploded, turning into a game of Star Wars as red and green tracer fire created a storm downrange from the mercenaries. Bullets sparked against the hovercraft and the submarine. Their remaining Carl Gustav and a half dozen RPG rocket launchers shook the ice as they blasted the submarine. A few shots went wide, but more than a couple scored direct hits, creating brilliant yellow flashes that briefly illuminated the ice floe around them.

Muzzle flashes continued to light up the darkness, looking like dozens of strobe lights at a dance club as Samruk peppered the enemy with automatic fire. Deckard's radio started blowing up with a flurry of traffic that he wasn't able to keep up with over all of the shooting.

Garbled transmissions rang out as squad leaders attempted to give orders over the cacophony of machine gun fire.

"Cease fire! Cease fire!" Deckard yelled.

After a few more sputters of gunfire, the Samruk mercenaries managed to ratchet it down. They lay in the prone, watching for signs of life. The submarine mast was now a smoking tower. Getting his thermals back up for a few seconds after having it under his parka, Deckard could make out several gaping holes in the submarine where anti-tank rounds blasted it.

"Six," Cody said over the radio. You've got a lot of movement back at their ship. It looks like they are prepping a couple more vehicles."

"Launch the snowmobiles to intercept."

"Roger."

They watched and listened for signs of life in the kill zone, but nothing moved.

"Assault!"

The mercenaries loaded fresh magazines into their rifles and new belts into their machine guns before getting to their feet. They rearranged themselves into a tighter assault line and began stalking forward across the ice floe. A loud groan could be heard over the sound of the wind in their ears, the submarine scraping against the ice as it slowly began sinking.

"Six, this is Frogman," Rochenoire said over the radio. "We are en route to intercept the enemy snowmobile team, over."

"Roger, Deckard confirmed. "We're counting on you to cover our six."

Scanning for targets, none of the Kazakh, American, or European mercs saw anything moving. They were a couple hundred meters away from the hovercraft and the submarine, which was still sinking, when they noticed the ice beneath their feet vibrating.

"Another lead opening in the ice?" Fedorchenko said from Deckard's side.

"Could be."

The ice was now visibly vibrating, bouncing around the snow on the surface. Several of the mercenaries slipped and had to be helped back up to their feet. They stumbled along, heading toward the hovercraft.

Then the ice snapped open, flashing like a bolt of lightning right in front of their eyes. The chasm opened, the ice tilting, sending the mercenaries falling to their knees or flat on their faces. The crack continued to grow, racing up between the submarine, the hovercraft, and the Samruk troopers.

Deckard's mouth hung open as the ice tilted backwards, sending them slipping away from the submarine. They skidded across the floe, and without any ice axes to help them gain purchase, they were at nature's mercy. The mercenaries slid about half the length of a football field. Deckard's stomach turned upside down. The sheet of ice was now pitching forward. An object in motion stays in motion. They were about to slip right off the side and into the crack; then, into the dark waters below.

"Brace yourself with something!" he yelled.

Down on his knees, Deckard slid toward the ice valley in front of them. As the floe tilted down, he could see the churning Arctic water. No one would be able to pull him out this time. Letting his AK-103 hang by its sling, Deckard slapped at his chest rig, his hand closing around the handle of his knife. Yanking the blade from the Kydex sheath, he twisted to face the ice, then slammed the black fixed-blade knife into the ice.

The knife successfully stopped his collision course with death. One of the Kazakhs was not so fortunate. As he careened across the ice, Deckard reached out and grabbed him by the sleeve, holding on to his hard point in the ice with one hand. It felt like his shoulder was about to be pulled out of its socket, but he had held on to his teammate.

Deckard and the young Kazakh watched in horror as several of their friends got too close to the chasm, unable to find something to break their trajectory forward. Two Samruk mercenaries slipped right off the side, their howls disappearing into the night. Another formed claws with his hands, trying to dig into the ice. It was to no avail; he was unable to scramble away from the edge. He too disappeared into the water.

The sheet of ice they were on was leveling out, but there was now a huge lead in the ice between them and the enemy. Echoes could be heard all around them as the ice floe cracked again and again. The entire island-sized sheet of ice was breaking up.

"What the fuck is this shit?" Deckard grunted.

It was no coincidence that the ice floe started breaking up just as they got the drop on the enemy.

Reaching down, Deckard pulled his knife out of the ground and slid it back into its sheath. It was a Company Knife, made for commandos, mercs, and black-helicopter types by expert knifemaker Newt Livesay. Reaching down, he helped the Kazakh trooper to his feet.

"Six, we're not going to be able to intercept. The ice is cracking up all around us. What the hell is going on?" Rochenoire radioed him.

"Good question. Just get back to the Carrickfergus."

Just then, two black snowmobiles powered over a pressure ridge in the distance. From across the chasm,

Deckard watched them tear through the snow and pull up alongside the destroyed hovercraft. They got off their snowmobiles and began unloading something out of the back. Deckard pressed the thermal sight against his eye.

Four men in black balaclavas unloaded a large plastic case that looked to be about the size of a refrigerator. They held onto the carry handles at the sides of the case and set it down on a sled attached to the back of one of the snowmobiles. Meanwhile, the submarine had completely slipped back beneath the ice, its status unknown, but it couldn't be good.

"On my tracer fire," Deckard ordered.

Leveling his AK-103, he sent a stream of red tracer rounds at the snowmobiles on the other side of the ice floe. The Samruk mercenaries joined in, cutting loose on the enemy one more time. The balaclava-clad men were already on their snowmobiles, vanishing into the dark.

Deckard's jaw tensed as he lowered the smoking barrel of his Kalashnikov.

Everything about this was wrong.

Chapter 12

"Which way are we going?"

"Dammit, we can't go that way!"

"Nyet, nyet!"

"It's blocked, it's blocked!"

"Go back the way we came!"

"We ain't going back that way, the ice just cracked again."

"What's on our right flank? I can't see shit!"

Deckard could hear the panic rising in their voices as his men radioed back and forth, desperately trying to find a way off the ice floe. They had spent two hours weaving across the ice, dodging fresh breaks as the ice island continued tearing itself apart. Every time they thought they had found an opening, they would run right into another lead—20-foot openings with sloshing sea water at the bottom.

"That's it," Deckard finally ordered over the radio. "Put them in a file. Dag, get us the fuck out of here now."

"Roger that," the the former Norwegian FSK commando replied. "On it."

The Samruk mercenaries broke formation and began moving in a single-file line, sacrificing security for speed. The ice was coming apart under their feet, and if they didn't rendezvous with the Carrickfergus soon, they would drown, freeze, or be left squatting on a car-sized piece of ice, floating toward Siberia like a lost polar bear.

Dag led them over a chest-high pressure ridge, then hand-railed alongside a fresh lead, driving them deeper and deeper into the darkness of night. The men were frantic, eyes darting around the ice, looking for ghosts that weren't there. One of the newer guys even let off a burst of Kalashnikov fire at an imaginary enemy before

Chuck Rochenoire blasted him in the face with a clenched fist.

Deckard was losing control of his element, and shit was getting more gangster by the second.

"Otter, flip on the IR strobe for thirty seconds."

The strobe light mounted on the Carrickfergus would blink on and off in the infrared spectrum, visible to those wearing night vision goggles but invisible to the naked eye. Asking for 30 seconds of strobe light wasn't because Deckard was worried about the enemy spotting their ship. At this point he could care less, but the batteries in their PVS-14 night vision monoculars would freeze after much longer than that.

"That's it, I've got them," Dag confirmed over the radio. "Five hundred meters due east."

The radio batteries would freeze as well, but they now made sure they wore their inter-team radios under thermal layers of clothing beneath their parkas.

"Get us there."

After another 15 minutes of stumbling around the ice, they could see the silhouette of their ship docked alongside the ice. Fedorchenko spread his men out in a half-moon formation to pull security while their sister platoon scaled the cargo net and climbed up the hull of the ship. Once they were on board, the other platoon collapsed down and climbed aboard as well.

Deckard was the last off the ice. Slinging his rifle, he grabbed onto the net with one hand and looked over his shoulder.

All he saw was darkness.

All he heard was the howling of the wind.

The enemy was out there. Somewhere.

Deckard swung around and stuck his foot into the net, then climbed up hand over hand, promising himself that he was going to find them.

Then he was going to kill every single one of them.

* * *

Flinging open the door to the bridge, Deckard dumped his kit on the ground and slammed his rifle down on a shelf.

"Where—"

Deckard interrupted the ship's captain before he even had the chance to ask.

"East. Just head east."

Opening his laptop, Deckard punched in the number for the JSOC guys in Tampa. He needed a word. The VTC opened and he was looking at the usual four-man cast of characters.

"Deckard, what happened?" Gary asked. "Did you get them?"

"Prevented them from transferring the weapon. It was a submarine, not an airplane, but they got away."

"What? How the hell did that happen?"

"We need to talk. You level with me right now about what I'm up against or I'm assaulting my way to Tampa to skull-fuck the four of you once I'm done up here."

"Whoa, hey, what are you talking about?"

"What. The. Fuck. Am. I. Hunting."

"We told you, we're still trying to fit the puzzle pieces together. We don't know who this is."

"Beyond that. Whatever the fuck it is they stole, it isn't nuclear."

"The Urals compound they hit is a nuclear research facility."

127

"Bullshit," Deckard said as he slammed his fist on the table. "Whatever that thing is, they activated it just as we were moving in for the kill. It shook the ice beneath our feet. The next thing I know, the ice floe was coming apart right under us and my men were getting sucked into the ocean. They made the entire ice floe destabilize so that they could get the device back to their ship and escape."

Everyone in Tampa was silent.

"What the fuck am I up against here? I want an answer and I want it right fucking now."

Will cleared his throat.

"There have been stories—rumors really—coming out of Russia since the Soviet years."

"Rumors of what?"

"An entirely new generation of weapons. Direct-energy systems, psytronics, stuff that can even steer weather patterns. Sometimes defectors or recruited assets would pass on whispers about this kind of stuff."

"Consider the rumors confirmed. They've been holding an ace up their sleeve."

"None of it makes sense. We've had scientific review boards come up with classified findings. None of the math adds up."

"Humor me."

"We know that it is possible for man-made earthquakes to be induced. It has been done accidentally in India and China by building massive water reservoirs on top of fault lines. Some scientists have theorized that nuclear testing is also responsible for increased earthquake activity, but there isn't much proof of that," Will said.

"What about actual weaponization?"

"Well, even scientists more open to this idea only believe that it's possible to tickle seismic activity where there is already great tectonic pressures, basically inducing an earthquake that is already going to happen at some point, maybe making it a little stronger."

"There are already frictions on an ice floe; we know that because of the leads and pressure ridges present. But that is nothing like the tectonic forces of the earth's plates," Deckard replied.

"No, it isn't," Will agreed. "Which means the Russians may be much further along with the weaponization process than any of us had suspected. SCOPE employs a number of scientists as consultants who we will have to call in to work on this."

"We are in the shit right now. How is it possible for something like this to work?"

"If I was to speculate," Will said. "I would guess it utilizes electromagnetic energy. Nikola Tesla claimed to have nearly shaken a building to the ground with a device he built based upon what he termed 'telegeodynamics.' From there, we are getting into conspiracy theory territory."

"An area of expertise for you, isn't it, Will?" Craig said as he turned to face his co-worker.

"Mine too," Deckard added. "I've seen too many black helicopters to discount it. Especially when it is right in front of my eyes."

"Where does this leave us?" Gary asked.

"We are heading east. With the Bering Strait cut off, they won't make it into the Pacific, and they won't be double-backing right into Russia's Northern Fleet."

"The northeast passage, then?"

"That is their only way out of this, through Canada and into the Atlantic. That submarine took direct hits and won't be resurfacing anytime soon, if ever. What is the status of the Global Hawk UAVs?"

"We have one platform flying up from Montana right now. It will have to refuel in Fairbanks. ETA is almost twenty-four hours."

"I'm going to pursue. We can't wait for you guys to get your shit together."

"Deckard, we need—"

Slamming his laptop shut, Deckard grabbed his rifle and threw the door open on his way out.

* * *

Opening his eyes, Deckard was immediately awake.

Despite only sleeping for five hours, he felt like he had just woken up after hibernating over the winter. When you are so exhausted that you start droning, even a little bit of sleep can make an amazing difference when it comes to recharging your brain.

Tossing a Woodland camouflage poncho liner off, he rolled out of his cot and pulled on a layer of thermal clothing before walking through the ship. Most of the men were still asleep, but a few others lay awake watching movies on portable DVD players or laptops. A few Xbox One and PlayStation Four consoles hummed in the darkness; the guys bunked in that particular area had fallen asleep watching movies or paused the screen in the middle of a Call of Duty death match.

Climbing up the steep metal steps, Deckard entered the bridge. Otter's second mate, a younger sailor in his late twenties named Squirrel, was on watch.

"Any updates?"

"Not much on our end. We are on course, heading toward the northeast passage as you instructed. Back home, half of Los Angeles lost its power grid and ISIS set off a couple car bombs in Paris," Squirrel answered.

"Someone keeping the pressure on us."

"Huh?"

"Nothing."

Sitting behind a desk, Deckard opened his laptop.

* * *

The blade master pulled back on the crossbow's string. Most warriors couldn't draw back the bow on this particular weapon, but with a flex of his shoulders, he was able to set the string in the weapon. Inserting a poison-tipped quarrel, he scanned for his quarry.

The humidity of the jungle was thick in the air, enveloping him in a haze into which the tangles of vines over his head eventually disappeared. Somewhere, through the mist, was a Drakkenborn. Ducking under a fallen tree, the blade master stayed as stealthy as possible as he stepped into a stream. Decaying machines of war lay scattered throughout the jungle. The one in front of him, powered by steam, had been used in the Third Aqualonian War. It was the technology that gave them life, long since lost. Now they were just remnants of the past.

Moving around the arms of the broken mechanical cyclops, the blade master noticed movement in the distance.

Jackpot.

The Drakkenborn was stalking something, not realizing that he himself was the prey. As the blade master inched closer, the mist parted, revealing the half-breed spawn of a human and a dragon, made possible by the dark machinations of sorcerers and warlocks. He was as tall as he was wide, wearing a golden tunic with heavy metal armor on his shoulders and chest.

Holding a lance above his head, the Drakkenborn prepared to launch his weapon at a giant neon-green spider creeping up a tree.

Leveling the crossbow to his shoulder and taking aim, the blade master fired first. Depressing the lever on his crossbow, the quarrel shot through the air and speared the Drakkenborn in the neck. He recoiled as the poisoned dart struck its mark. Turning to face the unexpected threat, the Drakkenborn cast a bolt of lightning.

The blade master strafed to his left, narrowly avoiding the flash of electricity. Now the Drakkenborn came crashing through the brush, his sword drawn.

"Get the hell out of there," a voice sounded in the blade master's ear. It was his dark elf mentor, communicating with him via an enchanted gemstone he wore around his neck. The dark elf wore an identical one magically bound to his own.

Executing an about-face, the blade master ran toward the shard. If he could make it in time, the poison would do the rest. Slinging the crossbow over his shoulder helped him run faster. He was going to need all the help he could get.

Dodging around the overgrown war machine, the blade master cringed as another bolt of lightning hit a tree just in front of him, setting it ablaze with fire. The ferns were waist high, leaving an obvious trail in his wake, not that any was necessary. The Drakkenborn was nearly on top of him. The blade master climbed on top of one of the war machines and slid down the oversized metallic face on the opposite side.

His enemy was still in pursuit, cursing at him in some foreign language.

The shard was right in front of him in an open clearing, glowing with ancient magic. The blade master sprinted toward it. Halfway across the clearing, a dagger stuck into his back. The Drakkenborn had depleted his reserve of magicka, but was not out of the fight. Another throwing dagger sank into his shoulder.

Without looking back, the blade master dove into the shard.

The world blinked and he rolled into a dusty dirt road. A village full of small houses with thatch roofs was laid out in front of him. His hand went to his katana, and he drew it from its sheath. A dead body fell out of the shard at his feet. The Drakkenborn had succumbed to the poisoned quarrel.

Normally, poisons only degraded an enemy's abilities during a battle. They could be lethal if they went untreated for more than a day, but that was almost always enough time for those stricken to seek intervention at an apothecary shop in a village. The blade master has utilized the unique time dilation effect that took place when the shards teleported them across the world. While it happened instantaneously for those going through the slipstream, several days passed back in base reality. The Drakkenborn had been upset and did not think this through before chasing the blade master into the shard.

"Not bad, but you got lucky." The gemstone around his neck glowed with each word.

"Luck is one of my skills."

The blade master sheathed his sword and yanked the two throwing daggers out of his back.

"That remains to be seen. I'll be more interested to see how you deal with the next target."

"Where is he?"

"Head west through the village."

The blade master crouched down next to the corpse of the Drakkenborn and got some mad loot off of the body. Walking through the village, piglets and baby goats parted as he walked between them. Pollen floated through the air as the townspeople worked at the mill and merchants sold their wares from stalls alongside the road.

"Dwarven armor for sale!"

"Magicka elixir, plus ten mana!"

The hustle was unreal, even in such a small village.

"Hey," a tinkerer said as he approached the blade master. Half of his teeth were made of wood and he carried a heavy load on his back, pots and pans strung into his pack. "Want to watch Kim Kardashian suck a cock?"

"Goddammit," the blade master cursed. "Get the fuck away from me!"

Climbing over a wooden stake fence, he walked through someone's farm and then out into the countryside. Lazy white clouds floated through the sky. Cows were not supposed to have horns and farms were not supposed to have jackalopes, but they were here in spades.

The blade master slid down an embankment and disappeared into the forest.

"I'm going to love seeing how you will pull this one off."

He spun, the katana materializing in his hand.

The dark elf threw his hands up in front of him.

"Hey, take it easy."

"You take it easy."

"You are going to love this. The next one is a barbarian. Maxed-out legacy status. Level 150."

"Oh, is that all?"

"Luck is one of your skills."

"Shit."

"Listen, it's working," the dark elf said through cracked lips. "A lot of people are looking for the new blade master who's burst upon the scene on the PvP server. You are getting attention, and that is exactly what we want."

"And here I was thinking I was just helping you guys level-up your RPG character."

"You are making fast progress, not to worry. You have already killed seven of their people. If you take down this barbarian, you are going to be on their radar in a big way."

"Is that a good thing or a bad thing?"

"Time will tell, but your unorthodox methods are working in your favor. Still, about this barbarian...."

"Just show me where he is."

"Follow me."

The blade master did. Climbing up a steep cliff, the duo crossed a rickety rope bridge over a gushing whitewater river a hundred feet below them. On the other side was a clearing. Another shard floated in the air, glowing white light.

"Where are we going now?" the blade master asked.

"You'll see," the dark elf replied as he disappeared into the light. The blade master followed and found himself in a windswept tundra. He squinted as wet white flakes of snow stung his eyes.

"Icedale? I really don't need any more of this shit in my life."

"I thought it might be growing on you," the dark elf said, once again taking the lead.

"My balls still haven't emerged from hibernation."

"What the hell do you need those for?"

"You have no idea."

"Yeah, I'm sorry I asked."

After few minutes of walking, they found the player character they were looking for. He was of the barbarian class, nearly seven feet tall and wearing heavy bear furs tied around his body. Swinging a massive broadsword, the barbarian split open a griffon's skull, painting the snow crimson.

"One of the legends of Infinity Blade," the dark elf said. "King Krag."

"Great."

"So what's the plan, hotshot?"

The blade master scoured the terrain.

"Hmm. Wait here."

The dark elf watched the blade master go into stealth mode and keep a distance from the non-player character monsters. Icedale was an expansion pack for Infinity Blade and had only been released a few months prior for the most high-level players in the game, allowing them to advance to level 150. His protégé wouldn't last long tangling with the ice giants and frost spiders, not to mention King Krag.

As the blade master advanced toward a cave opening he had spotted, the dark elf could see King Krag cast a spell, surrounding himself with blue light as the healing potion took effect. Then he charged at one of the ice giants. Behind Krag, the blade master slid down a snowy slope and disappeared into the opening of a cave.

"What in the hell is that guy doing?"

King Krag continued to swing his broadsword, blocking the ice giant's club with his shield and then slashing again until finally, the giant collapsed with a thud. In the meantime, a mammoth had stormed across the tundra and joined the fray, engaging Krag with his tusks.

Minutes went by with Krag turning the tundra into a bloody killing ground of dead NPCs. The blade master suddenly burst out of the cave, running straight toward Krag, who was now fighting it out with another ice giant. Right on his tail, a long line of ghouls, ghosts, and orc lords chased the blade master.

"A dungeon train," the dark elf said to himself. "Son of a bitch."

The blade master bumped right into Krag as he parried an attack from the giant, then cast a potion of invisibility on himself and disappeared. The entire dungeon train then crashed right into Krag. He was surrounded by a dozen high-level NPCs and was soon taking a beating. He cast another healing potion on himself, but there was no way he was fighting his way out of this one.

"That should do it," the blade master said, reappearing at the dark elf's side as the potion wore off. Krag was hacking and slashing furiously. The ice giant was down, but Krag was getting pounded by dark magicka from the ghouls and from the war hammers wielded by orc lords.

"But you need to get credit for the kill. It won't count if he gets slain by NPCs."

The blade master drew his crossbow and loaded it with an explosive quarrel.

"You sneaky bastard."

He hefted the crossbow to his shoulder and sighted in on King Krag as he was knocked down to his knees. Staggering back up, he was now covered in his own blood.

"Wait for it."

The two watched as Krag's HP points diminished. The blade master waited until the final moment, then let the quarrel fly. It struck Krag right between the shoulder blades and exploded in a brilliant phosphorus flash. Krag fell face-first into the snow, dead.

"Let's get out of here before he respawns and comes looking for us," the dark elf suggested.

The blade master was silent.

"Hey? You hear me?"

He just stood there, not saying a word.

"Hello? What the hell is going on?"

Chapter 13
American Arctic

"What the hell is going on?" Deckard asked as he looked up from the computer screen.

Off in the distance, the ocean was glowing orange.

"I thought it was the Northern Lights at first," Squirrel said. "But that's a different kind of light. We're not far off the coast of Alaska now, and those are the offshore oil fields."

"Holy shit."

Engineers and scientists had demonstrated that the Alaskan Arctic contained 40 billion barrels of recoverable crude oil and in the neighborhood of 210 trillion cubic feet of recoverable natural gas. America's long-term energy plan to become less reliant on the often unstable Middle East only helped speed up the process of drilling off the coast.

Companies like Exxon, Royal Dutch Shell, Gazprom, and their own employer, Xyphon, had developed crash programs to build offshore oil rigs all over the Arctic, a region reputed to hold up to a quarter of the world's fossil fuels. While Saudi Arabia's oil reserves amounted to about 260 billion barrels of oil, the Arctic may have as much as 580 billion barrels. Like the Middle East, the Arctic was now ripe for conflict.

"They did this because of us," Deckard said.

"What?"

"Just like Saddam set the oil refineries ablaze to try to delay the coalition advance during the Gulf War, the enemy blew up at least one of the oil rigs to try to prevent our pursuit."

"We're on their tail, then."

"Probably closer than we suspected, and they are out of options. Get us around the fires. We're going into the northeast passage."

The radio bolted above the helm suddenly chirped.

"Mayday, mayday, mayday, this is the surviving crew of Hillhorn platform! Mayday, mayday, may—"

"Shit," Deckard said. "I'm going to wake up the boys and get Otter up here. Then we're going to find out where the hell Global Hawk is and hunt these bastards down."

Squirrel looked into the looming flames, his eyes filled with uncertainty.

* * *

Jeff Dombrowski was the junior driller on the Hillhorn gas and oil platform, or at least he had been until an hour ago. Huddled under the plastic tent that protected them inside the octagonal inflatable life raft, he stared across at Alan, the assistant rig manager; Roger, the senior toolpusher; and John, their rig maintenance supervisor.

The wind had shifted, and now the four men watched helplessly as their life raft was pushed back toward the sea of fire. The Hillhorn and the Fitzpatrick platforms had both exploded at the same time, something that wasn't supposed to be possible outside of sabotage. As far as any of them knew, they were the only survivors.

A wave lapped over the side of the raft, cold ocean water seeping inside. Roger was staring into space. Somewhere else. Anywhere but here.

"Mayday, mayday, mayday," John cried into the handheld emergency radio.

A burst of static emitted from the radio.

"Roger, Hillhorn," a scratchy voice said on the other end. "This is the Carrickfergus. Give us a grid, over."

Jeff nearly jumped out of the raft as he grabbed the GPS.

"It's not working," he said as he played with the settings.

"Satellites have been acting weird for a couple of days," John said. "We have a hell of a big Roman candle out there to act as a beacon, though. I'll try to guide them in."

Jeff unzipped and tossed open the plastic covering. The sea slapped against the side of the raft, spilling more water inside that sloshed around and gathered around their feet.

John poked his head outside.

"Carrickfergus," he said into the radio. "GPS is a no-go. What is your current heading?"

* * *

The exhausted survivors of the Hillhorn blast were pulled aboard the Carrickfergus nearly an hour later. Their beards were soaked and frozen, their eyebrows drooped. Each of them walked around like a zombie, not even aware of the strange ethnicities of the crew members who pulled them onto the ship.

"Hey," a tall American with a chiseled jaw said. Jeff looked up at him.

"I'm Pat. The boss wants us to get you in some warm clothes, and then he wants to see you four on the bridge."

"Yeah, OK."

He looked up above the ship. Fluttering in the wind and glowing orange as the oil rigs burned in front of them waved the Jolly Roger. Looking back down, he then noticed the pistol and spare magazines Pat had strapped to his belt under his open parka.

"Let's roll."

The four survivors followed after Pat as he led them inside. They could already feel the Carrickfergus shifting under their feet, turning to go around the fields of fire. The Hillhorn crew members blinked in disbelief. There were machine guns, rifles, hand grenades, open metal cans of ammunition, and porn mags lying all over the place. Men wearing snow camouflage who looked to be of a dozen different nationalities were prepping their gear, looking like they were ready to launch World War Three.

Pat took them down a flight of metal steps to a changing room in front of the showers where they had some space. Another camo-clad man stepped in behind them, said something in Russian, then dropped a box at their feet. After looking inside, they didn't need Pat to tell them what to do. The crewmen stripped off their soaked clothes and then tore into the box of brand new thermal underwear, pants, and jackets.

"What is it you guys do, exactly?" John ventured.

Pat leaned to the side with one hand propped against the wall, the other at his hip.

"We're corporate trouble shooters."

"Oh yeah? Does trouble shoot back?"

"Oh, fuck yeah. C'mon, grab some towels to finish drying off and we can go get this meeting over with. Then we can get you some chow."

Back in the bay, they then climbed another set of stairs that was vertical to the point of being a ladder, then ascended to the bridge. It was pretty easy to identify the ship's captain behind the helm by his big, bushy beard and coffee cup in one hand. The younger guy working the sea charts was obviously the first mate. A third guy, who wore a Patagonia pullover, looked up from his laptop with bloodshot eyes.

Walking around the desk, he sized up the four oil rig workers.

"We owe you big time, man," Jeff thanked him.

"Don't mention it. I'm Deckard."

He shook all of their hands, but the boss didn't look happy. As he lit up a cigarette, Jeff noticed the scars on his knuckles. He'd worked around the oil industry long enough to know that this guy had been in a few brawls.

"If you don't mind me asking," John said, "what exactly is it that you guys do?"

"We're mercs," Deckard said without missing a beat. "We kill cunts."

"Um, what?"

"Let me put it to you this way. If some jag-off dictator takes over a country somewhere, they call in the 82nd Airborne or the Marines. If some douchebag hijacks a nuclear weapon, they call in SEAL Team Six or Delta Force. But if some X-factor comes out of left field in a blur, steals a super weapon that can end the world, and then takes off in a high-tech stealth boat, they call me and my boys."

"Really?"

"I'm afraid so," Deckard said as he frowned and looked out the window. "Every fucking time."

The four survivors looked at each other, wondering if they had just entered the Twilight Zone.

"You lost a lot of men on those rigs," Deckard said, his voice detached from the human toll of the disaster.

"I think we're the only ones left," Jeff said.

"I'm sorry, this is my fault."

"What are you talking about?"

143

"I'm chasing someone who doesn't want to be found. They ordered this strike against your oil platforms to delay us."

"What strike?"

"I just found out myself. Ballistic missiles launched from civilian container ships traveling along the northwest sea passage. Russian authorities are moving in now, but the ships are flagged in Liberia and the crews probably had no idea what they were carrying. Knowing the MO of the guys I'm after, the cargo containers on board were probably fully automated and received an electronic go-code from afar."

John shook his head. None of it made sense.

"Look, you guys must know this area and I could use your help."

Deckard walked over to the first mate, who was looking over the sea charts.

"The vessel we are looking for is about a two hundred-footer. We think they've been leaking a lot of fuel and probably haven't been able to make a lot of repairs while underway. If they had to make a quick stop to refuel and try to patch up their hull, where do you think they would go?"

"Only one place to go."

Everyone turned to look at Roger, who had only just spoken for the first time.

"Where?" Deckard asked.

"Barrow, Alaska," he answered. "The northernmost city in America."

Chapter 14
American Arctic

Old Uncle Joe teased his fishing line one more time, watching it dance in the hole he had cut through the ice. Holding the fishing pole between his knees as he sat on a folding chair, Joe reached down and palmed a Mason jar, moonshine sloshing around at the bottom. His fingers spun off the top and he took a swig from the half-empty jar. It burned all the way down, filling the fisherman with warmth.

Squinting his eyes in the darkness, he tried to focus. Maybe it was the moonshine playing tricks on him, but he thought he'd heard something out on the ice. Well, never mind. He screwed the cap back on the moonshine and set it on the ice. Exhaling a cloud of vapor into the cold air, Joe wondered if he would ever get a bite.

Suddenly the ice split and cracked in front of him, nearly tipping over his chair. Joe looked up with wide eyes as a 200-foot behemoth crashed through the ice, sandwiching him between the black ship and the shore. Old Uncle Joe rubbed a gloved hand over his stubble. There were not any icebreakers due in on Tuesday night.

Was this Tuesday night?

Come to think of it, Joe wasn't sure if it was even a weeknight.

Joe reached for the moonshine.

A metal hatch slammed open at the top of the ship. Dark figures spilled out into the Alaskan night, armed to the teeth. Several of them looked over at Joe as they slid down the side of their ship. They looked at him with green eyes. Joe took a swig of moonshine, gulping it down and giving the alien visitors a wave.

They didn't return his greeting, but instead dashed up the shore.

Suddenly, the fishing pole was nearly torn from between his knees.

A bite!

Joe reached for the pole with both hands, forgetting that he was holding the Mason jar. As he grasped the fishing rod, his jar of moonshine shattered on the ice.

"Awww fuck," Joe complained.

Then he reached for one of the singles of Jack Daniels that he kept in his parka pocket for such emergency situations.

* * *

Tampa, Florida

"That's it! That's them!"

Will smiled as he watched the flat-screen monitor. The Global Hawk unmanned aerial vehicle was orbiting over Barrow, Alaska. The sensor suite onboard the drone was being manipulated by a technician sitting in a trailer next to the pilot in Nevada. The cameras zoomed in on the long black ship that had just broken through the ice and docked alongside the coast. The fisherman who had been pinned right between the ship and the shore appeared on the screen to be completely unfazed. Was he a spotter or just a drunk?

"Where is Deckard?" Gary asked.

"Ten minutes out," Craig answered.

On the screen, little figures ran around like ants toward a warehouse on the far eastern side of Barrow, on the outskirts of the town.

"Who owns that damn warehouse?" Will asked.

"Huh," Craig said as he looked as his computer screen. "It seems that we do. It is an old warehouse left over from World War Two. Right now it is being leased to a company called Arctic Consulting Group. I'll pull up their information."

"It will turn out to be a front group. They've obviously pre-staged a lot of logistical support for this operation. They have been running advanced force operations right under our noses in anticipation for this. Burying caches, buying off officials, setting booby traps, leaving behind fuel depots, and God knows what else."

"What kind of military assets does Uncle Sam have up there in Alaska?" Gary asked. "Even if they cannot arrive in time for the hit, they can at least back up Deckard's men, contain the objective area, and help provide resources for contingency planning."

"I made some calls," Will replied. "And the answer is not much. The U.S. military has been focused on the desert for fifteen years, and we've let our already minimal Arctic warfare capabilities atrophy. 4/25 has been shrunk down to a battalion-sized unit, so we basically have no large, rapidly deploying unit that can fight in the Arctic, which means all we have to rely on is 1st SBCT, the Stryker Brigade Combat Team."

"Well that's something," Gary said. "Can we spin them up?"

"Not really. Not in these conditions. They are a Stryker brigade," Will said, referring to the Army's eight-wheeled Stryker armored vehicles that carried infantrymen in the back. "Strykers hardly work in negative ten-degree temperatures, and don't work at all in the negative forty-degree temperatures we're seeing in the Arctic between November and March. And that is just a mild winter for northern Alaska. Besides that, they have the oldest

Strykers in the Army. Some of them are the original test vehicles from the 1990s. They break down all the time, and getting the replacement parts up to Alaska takes a long time because of the great distances involved. That, and even when they are running, they suck at driving in the snow."

"Doesn't a brigade combat team have attack helicopters attached to it as well?"

"Yeah, but same deal. The AH-64E Apache helicopters they have at Fort Wainwright can't fly in negative ten-degree conditions because their electronics freeze."

"This is unreal. We have an Arctic warfare unit that can't fight in the Arctic?" Gary asked no one in particular. "What about troops? Can we truck them in? Fly them in?"

"Would take too long, again because of distance," Will lamented. "Besides, about only ten percent of the troops assigned to the brigade combat team have attended the Northern Warfare Training Center in Fort Greely, and even then, they really only get survival and mountaineering training. They don't get shit when it comes to actually fighting in the Arctic. If you want to talk to someone who actually knows how to fight up above the Arctic Circle, talk to the Canadians or the Russians or the Norwegians, because we've got our balls cut off when it comes to operating in this region."

"I'm pushing this imagery to Deckard now," Gary said with a sigh. "He should get there just in time to crash the party."

Will took a deep breath.

He sure hoped so, because right now, none of them had a very impressive track record.

* * *

148

Mercenaries were throwing on their combat gear, sliding down the stairs, and opening and slamming doors as they made a mad dash to get ready. Deckard snapped his plate carrier on, threw his parka over it, then shrugged into his chest rig, snapping it closed behind his jacket. He finally had a solid fix on the enemy's location, and he wasn't going to miss this opportunity to get the drop on them.

The town of Barrow was stretched out across the Alaskan coast, running from east to west. One of the oil rig workers had spent a significant amount of time there and reported that the roads were well made and were kept plowed to clear the snow and ice off during the winter months. Once again, nothing beats some local knowledge. With this in mind, Deckard knew he had the opportunity to launch a two-pronged attack.

Stepping outside into the cold, Deckard slung his AK over his back and climbed down a ladder to the barge platform. The ice crashed around the Carrickfergus's twin-pontoon hull, smashing its way toward the shore.

The Samruk mercenaries had five of their Iveco assault trucks up and running. All of them had to have their batteries charged up or replaced. It was a good thing they had at least brought extra tires, fluids, batteries, and recovery items to keep the trucks in the semi-shit state they were in.

"One minute out," Otter reported over the radio.

"One minute!" Deckard yelled.

The mercenaries began undoing the ratchet straps that secured the assault trucks to the deck. Fedorchenko's platoon was going to hit the ground with Deckard for their amphibious landing. The rest of the men would stay on the ship for the coordinated assault.

"Thirty seconds!"

Otter lowered the barge down to water level. The ramp began to lower and the golden lights of Barrow sparkled like giant diamonds in the night. The mercenaries loaded on the trucks and began racking rounds into their machine guns. Aghassi jumped on the back of Deckard's truck and nodded to him. He was usually Samruk's human-intelligence gatherer, but there wasn't much human intelligence to be had out in the Arctic wasteland.

Their recce section was also useless when their target was constantly on the move and there was no way to infiltrate the six-man team. The mortar section was also in need of a Viagra. They were used as regular infantry because they'd had a hard time pinning down the enemy location. Everything was different up here, even the enemy. Deckard knew they had been up against the ropes this entire time, but tonight he planned on evening the score.

The ramp came down on the shore just 10 meters away from the first road. The assault trucks roared off the ship in four-wheel drive, then crept across the snow and over a hump at the edge of the road. The five vehicles were lining up in their order of movement as the Carrickfergus began backing out, smashing its way through the ice, heading farther down the coastline.

"Update?" Deckard asked.

"Global Hawk sees about a dozen personnel on the ground. They are still refueling the ship."

"Roger, we're moving."

Sitting in the passenger seat, Deckard looked at the Kazakh driver and pointed down the road. The five vehicles started down the street, heading east. The town of Barrow was kind of spooky at night. All of the residents had wisely escaped the cold and remained indoors. The houses were oblong and rectangular, painted yellow, purple, green, and blue, all lifted three feet or so on stilts above the ground to avoid the permafrost. The buildings flashed by as the driver took them down the main road. In seconds they were past the town and were driving by the salt lagoons.

It was warm inside the heated cabin of their truck; everything was quiet outside, but Deckard knew that was about to change.

The idea was to hit the warehouse and ship at the same time, coming at the enemy by land and sea. That would split their attention, making the enemy think for a few seconds as to what direction they wanted to counterattack. That kept Samruk International inside their decision-making cycle, and would give them the precious few seconds they needed to get the drop on them once and for all.

"Contact! Contact!" Otter yelled over the radio.

Through the windshield, Deckard saw yellow flashes blink a few hundred meters to their front.

"Go, go! Step on it!"

The driver floored the accelerator, and in seconds the PKM gunner in the turret above them was blazing away. They were in the middle of a war zone, 10 things happening simultaneously. As the truck slid across the ice to a stop in front of the warehouse, Deckard flung open the door and jumped out.

A long hose stretched out from the warehouse and ran all the way to the coast, to the knife-shaped vessel sitting in the ice. Several figures on top of the ship were firing RPGs at the Carrickfergus as it closed the distance. Muzzle blasts from their ship answered in return.

A handful of black-clad figures were caught out in the open near the warehouse. With the assault trucks

151

pulling in between them and their ship, they were cut off. Deckard's hood blew off his head as he pulled the stock of his Kalashnikov into his shoulder. One of the enemy soldiers had turned and was running toward the warehouse, hoping to find some cover and concealment. Deckard denied him this, pumping a two-round burst into his back, then walking his rounds up his back, neck, and into the back of his head in a technique called a failure drill. After firing center mass, the shooter walked his rounds up to the head and kept firing until the enemy failed. The grape popped at the top as Deckard walked his rounds up. The black-clad figure spilled across the ice, his Israeli-made bullpup rifle sliding in front of him.

Another of the enemy's number pivoted, turning around and popping off a few rounds in Deckard's direction. The PKM gunner on his truck cut him down with a burst that folded him in the middle like an accordion. The other machine gunners on the assault trucks turned their guns on the enemy ship, aggressively firing long bursts from side to side that chopped through the RPG-armed enemy firing on the Carrickfergus.

Turning back toward the warehouse, Deckard saw at least a half dozen more of the enemy disappear inside. He was already running toward the warehouse, smelling blood in the water as the Samruk mercenaries joined in the chase. As they ran toward the door, one, then two of the mercenaries collapsed to the ground. Deckard hadn't even heard the enemy gunfire.

"No frags!" he yelled. The explosion could set off whatever fuel source they had concealed inside. He was willing to risk a flashbang, though, and nodded to Fedorchenko as he yanked one off his kit and pulled the pin.

Deckard lobbed the nine-banger through the door. It went off again and again, the distraction device serving its purpose. Deckard stepped through the door as the banger was still popping off, his rifle sweeping through the darkness, hungry for targets. As the other mercenaries flowed through behind him, he picked up something in his peripheral vision. Shifting his hips and bending on one knee, he turned toward the threat.

Then something flashed, and Deckard's entire world went upside down. His vision was spinning inside his brain, his arms and legs feeling detached from his body. Stumbling forward, he thought he heard gunfire but couldn't tell. His brain had somehow been disengaged from reality, and now all he knew was that the world was coming up to meet him. Fast.

He landed on the hard concrete floor with a thud, barely able to get his arms out in front of him before he fell.

Two rifle shots cracked into his back, and then Deckard was still.

* * *

The SCOPE think tank sat with their mouths ajar as Global Hawk captured the carnage outside Barrow, Alaska. The enemy ship was pulling out of port, tearing away from the hose refilling their fuel tanks, spilling gas across the ice. RPG gunners were still firing at the Carrickfergus as it stormed toward them.

The warehouse was quickly surrounded by the five assault trucks before little figures dashed across the screen and chased some of the enemy inside. Machine gunners on shore and on the Carrickfergus were making quick work of the RPG gunners on the enemy ship, their bodies flopping over the side, into the dark water.

Leaving both their dead and their living behind, the enemy ship plowed through the ice, making way for the open water beyond. The Carrickfergus was in pursuit, at least until the bad guys steered their ship into a channel previously cut by an icebreaker heading into or out of Barrow. Once inside the channel, the boat lifted up out of the water, moving like a speed boat away from Barrow as quickly as possible.

The think tank listened to the radio chatter as the mercenaries yelled at each other in three or four different languages. At times, the voices were washed out by gunfire.

"Objective secure," someone finally announced. "Starting sensitive site exploitation."

Gary leaned over and pressed a button on the comms panel that linked them to the Carrickfergus. "I want full biometrics on the enemy bodies as quickly as possible," the think tank leader said.

"Right, let me put out the fire on the deck of my ship if you don't mind," the Carrickfergus captain guffawed.

A minute later, the biometric readings from the bodies started coming into the SCOPE office. Pictures of faces, iris scans, and fingerprints could all be taken by the Samruk mercenaries with a handheld device manufactured by Crossmatch. The data would then be streamed to the Carrickfergus and uploaded via satellite to JSOC servers.

The four men were tense as the data began loading onto the flatscreen mounted to the wall in front of them. Craig swallowed. Will interlaced his fingers in front of him as he sat forward in his chair.

The first face to show up on the screen was Asian.

"We're running it through our databases now," Will said. "We'll see if we can get a match on ID."

The second face looked Arab, maybe, but definitely Middle Eastern.

Craig looked over at Will.

The third face was Caucasian.

Will smiled.

The data continued to flow in as the Samruk mercenaries took biometrics of each of the bodies. Two more pictures of Asians came in, then another with a face so caved in by gunshots that it was hard to tell his ethnicity. Then there was another white guy and another Middle Easterner.

Will stood up and walked around the table.

"Chinese," he said, pointing to the Asians displayed on the screen.

His finger drifted over to the Middle Easterners.

"Iranians."

"Holy shit," Craig said as he held his head in his hands.

Will pointed to the Caucasians.

"Russians."

"You were right," Gary said, almost under his breath.

"These are the players in the game."

Craig shot up in his chair.

"What the hell," he said. "The database got a match on one of them."

Will turned around, seeing a new picture of a white guy with his eyes closed. The JSOC database did get a hit —he was one of theirs.

"Army? CIA?" Gary said it almost as a curse.

Scrolling down the screen, they saw his name.

"Deckard?"

Chapter 15

"Put that down, you fucking idiot!"

One of the Kazakhs looked up at Kurt Jager as he walked into the room. He was pressing the limp hand of one of the bodies onto the glass fingerprint reader of the Crossmatch scanner.

"He's one of ours."

Kurt looked down at the Samruk commander. He was motionless. Everyone else in the room was dead. Four of their men including Deckard had been shot by one of the bad guys before the rest of the mercenaries had burst in and blasted him.

The former GSG-9 commando turned on a Petzl headlamp he wore around his neck and ran his hands over Deckard's body. He was confused, as he didn't see any sign of blood or entry or exit wounds. Thinking he felt something, Kurt pulled off one of his gloves and felt around Deckard's back. His middle finger entered through a hole in Deckard's parka.

"Ow, shit!"

He snapped his hand back to his body, recoiling away as something burned him. Rolling Deckard on his side and looking at his back with the white light, Kurt realized he had burned himself on a bullet embedded in the plate carrier under Deckard's jacket.

"Wake him up," Kurt told the Kazakh. "He is just unconscious."

The Kazakh pulled a water bottle out of his chest rig and emptied it over Deckard's head. The wounded man immediately shot up on his elbows, panting as if he had been holding his breath. Deckard's bloodshot eyes began to open.

156

* * *

The room had stopped spinning, but Deckard still felt nauseated from the severe vertigo he had experienced. He had gone from balls to the wall combat mode to having his world turned upside down and put on queer street faster than he could blink his eyes. His vision began to come back into focus. He squinted, trying to make out something moving on the other side of the room.

"You're OK, you're OK," Kurt assured him. "You took a round or two in the plate. We killed the shooter before he could finish the job."

Deckard continued to stare forward, not daring to turn his head and induce the brain-spinning vertigo again. Finally, his sight cleared up, the fidelity of his vision zeroing back in. There was a dead body lying across from him. The movement was the dead mercenary's foot wiggling back and forth as his nervous system continued to fire on auto, some part of the body still working after everything else had shut down.

"What happened?" Deckard asked.

"The ship escaped again, but we killed about ten of them in the process."

"Help me sit up."

Kurt grabbed Deckard under his armpits and helped him sit up. Of the four wounded men who had entered the room, Deckard could see that he had been the only survivor. Something had put them all on their ass and then one of the bad guys had walked up to each and plugged them. Deckard had gotten a couple rounds in his back and the next would have been in his head if the shooter hadn't been stopped in time.

"OK, I feel a little bit better," Deckard lied. The vertigo was gone but had been replaced with dread. Some of his men had been killed and, once again, he had skated right past the Reaper.

"Good," Kurt said. "We've been uploading the biometrics on the bodies back to the States, but you don't need fingerprints and iris scans to know that something doesn't add up here."

"What do you mean?"

"They are different nationalities. Asian, Middle Eastern, and white guys too."

"Sounds like a joint coalition task force."

"Well, that is what we would call it, but I've never seen anything like this from the opposition."

"All the villains in Gotham City."

"Huh?"

"They're having a team-up. But what the hell was it that made us all collapse like that? I saw a couple other guys go down outside on the way in."

"They were blinded," Nate said as he walked into the room. "With this."

In front of him he held one of the Tavor assault rifles chambered for the 5.56mm rounds the enemy used. Attached to the side of the rifle was what looked like a large flashlight. The former MARSOC Marine pointed the rifle at the wall and activated the flashlight. It blinked on and off, flashing a ghostly green on the wall.

"It is a visual disruption laser. The guys hit with it were blinded, but their vision is already clearing up."

"Why use non-lethals?" Kurt asked.

"Because they didn't have any machine guns or other suppressive weapons on shore; they didn't have this site prepared properly because they never planned on coming here. We caught them with their pants down and they used the non-lethals because they can be used as area weapons, putting down a large group of us quickly.

158

With that done, they can casually walk around and flip our off switch with a bullet," Deckard finished, pointing toward the bodies.

"So that is what they got you with."

"No, I wasn't just blinded," Deckard insisted. Planting one hand on the ground, he pushed himself up to his feet. "It was more than that. Complete disorientation."

Just then, Chuck Rochenoire walked into the room. "Hey, what is this?" He reached down and picked something up off the ground. It was boxy and black, with some kind of pull lever at the top.

"No, no, stop!" Deckard shouted just a moment too late.

The black box flashed.

Kurt Jager immediately vomited all over himself. Deckard went crashing back down to the ground as if someone had cut his legs out from under him. Rochenoire's eyes rolled back in his head as he fell backwards and slammed into the floor.

* * *

Old Uncle Joe's hands dug into the snow like claws as he pulled and struggled his his way over a berm that could not have been more than knee height. Safely back on shore, he got to his feet and dusted himself off. Reaching into his jacket, he palmed another single of whiskey, unscrewed the cap, and swigged it down in one gulp.

Surveying the carnage around him, Joe shook his head.

"What a time to be alive!"

Chapter 16

The blade master climbed over the brambles. He had been struggling through them, the thorns leaving long red streaks on his forearms and face as he scaled the approach leading up to the dark castle. Storm clouds were gathering overhead, heat lightning fanning out high above his head in surges that radiated across the sky in all directions.

The invitation had come by courier and was waiting in his inbox for him when he arrived back in Pangea. He had gotten their attention. Now they wanted to see him.

Past the thorn bushes, the path opened up slightly, turning into a series of switchbacks that cut back and forth. The footpath was only wide enough to inch forward by placing one foot in front of the other. The blade master considered himself lucky. At least the orc lords at the first gate had let him through, and then the sorcerers at the second gate had also granted him safe passage. All he had to do was walk.

Finally, he arrived at the castle. As he stood in front of the drawbridge, it slowly lowered and spanned the gap between him and the moat. He stepped across the wooden drawbridge, peering down into the spike-filled moat. It was filled with rotting body parts.

Inside the barbican, he was greeted by someone sent to collect him.

"Hail, blade master," a voice echoed through the corridor.

"Hey, what's up?" the blade master responded.

Stepping forward, he saw that he was being greeted by Azarian, one of the reptile people from the faraway island of Dresh. He was of the knight class and wore ornate plate armor that reflected his stature in the paladin guild.

"Follow me if you please," the knight said.

The blade master was led into a courtyard surrounded by high walls and circular towers with spires on top. Nothing moved. Even the moisture seemed to hang in the air. A burned-out carriage had caved in on itself and now rested in the center of the courtyard, its wooden struts blackened from flames. His hand drifted toward the hilt of his katana.

"You won't need that here," his escort said casually.

Inside one of the towers, they climbed a circular staircase. Their footsteps echoed on into forever, bouncing around inside the castle and swirling around them like phantoms. At the top, they entered a dark corridor illuminated by only a few torches. Down the hall, his escort stopped in front of a door.

"You are our guest," he said with a nod toward the blade master.

"That's good to hear."

"Just inside please."

The blade master opened the door and stepped inside. There was a stone pedestal in the center of the room, covered with some kind of fur. A single torch flickered against the stone walls.

This was it.

"Thank you for joining us," a voice said, cutting through the darkness.

The blade master didn't flinch. He had been expecting it.

"I already crashed the party. Saying hello seemed like the least I could do."

"We appreciate that very much," the voice said from the shadows.

"We?"

"Never ask about the weight of the cauldrons."

"Excuse me?"

"It is a proverb, meaning that you show your hand too soon."

The blade master watched the mage materialize in front of his eyes. Gradually, the shadows moved, turning to ectoplasm, an ethereal phantasmagorical entity consolidating in front of him. The mage stepped forward, his eyes burning like coals.

"I've waited a long time to meet you, Deckard."

The blade master was silent.

"You're surprised? I think we have demonstrated our capabilities at this point."

"You have, but it seems that you have me at a disadvantage."

"Perhaps in the opening gambit. But things did not go according to plan. You escaped several of our contingency plans and we underestimated the amount of havoc you could spread. No one expected such a mess in the Arctic."

"Well, if you know me, you know I have a habit of doing just that."

"Yes, you do." The old mage stepped closer, standing just across the pedestal from the blade master.

"Still, you've given me a good run for my money."

"Deceive the heavens to cross the ocean," the mage said. His English was impeccable, but it was clear that he had first learned British English, not American.

"God plays his games and we play ours."

"Indeed. Do you know what my job is Deckard?"

"War by proxy? International terrorism?"

"Those are simply tactics. My job is to manage the decline of your country."

162

"Isn't that a bit presumptuous?"

"America is finished as a global power. It is only a matter of time now; the data is very clear on this. Your economy is slowing down, your thoughts are crystallizing, and your military can no long win wars. My job is to help ease your country into its place as a second-rate power."

"Ouch."

"This is a dangerous time. Dangerous because a declining power is capable of lashing out in desperation as it tries to hold on to what power it has in vain."

"Or it could be dangerous because a rising power has miscalculated by several moves, assuming that an attempted power grab will be far easier in theory than in practice."

"This is not the *fait accompli*, Deckard, this is just setting the stage. My job is to harmonize your country with the coming global order. Unlike yours, our order will work. It will value order over freedom, place elite governance ahead of the ridiculous idea of democracy."

"Democracy has worked out pretty well for us, and for much of the world."

"It did work very well for you, but the world has changed. The rules have changed. America is the butcher of the world. You can never put down the butcher knife and become a Buddha. Our actions against America are nothing more than looting an already burning house."

The blade master looked away.

"Do you know what one factor convinced me that now was the time to act, Deckard?"

"No, I don't."

"Factional infighting amongst your most talented generals. The mysterious death of General McCoy. Then, several very powerful elites die just as mysteriously in New York City. The Biermann brothers, for instance."

"I seem to recall reading about that somewhere."

"As America comes apart at the seams, your elites are turning on each other."

The blade master knew he was being baited.

"But it was something else that really convinced some like-minded people, Deckard. Convinced us that the end is near for your country. That was the Crown of the Pacific incident. A maritime accident? Please. Someone liquidated much of the elite class that night. What do you think really happened?"

"People keep asking me and I keep telling them not to believe every conspiracy theory on the internet."

"It's not a conspiracy if you lived it, Deckard. We have studied American political fault lines very closely. We know your political cliques, we know your technical capabilities, we know your stovepipes, and over the last several days we have taken advantage of this knowledge. While we set the stage for a new global order, your government is preparing to wage another misguided campaign in the Middle East, blaming the Islamic State for the actions that I have orchestrated."

"I thought you weren't supposed to tell me that."

"Perhaps not, but it hardly matters. You can't prove anything, and even if you could, your bureaucrats are in such a deep case of path dependency that it is far too late for them to change their minds."

"I got the drop on you in Barrow. So what's our next play?"

The mage smiled.

"We run, you chase."

Chapter 17
Canadian Arctic

Deckard stood on the bridge as the Carrickfergus entered the northwest passage. Blue water with floating chunks of ice bobbed everywhere around their ship. In many places, the ice had not completely melted and Canadian icebreakers had smashed channels through for commercial ships to pass. Now a major maritime shipping route, Canada's maze of waterways between its northern archipelago of islands was little more than a fable until recent years.

The European powers had sought out a northwest passage connecting Europe to Asia since the 1500s, but the passage wasn't actually navigated until the early 1900s by Norwegian explorer Roald Amundsen. The northwest passage was still considered far too hazardous for commercial shipping, even when the ice cleared for a short period during the summer months. Until now. The climate was changing, leading to more ice melting than ever before, which opened up the northwest passage like never before. Just like the Russian northeast passage, Canada's northwest passage promised to shave hundreds of miles off commercial maritime routes.

Some even feared that an Arctic gold rush would soon happen, something that was already coming to pass as oil companies built more and more platforms in the high north. The long-term results remained to be seen. Deckard tended to believe that the climate moved in cycles, and the most grave predictions of environmentalists—that the Arctic would soon be completely free of ice—had been proven completely unfounded.

The main security concerns for Arctic nations focused on increased sovereignty disputes due to claims on mineral and fossil-fuel rights, environmental concerns due to commercial exploitation, and the fact that their now-open Arctic waters could be used by adversarial nations or even non-state actors like terrorist groups and drug smugglers. As it turned out, the fears of America, Canada, Norway, and Denmark were not as alarmist as they may have sounded a decade ago.

Deckard turned as his laptop began to beep. It was Tampa.

Clicking on the icon to accept the call, he was connected with the JSOC think tank.

Gary appeared on the screen. "Deckard, we have Global Hawk refueling, then we're putting it back out to run ISR for you," he said, using the acronym for intelligence, surveillance, and reconnaissance.

"Good news. We're looking over our sea maps and the latest updates from the Canadian government on the status of the ice out here," Deckard informed Gary and his team. "The waters are navigable for the most part, but the bad guys are still restricted, channelized between the islands and ice that hasn't thawed. We are traveling on what we suspect is their most likely route and will send a list of the number two and three most likely routes for Global Hawk to scan."

"We are also coordinating with the Canadian government. They take any violation of their sovereign waters very seriously. The Canadian prime minister also had a brief phone call with the president yesterday, expressing his full support and cooperation in standing with us during this crisis. Currently, Canadian icebreakers are heading out to help us sweep the northwest passage. Canadian Rangers are being called up as well."

"Canadian Rangers?" Deckard asked.

"Not like American Rangers," Craig spoke up. "Most of them are Inuits who have lived their whole lives up in the Arctic. They are better acquainted with Arctic military operations than anyone in the U.S. military, so they could prove to be a huge force multiplier."

"We need all the help we can get up here."

"We'll make sure you guys are put in touch so you can liaison and deconflict with each other."

"I also want you to figure out which airstrips are active in the Canadian Arctic," Deckard said. "If we can land my C-27J airplanes somewhere up here, we can carry out a relentless pursuit, keeping the heat on them, leap-frogging ahead of their positions. I doubt the Russians will clear airspace to let my pilots take off at this point, though."

"We'll let you know."

Deckard signed out and looked back out at the ocean.

The enemy was out there, and he knew they were planning something.

* * *

The mage slid the furs off the portal. The dark lords continued their quest through the Arctic wasteland, a glowing dot on the portal's map showing their path.

"You're sure the submarine can't surface?" The mage asked.

"Yes," the necromancer answered. "Too much damage to the mast."

"And the dry dock?"

"Still usable."

The mage nodded.

"Deploy our reinforcements at the soonest opportunity."

"As you wish," the necromancer said, already preparing a communiqué.

Chapter 18

"There they are!" Nikita yelled over the radio.

The sniper had spotted the enemy ship from up on the deck.

With the Carrickfergus traveling at full speed, they had caught up with the dagger-shaped ship in a channel carved out by a passing Canadian icebreaker. After taking watch in shifts, Nikita had finally spotted something through his sniper scope as they traversed the Prince of Wales Strait. The strait was about 20 kilometers across, and it took them deeper into the northwest passage. An icebreaker had opened a path through the ice, but since it had been cut, the wind and shifting tides had turned a straight line through the ice into a haphazard-looking zigzag path forward.

"Gotcha," Otter said from the helm.

Deckard stood next to the ship's captain as he maneuvered them through the cut in the ice.

"We've got them now," Otter continued. "They can't hydroplane their ship in a narrow passage that cuts back and forth like this. I can close the distance." Otter looked over at Deckard. "The rest is on you."

"Get us in range," Deckard ordered. "We'll handle them." Reaching for the PA system, Deckard mashed down the transmit button so he could talk to everyone on the ship. "All hands on deck; the enemy is in sight. I want snipers to report in to Nikita. First Platoon, split in half and cover left and right flanks from the deck. Second Platoon, prepare to support 1st Platoon and be ready for follow-on operations."

For now, it made sense to keep one platoon inside and behind cover for a boarding action while the other platoon engaged the enemy using maximum standoff.

169

"They've spotted us too," Nikita's voice crackled over the radio from outside.

"They sure have," Otter confirmed. "You can see them kicking up a wake behind them as they try to speed up, but this channel jackknifes left and right so often that they will get nowhere fast."

Sure enough, Deckard watched as the black ship alternated between lifting out of the water for a hundred meters and then sinking back down before repeating the process. They were bottlenecked by the ice. Deckard laughed.

The Arctic was a bitch like that.

* * *

Nikita watched through the 10-power scope on his HK417. Behind him, Aslan, his sniper partner and spotter, was assembling one of their .50 caliber Barrett sniper rifles. The second Samruk sniper team was also getting into position on the other side of the ship, climbing to the roof over their living quarters. Looking over at the other team setting up in the open, Nikita clicked his radio to talk to the other sniper team leader.

"Find some cover," he said in Russian and then again in English. The sniper team had dual nationalities. One of them was a Kazakh and the other was an American who had served as a sniper in a Ranger battalion. "We had some guys blinded on the last mission."

Finding cover would help, but the reality was that they didn't have any real countermeasures to deal with the laser weapons or the seizure grenade that had taken out Deckard and his entry team.

The other sniper team scooted under the lifeboat attached to the roof and set up shop. Nikita and Aslan used the actual control tower of the ship as cover, just barely poking out from the side to glass their target. It wasn't ideal, but it was better than nothing. For concealment, they had taped a tarp around the metal railing on the deck and cut a hole in it to shoot through.

Their firing position had been built little by little as each sniper rotated on and off guard duty. One of the chairs that had been torn out of the living area belowdecks was used to sit on, and the railing in front had been lined with foam padding to rest the rifle on. Between the two, it was hoped that much of the vibration from the ship would be eliminated while trying to acquire and kill targets. Life was filled with sub-optimal decisions, especially in combat. You chose the least of two evils and rolled with what you had. They were close to the centerline of the ship, which would help mitigate the movement of the vessel on the water and was far away from the vibrations caused by the engines. That was about as good as it was going to get.

Aslan slid up next to Nikita with the Barrett. Handing him the HK417, he hefted the weight of the anti-material rifle and began settling into a steady firing position. Turning the adjustment ring on the Night Force scope, he dialed it down from 10 power to 3.5 power. At high magnification, it was too easy to lose sight of his target on the rolling ocean. The .50-caliber round of the Barrett had some ass behind it, something they would need in high winds. The lighter 7.62mm rounds would be easily blown off target as high-pressure systems collapsed into low-pressure systems, causing gusts of wind around the Carrickfergus. The .50 caliber was primarily used for destroying equipment, but in this case, it wasn't as if they had to worry about blasting through bulkheads and hurting friendlies. They were in combat.

Nikita looked over the enemy ship, prioritizing his targets. Four crewmen were on the deck moving around. They looked to be preparing some kind of hard points. Then a hatch opened and two more enemies wearing black uniforms emerged carrying a long tube. It looked like a recoilless rifle. Sweeping across the deck, he spotted several antennae, a small radar dome, and he could see the wash created by the rudder and prop. He needed to take them all out as fast as possible, if possible.

"Range?" Nikita asked.

Aslan sat next to him with the HK417 at his feet and sighted in with his laser rangefinder.

"Two thousand three hundred meters," he answered. "Two thousand two hundred. Closing fast." The Carrickfergus would be on top of the enemy soon. Meanwhile, the enemy was getting the recoilless rifle mounted on a tripod on the deck.

Nikita changed channels on his radio and called down to Otter on the bridge.

"Wind check."

"OK, I have twenty knots of relative wind and fifteen knots of true wind, moving from west to east."

The ballistic solution for this shot was already complicated, and the difficulties in making a wind call only made it that much harder. As the numbers ticked down in Nikita's head, and as the ships grew closer to one another, he realized this would be the most difficult shot of his sniper career.

Thankfully, the ship had an anemometer and wind vane, which allowed him to separate relative wind from true wind. Relative wind was the actual wind plus that created by the forward movement of the Carrickfergus. Relative wind would affect the ballistics of his rifle when he fired, but become less relevant as the bullet continued along its trajectory toward his targets. Beyond that, unlike on land, there were no trees or mountains to interfere with wind speed. Fifteen knots put him at a 17 miles per hour crosswind from left to right.

With both vessels constantly moving and adjusting course through the channel in the ice, there would be no perfect ballistic solution. The ballistic computer in his brain would never have been able to keep up with the constantly shifting variables at play. Nikita dialed the range into the ring on the top of his scope and used a hold-off for wind using the Mil-Dot reticle in his scope.

On top of adjusting for the wind, range, and the constant movement of both ships, Nikita also had to compensate for the up-and-down pitch of the waves that were lapping up against the sides the Carrickfergus. The Kazakh sniper breathed evenly, preparing to squeeze the trigger. If he pulled the trigger when his crosshairs were perfectly aligned with the target, his bullet would miss because his crosshairs would be off the target by the time the bullet left the barrel. The Carrickfergus continued moving up and down with the waves.

Air humidity had already been accounted for in their previous engagements in the Arctic, so Nikita simply compensated for one minute of angle, or one inch at a hundred meters, as he had last time. The same went for temperature. A 20-degree decrease in temperature would cause a bullet to drop by one inch at 100 meters...or 10 inches at 1,000 meters. The Arctic temperature was relatively stable, but the temperature of the water sometimes changed, affecting that of the air.

"Wait until we are within AK range," Deckard said to Nikita over the radio. "I want everyone to open up on them at once."

Nikita looked at the three enemies setting up an SPG-9 recoilless rifle on the deck. Wearing black uniforms, they scurried around, preparing the crew-served weapon. He knew he had them dead to rights. There was no reason to wait and risk lives, hoping that they would not get a shot off at the Carrickfergus.

"Did you hear me?" Deckard asked.

Nikita did not acknowledge the order.

He breathed out, timing his breath with the harmonics of the waves that rocked their ship up and down. Having made his corrections for windage, distance, and atmosphere, he now had to time his shot perfectly, anticipating where his crosshairs would land a split second after he squeezed the Barrett's trigger so that the bullet hit its target. Shooting from one moving vessel to another would be anything but easy.

Chatter kept coming over the radio, but Nikita ignored it. He knew he had the shot and nothing was going to stop him now. The enemy had the SPG-9 tube on a tripod they'd bolted to the deck, and were making some final adjustments. The bow of the Carrickfergus dipped down over a swell. Nikita let out his breath as the ship began to rise over the next wave. His sights drifted across the hull of the semi-submersible ship in the distance, gently gliding toward one of the recoilless rifle crew members. The .50 caliber sniper rifle bucked hard into Nikita's shoulder.

It was the longest two seconds of Nikita's entire sniper career as he stared through the scope, waiting to see a splash.

"What the fuck—"

Deckard's angry voice came over the radio just as the shoulder of the crewmen Nikita had shot at exploded into a red mist. Spun around by the massive .50 caliber bullet, he fell backwards, bounced off the deck, and then rolled off the side and splashed into the ocean.

"I said hold your fire. We can't mass our fires yet!"

Deckard was pissed.

Nevermind. Nikita sighted on the next target and fired. Knowing that his rifle was sighted in correctly, he only had to time his shots correctly. Without waiting to see if he had a hit, the sniper transitioned from target to target, indexing them with the correct hold-off and then squeezing the trigger.

"Another hit!" Aslan cried out as he glassed the target with his laser rangefinder binoculars.

The second crew member was nearly cut in half as the second shot tore through him, spilling intestines across the deck. The third turned toward the carnage just as Nikita's third shot drilled right through his knee, severing his leg. The next order of business was taking out the SPG-9 itself, then the radar and any other sensors he could spot.

Getting his sights on target, Nikita was about the empty the rest of his magazine on the recoilless rifle. With a grin on his face, he was just about to pull the trigger when the curtains fell and everything went black.

* * *

"I'm hit!" Nikita's voice came over the radio.

"Son of a bitch," Deckard cursed. "That fucking idiot."

"I don't see the wound," Nikita's spotter said over the net in Russian. "He is holding his eyes."

The gears in Deckard's brain cranked for a hot second as he mentally transitioned from English to Russian. He had learned the language from spending so

175

much time around the Kazakhs, but he was far from being completely fluent. Then it dawned on him.

"Get down," he blurted as he reached out and pulled Otter down behind the wheel of the ship.

Shooting a look over his shoulder at Squirrel, he repeated the command.

"Duck!"

Squirrel dropped the triangle he was using to measure his sea charts and disappeared behind his desk. Deckard wore an ear bud and had a small microphone clipped to his shirt that connected to his MBITR radio. Clicking the push-to-talk, he transmitted over the assault net.

"Everyone get down behind cover. No eyes directly on the target vessel. They're deploying visual-disruption lasers. We've got one friendly blinded already."

"This is Shooter-Three," the second sniper team reported in. "Make that two. My spotter just got tagged and is flailing around like Helen Keller."

Once again, the enemy was turning the tables on the Samruk mercenaries.

"Get below deck," Deckard ordered the sniper teams before turning toward the ship's captain. In the distance, a cannon boomed.

"Must be that smoothbore they were mounting on the deck," Otter said with wide eyes.

Deckard crawled past him to look out a side window where he would not have visuals with the enemy ship. Sure enough, a spray of white foam splashed down in the water just 30 meters off the Carrickfergus's starboard side. Another blast sounded, and this time the 73mm recoilless rifle round slammed into the ice surrounding the channel, cracking it before the round exploded, creating a geyser of ice and water like that of a fat kid doing a cannonball off of a diving board.

Out of the corner of his eye, Deckard saw the screen of his laptop. He had left it open while playing Infinity Blade and he could see that someone had opened a shard right in front of his blade master. Crawling on all fours, he slid the laptop off the table and set it in his lap. Pressing the forward arrow, he moved his character into the shard.

He was immediately transported into the castle up on the mountain. The old mage was smiling at him.

"Busy?" the mage mocked him.

"Wait one," Deckard typed. "It's surf and turf night down in the galley."

Setting down the laptop Deckard moved to the door. "Otter, back us off. We've closed the distance to about a kilometer, which keeps us out of their maximum effective range with that SPG-9, but not out of their maximum range. They can't place accurate fire, but they are going to score a lucky shot—"

No sooner had the words left his mouth when Deckard winced, a hole suddenly blown through the ramp folded vertically upward for travel on the barge deck below. A 73mm anti-tank round carved right through the metal and was only stopped by the front end of one of their assault trucks. With the round slowed down, it still lifted the two front tires off the deck before blasting open the vehicle. A fireball burst into the air as the fuel tank went up, turning their world yellow and red.

Otter throttled down the engine while simultaneously yanking the hand mic off the wall and speaking over the ship's PA system.

"Fire crew on the deck! We just took a direct hit!"

177

Chapter 19

A squad from Shatayeva's platoon was out on deck with a hose and chemical fire extinguishers, quickly getting the blaze under control. Deckard was impressed. He hadn't been paying much attention to the fire drills that Otter had insisted they perform during down time, but now it was paying off.

While a cloud of fire extinguishing dust was being carried away by the sea breeze, another SPG-9 round fell short, splashing into the arctic water just in front of their ship. Another landed right off their port side. Otter had slowed them down, keeping them at a distance of about two kilometers from the semi-submersible ship, which of course was exactly what the enemy wanted.

Deckard's pirate ship was packed to the gills with heavily armed mercenaries. In a stand-up fight, the enemy wouldn't last, but every single action they had taken thus far told Deckard they had absolutely no intention of going man to man and gun for gun. The numbers were ticking down, and before much longer, they would be out of the strait and back into open water where the semi-submersible would be able to outrun them again.

They were out of range of the enemy's weapons systems, but the enemy was also out of range of their own. Stand-off had been achieved by both parties, but it only benefitted the enemy, as it delayed Samruk, allowing them to make their escape deeper into the Arctic.

"Keep us two kilometers off their ass end," Deckard said as he threw open the door and left the bridge. Scrambling down the stairs, he ran into the billets where both platoons were preparing their gear and standing by for orders.

"Ivan? Where the hell is Ivan?" he asked.

One of the Kazakh mercenaries came running up. In his mid-thirties, Ivan was the nickname for one of the original soldiers Deckard had hired out of the Kazakh military services. He'd had extensive training on mortar systems during his military service, and he had only become more technically and tactically proficient under Mendez, an American who led Samruk's mortar section— until he had been killed during a previous mission. Much like Nikita, the Kazakhs had stepped up to replace their foreign mentors after they had been killed.

"Zakazy?" the Kazakh asked.

Deckard gave him some basic instructions to prepare the section's mortar tubes for action. Ivan and his six-man mortar team had been sidelined in the Arctic until now. Once Deckard finished, Ivan darted away to round up his men and get to work.

"Why are we backing off?" Fedorchenko asked as he stepped forward to confront Deckard. "Let my men take them down."

This was not the kind of conversation they should be having in front of the men, but Deckard fully understood how frustrated the platoon leader was.

"Did you see Nikita doing the clucking chicken? Serves that dumbass right. We need to set the conditions before we take another pass at them."

It had taken Deckard a long time to adjust to his role, even though he still slipped the leash at times. Not long ago, he had been in Fedorchenko's shoes, always gnawing at the bit. Their campaign against a Mexican drug cartel had taught him to bide his time. The Russians and Chinese nationals they were fighting knew the American character well and were counting on him blundering into situations unprepared.

"Use some tactical patience and I'll get you on target," Deckard assured him.

Then he heard heavy footsteps coming up behind him and knew that Cody had just entered.

"HEY!"

"Turn down the volume, Cody," Deckard said as he turned to the computer hacker.

"You guys are morons. The lasers are easy to defeat."

"Why didn't you clue us in earlier, then?"

"I didn't think about it, OK? Fuck."

"Spit it out already."

"Use your night vision and leave the daylight cap over the lens. Then put a fucking pirate patch over your other eye since the PVS-14 monocular goes over the other one."

"Shit, why didn't I think of that?"

"Because you are a fucking moron."

Cody was the only one who got away with talking to Deckard and many other people on the Carrickfergus like that. He was an electronics whiz kid, but also a dirty civilian who never served in uniform. They just had to put up with him and his autistic, Tourette's shit sometimes.

"The laser might burn out the tube if you take a direct hit," Cody warned.

"But it is still better than being blinded for the duration of the battle," Deckard finished. "Fedorchenko, let Shatayeva and Ivan know. Bring extra batteries because they will freeze in ten or fifteen minutes when you are exposed to the elements. I want all of you ready to go for the next round."

Taking a look from one of the windows, Deckard could see the fire brigade wrapping up now that they had extinguished the flames. Meanwhile, Ivan's mortar section

180

and a few other men were helping him on the deck. They had pulled out some lumber, and one of them already had a hammer and nails out and had begun banging away. A few others were hauling up bags of rice they had to help ease the pain of a steady MRE diet.

Deckard climbed up the stairs and back onto the bridge. The ship's captain was crouched down and steering the ship by looking at one of several deck-mounted cameras. One had been taken out by whatever ship-mounted laser the enemy was using, but the other was thankfully still functional.

Nikita would be lucky to keep his job after that last stunt, but with him out of the way, Deckard would be getting directly involved in making sure the second attempt wasn't a clusterfuck. Keeping his head below the window, Deckard donned his kit, throwing on the body armor that had already taken two direct hits from a Tavor assault rifle. Then he pulled on his parka, chest rig, wool watch cap, and gloves.

Finally, he pulled on an Ops-Core helmet and attached PVS-14 night vision goggles. Reaching up in front of him to feel around, he made sure that the black rubber daylight cap was attached to the front of the monocular. The 14s were designed to amplify existing light, so during the day, when testing the NVGs for functionality, the cap was left on to protect the sensitive lenses inside. In this case, they would be using the goggles in broad daylight.

"Otter, when I give the word, I want you to start closing the distance. Where are we now?"

"Two point two kilometers."

"Keep us there for now."

Pulling the edge of his watch cap down from under his helmet, Deckard used it to cover his left eye while the night vision monocular covered his right. Stepping out onto the upper deck, he found Aslan hiding behind cover with the Barrett and Nikita's HK417. The blinded sniper had been taken below deck to see the medic.

"Give me the Barrett," Deckard said in Russian. "Make yourself look like me. Cover one eye and use night vision over the other with the daylight cap."

"Roger."

Deckard reached into Nikita's Drop Zone assault pack and withdrew his PVS-22 universal night sight or UNS. Attaching it to the Barrett's picatinny rails in front of the Night Force 10-power scope would also protect his eyes if the enemy decided to laze them again. Closing his eyes, he flipped up the PVS-14 on its pivot mount and then stared through the green tint of the UNS and Night Force scope combination.

The mercenary commander let out a deep breath as he snugged the rifle stock into his shoulder. Although a school-trained sniper with actual combat experience behind a long gun, precision marksmanship at long distances was a perishable skill. Being able to effectively place rounds at over a thousand meters required not just school house training, but constant range time to maintain proficiency. Deckard hadn't worked as a sniper in a long time, and as much as he hated to admit it, Nikita was now a better shot than him when it came to long-range engagements. Much better.

But Nikita was flopping around the med bay right now, so it was what it was. Now Deckard would make sure that their fire was synchronized and massed for maximum effect.

Down below, the mortar section had finished framing out a wooden box and was filling it in with the bags of rice while two of the men prepared 82mm high-explosive rounds to drop down the tube. Deckard glanced through the scope; the semi-submersible ship was still cutting back and forth through the channel in the ice.

Ivan was yelling orders to his section as they dropped the mortar base plate on top of the rice bags. Their improvised platform would stand in for the dirt in which the base plate would normally be set. With the plate in, they then slid the actual mortar tube onto it by the pivot knob at the end and attached the bipod legs.

"Ivan, are you set?" Deckard asked over his comm link.

Below, he saw the mortar section leader speak into his radio.

"Roger."

"Otter," he radioed to the helm, "get us within one kilometer. Close the distance."

Aslan had his night vision goggles on and slid in next to Deckard with his HK417.

"7.62mm is going to get batted around something fierce in this wind," Deckard said to Nikita's spotter. "But you can spot for the mortar section and make corrections."

"Da," the Kazakh answered, curt and to the point as always.

The Carrickfergus hummed as Otter throttled the engines, again closing on the enemy. The ship swayed beneath them as he dodged through the ice channel, making corrections as he sped them up. As they got closer, SPG-9 rounds began raining down around the Carrickfergus. They were out of maximum effective range, but the enemy was going to try to put some suppressive fire down to keep the pressure on the Samruk pirate ship.

"All stations on this net," Deckard transmitted over the assault net. "Everyone hold. Initiate on my fire. Acknowledge my last, over."

Ivan, Fedorchenko, and Shatayeva radioed in to confirm his order.

"Closing in on one kilometer, boss," Otter crackled over the comms.

Another 73mm round slammed into the ice off their port side, creating another mini-volcano of water and ice. Deckard looked through the green-tinted rifle sight and homed in on the recoilless rifle crew. Unlike Nikita, he was going to take out the weapon system itself, which in this case was more important than the humans crewing it. They could actually be replaced.

"One point two kilometers," Aslan reported, reading off the red digital numbers in his rangefinder as he lazed the target.

Deckard winced as the Barrett's sights bounced around with the movement of the Carrickfergus. This was a shit show if he'd ever seen one.

"One point one," Aslan updated him.

Deckard tried to understand the pattern his rifle sights were following as they rocked up and down with the ship. It would be damn hard to get off more than one shot before his sights were off target again. Thinking he had it more or less figured out, Deckard flicked the safety off and breathed out. His finger tightened around the trigger.

"One kilo—"

Aslan's words were cut off as a .50 caliber round exploded in the Barrett's chamber, the sudden inflation of gas pushing the thumb-sized bullet out of the barrel. Before his round had even entered the terminal phase, Ivan's men dropped an HE quick round down the mortar tube.

A spray of silver sparks flew into the air as Deckard's shot rang the recoilless rifle tube. Deckard fired again and again, each squeeze of the trigger sending the anti-material rifle bucking back into his shoulder. It would leave a hell of a good bruise, but this was a good kind of pain.

The first mortar round came down 50 meters behind and 50 meters to the starboard side of the enemy vessel, exploding just before it hit the water. Aslan began calling on corrections, the first shot not bad at all. Like Deckard, Ivan had to compensate for the forward travel of the enemy ship, intentionally overshooting it and hoping that they would sail right into the burst by the time it landed.

Deckard dropped the empty magazine and reloaded.

"Not sure about the status of the SPG-9," Aslan reported. "But one of the crew is lying face-down on the deck. Another one is missing, probably in the water somewhere. The third is standing back up. Looks like some more movement, guys getting ready to come out of the hatch."

"Let's see what we can do about that," Deckard said as he racked the Barrett's bolt.

"Shot, out!" Ivan declared over the net.

"Shot, over," Aslan responded as he watched for the impact.

The nose of the mortar rounds could be dialed to explode on impact, on a slight delay for destroying dug-in enemy, and in this case, set to quick, meaning they would explode slightly before impact—great for hitting troops in the open. A puff of black and white smoke appeared above the enemy ship, clearing off the deck of remaining troops and toppling the SPG-9 over on its side as one of the tripod legs was severed.

"Fire for effect!" Aslan told the mortar section. Ivan's men immediately began sliding round after round down the tube as fast as it would fire.

Deckard trained his sights on the open hatch where they had spotted movement and started dumping rounds at it whenever his crosshairs drifted over it. Pausing for a moment, he fired a shot off at the small radar dome, which exploded in a spray of black plastic. Unfortunately, he was unable to spot the direct-energy platform that had been dogging the Carrickfergus with its lasers.

82mm HE quick rained down in the vicinity of the ship, puffing up a ring of a smoke all around it as the mortar section sent a hail of hate their way. None of the rounds appeared to be quite as direct a hit as the first, but mortars were an area weapon, not a point one like a sniper rifle. This was hand grenades and horseshoes; close was good enough.

Now the captain of the black ship threw caution to the wind and floored the throttle. The ship rose out of the water like a black needle shooting through the sea. The mouth of the strait was close, and they knew that the pirates on their heels were just clearing the decks in preparation for a ship boarding. It was now or never.

The ship powered away, another storm of HE quick exploding right behind it. The ship's captain was good, Deckard thought as he watched them make a last-ditch effort to reach the open ocean. He took them through the rest of the weaving channel, chipping away ice at the sides on several occasions as he sped away.

"Three kilometers out," Aslan reported.

Deckard smiled. Through his scope, he saw the ship trailing a plume of black smoke. The enemy just had their shit pushed in, and it was about goddamn time. Setting down the Barrett, he walked back inside the bridge.

Picking up his laptop, he set it down on the table and typed a message to the mage, who was still standing there waiting for him.

"Is it getting hot in there?"

The mage was silent for a long moment.

"Well played."

Waving his hands, the mage cast a spell. Yellow fog billowed up around the blade master and banished him from the dark castle.

Chapter 20

The JSOC think tank was deathly silent.

Craig reached for the remote and clicked off the television as the press conference they had just watched concluded, the president walking from behind his podium at the White House.

"That's it," Gary said solemnly.

"Are you surprised?" Will asked, his words cutting through the air like a knife.

"America gets hit with the most sophisticated and well-planned terrorist attack in history, and the administration is not seriously considering state sponsors? ISIS takes the blame just like that, case closed?" Craig said.

"They are a convenient scapegoat. Blame a bunch of Arabs with long beards who nobody likes anyway, drop some bombs, and declare mission accomplished, all while the real puppet masters get away clean," Gary thought aloud.

Will turned to look at him.

"Everything is going according to the enemy's plan," Will told him. "ISIS has had some state-sponsored support since shortly after they rose to power. Their propaganda campaign is slick, like something straight out of Madison Avenue, showing a deep awareness of American cultural motifs and norms."

"What are you alluding to, Will?"

"It is called reflexive control, a form of information operation the Russians have been studying for over forty years. Essentially, how it works is that you insert socially loaded information into the enemy's decision-making process in order to elicit a response that favors your strategy. For example, the Russians consider our so-called

188

Star Wars program in the 1980s to have been a reflexive control information operation."

"We knew that the Russians would seek to counter any type of horizontal weapons proliferation, so we invented a fake weapons program we knew would bankrupt their economy when they tried to match it?" Joshua offered.

"Correct. ISIS has used a propaganda campaign against the West for years now, one which uses our own media outlets to disseminate information they want our public to see. The main images and video they want us to see are the destruction of ancient antiquities across Syria and Iraq, the execution of homosexuals, their use of young girls for sexual slavery, and the mass executions of Christians and Western hostages. These images are peddled to us knowing they will provoke a reflexive response from the West. It was only a matter of time; they just let the pressure build. And the Russians, Chinese, and Iranians behind the terrorist attacks have spent years preparing the West psychologically for this. We are emotionally committed to blaming ISIS. All it took were a few false leads for the enemy to lay out for us to find," Will finished.

"You are so sure of this simply because ISIS uses a propaganda strategy the Russians have studied in the past?" Craig asked.

"Yes, partially. But you can also look at the Russians, Chechens, Georgians, and others who traveled to Syria to join ISIS. Many of them openly fought as GRU proxy forces in Dagestan, Georgia, and Nagorno-Karabakh. Then they suddenly flip the switch and become committed jihadis in Syria? I think not. They were deployed to Syria. Deployed by the Russian security services."

Gary's chair creaked as he sat back and rubbed his temples.

"Good god."

"He has nothing to do with it," Will said. "Think about it. In 2011, JSOC was trying to vet rebel forces in Syria who we could sponsor and support with arms against the Assad regime. By sending Chechens and others to Syria, the Russian intelligence services used jihadis as a spoiler force, knowing that we could never arm Islamists. They effectively re-contextualized the conflict from being about Syrian nationalism to being about international jihad. This was the same technique they used for their second war in Chechnya.

"And if Deckard can't capture or kill these guys in the Arctic, then the enemy will get away with the entire scheme. Not only will they walk away clean with a geological weapon that can never be traced back to them after it is used against us, but we'll also be committed to fighting another useless bushfire war in the Middle East."

* * *

"Take a look at this, Deckard," Otter's first mate said with a smile.

"Good news, I take it?" Deckard asked as he walked over to the sea charts Squirrel had been looking at.

"Yeah, finally. We're moving deeper into Canada's Arctic archipelago, which would give the bad guys more places to hide, but the Canadians are stepping up in a big way. They take any violation of Canadian sovereignty very seriously, especially in light of what has happened over the last week. The Louis S. St. Laurent and the Des Groseilliers are moving toward us to cut off several key escape routes through the northwest passage."

Deckard looked down at the charts. The archipelago of islands created a kind of maritime labyrinth in the Arctic Ocean. There were also key choke points that could be cut off by friendly Canadian forces. Squirrel was pointing out several such choke points that would soon be locked down by the Canadian Coast Guard. The Des Groseilliers was moving up the M'Clintock Channel, which separates Prince of Wales Island and Victoria Island. Farther east, the Louis S. St. Laurent was chugging up the Prince Regent Inlet.

Soon, both icebreakers would enter into the Barrow Strait, blocking the enemy from moving any farther east.

"That will force them to head north," Deckard commented.

"Right, straight into the perma-ice of the polar ice cap. We have them trapped."

Deckard frowned, knowing it was never that simple.

"If we keep the pressure on, they will have to keep moving. That means running aground somewhere in the Queen Elizabeth Islands or Ellesmere Island."

"They will probably try to hide out in one of the fjords and hold out for some alternate form of transportation, maybe even try to hijack one of the commercial ships sailing through the northwest passage, but you're right; if we're still on their ass, they will have to abandon ship and move into the interior of one of these islands."

Deckard cracked his knuckles.

Doing some quick math, he estimated that it would be about another 12 hours of navigating through the Arctic archipelago before the enemy ran into a dead end and had to abandon ship.

It was time to get the boys ready for the ground war.

* * *

"The *shi* is moving quickly."

"*Shi*?" The blade master shook his head.

"Yes," the mage lectured him. "This is hard to explain for your ears. You might describe it as the strategic momentum of an event or an alignment of forces."

"So *shi* is tactical patience?"

"No, but a cunning leader uses long-term strategic patience to wait for *shi* to fall into his favor. Many, many years ago, the emperor would employ a sage who could divine such information. The sage would know exactly when to strike, when the situation had been properly shaped, when the balance of power was in the emperor's court."

"And now?"

The mage turned to face the blade master, his eyes sunken like bottomless pits.

"I am probably the closest thing to the emperor's sage, but we also use computers today for the raw calculations. I wait patiently, sometimes shaping the *shi* as I see fit. We call it *fighting with a borrowed sword.*"

"Information operations. Proxy soldiers. Black operations."

"These are military terms, but your people have only just discovered these concepts. We have been doing this for over a thousand years. Use the strength of another to do your fighting for you. More recently, we used the Russians to this end; they helped us modernize and industrialize our nation."

The blade master smiled. The mage was not even trying to hide it anymore. He was speaking of the People's

Republic of China and their eventual ideological split from the Soviets in the 1950s.

"And after the Russians, it was us. America gave you favored-nation status, entry into key economic summits, and shared our military technology."

"*Wai ru, nei fa*. It means, 'On the outside, be benevolent; on the inside, be ruthless.' This would be obvious to anyone who was properly educated. Americans simply do not learn how to think."

"I got a crash course in your methodology back in Cairo," the blade master said casually.

"Cairo?"

"Major Shen Banggen of the General Staff Development's Third Department."

The mage looked away.

"Yes, I knew him."

"I put a bullet between his eyes as he was in the process of purchasing a very sensitive piece of American technology used during Egypt's Arab Spring."

"I did not know that you were involved. Banggen was very useful to us. He traveled to Afghanistan and Pakistan to procure American military equipment that had been captured or lost. Without his help, we would not be able to jam your communications or defeat your defensive systems as easily as we have."

"You have been planning this for a very long time. Waiting for the *shi* to align with various other forces?"

"Correct. To engage in a large military build-up, to take overly aggressive military actions, or to announce to the world that we seek unipolar dominance over the United States would have been to invite a catastrophe. We cannot meet America jet for jet or ship for ship, so we have sought out other strategies. But now we are nearly ready to emerge from the shadows and challenge the hegemony of your country. America is in decline and it is now our time. The *shi* is in our favor."

"It seems that your plans are currently unraveling."

"You are attempting a strategy of encirclement against my forces in the Arctic," the mage said. "Very typical of Americans. It will not succeed. We have reached the point of maximum opportunity; the situation has been shaped for this success."

"Setting the conditions for success?"

"Ah, yes, this is the American military expression? I like it. We still have great freedom of maneuver, thanks to your Islamic bogeymen in the Middle East. Your president's advisors are very easy to manipulate. They do not want to see the truth. Even if they did, I wonder if they could."

"Our *shi* is speeding up as well."

"Yes, our little corner of *wei qi*."

"*Wei qi*?"

"A game. Translated, it means encirclement board."

"I think I've played this game before."

"Shall we play another round?"

Chapter 21
Tampa, Florida

"This is most irregular to say the least," the nuclear seismologist said.

"Irregular is about the most polite word you could have used," Deckard replied.

The JSOC think tank in Tampa had brought in one of their consultants, Dr. David Flynn. He was one of the leading seismologists in the country. His speciality was monitoring for potential nuclear detonations around the world, his work mostly focused on North Korea and their alleged nuclear test detonations below ground.

"Simply put, tectonic weapons are not even supposed to exist. Such a thing would violate several scientific principles. There has been speculation, of course, by people like Aleksey Vsevolovidich Nikolayev at the Russian Academy of Sciences. We have done some feasibility studies, but the math doesn't add up."

"What is your best guess, then?"

Dr. Flynn squinted on Deckard's computer screen. The bearded scientist was hesitant.

"Between us girls," Deckard urged him. "I'm not quoting you in a scientific journal here."

"The Soviets were rumored to have a class of weapons called energetics. Action-at-distance, directed energy, even a sub class called psytronics that involves things like telekinesis and mind reading. Personally, I always felt that it was bunk, but the Russians apparently took it seriously, which led to some of our scientists taking it seriously as well during the Cold War. Secretary of Defense Cohen was even briefed on the threat in 1997."

"On tectonic weapons?"

"And weather weapons as well. The technology that would be used to induce an earthquake would be a scalar interferometer. Again, this is not my hypothesis. Using this type of device, theoretically speaking, electromagnetic energy could be introduced into the fault lines. This could increase stress and cause the tectonic plates to eventually slip."

"Worst-case scenario, what kind of damage could be done with a tectonic weapon?"

"Well, they would have to use it to trigger an earthquake where there is already natural geophysical pressures present. I think the worst damage they could do is if they were able to push along the caldera under Yellowstone National Park. It is a supervolcano with a magma chamber 50 miles long and 12 miles wide. Eruptions have occurred 2.1 million, 1.3 million, and 640,000 years ago."

"A tectonic weapon could also trigger a volcano?"

"If such a thing exists, then yes. Electromagnetic energy could be introduced into the volcano's magma chamber, building up internal pressures until it finally erupts."

"What would happen if the Yellowstone caldera erupted again?"

"Well," the scientist said with a shrug. "Maybe not an extinction event, but...."

"What?"

"America would cease to exist as we know it, at least for the foreseeable future. The eruption would go on for about a week, but the real damage would come from the blanket of ash that would cover the entire country and float in the sky above our heads. Agriculture would be wiped out, and as a country, we could even be brought to the brink of starvation."

"Unless an allegedly friendly power stepped in to help us out," Deckard said, cutting himself off before he said too much. In his mind, he could not help but think about Chinese troops landing on American shores as a part of some humanitarian aid program, with god only knows what strings attached. By then, the American government would probably welcome them with open arms.

"All I can say for certain," Flynn told Deckard, "is that if the Yellowstone caldera goes up, it will change everything we know about America for generations to come."

"You forgot the best part," Deckard replied.

"What's that?"

"Our government would never even know that a weapon had been used against us."

* * *

"Canadian Rangers out on a patrol near Resolute Bay spotted the semi-submersible ship passing Little Cornwallis Island," Otter said, setting down the radio microphone as Deckard walked onto the bridge. "The Canadians have the other passages through the northwest passage blocked off. North is the only direction they can go."

Deckard's eyes scoured over their sea charts, counting down the numbers in his mind. "Ellesmere Island," he said, pointing to a large land mass on the map. "That's where this is going to go down. They will be trapped up in these fjords. From there, they will either stand and fight or try to cross overland."

197

"We're only a few hours behind them," Otter added. "Considering we interrupted their refueling in Barrow, they must be running low on gas as well."

"I'll make a call and try to get Global Hawk back up, but it is already outrunning its operational range out of Alaska. Hopefully the Canadians can step up their air patrols now that the Rangers spotted them."

"They already have birds in the air," Otter replied. "They will let us know once they get eyes on."

"Good to hear. We'll get the men prepared."

"What now?"

"We've kept the pressure on the enemy, forced their hand, and made them expend resources. Now it is time to run them to ground, exhaust them, and kill them."

* * *

Canadian Arctic

Jiahao closed his eyes as bubbles gurgled up from the regulator in his mouth, the oxygen pooling into one large bubble at the top of the 553mm torpedo tube.

The submarine mast had been so badly damaged, it made surfacing too dangerous—if not impossible—until they would be able to receive repairs at the underground Yulin naval base on Hainan Island. Until then, the divers would have to make do with an egress through the torpedo tubes. Four divers were crouched over inside two delivery vehicles, one in each tube.

Jiahao smiled, biting down on the regulator to prevent water from leaking in from the corners of his mouth. The great irony was that the specifications for the construction of the torpedo-launched delivery vehicle had been stolen from the United States by cyber spies on the

198

mainland. Instead of delivering Navy SEALs onto some Third World battlefield, Jiahao's special team would be making use of them in the Canadian Arctic.

Suddenly, he was jerked back, his hands clinging to the controls as water passed around his head and shoulders like a cold breeze. On their flank, the commando could make out the second submersible delivery vehicle humming along. Initiating the prop, the delivery vehicle began maneuvering toward the surface.

Jiahao had been given a mission by his mage, and he fully intended to carry it out.

* * *

Twelve hours later, the Carrickfergus entered into the fjords of Ellesmere Island. Covered in glaciers, with steep V-shaped valleys and weathered crags poking up from beneath the ice, Ellesmere Island was one of the world's last frontiers, dividing Canada from Greenland. From the sea, the terrain looked both unforgiving and surreal. Glaciers crept into the ocean, the water itself a brilliant turquoise color.

In the distance, black smoke rose into the air where the China-Russia-Iran confab had jettisoned their semi-submersible ship and destroyed it with explosives. Canadian surveillance aircraft had spotted the explosion, but had yet to pick up where the enemy had moved on to. Canadian Rangers were being mobilized, but it was unclear if they would arrive in time to do anything. Most Canadian military assets were already being prepared for a coalition ground war in the Middle East, a knee-jerk response to terrorist attacks back home, leaving the Arctic forces with even less resources than usual.

The Carrickfergus dropped ramp one fjord before where the remains of the enemy ship were located for an off-set infiltration. The Samruk International mercenaries stormed off with their gear and sank into the snow under their heavy rucksacks despite the snowshoes they wore. Arranging themselves in a security perimeter, they took turns donning their skis. Samruk hadn't skimped on winter equipment, and they would need every edge they could get on Ellesmere Island.

Deckard stowed his assault snowshoes in his pack and snapped on a pair of Carbon Aspect skis manufactured by Black Diamond. Ski skins and climbing crampons would be kept on hand, as they would definitely be needing them soon. At two platoons plus a mortar section, Samruk consisted of a large element when trying to move around in an arctic environment. It would be slow going, but the tools they brought with them would hopefully give them a mobility edge on the enemy.

With his kit set up, Deckard yanked two ski poles— called whippets—off the back of his pack. They could collapse down when climbing uphill, and also had a small ice axe at the top of the pole for self arrest in the event that a climber began sliding off the edge of a cliff. Additional ice axes were lashed to their belts. They anticipated some tough climbs.

Once men, weapons, and equipment were prepared, Fedorchenko's platoon moved out, breaking a fresh trail. They moved in a file, cross-country skiing across the snow and ice. Two point men took the lead with a squad leader behind them making sure that they stayed on azimuth. Shatayeva's platoon followed a few minutes later, in a military formation called traveling overwatch. The two elements would remain separate, but close enough to each other to provide mutually supporting fire. The mortar section traveled in a third element with Deckard, the snipers, and their recce team.

Sliding across the ice, Fedorchenko's men made good time as they skirted the water's edge, heading toward the spur ahead that separated one fjord from the other. Once they hit the elevation change, the movement quickly slowed down. Skis had to be stowed on packs as they moved hand over hand up the crest with ice axes. At the top, the platoon got eyes on the smoking hulk of the scuttled enemy ship in the distance.

"Looks deserted," Fedorchenko reported over the radio. "No signs of the enemy. It appears that they ran the ship aground and then destroyed it with explosives."

Deckard looked up the slope at them. Nikita and his sniper partner had taken off on their own to glass the target with their high-powered optics. He didn't know what the private military company version of a court martial was, but Deckard was going to dock Nikita's pay and put him in the time-out corner once their Arctic mission was over. For now, he needed every gun in the fight.

"Keep eyes on until we get there."

Deckard collapsed his ski poles before tying them down to his ruck along with his skis. He then slipped crampons over his Dynafit ski boots and retrieved his Petzl ice axes. Step by step, he sank the crampons into the ice, swinging the ice axes one over the other to gain purchase, before repeating the maneuver and hauling himself up inch by inch. Once the mortar section and Shatayeva's men were up the side of the spur, Fedorchenko's men had time for a good rest before they put their skis back on.

Squad by squad they pushed off, skiing down the slope toward the enemy vessel that had dogged their every move in the Arctic. In their winter camouflage, the mercs blended seamlessly with the terrain on Ellesmere

Island, confusing the eye and nearly disappearing at times. They were not Arctic warriors on par with the Canadian Rangers, but they were learning fast.

After a half-hour climb, the entire platoon reached the opposite side of the slope and began cross-country skiing toward their target. Deckard led the way for the second element, his facemask and goggles protecting him from what would have been a debilitating case of frostbite, the cold air whistling past his ears. The crags at the bottom of the downhill run came up to meet him even faster than he had anticipated, forcing him to pivot his knees and ski away at the last second, a boulder rushing by before he leveled out at the bottom.

With the rest of Samruk at the base of the slope, Deckard radioed Fedorchenko.

"Go scout out that ship and watch out for boobytraps. There is no need to get too close; we just need to pick up their spore."

Spore were signs of human passage. Normally, this would consist of footprints in the dirt and broken branches. Maybe the only thing the Arctic had going for it from a military standpoint was that following human footprints in the snow was an easy affair.

The ship was only 500 or so meters away, so once Fedorchenko's men moved out, Deckard took his element closely behind. With his ski poles extended, he dug into the ice, pushing along as he skied forward, quickly working up a sweat under his jacket. Once they caught up with the lead platoon, Deckard saw Dag crouched down, looking at something. Skiing over to him, Deckard immediately saw the tracks.

The enemy were moving out on snowshoes. The trail was well beaten and heading east toward the mountains in the distance.

"Maybe a hundred of them," Dag said. "The tracks have not degraded much. The wind has not even blown them away. They are only a few hours ahead of us. We can catch up quickly. No rests."

"That's what they expect," Deckard said. "They'll double back and mine their own spore. Do a map reconnaissance and find an alternate route. We'll get ahead of them and lay an ambush of our own."

"I will take a look and plot a route," the Norwegian said.

Deckard felt something vibrating in the inner pocket of his parka and jumped in surprise.

"What is it?"

"Nothing," Deckard said as he unzipped his jacket and reached inside. "It's this tablet that Cody gave me. He called it a Pwn Pad. It can isolate electronic signals."

Pulling out the Nexus tablet, Deckard held one of his gloves in his teeth and yanked it off. Scrolling through the apps, he saw that the Pwn Pad had picked up on a signal being emitted nearby.

"Found something?"

"I don't know. Maybe it's coming from the ship? Maybe they set a repeater in the snow somewhere?"

Reaching down, Deckard keyed his hand mic.

"All stations on this net, this is six. Heads up, I'm seeing some weird electronic signals. Hard to say what it is —"

His words drifted off as his eyes tracked along the shore of the island. Something was churning the water in a circular pattern just outside where the waves were breaking against the shore.

"Fire! Fire!" Deckard yelled. "In the water!"

One of the Kazakh mercenaries was Johnny-on-the-spot, firing a burst of 7.62mm into the churning ocean water. Something beneath the surface exploded, sending a spray of water into the air. More signatures suddenly appeared from beneath the surface, then blasted up into the air, splattering sea water in all directions.

"Drones!"

Chapter 22

The quad-rotors emerged from the ocean where they had been concealed and shot up into the air. The amphibian drones transitioned from navigating water to open air in the blink of an eye. About as wide as a manhole cover, the drones lifted off and sped toward the mercenaries.

Deckard could see the black boxes heading toward them. Four arms reached out from the main control unit, each with a separate plastic rotor blade on it. Fluid dynamics and aerodynamics responded in very similar ways, making it possible for a multifunctional drone to be equally at home in the water as it was in the air, but none of them had time to contemplate that fact as they came under attack.

The drone swarm was racing toward their position. The first one had blown up when fired upon, leaving little doubt as to the payload they carried. Each was a remote-operated improvised explosive device.

The mercenaries opened fire, tracers going wide, high, and low as the swarm came straight at them. Someone finally scored a hit and the drone immediately took a header into the ice, where it detonated less than 50 meters in front of their security perimeter. Ice and black smoke radiated from the blast.

Deckard saw one drone break from the swarm's formation and head directly toward him. Somehow he knew. It was the mage, an electronic puppeteer behind the scenes.

Flicking the Kalashnikov's selector to auto, he let off a burst that clipped the drone, severing the rotors on the left-hand side. The quad-rotor then went into an uncontrolled spin as the rotors on the other side continued to generate lift. The drone spun end over end as it burned in and crashed 10 meters in front of him before exploding.

Ice chips cut into his pants and parka as Deckard and Dag both instinctively brought up their hands to protect their faces. Meanwhile, the Samruk mercenaries were dropping the drones one by one. Deckard watched as they fell from the sky like sparrows shot by a slingshot, except these sparrows went up in a ball of fire when they went down. One of the drones dropped elevation in a sharp jerking motion, then cruised right up to the frontline of mercenaries. The Kazakhs managed to shoot it down at the last possible second. The resulting explosion flung three of the mercenaries down on their backs.

One of the drones managed to infiltrate through their security perimeter and landed in the middle of the mercenary formation. Sergeant Major Korgan and Aghassi ran for their lives along with several of the Kazakhs. They saved themselves by the skin of their teeth, slipping and falling as the shock wave from the exploding drone washed over them.

The remaining drones were coming in hard and fast. The mercenaries raked them with PKM and AK fire, causing the drones to explode right in front of them. A Carl Gustav gunner loaded a round into his recoilless rifle and pushed several mercenaries out of his way to get in front of them.

"Back blast area clear," he shouted over his shoulder. But it wasn't really clear. One of the mercs dived out of the way just as he fired.

The 84mm ADM round fired a spray of 1,100 flechettes. Designed for taking out enemy troop formations in urban and jungle warfare, the ADM round delivered its lethal payload into the drone swarm. Plastic rotor blades were shredded and torn away from the drone control units by the flechettes, driving them down to the ground as if someone had just flicked their off switch. Smashing into the ice, they exploded one by one.

Once again, the enemy had used a combination of surprise and high technology to gain the advantage over Deckard's men. They had survived, but only because of the quick thinking of their goose gunner.

Reaching down, Deckard helped Dag to his feet.

"Fuck these assholes."

Dag nodded.

"Let's finish this."

* * *

Will sat back in his chair, watching the feed coming in from their Global Hawk drone circling above Ellesmere Island. The drone's loiter time was severely constrained, it had only half an hour before it would have to return to base for refueling, but until then they would relay what they spotted on the video feed to Deckard's men through the Carrickfergus, giving them as much situational awareness as possible.

They had yet to locate the enemy force, but the Samruk International mercenaries were at the edge of a glacier, preparing for their crossing. Looking at the terrain, Will could make an inference about Deckard's tactics. Crossing the glacier and then a mountain ridge in arctic conditions was exceedingly dangerous, the definition of a bold maneuver. Deckard thought he would be able to take a shortcut and pop out in front of where he projected the enemy to be moving to next.

Craig sat in the SCOPE conference room with his arms crossed.

"How did we not see this coming?" he asked absently.

Will swallowed.

"We're America. It is our national style to not see slowly escalating threats. What he have here are three challengers to the throne. America is the power that has shaped global order since the end of World War Two. China, Russia, and Iran are seeking asymmetrical means to re-calibrate that order."

"We knew they were trying, but no one anticipated anything on this scale."

"The fact that they wanted it should have set off alarms a long time ago. They may be separate, competing powers that don't particularly like each other, but hatred for America is what they have in common. It has aligned them against us. Iran's at best a regional power in the Middle East, but because of their history and cultural legacy, they see themselves as being more important in world affairs than they will ever be. In fact, the only element that the Iranian regime has to galvanize their people is anti-American and anti-Israeli sentiments.

"Meanwhile, Russia has always suffered from a profound sense of insecurity. They have always had Mongols, Tatars, and Europeans on their doorstep. During the Cold War, they sought strategic depth to prevent NATO from getting a clear shot across the steppes to Moscow. Today, they perceive us as strategically encircling them with a anti-ballistic missile shield.

"Then there is China. They are the real problem. Of the three, they are the only country with a real chance at restructuring global order in their own image. In another decade, the Chinese economy will surpass America's. They have spent decades sharpening their knives, pretending to be our friends, and playing the victim. The reality is that they also see themselves as victims of the West, at least some of it stemming from events as far back as the Boxer Rebellion. The Chinese have bided their time, and now they are striking against us."

"While our own bureaucracy launches a war against the wrong enemy. Our government can't even figure out who to fight."

"What makes you think they can't figure it out?" Will asked rhetorically. "Perhaps they don't want to fight the Chinese. Our economic interests are too closely intertwined. This isn't a mistake, it is part of a calculated strategy the Chinese have devised to insulate themselves from American power. At the same time, the American public is scared out of their minds right now. They demand that we find an easy-to-define enemy and then bomb them into the Stone Age. ISIS is the perfect fit. Kill them all, and with minimal political repercussions on the world stage."

"In other words, we're fucked."

"Now it is up to them," Will said, watching little black dots move across the screen.

"Hey, do you see that?"

Will squinted at the screen. The Global Hawk had passed over the glacier and then over a ridgeline, looking down into a valley that led away from the western coast, heading in a northeasterly direction.

"That's them."

* * *

Deckard pulled his mask down and drank from an insulated thermos as he stared out across the glacier. Spread out in front of him, the glacier was stunning in scope. It inched down the entire valley, only stopping a kilometer away from the shore. From that point on, the melting ice churned that lonely patch of valley into a rock-strewn mud puddle they had thankfully avoided. The glacier itself filled the valley and crept up the rocks on either end.

The occasional faint groan was just barely audible, heard from the subterranean ice below. It would have been far better to begin crossing the mass of ice in the morning, before the sun had begun the daily melt that started each day before freezing again at night. Now it was the middle of the day, and the glacier would be much more dangerous. As the sheet of ice flowed down the valley in slow motion, it grated across elevation changes on the valley floor, which caused the ice to split, creating crevasses on the surface. A similar physical dynamic took place where the glacier was forced to turn in the valley, which also led to crevasses appearing on the outer edges.

The men were already preparing their equipment, crafting improvised harnesses out of lengths of rope and then tying into one another in groups of four in case someone fell into a crack, which was easy to do if it was still concealed by a layer of snow.

It would have been better to make camp, let the glacier freeze again overnight, and make their crossing in the morning, but this wasn't some Ranger Rick expedition for a Discovery Channel special. They were at war.

"Bird in the sky's got eyes on the enemy," Otter's voice cracked over his radio. "You were right about them skirting through the next valley and then up into the mountains. The drone only caught sight of them for a minute before having to head back to the refueling station, but they estimated about a hundred personnel, over."

This was combat. They would cross the glacier now, make camp at nightfall, and find a way over the mountains to intercept the enemy. There was no time to waste.

"Roger," Deckard radioed back to the Carrickfergus. "Thanks for the SITREP, over."

"They think that the device is being hauled on a snow sled."

"Good. That should slow them down a bit."

"Roger, out."

Deckard slid through the snow, down an embankment, to the edge of the glacier.

"We're almost ready to roll out," Kurt Jager announced. "You ready to tie in?"

"Let's go."

Kurt was tied into the leading edge of the rope with a figure-eight knot that went through his harness. Sergeant Major Korgan was tied into the trail end, and Pat was tying into the middle. Spacing himself between Pat and Kurt, Deckard tied himself in. With that done, each of them used another length of rope to fashion a chest harness, secured across the front with a carabiner. The chest harness was then also clipped into the main line. Considering the heavy rucks they were carrying, without a chest harness, they would have risked not being able to sit upright if they fell into a crevasse, or worse yet, breaking their backs during the fall.

While the harnesses and main lines were done with 11mm dynamic rope, smaller 9mm static ropes were used to form Prusik knots along the main line on each side of the figure-eight knot they had tied in with. The free-running ends were tied off into hand and footholds, then jammed into pockets. These were friction knots that could be used to scale the main line back to the top if they fell into a crevasse. The entire PMC was rigged up the same way, ready to cross the glacier's expanse, a nearly five-kilometer trek.

"This is Six. Ready when you are," Deckard announced over the radio.

Dag and Jacob would be the lead element for the movement. Having served in Norwegian and Danish special operations units, respectively, they were the most qualified.

"Roger," Jacob responded. "Heading out now, over."

Deckard flinched as a piece of ice broke off from the cliff above them, crashed in the rocks, and showered him with powdered snow. The ice was melting and Mother Nature had given them fair warning.

* * *

Dag made sure his safety rope was fully extended between himself and Jacob, taking out any slack before pushing off on his skis. He could glide across the glacier at a fairly fast pace as things stood, but he had to take it slow, probing the snow in front of him for gaps in the ice that could be covered over. The good news was that going across on skis helped keep their weight distributed, making breakthroughs less likely.

Once out on the glacier, Shatayeva's men came up behind them, each trooper staying on Dag's original ski trail he had made. Fedorchenko's men had been breaking the path all morning, and now the platoons were changing up the order of movement so the ones bringing up the rear could rest a little.

The former Norwegian commando proceeded forward, watching for trenches in the snow that would indicate a hidden crevasse. He would spot the signs of it if he was lucky, otherwise he would just have to hope that probing the snow with his ski poles would warn him before he fell in. With Jacob's help, Dag had to focus all of his attention on navigating the glacier, staying on azimuth, and avoiding the crevasses. He couldn't divide his attention by concerning himself with the enemy. For that purpose, a PKM machine gunner and Nikita, one of their snipers, were tied in behind Jacob.

Although the dynamics were different, the glacier also had friction points like the ice floe they had been on a few days ago. If the enemy knew they were out on the glacier, could they activate the device a second time and open a chasm so big that it swallowed them whole? Dag cast the thought out of his mind and focused on the job at hand.

Under the sun, Dag was working up a sweat and stopped several times to drink water. He rolled his eyes, remembering an American infantry saying: "Travel light, freeze all night." The travel light part never seemed quite accurate, but the second part certainly was. He had been skiing for an hour when he spotted a crevasse field up ahead, about halfway across the glacier. Looking over his shoulder, he could see a file of soldiers winding back almost as far as he could see.

"Crevasse field up ahead," Dag radioed back. "Keep an eye out and remember to keep your ropes taut." Having too much slack would result in a harsh snap for everyone tied into the rope if someone fell, which could possibly pull others in before they could self-arrest with the axe blades on their ski poles.

"Dag, let me take lead for a while," Jacob offered. "Rest your eyes for a bit. You've almost taken us halfway there."

213

"I'm good for now. We'll switch out after we clear this crevasse field."

Pulling off his face mask and cramming it in a pocket, Dag skied forward with his three teammates trailing behind him, attached by the climbing rope. Probing just in front of him, the Norwegian's ski pole punched through the snow. Bucking over at the waist, Dag recovered quickly, caught by surprise. He continued probing the area, knocking the thin layer of snow down into what had been a concealed crevasse. Peering down into the chasm, Dag saw nothing but ice descending into the darkness below.

"We hit our first crevasse," Dag said over the assault net. "Skirting around it now."

Dag used the ski pole and probed his way around the gap, taking his lead element around it. It was a technique called an end run, one of many the Nordic warrior knew he would have to employ to get them across the glacier.

Moving on, Dag took them into the visible crevasse field in the middle of the glacier, where the elevation change, the declination of the valley floor, caused the ice to crack. Because of this, the crevasses were running mostly perpendicular with their patrol. Taking another drink of water, Dag examined their options.

"Take it at an echelon?" Jacob asked from behind him.

"Exactly what I was thinking," Dag replied.

Instead of following in Dag's ski tracks, the lead element shook out and got parallel with one another. They would travel in this manner instead of a single file to keep a good pace without compromising safety. Their safety lines would dangle over the crevasses as the mercenaries traveled between them. Once they were situated, Dag motioned forward. At the opposite end of the rope, Nikita skied with his HK417 rifle slung across his back, barrel pointed up.

The skiers crossed the crevasse field individually, finding their own ways forward as they carefully probed and zigzagged their way between the gaps in the ice. Under his skis, the ice undulated as Dag wove his way across. Loose snow caught in the wind and blew over the edge of the crevasse to his left, then began swirling around in circles inside. Dag would probe and then edge forward, then repeat the process again and again. At one point, the crevasses became so wide that the lead four men collapsed back down into a file.

The entire field was only a few hundred meters, but they all breathed a sigh of relief when they were past it. The opposite end of the glacier could be clearly seen. Turning, Dag looked up at the glacier coming down out of the mountains. It was an amazing sight, and one that very few people got to see since it was tucked away so far up into the Canadian Arctic.

"Ready?" Jacob interrupted. He was already untying himself from the harness.

"*Jo*," he confirmed. "*Takk*."

"*Selv Tak*," Jacob replied in his own native language.

The pair worked well together, and had even trained together a few times in Denmark's annual counterterrorism exercise called Night Hawk. When they got together, you could hardly tell the difference between Denmark's Jaeger Corps, Sweden's SOG, Norway's FSK, and Germany's KSK unless you had an ear trained for Scandinavian languages. In MultiCam fatigues, they all seemed so similar until you heard them talking.

Dag pulled at his figure-eight knot for a minute before finally loosening it. He skied back to Jacob as he got himself free and headed to the end of the rope. The sun was beginning to sink in the sky, but they still had enough time to clear the glacier. Everything seemed to be going according the plan, which was what bothered the two senior alpine soldiers.

Jacob and Dag looked at each other as their radios crackled with static, someone trying to scream something over the net.

* * *

Deckard hit the ice hard and was immediately pulled toward the crevasse. Getting the ice axe at the top of his ski pole into the ice, he laid down on top of it as he was dragged through the snow. Up ahead, Kurt Jager did the same before reaching back with one hand, freeing an ice axe and swinging it into the ice, finally arresting them before they were sucked into the crack.

Taking a deep breath, Deckard looked back and saw Pat with both of his whippet pole axes stuck in the ice. His legs were dangling over the edge of the crevasse. With his eyebrows drooped and an upside-down smile, it was clear that the former Delta Force operator was less than happy.

Using his incredible upper-body strength, Pat muscled his way over the lip of the crevasse and dug back into the glacier with his ice axes. Pat was known for going into beast mode in the gym, not to mention in combat. Woe was the Samruk trooper who stepped into the boxing ring with Pat for morning PT, as Pat was also known for sparring with an entire platoon in a single session, one soldier at a time.

Attached by the safety line, Sergeant Major Korgan was dangling somewhere down in the crevasse.

"Korgan," Pat called. "You alive down there?"

A grumble came as a reply. "Da, I'm alive," Korgan said, his voice echoing around in the fissure in the ice. "Just get me out of here."

"We're working on it."

Deckard worked on setting in the initial anchor. He could already see the mortar section dropping their rucks and making their way over to them to assist in the rescue effort. Pushing the handle of his ice axe into the snow, he attached the handhold of one of his Prusik knots through a carabiner, then secured it to the ice axe. It wasn't a great anchor, but it would take much of the weight off of the safety line running from him to Kurt Jager, giving the German some slack, and some time, to set in a more substantial anchor.

Kurt buried a picket into the snow and then hammered it in with his ice axe. The free-running end of the safety line was then secured to the picket by tying it in a figure-eight knot and clipping it into another carabiner that went through a hole in the picket. With the mortar section arriving, Ivan and his men crept forward, first assisting Pat in untying from the safety line and getting free from the crevasse. Kurt and Deckard then untied, and the three used a new line to tie into.

Traveling across the glacier in such a large element was painstaking and cumbersome to say the least, but one positive aspect was that there were a lot of warm bodies around to assist in the rescue. Normally, it would be just two or three people.

"Hey," Pat shouted down to Korgan. "We're going to send a rope down so you can tie off your ruck, skis, and weapon. We'll pull them up."

"What about me!" his voice echoed up in reply.

"You're next, but this will make it a bit easier."

217

They dangled another climbing rope down the gap. It began getting tugged around.

"Need more rope!" Korgan's accented English shouted back to them.

The mortar section gave him some more slack. A long string of curses in Russian followed from inside the crevasse, but finally, the mortar men hauled up Korgan's gear. Meanwhile, Deckard lay on his belly and slid the shaft of an ice axe under the safety line that Korgan was hanging from to prevent it from becoming entrenched in the snow. The Samruk commander remained in place to manage the rope from the edge while the mortar section lined up around the safety line to begin hauling. With eight men, they had more than enough personnel for a quick recovery that would not involve a Prusik climb or complicated pulley system.

"Heave!" Kurt ordered.

Playing tug of war with gravity, the mortar men hauled Korgan toward the surface by hand. Deckard was still on his stomach, making sure the rope stayed over the shaft of the ice axe. Finally, Deckard could see Korgan emerging from the shadows below. He looked up, his eyes wide but alert. Once he was close to the top, Deckard, Kurt, and Pat grabbed him and pulled him to safety.

Korgan immediately jumped to his feet and began tugging on his rope harness. He'd been suspended in mid-air by the harness, and it had been biting into his thighs while putting his ballbag in an uncomfortable situation. The sergeant major was visibly relieved when his nuts were once again hanging free.

Deckard laid on his back for a moment, taking a rest. They were all saturated in sweat under their parkas at this point.

Just then, the glacier groaned, another crevasse opening somewhere.

"Jesus titty-fucking Christ," Deckard cursed. "Let's get the fuck out of here."

* * *

After the crevasse rescue, Samruk International made it across the glacier without further incident, which was a good thing because it was nearly dusk. They could only pray that the enemy was having as difficult a time negotiating the terrain as they were. Climbing off the glacier and into the foothills of a mountain, several musk oxen scattered and disappeared into the tundra.

Leading the mercenaries uphill into a draw, Jacob found a suitable place for a patrol base where they could lay up for the night. He would leave the men to dig out their shelters and see what kind of progress he could make on the next leg of their journey. If the glacier was difficult to traverse, he was not looking forward to what came next.

The Danish commando had to crane his neck all the way back to see the top of the mountain in front of them. Tactically, it made sense to scale the mountain, secure the high ground, cut the enemy off while they were channelized in a valley, and assault down on top of them. Realistically, a mixed alpine climb, which included climbing frozen waterfalls, rocks, snow, and ice, would make their rope installation and movement over the mountain one of the most challenging tasks of his career.

Mentally reviewing historical precedents, he could only think of one in recent military history: the 1999 Kargil conflict between India and Pakistan in Kashmir. Overnight, Indian military mountaineers did a similar rope installation, and then moved Indian soldiers up to the high ground, surprising Pakistani troop positions by attacking from a completely unexpected place. It was a bold maneuver, but it worked.

Dag gathered together the winter warfare experts in the unit. Nate, Maurizio, and Jacob came over while they discussed their game plan for the rope installation. They would be working all night to have it ready by morning. Looking up the mountain, they pulled out topographical maps and talked through their angle of attack, rejecting some ideas and going with others as they tried to plot the easiest route up the slopes.

Hearing the crunch of snow, they looked over to see Deckard stomping his way over with his rucksack. He had traded out his skis for his assault snowshoes.

"What's the plan?" he asked, slightly out of breath.

"It is a mixed climb," Jacob said. "No getting around it."

"We are going to have to use methods from alpine climbing, ice climbing, and rock climbing to get over this," Nate added.

"Do we have the gear you need to do that?"

Dag looked skyward.

"Ja," he replied after a long moment of thinking. "I believe so, but we may run out of equipment at some point. We're going to have to make compromises with safety, especially because we will have to install two lines if we want to get both platoons up without waiting until next Christmas."

"I'll bring Kurt as well, since he has mountaineering experience. You'll need all the hands you can get. Korgan will be in charge down here, getting the patrol base together. We'll wake the boys up before dawn and get them moving."

"Wait," Nate said. "You want to come with us?"

"Yeah, of course."

"Have you ever done anything like this before?"

Deckard pointed up to the summit of the mountain. "You see that?" He then pointed back at the human anthill of Samruk mercenaries digging into the snow. "You see them?"

"Yeah," Nate replied.

"No one has ever done anything like this before."

Chapter 23

Nikita flung his tri-fold shovel into the snow and unzipped his jacket. He was overheating now, but as the sun sank behind the mountains, he knew that would be changing shortly. It added some extra motivation to the troops to get their defenses and sleeping areas dug out. Korgan was marching around with a notebook in hand, pointing to where machine gun positions were to be dug and indicating the general arrangement of the trenches.

The mercenaries had crawled into a draw between two spurs coming off the mountain where they would prepare their overnight patrol base. The recon and mountaineering team had already departed, and the Kazakh did not envy how their night would be going. They were crazy to even attempt the climb in the darkness as far as he was concerned.

The patrol base was shaped like an extended crow's foot, with trenches being dug out in three directions and gun positions dug at each end to establish triangular, mutually supporting sectors of fire. The platoon CP, or control point, would be centrally located, as would the mortar pit. Putting their backs into it, and using the occasional ice axe, they cut through the snow and ice, carving out the trenches. Next, the men broke up into their individual squads to begin hollowing out shelters by tunneling under the snow from the trenches. Others worked to improve the gun positions, making sure that the gunners would have a good 18 inches of snow as a barrier to stop enemy rounds.

Meanwhile, Korgan assigned men to begin melting down water and refilling empty canteens and Camelbak bladders. Fedorchenko assigned two men to dig out the latrine and then began supervising the construction of individual shelters. The mercenaries lined their rucksacks and skis up outside the entrance to their shelter, squad by squad. Weapons were wrapped in a poncho and left even closer to the entrance so they could be quickly retrieved. Keeping their guns inside the warm shelters and then bringing them back out into the Arctic cold would result in "sweating," causing weapons malfunctions. During the night, each squad would light a small fire inside their shelter to stay warm.

The patrol base was nearly done being constructed by the time the sun finally set. Korgan was working his men into the ground, knowing their task would be a hell of a lot harder at night. Nikita and the other three snipers crouched down and entered their shelter at last. They dug out their bunks in the side of the snow shelter to keep them above the floor. Otherwise, they risked carbon monoxide poisoning.

Brian, the American and former Ranger, and Aslan carried out the remaining snow in their ponchos. Finally, the four men sat around a small gas-burning MSR stove drinking water and eating MREs. The four snipers were already dozing when someone yelled inside their shelter. Their heads bobbed up and down like a slinky going end over end down a flight of stairs as they woke up.

"Guard duty!"

* * *

When the sun went down, the temperature dropped rapidly. The six-man mountaineering team pulled their hoods down tight against their heads and did their best to keep moving, more of an attempt to stay warm than anything. Nate trudged through the knee-deep snow as the incline got steeper and steeper. Wearing assault

223

snowshoes, he was running a line up through the snow for the main body to use in the morning. Using his ice axe as a cane, he pulled and pushed his way forward. Behind Nate, Kurt dug small pickets into the snow and then attached the rope Nate was running into the pickets with carabiners.

As the slope became steeper, it turned into a sheer sheet of ice. Deckard volunteered to take the lead, knowing he could handle this portion of the climb. As they went vertical, he would have to turn the lead over to the more experienced climbers. Using one ice axe and one ice tool specially made for ice climbing, Deckard utilized what was called the American technique to scale the ice, having traded out his snowshoes for crampons. He kept his lead foot pointed forward and the trail foot perpendicular to the mountain. This allowed him to compromise between his speed up the slope and not completely exhausting his legs, as he was able to distribute his weight between his calf muscle and thigh.

Wind howled down the mountain, cutting through Deckard's parka. He hadn't experienced anything like this, not even in Afghanistan. The only element going in their favor was good illumination. The mountain rose up in front of him like a demon. It lurched over him, watching and waiting. A gust pushed Deckard back, threatening to topple him over and send him sliding. Swinging his ice axe overhand, he slammed it into the ice to regain his composure. Deckard's breath came in short gasps, each one freezing behind the mask he wore over his face.

Behind him, he could see his teammates shuffling in the dark. The sound of their ice tools and crampons came to him in dull tones, proof that they were still there. The sound of metal on ice offered him some security, maybe a false sense of it, like the Kalashnikov slung over his shoulder. Kurt continued to secure the rope at odd intervals by installing ice screws with the pick of his ice tool, turning them into the hard ice where they would freeze overnight. A carabiner would marry up the rope to the metal eyelet at the end of the ice screws.

Finally, Deckard reached a point where the mountain went vertical. He had been scaling an incline steep enough that he was touching ice when standing straight up and reaching out with one hand. Now they were going up at a 90-degree angle.

Dag broke ranks and climbed up beside Deckard to begin preparing his equipment. Adjusting his harness, Dag lit up his headlamp and started clipping gear to his rack for the climb. This included ice screws, ice hooks, his ice tools, carabiners, and nylon tubing for creating additional anchors. His Kalashnikov was slung over the top of all of it. They were the lead element, and there was an expectation of enemy contact at some point.

The Norwegian looked up at the frozen waterfall. Due to the plasticity of the ice, he had estimated that climbing the waterfall would be easier than attempting to scale older ice and inverted cliffs elsewhere. Swinging his ice tools into the ice, he monkey-hung from the ice, jamming his crampons in before beginning to climb. Bringing a tool down on the ice with his arm at maximum extension, Dag would then bring his feet up until he was in a vertical crouch, then stand up and repeat the process.

The five mercenaries at the bottom watched in awe as the former FSK soldier glided up the ice with his headlamp leading the way. Dag showed them how to get it done. Thirty meters up the ice, he paused to install the first ice screw. Taking a deep breath, Jacob was the next to follow Dag's lead up the frozen waterfall.

As he climbed, Dag was forced to take an irregular route. Going straight up was out of the question as rocks, hanging stalactites of ice, and impossible overhangs obstructed the way. Some of them he could traverse, but the rest of Samruk International was not as experienced as he was. For their sake, it would require a twisting route far easier for the others to climb. Using the rope and ascenders, their climb would be a piece of cake by comparison.

After installing his fourth ice screw, Dag began climbing laterally to go around an overhang. Once clear of the overhead obstacle, he screwed in another piece of gear and continued back up. Eventually, he found a solid pillar of ice as big around as a redwood tree. The pillar was the result of ice melting each morning and dripping down an icicle until it created a stalagmite at the bottom when the water froze again in the night. Eventually, the two joined into a solid pillar.

Dag worked for hours in the dark and freezing cold. His muscles froze, then were covered in slimy sweat under his jacket. Finally, his biceps and quads began turning to jelly, his every move labored as he hauled his body weight and equipment up the ice pillar, one swing at a time. Looking up, he spotted a large patch of cauliflower ice beneath a ledge and aimed for it. True to its name, the patch looked like giant white puffs belonging to the vegetable. Ignoring the pain in his muscles and strain in his back, he didn't stop until he reached the cauliflower formation.

The ice formation created large footholds; he could even lean up against the slope while standing on the ice and try to take a rest. Taking a few deep breaths, he used the hammer head on the back of his ice pick to pound in a few ice anchors to which he secured the safety rope.

"You OK up there?" Kurt hollered up from below.

"Yeah," Dag panted between breaths. "Almost to the ledge."

Scrambling up the ice formation, Dag slugged it out the rest of the way up. Ironically, getting over the ledge was perhaps the most difficult part of the climb. It was awkward scooting his ass end up as high as he could on the ledge while leaning forward with both of his axes over the top, his arms extended. Finally, he grunted over the lip. He didn't even want to look up. He was only halfway up the side of the mountain.

While the others continued their climb, he found a rocky outcropping to use as an anchor. He secured the rope around it and then finally took a rest. It felt as if his overheated body instantly froze. His joints locked up and became stiff. More than anything, he just wanted to lie down and go to sleep. The other five mercenaries muscled their way up and nearly collapsed as well.

"Drink some water," Nate mumbled against the cold. "You have to force yourself."

Ice cracked along the back of their pants and parkas, falling at their feet as they reached for insulated canteens and Camelbaks, trying to stay hydrated.

The next leg of the climb was not as technical. Jacob led the patrol and took them on a winding path between some snow-covered boulders. A narrow ledge then led the way up. Finding cracks between the rock, he inserted spring-loaded camming devices to which they would secure their rope. Eventually, they were bouldering, moving hand over hand laterally along the edge, heading toward a place Jacob had spotted in which they could walk up rather than climb.

The Dane's hands were numb, his face raw from his breath freezing against it. The harder he pushed himself, the more he just felt like lying down. Reaching for

227

a protrusion in the rock, he slipped. The mercenary was airborne for a terrifying second until the safety line jolted him to a halt as it caught against the last anchor. The wind was knocked out of him as he slammed against the rock face.

Slowly, he moved his arms and legs, forcing them to function. He had to use his ice axes against the cold rock to climb back up while the others watched. Minutes seemed like hours, his every movement done in slow motion. Nate reached down and grabbed him by the sleeve, tugging him back up. With the feeling in his hands and feet long gone, Jacob shuffled along the rocks until they came to another snowy embankment.

The Dane collapsed to his knees. Nate came in just behind him and sat down. They had been running on fumes an hour ago. Now the tank was empty.

"Come on," Deckard said as he shook Jacob awake. "We're not going to make it to the top tonight. We need to find a place to take shelter."

Deckard secured their latest safety line to another boulder, then pulled out a new rope. He went from trooper to trooper making sure they were all secured to it before leading the way. The mercenary commander put on a good show, but the truth was that he was just as smoked as the rest of them. He just needed to make sure his team survived the night.

A fresh gust of wind nearly blew the six men right off their feet.

Deckard gritted his teeth.

The mountain was going to have a say in their survival.

Chapter 24

The landscape froze, then melted, a single drop of water dripping down the side of a lonely cliff face. Snow fell, then collapsed down, flattened out by the the sun, only to begin drifting down from the sky again hours later. The glacier moved, too slowly for human observation to notice. What appeared static was constantly in a state of flux. Even the barren desolation of the Arctic contained a hint of life, even if it was desperate and barely hanging on underneath a rock, waiting for spring.

A fist punched up through the snow to the surface.

The surrounding snow collapsed as the fist was withdrawn and a human figure emerged on the side of the mountain. Deckard reached up and pulled his hood down, using the cold air to force himself awake. It had been a long night, but he was alive. Alive and pissed.

Pulling out his MBITR radio, he walked to the edge of the mountain. Using FM signals, the radio operated by line of sight. Having the high ground did him little good in this case, but he hoped he would be able to make contact with the main body.

"Any station on this net, this is Six, over," he said into the main mic.

Static was the only reply.

"Any station on this net, come in, over."

More static.

Backing away from the ledge, the radio came to life.

"Six—" the voice cut out as fast as it appeared, replaced by a gurgle of static. "No...over...jammed."

Their net was being jammed; he got that much.

"En route...hours..."

"Say again, what is your ETA?" Deckard asked.

"Thr...rs."

"Three hours," Deckard said to himself.

More half-frozen bodies emerged from the snow shelter. Kurt, Dag, Jacob, Nate, and Maurizio shook out their arms and legs. Dag started doing jumping jacks to try to warm himself up.

"I got someone over the net," Deckard announced. "They are about three hours out. The net is fucked, though. They're jamming us again."

"Radio batteries are heavy anyway," Jacob said. "Good to know there isn't any point in carrying them!"

The team took a quick inventory of their remaining gear before plowing through the snow to the summit. Thankfully, it plateaued out toward the top, where they donned their snowshoes. Struggling to blaze a path through the snow was still easier than hanging on to the side of an ice wall by their crampons. It took an an hour and a half, but they made it.

A valley spread out in front of them as they looked into the morning light. More snow. More ice. Going on straight into forever. The only movement below was a trio of white wolves stalking the tundra.

Deckard had done some map reconnaissance, and had been banking on there being at least one route down the opposite side of the mountain that could be traversed on skis. To his satisfaction, there looked to be several. Now they had to wait for the others to arrive, and hope that he was right about being able to intercept the enemy. He sighted through a pair of binoculars. There did not appear to be any sign of the enemy's passage.

They too had to deal with the arctic night.

"Got something," Nate announced as he looked through his own pair of binoculars. "Movement up on that mountain on the other side of the valley."

Deckard squinted behind his goggles.

"How can you even see anything that far?"

"Way too much time squatting in a spider hole in Afghanistan, boss."

Deckard scoured the mountain opposite to them. It took a minute, but he picked up several black specks moving across the ridge of the mountain.

"Who the hell is that?" Nate asked.

"More importantly, which side are they on?"

"Not ours, I imagine," Dag said, clearly not feeling a positive vibe.

"OK, Dag and Kurt, you head back to receive the main body when they arrive. The rest of us will look for some better cover and concealment to keep eyes on the valley. Make sure you get some food in you, too."

Despite the main body leaving their patrol base and starting their ascent before dawn, it still took all morning to get the platoons up the side of the mountain. The mountaineer team was grateful for the rest and spent the morning alternating on watch from the summit of the mountain and warming themselves in the sun while chowing down on military rations and protein bars.

The sun was high in the sky, the wind still biting at their cheeks when Jacob called out, "I've got something here."

Deckard lay down in the prone next to him.

"What is it?"

"Movement along the military crest of the mountain."

The military crest was Army jargon meaning they were moving on a path halfway up the side of the mountain. Deckard looked down the slope and to his nine o'clock.

"Yes, I see them."

231

"Maybe a scout patrol?"

Deckard scanned some more, but had a hard time making out details as they were still a few kilometers away. The enemy wore overwhites to blend in with the snow, and their Israeli bullpup rifles had been spray-painted white as near as Deckard could tell.

"I think so," Deckard finally replied to Jacob. "Maybe ten of them. They are an advance element, just like we are."

"Let them pass and then ambush the main force?"

"Not enough time. I don't think our guys will arrive here in time for us to have even a minimum force. The enemy is about 100 strong, outnumbering us by a third to begin with. If we attack before all of our boys are up here, we will be mowed down like grass."

"Delay them instead, then," the former Jaeger Corps soldier concluded.

"Exactly. But we are going to need—"

"Deck." Kurt waded toward him through the snow. "Fedorchenko just arrived with the first of his men. The rest are coming up behind him slowly, with Korgan pushing them up from the rear."

"Where are our rucks and skis?"

"They have set up some A-frames and pulley systems for hoisting the gear up, but it is going to take a while."

"Send the word down to send up six pairs of skis immediately. The enemy is inbound."

"What are you going to do?"

"You mean what are *we* going to do?"

Kurt smiled. A good man kept his sense of humor in these situations. "Even better."

"We're going to slow them down."

Kurt frowned.

"What?"

"Look behind you."

Deckard turned around and saw four open parachutes descending in a staggered formation well off in the distance. The parachutists were descending to the ground in broad daylight, after jumping from a plane that none of them had seen or heard, most likely at high altitude.

"Freefall jump," Kurt said. "Those look like ram air chutes."

"Between them and those guys we saw scrambling along the mountains way off in the distance today, you have to wonder how many more want to join our party out here."

Kurt smiled. "Let's crash it and find out."

* * *

Deckard sank his whippets into the snow and pushed off.

His peripheral vision immediately disappeared into a blur of motion as he blasted down the side of the mountain, his skis slipping right over last night's fresh snowfall. He kept his eyes fixed on the small dots moving below him, the enemy moving about in their overwhites, so far unaware of the mercenaries above them. Maurizio came up alongside him, the rest of Deckard's mountaineer team close behind.

The technique was called *mottis* by the Finnish winter soldiers who developed a fierce reputation in World War Two for outmaneuvering Russian forces. Patrolling deep behind enemy lines on skis, the Finns would encircle and cut off the Russian Red Army, separating the soldiers from larger elements and cutting off their logistical lines. By doing this, they would wear the enemy down, draining their resources and exhausting them until they were killed or surrendered. Deckard's men would do the same, cutting off the scouting team and delaying the main force until Samruk could effectively mass their forces and launch a successful counterattack.

It was a gamble, but Deckard had spent his entire career threading impossible needles.

The mountain angles were getting steeper, and boulders were coming up to meet Deckard faster than he had anticipated. Maurizio and Deckard veered in opposite directions, narrowly missing one of the ice-covered crags. Launching off a small ridge, the mercenary went airborne for several seconds before splashing down in a cloud of snow. Behind him, Nate and Dag were more or less following in the trail they were blazing through the snow. Kurt and Jacob were moving parallel to them, finding their own way down the slope.

Dodging another boulder, Deckard scoured the terrain ahead, trying to pick up signs of the enemy again. He looked back down at the ground in front of him as he went off another ledge and sailed into the air. He came down hard, his knees acting like pistons to cushion him from the drop. As the slope leveled out, the skiers began making large, looping switchbacks as they visually identified the enemy scouts in the distance.

By now the angles were getting even steeper and the ski soldiers were cutting through the snow until an arctic sandstorm of snow was flowing all around them. Deckard chanced a glance over his shoulder to see what looked like a white waterfall behind them. There was no way the enemy wasn't going spot them in a few seconds. Now he could make out the bullpup rifles the Chinese,

Iranian, and Russian troops were carrying. They were only a few hundred meters away.

Letting the whippets hang by their lanyards, Deckard reached for the Kalashnikov slung over his shoulder and racked the charging handle. Ten sets of dark-lens goggles looked up at five skiers descending down upon them. Deckard lined himself up on an assault lane with as few obstructions as possible and opened fire. Getting his iron sights on target while bouncing down the side of the mountain was impossible, so he simply point-shot at the nearest target, squeezing off a burst of auto-fire.

The burst went low, kicking up splashes of snow, but kept the enemy in react mode, preventing them from opening fire first. Maurizio and Nate opened fire next, the staccato bursts of fire echoing down the side of the slope. One of the enemy troops was spun around as he caught at least one bullet in the side, his bullpup dropping into the snow.

Deckard pivoted, his skis churning up a wall of snow that seemed to cut into his skin even through all of his cold-weather gear. He came to a stop just behind a rock poking up from the snow and took a knee. Crossing his whippets to make an X shape, he rested his AK on them and used the poles as a platform to shoot from. He got his iron sights lined up on one of the moving enemy less than a hundred meters away. He put a controlled pair downrange, the AK bucking into his shoulder but rewarding him as his target dropped in a spray that turned the white snow a bright shade of crimson.

Now his visibility was becoming obstructed. When he fired his rifle, the hot propellant gases in his ammunition interacted with water vapor that quickly froze in the subzero temperature of the air, creating a fog around him that interfered with his line of sight.

As the others were maneuvering to their own fighting positions, the cloud of snow came in from behind and whispered around the mercenaries. Several cracks announced return fire from downhill, but none of it effective. Deckard cracked off a shot at one of the enemy but missed again. Crouched over and trying to find something to use as cover, Deckard was losing the enemy in the background as their overwhites blended in. Giving one a good lead, Deckard made some bold corrections, chopping through the air with 7.62x39mm in front of where he last saw his target. Finally, he saw a figure flop over and heard him screaming between gunshots as the men to his left and right began raining down the fire.

Several rounds buried themselves in the snow in front of Deckard, forcing him to go prone as more gunfire cut through the space he had occupied a second before. To his flank, Nate's AK was also kicking up a fog of frozen water vapor. Despite the difficulty in shooting through the vapor fog created by their weapons, the Samruk men had the terrain advantage. One by one, the enemy fell.

Watching his friends quickly cut down, one of the enemy turned downhill and disappeared down a ridge on the slope. Deckard let his rifle hang, grabbed the handles on his whippets to pull himself to his feet, and quickly charged after him.

"Deckard, hold on!" Kurt yelled.

But it was too late. He left the others to catch up, unwilling to let one of the scouts get away. Deckard avoided the bloody corpses and weapons strewn across the kill zone, skiing through red snow and dropping down the mountain. He could see the back of the survivor who was digging in with his poles, desperately trying to escape.

Angling his skis straight downhill, Deckard used his whippets to dig into the snow, pushing himself even faster as gravity sucked him downward. He was quickly catching up with his target. Meanwhile, his teammates tried to catch up with him.

The terrain bounced underneath his skis as the world flashed by, his focus on the back of the fleeing skier. For several seconds, everything else disappeared. As he closed the distance, Deckard didn't dare reach for his AK and risk losing control. He held his right-side whippet in his fist and jabbed it forward into the back of the skier's head as he approached. The enemy tumbled forward in a big ball of fuck, the man's skis, rifle, and gloves flinging into the air as he somersaulted down the mountain.

Deckard slid sideways, his skis parallel with the slope until he skidded to a halt. Reaching for his rifle, he skied over to where the squirter lay in the snow. Both of his legs were twisted in impossible, unnatural angles. With the barrel of his weapon pointed under the injured man's chin, Deckard dropped a knee down on the seemingly lifeless body and tore away his goggles and face mask. His eyes stared up at the sky. He was Caucasian, Deckard pegging him for one of the Russians. Slowly, his eyes rolled toward Deckard.

His lips moved, whispering, "Kill me."

Deckard pushed his own goggles up and rested them on his forehead as the rest of his team skied to his position and surrounded the sole survivor of the scouting party.

"Who are you?" Deckard asked as he pulled down his own face mask.

The Russian closed his eyes, seemingly at peace.

"I can't feel anything past my neck," he said in accented English. "My neck is broken. I'm paralyzed. Grant me this one wish. I am a soldier, like you."

"Are you GRU? Alfa?"

"Zaslon."

Deckard took a breath. He knew the unit but had never crossed paths with them as far as he was aware. They were a shadowy paramilitary unit that operated under the FSB. Back when he worked for the CIA, Deckard had heard rumors that Zaslon had been deployed to Iraq during the final days of the Saddam regime, where they had gathered documents, weaponry, perhaps even equipment used in the construction of weapons of mass destruction prior to the U.S. invasion. Material that had originated in Russia. This was the type of incriminating evidence the Kremlin did not want Americans discovering in Iraq when they invaded.

"Zaslon," Deckard repeated.

"That is who I was," the Russian said, his breaths becoming fast and shallow. "Not who I am now." The Russian paused. "Will you let me die honorably?"

"If that's your wish, yes."

"We are called Oculus."

"Russians working alongside the Iranians and Chinese?"

"Yes, the product of American imperialism around the globe. Desperate partners who would otherwise hate each other."

"And they say America is a force for global stability," Deckard said, looking away and wondering how long it would be before the other 90 Oculus members would catch up with them. "Here we are helping you guys make friends."

"Congratulations," the Russian groaned.

238

"Who is the ground force commander for this operation? Who is in charge?"

"The commander from my old unit, but he is being relieved in the field. For incompetence."

"Relieved by whom?"

"Someone the Chinese are sending to rendezvous with us."

"Is that who parachuted into the valley this morning?"

"We saw them, but I don't think so. I don't know who that was."

Deckard thought about the other group he saw up on the ridgeline.

"In minutes, the rest of my team will arrive at this position. Keep your promise and kill me."

Getting back up on his feet, Deckard shouldered his AK and kept his promise.

* * *

Shatayeva and Fedorchenko maneuvered their platoons through the snow, closing on the enemy force as they in turn closed on Deckard and his advanced party. They skied carefully, each of them top heavy with all of the kit they carried on their backs, but morale was through the roof. Every one of them was excited to have finally fought through the cold and unforgiving terrain to close with and destroy the enemy.

Sergeant Shatayeva got his men up on a rocky embankment halfway down the side of the mountain. PKM machine gunners quickly kicked off their skis and got down in their firing positions. Below them, Oculus looked like little army ants crossing through the snow, making way toward the firefight they had heard when their scouts were taken out.

With the enemy a good 400 meters out, Shatayeva initiated the ambush with his Kalashnikov. The sound of his shot was instantly drowned out as three PKMs sent a spray of tracer fire downhill. The enemy turned to the sound of the guns and lit up the Samruk position, not wasting any time. But now they were fixed in position, and Fedorchenko's platoon was skiing downhill in a flanking maneuver that would also get between Oculus and Deckard's element, effectively shielding the mountaineering team from being overrun.

The base of fire on the rocky outcropping was quickly engulfed in a cloud of frozen vapor, faster and with more volume than any of them had really expected. Several machine gunners and their assistant gunners attempted to shift left or right to new positions, but to little avail. They simply kept the fire on to keep the enemy's heads down and prevent them from having freedom of maneuver or gaining the initiative.

Keeping the tracer fire skipping into where they had last seen the enemy, Shatayeva watched 1st Platoon continue downhill, trying to keep a shallow spur between them and the enemy to cover their advance. It was a textbook fire-and-maneuver concept, and no one was more surprised than the Samruk mercenaries that it was working so well in austere conditions.

Shaking out into an assault line, Fedorchenko's platoon began cross-country skiing toward the enemy position. As they got closer to the 90-plus enemy soldiers they expected, Shatayeva called a ceasefire. His machine guns fell silent, using the pause in the action to load fresh belts of ammunition.

The occasional gunshot cracked from below, but it was far from the firefight they'd been expecting. With the enemy concealed by the vapor cloud, the Kazakhs could only imagine what their teammates would find in the kill zone.

"Objective secured," Fedorchenko finally radioed up. "About fifteen bodies. The rest look like they slipped away into a draw, skiing farther down the mountain."

Tactically, it made sense. Outgunned, taken by surprise, and at a severe terrain disadvantage, there was no reason for them to stand and fight on someone else's terms.

"Break down those gun positions," the Kazakh platoon sergeant ordered his men. "We are going to consolidate with First Platoon."

In three minutes, the men of 2nd Platoon were on their skis and crisscrossing their way down the mountain toward Fedorchenko's men. Sure enough, there were bodies going into deep freeze on the Arctic tundra, sprawled out all over the place. Aghassi was going from corpse to corpse with their biometric scanner to collect fingerprints and pictures. However, everyone was aware that the bodies represented just a small portion of a much larger force that still numbered around 75 men. At least they had thinned them out a bit.

"Any word from Deckard?" Rochenoire asked aloud. With his face mask pulled down, his breath was already freezing on his beard, little icicles dangling off of it.

"He's on his way back to link up with us here," Aghassi answered as he finished scanning another body. The data would be uploaded back to SCOPE in the United States for analysis at the next opportunity.

Fedorchenko skied over to the edge of a cliff where the enemy had descended from and disappeared into the white. Dozens of ski trails marked their path. Farther below, he could also see that their passage had triggered a small avalanche, which was now picking up momentum as it rolled toward the valley floor.

"We'll pick up their trail once Deckard and his guys get here," Aghassi added from behind Fedorchenko.

The Kazakh mercenary frowned as he watched the avalanche plummet away from them. Just another hazard of operating in the Arctic. He would take their previous deployments to Afghanistan, Burma, Mexico, or Syria over this nonsense any day.

Suddenly, a hollow *bloop* sounded from somewhere at the bottom of the cliff. All eyes turned skyward as a black torpedo shape arced low and slow through the sky above them. Squinting in the bright sunlight, Fedorchenko could make out the tail fins of a 60mm mortar round that seemed to be moving at the velocity of a booger flicked across a junior high classroom. The mortar round reached its maximum altitude for the charge setting it was on, then its nose tipped back toward the earth and followed a trajectory that would have it land a few hundred meters above their position.

Finally, it slapped into the mountainside and detonated with a hollow thud. Above them, the mercenaries heard the snow and ice rushing down toward their position.

"You have got to be fucking kidding me," Rochenoire groaned.

Chapter 25

The Samruk International mercenaries made a mad dash for the closest boulders or cliff faces they could find, anything that might stand a chance at shielding them from the flood of snow and ice about to rain down upon them. Three Kazakhs from one of Fedorchenko's assault teams reached out toward their teammate as they took cover behind one of the crags, but he was just a second too slow.

The avalanche burst over them, sweeping the Kazakh off his feet and washing him over the cliff. Another one of the Kazakhs who had gotten behind the rock formation in time was nearly swept away as well, with snow coming up over the top of the rocks and pelting down on their heads. His teammates held on desperately to his parka, another grabbing onto the man's rifle sling, which threatened to strangle him as he lost his footing, undulating white sheets flowing around the rock on either side.

Fedorchenko was huddled under another cliff face with his platoon medic and another assault team. The avalanche flowed over them like a waterfall, crashing down in front of them. After a few seconds, it had passed, a relatively small avalanche.

"Nikita," the platoon sergeant barked, "get out there and figure out where the enemy is. Ivan, get those guns out," he said, referring to their own 60mm mortar. The mortar section carried two 60mm mortars with the hip plate and rounds. There was no way they would have been able to make the climb with the 82mm systems, so they had been left on the Carrickfergus.

Fedorchenko was ready to fight fire with fire. Nikita peered through the scope on his 417. Based on the

243

direction of the enemy's ski trail and where he thought their mortar shot had come from, he could only make an educated guess. Before they could get their act together, a second mortar round arced into the air and came down above the Samruk men. Thankfully, this one failed to trigger another avalanche.

Ivan's men scrambled to get the ball socket of the mortar tubes into the hip plate while others were setting 60mm rounds to explode on delay. They wanted the rounds to bury themselves in the snow before detonating.

"Put the rounds up there," Nikita said, taking a best guess as he pointed uphill and about 600 meters to their flank.

Ivan looked up at Fedorchenko, who nodded.

"Do it."

Both mortar gunners dropped rounds down the tube and fired up into the mountain. The rounds impacted and exploded, puffs of white snow flung into the air. Fissures appeared in the snow. Then, massive sheets of the white stuff came apart and began to break apart. The avalanche rumbled downhill as the snow came apart in big chunks and began flowing, becoming a river of snow.

"That should slow those fuckstains down a bit," Rochenoire said with a laugh.

"You know they might be able to activate that earthquake weapon they are lugging around with them and bring this entire mountain down on us," Aghassi reminded him.

Rochenoire stopped laughing, his expression frozen on his face.

"Not to worry, we're too close to them. They would kill themselves in the process."

"On your feet," Fedorchenko ordered the men. "We need to vacate this position before they fire on us again."

244

* * *

Nate slid to a halt and looked at the avalanche gushing down the mountainside in a white cloud. It made a thundering sound as it tumbled, echoing through the valley.

"I think we've got a problem here," the MARSOC veteran called back to the others.

"*Cazzo*," Maurizio cursed as he came up alongside Nate.

"That's where our guys were firing from, isn't it?" Deckard asked as he skied forward, the third in the order of movement.

"Yeah, just about," Nate said with worry in his voice.

"Let's get a move on," Deckard said as he took the lead, pushing into the snow with his whippets. The mercenaries huffed and sweated for another minute of travel until they heard several mortars fire from the Samruk position, causing another avalanche farther away.

"Neither knows where the other is, and neither have a direct line of fire, so they're trying to create avalanches on one another," Dag said, raising his voice so Deckard could hear him.

"Let's pick up the pace; we need to consolidate with the rest of our element and find out what the hell is going on."

With little choice in the matter, Deckard plowed forward, hoping he wasn't skiing his way into another avalanche or a stray mortar round.

* * *

"Oh, that's a good one," Aghassi said.

Having moved their element 500 meters laterally across the mountain, Samruck's mortar section dropped a few down the tube, firing into the cliffs above. They couldn't wait for Deckard to show up when the enemy knew their location.

The mortar maggots had outdone themselves. The avalanche picked up steam as it slid down the mountain to their front. Sheets of snow crumbled into a rolling mess of debris that flowed right by the Samruk mercenaries before continuing downhill to where they suspected Oculus was located.

Fedorchenko pulled down his hood and held up his fist, halting their movement. In military terminology, it was called SLLS, or stop, look, listen, and smell. Careful observation helped push the human senses out into the surrounding terrain to detect signs of the enemy. Sure enough, shouting could be heard somewhere below them. The avalanche had hit pay dirt.

The platoon sergeant smiled. "Let's go finish them off."

* * *

The enemy's counter-fire sailed right over the main body of Samruk mercenaries, to their relief. Instead, the 60mm rounds exploded a few hundred meters above Deckard and his advance team. The mountain above them seemed to crack and come apart as another avalanche was triggered.

"Go, go, go!" Deckard yelled.

The order didn't require any further explanation. The avalanche streamed down the draw between two spurs coming off the side of the mountain. The mountaineers quickly realized they had mere seconds before they were swept away, not nearly enough time to move out of the way by climbing up the side of the nearest spur. Their only option was down.

Almost in unison, Deckard, Nate, Dag, Kurt, Jacob and Maurizio hopped and pivoted their skis at a 90-degree angle, nosing them straight downhill. Launching down the mountain, they skied like they never had before. The avalanche was already tumbling over the ski trails they had left behind just a moment ago.

Normally, the best way to survive an avalanche was to hug a tree, but of course there were none on Ellesmere Island. All of them knew that outrunning it was close to impossible.

Deckard picked up speed as he went over a bump and then down a sharper angle while he propelled himself forward with his poles. Swerving to avoid another rock, he kicked up a wave of snow to his side. In his peripheral vision, he saw Dag angle toward a boulder sticking out of the ground. Sailing right up the side of it, he kicked off his skis and scrambled the rest of the way up, saving himself.

He was one of the lucky ones. The avalanche was right behind Deckard. The snow was cracking and coming apart right under his feet, and he was still nowhere near the bottom of the mountain. His arms burned with lactic acid as he pushed harder and harder, trying to escape his own imminent destruction. His skis stayed just forward of the leading edge of the icy landslide, and for a brief second, he actually thought he was going to make it.

Then his world turned upside down, his limbs thrown in all directions. The world spun end over end, his vision blurred by snow whisking over his face. Then everything seemed to roll, like being trapped inside a garbage can spinning down a hill. He heard the crunch of snow, and again he was going end over end. His body was racked with spasms as something hard smashed into his lower back.

Finally, the disorientation came to an end as everything faded to black.

Chapter 26
Canadian Arctic

Quiet, lonely, and empty in all directions. The arctic desert existed as if it had always existed. Isolated from prying eyes and human projections, it simply was. Scant vegetation poked through the snow on the valley floor, waving back and forth in the wind. There were 20 of them in total, moving in a single-file line. The predators moved slowly, almost warily, but still steady and confident. Like the ridges, spurs, and valleys, they had been there for a very long time.

The white Arctic wolves hunted game, big game that required an unusually large pack. Musk oxen could weigh as much as 900 pounds in the Canadian Arctic. The pack had suffered decline; all of their kind had in recent years as their food sources were diminished.

The alpha female stopped in her tracks, her paws sinking into the snow as she sniffed the air. Somewhere in the distance, toward the mountains, there was death in the air. Where there was death, there was meat. Changing direction, she led the pack across the tundra, toward their next meal.

* * *

Four skiers wearing digital snow camouflage and heavy rucksacks moved roughly parallel to the wolf pack a half of kilometer off their right flank. Both parties were unknowingly heading to the same location. Warrant Officer Barry Cloutier led two sergeants and one master corporal across the frozen valley, the indirect mortar fire leaving them without any further doubts as to the location of the two belligerents they were searching for. With a pair of binoculars, Cloutier had seen troops on both sides caught in avalanches and swept into oblivion.

Arriving at the foot of the mountain, they spread out and began searching for one of the distant skiers they had seen go under in the avalanche. He had almost made it to the bottom, but had been swept up by the leading edge of it and buried under the snow. In an avalanche, the snow starts moving downhill so quickly, the friction causes it to melt into freezing water. Trapped under the snow, that water then quickly freezes again, entombing the hapless passerby. Whoever it was may very well be dead already.

"Hey, I found a ski!" the corporal said as he pulled it out of the snow and held it over his head.

Barry continued over the bumpy snow as his eyes picked out something as well. Slinging his C8 rifle, he reached down. His gloved hands found purchase on something flat and slick.

"I think I have the other one," the warrant officer said.

Grunting and yanking, he pulled the ski from the snow.

"Hold on," one of the sergeants called out. "Quiet!"

Barry set the end of the ski down in the snow and listened.

"There!" the sergeant said. "Did you hear that?"

"No," the warrant officer said with a frown.

"There's something down there, eh?"

Skiing over to the sergeant, Barry listened carefully. The wind blew gently in his ears for a long moment before he heard it. A muffled but audible cry.

Barry and the non-commissioned officer looked at each other.

"He's alive."

Each of the four soldiers took the snow basket off one of their ski poles and began probing the snow.

"I think I've got something," the corporal said, prodding his ski pole into the snow a few times to make sure it was hitting something solid.

The four men bent down and begin digging. They piled the snow behind them as they tunneled down. After clearing a foot of snow with their hands, they found a piece of fabric. The snow underneath it was moving; someone was trying to push to the surface.

"I think we have an elbow here, boys," Barry said.

As they continued digging him out, they noticed that he had at least been smart enough to get his arms up and create a small air bubble under the snow. Heaving armfuls of snow away, they freed his arms and could see his face. His goggles hung around his neck, filled with snow. Amazingly, his ski poles were still held around his wrists by their lanyards.

"I don't know who you guys are," the survivor said in an American accent. "And I'm not sure I care at this point."

One of the sergeants held his C8 rifle at the ready.

"We care very much as to who you are," Barry replied. "Say something American right now."

"Hey, wait a damn—"

"Say it!" The sergeant standing nearby with his rifle did not look like he was messing around.

"Ah, dammit. I like titties, beer, and cheeseburgers, OK?"

"What do you think, Barry?" the sergeant asked.

"Hmm," the warrant officer said, rubbing his chin. "OK, he sounds legit."

The survivor sighed as the sergeants and corporal continued digging him out of his frozen grave. It was the second time he had nearly met a ghastly fate since almost drowning in the arctic waters of northern Russia just days before.

"You guys are Canadian, I take it?" he asked as his torso was freed and his rescuers began pulling him up and out of the snow.

Barry nodded.

"JTF2?"

"CANSOF," Barry said. Canadian special operations. The Canadian government did not confirm nor deny JTF2 operations, and their operators were notoriously low profile, their leader not even willing to say the name of his unit during a combat operation.

"I'm warrant officer Cloutier. I take it you are part of the American element that your government legitimized with a letter of marque?"

"So you've heard of us?"

The survivor was finally free of the avalanche and walked in small circles trying to warm his body up, even though he was moving around like the Tin Man.

"Yeah, we got the brief before we jumped in."

"Yeah, that makes sense. We saw the drop but didn't know who it was."

"No way to let you know. Comms are being jammed."

"Hey, we have incoming," one of the sergeants warned.

Four skiers in PenCott SnowDrift camouflage cruised downhill, rushing up to their position fast.

"It's OK, those are my guys."

The Canadians lowered their rifles.

"Who are you?" the warrant officer said in a low tone.

"Deckard."

The Canadian hesitated.

"You're the ground force commander for the friendly element up here?"

"Yup, but you guys just cost my XO his new job before he even knew he had it."

"Well, I regret to inform you that this is sovereign Canadian territory, Deckard, and as the senior ranking Canadian military member here, I'm now in command. I've been instructed to link up and work with you, but there can be no misunderstanding as to the chain of command."

"Your mission is my mission."

The four skiers stopped in front of Deckard. He eyeballed Kurt, Dag, Nate, and Maurizio.

"Jacob?"

Kurt shook his head.

"We saw him go under," Dag informed him. "It happened almost right away."

"Fuck," Deckard cursed, trying to shake from his mind the mental image of one of his men freezing to death alone under tons of snow.

"I'm sorry," the senior JTF2 operator said. "I didn't know that you had lost one of your men."

"We have lost a lot of men on this operation," Deckard said as he looked up at the mountain. "But so has the enemy."

The nine men watched a pack of wolves begin to climb the mountain, searching for corpses to feed on.

* * *

The JTF2 operators cheated forward of the main element, moving out with the Samruk International recce and sniper personnel. The Canadians simply outclassed

253

the vast majority of Deckard's men on skis and seemed to float just above the snow.

Linking up with his two platoon sergeants, Deckard's men renewed their hunt. They had gotten the drop on Oculus with an unexpectedly bold maneuver over the mountain ridge, but they were unlikely to pull off another ambush. As he looked at the enemy's ski trails, Deckard thought that the odds were high that this time it would actually be them getting caught in an ambush, as the enemy button-hooked back on their own spore. The scouting elements were to help prevent that from happening.

The Oculus skiers moved in twin files, making sure they skied in each other's tracks to disguise their numbers. Much of the trail was also covered over by those dragging their ski sled, carrying the device with them. However, Dag had taken a count when they discovered an enemy rally point near the mountain, and estimated that there were around 60 of them left, a large chunk of them killed by Samruk gunfire and avalanches.

It was late in the afternoon now, but Deckard was feeling better as his body warmed up with the exercise, especially after nearly freezing to death a few times in the last 24 hours. He was also gulping down water, knowing how easy it was to get dehydrated. In the cold, you didn't even realize you were perspiring. Warrant Officer Cloutier came skiing over alongside Deckard, having come back from one of the scouting parties.

"I know where they are going," he announced as he pulled out his topographical map. "It is nearly a one hundred kilometer straight shot across the tundra. Then you come to a fjord that feeds Rawlings Bay. It will be mostly frozen this time of year, giving them easy egress to the coast."

"Is there a Canadian military base there or something? How will they get off of Ellesmere?"

"No idea. I heard there was some private sector work going on around here, laying deep-water fiber optic cables, but without being able to get a solid comms shot to headquarters, there is no way to know where that company's trawlers are right now."

Deckard looked down.

He could feel it in his bones. Like the rest of his men, he was running on fumes. The Arctic put tremendous stress on the human body and now he was suffering from low caloric intake combined with dehydration and sleep deprivation. He could tell himself that he would give his boys another Leonidas speech and walk the lines screaming about war like in *Braveheart*, but the reality was that he was going to keel over before much longer.

"We're going to have to make camp for the night soon," Deckard said wearily. "Can you help my guys scout out a suitable location?"

"No problem," the Canadian warrant officer replied, seeing the look on the American's face. The truth was that the JTF2 officer had been extensively trained in winter and Arctic warfare, but had absolutely no idea how the mercenaries had managed to have two full platoons scale the mountains of Ellesmere Island in such a short amount of time.

Speeding up to link up with his men, Barry was already looking for a place that they could lay up for the night, a location where they could lay ambush on their own trail and hopefully avoid a counter-ambush.

Chapter 27
Canadian Arctic

Four figures jogged through the snow as dusk arrived, but these were no Canadian commandos. The four Chinese nationals had surfaced after being deployed by submarine, scuttled their two launch vehicles, ditched their subsurface gear, and ran non-stop to link up with the rest of the Oculus strike force. They had climbed over a mountain on the opposite end of the valley from where the Americans had crossed, but did so with minimal climbing equipment and without stopping to sleep. In fact, they had hardly stopped moving since surfacing in the Arctic Ocean.

Viktor Serov watched them approach while the rest of his men dug into the embankment they had found, hollowing out hide sites for the night. As detachment commander, he had watched his force of well over 100 men steadily whittled down by the foreign mercenaries in recent days. Now they were down to just over 60 men. They had exacted a price on the mercenaries as well, to be sure, but each day their capabilities were weakened, their numbers diminished, and their strength was sapped from them.

He was an older man now, without a doubt, but age had made him more effective, more reliant on careful preparation—preparing the operational environment for success and exercising tactical patience. His career in GRU Spetsnaz had matured him over the years. Despite being older than the men he commanded, Serov maintained his physical conditioning and was proud of the fact that many of the younger Iranians, Chinese, and fellow Russians could not outpace him.

Now the mage had dispatched a new team, the old man, Zhongnanhai, having grown impatient as an expensive and intricately planned operation continued to come apart at the seams. The former Russian colonel took a deep breath, but otherwise showed no outward signs of stress over what he knew to be true: The old men were losing confidence in his leadership.

The four men were getting closer, their snowshoes kicking up white clouds with each step as their boots pounded the snow.

Serov would not let his men see his concern as they continued to dig in. This was far from his first operation. He had taken part in both Chechen civil wars, seen action in Dagestan and Georgia, and waged nasty war-by-proxy in Nagorno-Karabakh. He had led covert operations in Iraq, Syria, and most recently, in Ukraine, making him one of the Kremlin's most experienced paramilitary operatives. That had brought him to the attention of a former mentor, one of the old men in the castle who had recruited him into Oculus.

The Chinese operatives stopped at the edge of the embankment, just in front of Serov.

"Are you Dragon Caster?" one of them asked as he threw back his hood. The Chinese operative was younger than the Russian would have expected, but also bigger, more muscular and taller than any other Chinese soldier he had ever seen. That much was clear, even under the bulky parka he wore.

"I am," Serov responded. The code name was to maintain compartmentalization. None of them knew each other's real names.

The Russian colonel never saw the pistol, just the flash from the weapon that materialized in the Chinese operative's hand at an impossible speed. The suppressed shot sounded like a cough, and Serov's head kicked back in a spray of blood, a third eye appearing on his forehead.

The Oculus commander was dead before his body hit the ground. It rolled to a stop at the bottom of the embankment, leaking a swirling trail of dark red in its wake.

The body came to rest next to a refrigerator-sized box sitting on top of a sled with a white camouflage net tossed over it. The device was surrounded by four guards, standing by with Tavor assault rifles at the ready. All three nationalities of operatives set their shovels down and looked up at their new leader. The young Chinese man stepped forward.

"My name is Iron Hammer. I've been sent to take control of this element and get this mission back on track. That starts tonight."

His smile left the men of Oculus with an unsettled feeling; it wasn't that they had any particular loyalty to Serov, but they all feared what their new commander had in store for them.

* * *

Tampa, Florida

"Anything new from the Global Hawk feed?" Craig asked.

"Nothing yet," Gary answered.

With communications being jammed off and on, it was hit or miss. At the moment, they had the feed live on the flatscreen but had been unable to locate any personnel.

"From the bodies we've seen we can at least tell that they are heading in a generally eastern direction," Will offered. "We should make contact with the captain of the Carrickfergus and instruct him to head to the other side of

258

Ellesmere Island. It is going to take him a few days anyway."

SCOPE had not had contact with Deckard or his men in over 24 hours, but knew there was a pitched and running gunfight underway as their eye in the sky would sometimes spot a dead body, red splotches in the snow, or ski tracks. On one grisly occasion they had seen a pack of Arctic wolves tearing into a corpse at the foot of a mountain, but had been unable to tell if the body was that of a friendly or an enemy.

Meanwhile, the national security complex was slowly getting back on its feet. ISIS was officially taking the blame, but the media was still in a frenzy of contradictory narratives, blaming attacks on Iran, Black Bloc anarchists, white supremacists, Islamic terrorists, and even drug cartels. The media had been the ultimate force multiplier for the recent terrorist attacks, taking a dire situation and then churning it up into a full-on frenzy as citizens expected to wake up the next morning to find mothers cannibalizing their own children for sustenance in a post-apocalyptic world.

Will stood to go take a smoke break.

He knew what he was seeing was a concerted effort by Iranian, Russian, and Chinese elements working together to counter American influence. Thanks to Deckard, he could finally prove it rather than be the laughing stock of the intelligence community. This three-nation alliance was the inevitable consequence of America's creation of post-World War Two global order. The Iranians, Russians, and Chinese were not evil people, simply self-interested actors pushing back against a world order they had no say in crafting.

America had shaped the global economy through Bretton-Woods, the conference that laid the framework for the modern monetary system, which was then backstopped by the IMF and World Bank after World War II. The Westphalian system, which moderates international politics and how states interact with one another, was created by dozens of envoys, ambassadors, and politicians after the Thirty Years' War in Europe in 1648.

Other great powers like Russia, China, and Iran had no say in the establishment of Bretton Woods or the Westphalian system, both of which led to a Western-dominated world. But Will was a pragmatist. Say what you will about the decadence of the Western world, if the globe were to come to be dominated by the likes of Russia or China, it would not be a very nice place to live. With Russia or China as a global superpower, the world would become less democratic, have less respect for human rights, and leave little room for individual creativity, initiative, or innovation. These were autocratic regimes whose main driving interest was regime preservation. Self-perpetuation, almost as if the state itself was a living organism. Perhaps it was.

Stepping outside into the warm Tampa air, Will wondered where the world would stand tomorrow.

* * *

The plan was simple: chaos and terror.

Many of the Chinese in Oculus has been recruited out of the MSS intelligence service or military units like Sea Dragon, Snow Leopard, Arrow, and Night Tiger. However, the newly arrived Chinese operatives were assigned to a special project that was a part of a larger effort at weapons modernization called *shashoujian* or Assassin's Mace. More accurately, they *were* a program within Assassin's Mace.

260

The four operatives had crossed frozen arctic terrain faster than the most talented and experienced mountaineer could have, with very little equipment to help them on their way. It would have been a suicide mission; anyone else would have frozen to death within a few kilometers. But this was not the case for Jiahao and his men.

Jiahao holstered his pistol and looked to his three men.

"Shun."

The Chinese operative stepped forward, ready to follow his commander's orders.

"Now that it is dark, I want you to follow the ski trails back. The enemy has no doubt followed them and even now plots an ambush. I want you to teach them a lesson that they will not soon forget."

"Consider it done," Shun answered. Unslinging his Tavor assault rifle, he handed it off to one of his teammates. "This will just slow me down."

With only a pistol, knife, and snowshoes, Shun ran into the darkness and disappeared.

Jiahao smiled. He would have gone himself, but as the new leader, he had to spend the night in preparations, ensuring that the men were ready for the next day's movements. In the meantime, Shun would strike terror into the hearts of the Kazakhs and their American puppeteers. Soon, they would get a taste of what Assassin's Mace was capable of.

* * *

Wind howled through Samruk International's patrol base, extinguishing the small fire that had been lit to melt snow for drinking water.

261

Pat held his Kalashnikov close, attempting to stay warm while on guard duty. The JTF2 operators had done an excellent job finding a depression in the ground that offered them some cover from the wind sweeping across the tundra, but there was only so much that could be done with temperatures easily reaching -30 degrees. In the low ground, the mercenaries dug out their crow's foot-shaped patrol base and four-man snow shelters.

The former Delta Force operator balled up his fists and his toes, attempting to keep them from freezing in the night.

Suddenly, he stopped in his tracks, his eyes instinctively turning toward something. Nothing was moving, everything was silent apart from the arctic wind. Pat stepped forward. It wasn't something he saw, but something he heard, barely audible but certainly there. He heard the sound again. Something falling? Pat moved closer to the snow shelters, walking down to the far end of the crow's foot.

Snow being kicked. A body hitting the floor.

Pat ran straight toward it.

He burst into the snow shelter that he heard the sounds coming from, his Kalashnikov leading the way. Flicking on his Petzl headlamp, he scanned for threats.

The roof of the snow shelter had been collapsed toward the back end. Bodies lay on the ground, Pat's face twisting in a grimace as his headlamp illuminated their wounds. Their joints were broken, arms and legs twisted in unnatural directions. Faces were lumpy and blue, like they had been worked over with a lead pipe. A shiver went up the American's spine.

Wolves?

No, impossible.

Pat felt it still in the shelter, right there with him. Then its eyes opened. In overwhites, it blended right in with the sides of the shelter. The former Delta operator went to bring his weapon into play, but wasn't even close. The rifle was slapped aside and then torn right off of him, the sling propelling his head forward as he lost control of the Kalashnikov. For a samurai, there were few greater dishonors than to be disarmed by an opponent.

The rifle spun away into the snow and Pat found himself in a fight for his life. Blows rained down on him as he backpedaled. As someone who routinely boxed his entire Delta squadron for physical training, it was the first time he had squared off with a martial artist who was faster than he was. Fists, elbows, and knees came at him faster than he could react.

Suddenly, he was picked off his feet and hurled skyward, rocketing right through the roof of the snow shelter. In a burst of ice, he was flung into the night and came down hard on the tundra. Trying to shake off the shock to his system, Pat rolled over on his back and struggled to his feet. His attacker shot straight up into the air, jumping twice his height and landing in a crouch a few feet away from Pat.

Now able to see his attacker, Pat understood that he was facing off against one of the Chinese members of Oculus. His movements were nothing short of supernatural. Settling into a boxer's stance, he prepared for the onslaught he knew was coming.

This time, he was ready, ducking and weaving away from fists and open palm strikes. Pat took small steps to his right, then his left, then back, narrowly avoiding the Chinese commando. He didn't dare reach for any of the hand weapons he kept secreted on his body. The moment he reached for a knife, garrote wire, or brass knuckles, he knew the commando would launch another fusillade of strikes, taking advantage of his momentary distraction.

A low kick striking Pat on his thigh caused him to buckle at the knees. Continuing the movement, the attacker stomped on his booted foot, pinning him in position. Keeping his hands up, Pat protected his face, but his attacker's fists had more power behind them than anything he had ever experienced inside the ring or on the streets. Tearing his foot free, Pat stumbled backwards, struggling to stay upright.

In the blink of an eye, he saw the opening. The kung fu killer attempted a roundhouse kick. In the nanosecond that he gave up his back, Pat blitzed forward. His quick footwork closed the distance and he landed a left and a heavy right on the Chinese commando's skull. This time, it was his opponent who stumbled. The man quickly recovered before the former Delta operator could follow up his assault.

"Impressive."

The word was carried in the wind in perfect English.

"Not so bad yourself, Jackie Chan."

Pat didn't wait for a response but strode forward while shooting out a punch far before before he closed the distance, it was designed to distract rather than do damage. Then he launched his boot up into the commando's groin. The Chinese soldier smirked, easily deflecting the attack. A counter-kick hit Pat in the mid-section, opening him up for a fraction of a second.

Then the fists came down on the American in rapid succession. It was a Wing Chun technique called *Do Lin Wan Kuen*. The chain attack emphasized a series of short, rapid punches that brutalized Pat's rib cage. Ignoring the pain in his side, Pat punched, but his attacker blocked,

264

then chopped the American in the neck. Pat's vision went blurry. He felt like he had nearly lost his head.

Pat threw another punch, but the commando blocked it with his elbow and executed a low kick. Pat felt something snap inside his leg, causing him to limp backwards. The killer who had infiltrated their patrol base was now stepping on the gas pedal to finish the fight. His speed and power were trained—well trained—but also supernatural.

Pat dodged another punch that flew over his head in a blur of motion, but then took an overhand right to the side of the head that spilled him to the ground. He fought the black walls closing in. What little of the world he could see was spinning.

The Chinese assassin reached under his overwhites and withdrew a dagger. Smiling, he reached down to begin carving his turkey.

Two shots cut through the night. The assassin pancaked himself into the snow as another shot passed over him and his victim. Pat squirmed, his hand searching until it landed on the hilt of his own knife, which he yanked free of its sheath.

Curses in Russian greeted his ear.

"Pat? Pat? What the hell happened?"

It was Korgan, their burly sergeant major now at his side.

"Where is he?" Pat croaked.

"I don't know. Who was that?"

Pat rolled over and saw nothing but snow stretching out into the darkness.

Chapter 28

"The boys are whispering about a ghost that snuck into our patrol base last night," Sergeant Major Korgan said as he skied alongside Deckard.

"A fucking ghost didn't gut four of our men and go Hong Kong fooey on Pat."

The former Delta operator was now strapped into a plastic stretcher called a Skedco, which was being pulled through the snow by four mercenaries. The bodies of the dead had been buried in the snow for later retrieval.

Samruk had initiated their movement at dawn, handrailing the enemy's trail. The Canadian JTF2 counterterrorism operators were leading the movement since they were the most fresh of the group, not to mention the most experienced in the Canadian Arctic. Their warrant officer had been correct about the enemy heading for the frozen fjord.

The ski trail led right into it. Frozen over, the fjord acted as a natural line of drift and a flat, high-speed trail for humans to traverse.

"Who could have done something like that? Pat said he only saw one man."

"I don't know," Deckard said, shaking his head. "I've seen Pat surrounded in a bar by unconscious bodies stacked around him like cordwood. He's an animal who could take any one of us apart in hand-to-hand combat. Whoever did that to him...." His words trailed off. "Shit, I just don't know."

"I fear that we may have awakened something," the sergeant major responded, the old superstitions from the steppes of Kazakhstan still strong in the veteran soldier.

Deckard frowned.

"C'mon, let's get the hell off this rock," he said as he skied out onto the frozen river. In a few more hours they would reach the coast.

* * *

The Arctic fiber optic station looked abandoned and empty from a distance, with a door open and swinging back and forth in the breeze. Deckard had walked into one too many traps recently to take those impressions at face value. It suddenly dawned on Deckard that they were standing atop a frozen river, meaning that if they took indirect fire, they would be in a real shit state with no cover and nowhere to retreat to. Combat in general consists of a series of sub-optimal decisions to make, but this was especially true in the high north.

"I don't see their trawler," Aghassi said as he looked through a pair of binoculars.

"Oculus probably hijacked it and left, but they may have left some party favors for us."

"Drones, land mines, boobytraps, lasers, automated gun systems—"

"OK, yeah, thanks. I got it."

The former Task Force Orange operator scanned the one-story building, looking for signs of life.

"Interesting that they left the communications mast standing. The first thing I would have done is cripple the communications in the building before escaping."

"Maybe they are baiting us in."

Aghassi lowered the binoculars and looked at Deckard. "Or maybe someone wants to talk to you."

The mage.

"All right, get gun positions up and set intersecting fields of fire on the structure. Put the assault line a few hundred meters away from the building and cheat a small element forward. No one goes through the doors. Use windows or create another entry."

"Hey, hold on, we've got something," Aghassi said as he looked through the binos again.

Sure enough, a lone figure had stepped out of the building and was walking toward the Samruk International mercenaries with his hands held high in the air. Rochenoire snatched up a squad of Kazakhs and set up a hasty blocking position, with one PKM machine gun pointed downrange, ready to rock and roll.

"Advance forward," the former SEAL yelled at the lone figure. As he got closer, they could see that it was a male, wearing commercial cold-weather gear, and that he looked to be about 50 pounds overweight. Fit the bill for a civilian working at the Arctic fiber optic cable station, but they had to be sure.

"My name is Toby Baker!" the civilian yelled out to the mercenaries. "I'm an electrical engineer!"

"What the fuck ever," the former SEAL shouted back. "Take off your jacket and drop trou!"

"What?"

"Fucking do it if you don't want to get shot!"

Toby reluctantly unzipped his blue and gray parka, setting it on the ground next to him before undoing his belt buckle and dropping his pants.

"Now lift your shirt up!"

"Is this really necessary?"

"Just do it!"

Toby lifted his shirt, exposing his sizable belly to the elements.

"Now do the truffle shuffle!"

"The what?"

"Knock it the fuck off," Deckard said from behind Rochenoire.

With a sigh, the former SEAL told Toby he could put his clothes back on. Zipping his jacket up, the engineer waddled over to the mercenaries.

"What the hell was that about?" he asked with a scowl.

"Had to check for an S-vest," Rochenoire told him.

"S-vest?"

"Suicide vest."

"You mean like explosives?"

"Yup."

"Damn, man, they never got me. I was hiding in the rocks by the shore when they came. Killed four of our employees. The rest of us ran for our lives."

"Where are they?"

"Inside. There are three of us left."

"And the boat?"

"They took it and continued east."

"You still have comms?" Deckard interjected.

"Yeah, I already sent out a distress signal. The Canadian Navy is sending someone. They warned us that you were probably going to show up."

"True, and the Canadian Army is already here."

Barry stepped forward and shook his countryman's hand.

"I'm sorry about what happened here today. It is unacceptable and I promise that we will bring those responsible to justice."

"One way or the other," Deckard said under his breath.

Barry glared at him.

* * *

269

"We've been laying thousands of kilometers of fiber," Toby explained. "It took a long time to map out the bottom of the ocean at first, but with the Arctic Ocean no longer frozen solid all year round, we will finally be able to connect New York, London, and Tokyo with high-speed fiber optic communications, with a lot less fiber than if we had to cross the Pacific and Atlantic oceans."

The electrical engineer was getting carried away talking about his work, seemingly oblivious to everything that had happened in recent hours.

"Our cable ship toots along at just two kilometers an hour, and the fiber is slowly unwound from giant spools on the deck of the ship," the engineer paused. "Or at least it was until those Chinese and Russian dudes stole it."

"Let's take this one thing at a time, dude," Deckard replied. "First things first, we need to find a way to get off this rock and track them down."

"If I can get some connectivity, I'll reach back to CANSOFCOM and see what assets are in the area," Barry said, stepping into the fiber optic station behind Deckard.

"Good idea. I'll hit up my people as well."

"I'll take you to our comms center," Toby said to the Canadian warrant officer.

"Lead the way."

While the Canadians went to the other room, Deckard turned his attention to another engineer who worked at the fiber optic station. She was in her fifties, with shoulder-length straw-colored hair held back in a ponytail.

"Is this facility private sector or government funded?" Deckard asked.

"It's a joint venture between several governments and corporations. We're with Deep Fiber Incorporated and handle the laying of the physical cables along the sea bed."

"Gotcha."

"I'm Linda, by the way," she said, attempting a smile and holding out her hand.

"Oh, sorry. I'm a bit distracted. I'm Deckard."

"No worries. I guess we all are after losing Gus, Tony, and the others."

"Those responsible are going to pay for their crimes," Deckard assured her. "We just need to source some transportation off of Ellesmere Island and catch up with them."

"What kind of transport?"

"Sister, I could care less as long as it can move my men and equipment. Even better if it is fast enough to catch up with these bastards sooner rather than later. We have a ship, but it will take a few days for it to circle around from the other side of the island."

The female engineer paused, staring off into space for a moment.

"Linda?"

She opened her mouth as if she was about to say something, but the words didn't come out.

"Linda?"

* * *

"Deckard," Barry looked over his shoulder as he heard the mercenary walk into the comms room. "My command is having F16s scrambled on a search and destroy mission for that cable-laying trawler."

"Linda just got off the phone as well. We have transportation arriving for us within the hour."

271

"Within the hour? They told me they didn't have anything available in the area."

"Commercial, not military."

"What?"

"If you're done, I need to jump on the line. Can you do VTC?" Deckard asked, turning toward Toby.

"Yeah, we do it all the time with our HQ in Ottawa."

Barry stood and Deckard took his seat, then dialed up SCOPE back in Tampa, Florida.

The four-man think tank immediately appeared on screen.

"Holy shit," Craig answered. "We were starting to worry."

"Let's cut the shit. I don't have a lot of time."

Deckard quickly brought the think tank up to speed on the events of the last 48 hours, revealing that they had transportation inbound.

"Listen, Deckard, they can't have gotten far in that trawler. We'll mobilize NSA and NRO assets to start searching for them. Some of these platforms are starting to become available now that things are finally quieting down CONUS," Will informed him.

"Let me know. In the meantime, I have something else I need to run by you. This mission just keeps getting weirder and weirder."

"What is it?"

Explaining in depth what happened the previous night, he gave Pat's account of the lone Chinese super soldier.

"Pat is one of the meanest guys you never want to encounter in a dark alley, but he got taken apart. He described his attacker as having superhuman speed and agility, saw him jump like ten feet straight up into the air."

Several members of the think tank looked at each other. Will crossed his arms.

"What is it?" Deckard demanded.

"More rumors, that's all," Will said.

"Rumors are quickly becoming facts these days. Rumors about earthquake machines, for example."

"There are a few competing theories amongst some circles within the intelligence community," Will replied, his voice coming in a little scratchy over the satellite uplink. "One theory is that the People's Republic of China is running some kind of super-soldier program."

"And the other?"

"That the Chinese government is engaging in the largest eugenics project that the world has ever seen—the reshaping of their entire population and the creation of a new man."

"You mean the one-child policy?"

"It starts there and only gets creepier. In recent Olympic games, we have seen thirteen-year-old Chinese gymnasts do extraordinary things. Impossible things. I'm not talking about just a gold medal performance, I'm talking about athletic moves that have literally never been seen before. Again, there are two theories here."

"I'm listening."

"The first is that they are gene doping their athletes. The other is that these kids are grown in a lab."

"Jesus."

"Yeah, this ain't no Captain America super-serum. Frankly, I think it more likely that they are gene doping, not just athletes, but selected units in the People's Liberation Army as well."

"Is that like blood doping?"

"No. Let me put it like this: Some people have abnormal but completely natural abnormalities in their genetics that allow them enhanced performance by comparison to normal people. Most Olympic sprinters have the ACTN3 gene, for instance. Eero Mäntyranta was a Finnish gold medalist skier. It turned out that his entire family had abnormal responses to erythropoietin, meaning he had more oxygen-carrying red blood cells, essentially giving him superhuman endurance. Even you, Deckard, probably have some abnormal genes that have helped you perform in your career field where the average person would fail.

"Now imagine that we were able to play with these genetic characteristics. Using myostatin inhibitors, we could give a normal person superhuman strength. We could make the person, the soldier, faster, even smarter than his genetics allow."

"How can that be done?"

"A series of injections. The technology has been there for decades, but our Western medical ethics make it impossible for us to further research and experiment with this type of technology. Needless to say, the Chinese have no such restraints."

"Holy shit."

"Deckard, the fact that the enemy, this Oculus group you talk about, has put so much on the line, exposed so many tactics and techniques for the first time, demonstrates that they have placed all of their bets on this operation. Maybe they really are planning to explode the Yellowstone caldera, or something equally devastating. Otherwise, their actions don't make any sense. China has always believed that they should bide their time and build their capabilities, unwilling to face a direct military confrontation with America until the time is right."

"It seems that the time has arrived," Deckard said as he sat back in his chair and rubbed his face.

"Stay in touch. We may be able to provide further support on our end. Hopefully we'll come through with a fresh lead."

"Start coordinating with the Danes now."

"Danes?"

"Yeah, Oculus is heading toward Greenland. No idea if that is their destination, but the Danish government will want to know we are in the area. It would only take that trawler about five hours to make it to Greenland, and they already have a three-hour head start."

"We'll contact Thule Air Base as well."

"Sounds good," Deckard replied, his finger hovering over the button to shut down the video teleconference. "I have one more thing to take care of before I leave."

* * *

Airspace over Greenland

Vampire One-Zero hit the afterburners as Greenland's snowscape screamed by below him, heading toward an intercept with a Canadian CF-18 fighter. The Danish F-16 banked slightly as the pilot juked the sidestick controller, nudging the aircraft toward the proper intercept trajectory at Mach 2, the g-forces pushing him back in his seat.

"Rabbit Two-Two, this is Vampire One-Zero," the pilot announced over the radio as he watched the foreign fighter jet move across his radar display. "Be advised, you are now entering sovereign Danish territory. Turn your aircraft around immediately, over."

"No can do, Vampire," the Canadian-accented voice came over the Dane's headset. "Be advised that you are approaching sovereign Canadian territory. Advise that you turn back immediately, over."

Vampire's flight helmet bounced off the back of his seat as he sighed inside his oxygen mask. What he wouldn't give to jump into the fray with Operation Inherent Resolve in Syria or Iraq instead of having dick-measuring contests in the Arctic with supposed NATO allies.

The coast of Greenland was coming up fast, the snow giving way to the icy straits of Kennedy Channel between Greenland and Ellesmere Island. Vampire's pale blue eyes could already make out Hans Island in the center of the channel. The F-16 fighter pilot had sat in on enough briefings to be sick to death of hearing about the barren outcropping of rocks out in the middle of literally nothing.

The Danish government claimed the island as an extension of Greenland's landmass. Meanwhile, the Canadians made their own legal claims based on their past use and occupation, studying sea lions and snowflakes, no doubt. Apparently, possession really was nine tenths of the law. With oil and natural gas deposits being discovered in the waters surrounding Hans Island, tensions had only ramped up in recent years.

With maritime trade drastically increasing in the Arctic Circle, both countries were speculating that Hans Island would soon become an important maritime choke point for merchant vessels, maybe even rivaling the Panama and Suez canals one day.

But really. Both pilots had better things to do today.

"Rabbit, I've been dispatched on a search grid for a vessel potentially violating Danish sovereignty in our waters. Just stay the hell away from Hans Island today, over."

"They got me on the same mission, Vampire, but you know the rules. Hans is Canadian, over."

Vampire clenched his eyes shut, fantasizing about activating an air-to-air missile or two.

* * *

"You have nothing to feel ashamed of."

The blade master looked at the mage wearily.

"You fought honorably and failed. There is no shame in this," the mage said as he circled the cauldron in the center of the room.

"I'm not quite out of the game yet," the blade master countered.

"Yes, you are," the mage said as if he were stating a fact. "This is over. You will never be able to find my men where they are going."

"Oculus."

The mage spun around at the mention of the name and faced the young blade master.

"You mean I won't be able to find Oculus where they are going."

Flicking his hand dismissively, the mage continued around the cauldron. "It is of no matter."

"It is of some matter. You directed your minions to leave the communications at this facility running because you wanted to talk to me one more time. You know, the Chinese dudes you have on super-serum."

"Excuse me?"

"Gene doping. We both know that isn't natural strength."

"Ah, so you've come in direct contact with them. I am even more impressed."

"Oh?"

277

"Impressed that you are still alive. This is why I wanted to talk to you. You're a survivor, and despite what is coming, I have a feeling that you may survive. You're strong. Somehow, I know that we will meet again."

The blade master smiled. "Sooner than you think."

Chapter 29
Canadian Arctic

Linda cupped her hands above her forehead to shield her eyes from the sun, squinting to see better.

"There she is."

"Holy shit," Deckard said, he jaw nearly hitting the ground.

Even from a distance, the mass of the craft was overwhelming. It skimmed just above the Arctic Ocean, kicking up a white spray in its wake that shot up above its fuselage.

"That plane is unreal."

"Technically, it isn't a plane," Linda informed him. "It also isn't a ship or a hovercraft."

"Well what the hell is it then?"

"An *ekranoplan*—a completely unique class of transportation craft."

As it got closer to Ellesmere Island, the mercenaries stared in awe alongside the fiber optic engineers. It seemed to hover just above the water, massive turbine engines propelling it forward on short, stunted wings. The fuselage looked big enough to fit several city buses inside.

"Our benefactor had it built as an experimental craft to serve as a proof of concept," Linda continued. "He dusted off older Soviet designs used to engineer the so-called Caspian sea monster, hoping it will demonstrate a faster and more efficient means of cargo transport than today's container ships."

As the ekranoplan got closer, Deckard could see that it was coasting about 20 feet above the water. Thinking about his experience around military helicopters, it dawned on him. "Ground effects," he said with a smile. "It is creating a cushion of air under it to float on."

"Right. The closer the wings are to the water, the less drag it creates. The ekranoplan has to get its start with the turbines until it lifts off the water and air passing under the belly of the craft creates a bubble of air pressure."

"Unbelievable."

Powering down the turbines, the pilot of the ekranoplan set its mass down in the ocean, causing a splash of icy water less than a kilometer away from the fiber optic station. The short wings rotated toward them as the plane turned and began churning through the water toward them.

"Who did you say your benefactor is again?" Deckard asked.

"John Mann. He owns our company, DFI, and a number of other subsidiaries. I'm sure you've heard of him."

"Sorry, I've kind of been living outside the mainstream for a while."

"I bet you have," Linda said, shooting the mercenary commander a look. "The commercial manned mission to Mars planned for 2030? Powered armor systems for the Department of Defense? Any of this stuff ringing a bell?"

"I'll have to do some reading."

"No need, John is on his ekranoplan right now. After talking to him and putting in your request for transport, he sounded excited to meet you guys."

Deckard frowned.

The noise created by the turbines was overwhelming. A white haze blew across the mercenaries as the ekranoplan spun around on its belly and began backing toward the shore. Deckard held his arms up to shield his face from the snow stinging his face. As the turbines spun down, the ramp lowered. A loadie, wearing a fight suit and heavy parka, stood next to a control panel inside the fuselage, operating the hydraulics until the ramp set down on the rocky shore.

Off the back of the massive aircraft, a figure, flanked by a half dozen-man entourage, emerged. Two looked like bodyguards from their bulk. The others, more like executive assistant types.

"That's John Mann?" Deckard asked.

"The one and only."

Mann was in his mid-fifties, with crow's feet at the corners of his eyes, but otherwise looked and moved like a man several decades younger. Clearly he took care of himself. His hair was a mane of white that flowed back and almost down to his shoulders.

Deckard stepped forward and offered his hand. Both bodyguards moved to intercept him, cautious of a stranger decked out in paramilitary gear like a storm trooper on Hoth.

"It's quite OK, gentlemen," Mann said, ordering his bodyguards to stand down. The billionaire reached out and shook Deckard's hand vigorously.

"I just want to tell you what an honor it is to meet you," Mann said with a toothy grin.

"Honor?"

"Yes, I want to thank you for your service. So many are being asked to sacrifice so much in over a decade of war. You're true patriots, which is why I sponsor a not-for-profit called Honor Our Heroes. It is a registered 501(c) that promotes healthy lifestyles for veterans and their families. We've had some great successes, and if you look at our website you can see the numerous testimonials that —"

"Hey, uh," Deckard interrupted. "I really appreciate your support for this operation, but we're kind of dealing with the end of the world here. Civilization at the brink and all that."

Mann blinked. "Oh, I see."

"Yeah, we kind of need to get a move on here."

"How can I help?"

"I'm waiting to hear back from some national security types back in the States, but we need to get everyone on board and prepped for movement. I'm not sure of the destination yet, but I'm sure you know that the enemy hijacked your cable-laying ship and headed east."

"And I would very much like to recover my property!"

"We'll see what we can do about that as well. I also have an injured man here. Pat needs a medical evacuation as soon as possible, but we can coordinate that with the Canadian military."

Deckard turned as he heard a door slam. Aghassi had emerged from the station and was marching toward him.

"Hey," he called out. "It's Greenland. NSA has a hit from a Danish mine. Weird commo signals showing up all of a sudden. No way it is unrelated."

"What about the ship?"

"Danes and Canadians are having a bit of a pissing contest over jurisdiction and so far nothing has been sighted."

"We need to move on any lead we have right now. There isn't any time to develop the situation further."

"Greenland and sovereign Danish territory," Mann protested. "I can't just—"

"It has already been arranged," Aghassi informed the billionaire. "We will meet with Danish military liaisons when we hit the ground."

Barry coughed behind Deckard. "Speaking of liaisons," the JTF2 warrant officer said, "please obtain them the next time you decide to visit Canada."

Deckard shook the Canadian's hand.

"I will. Is this the end of the line for you?"

"My government would never approve us to conduct military operations in Greenland, especially alongside a private military company. I have to admit that it is quite tempting to slip the leash, but it could cause an international incident."

"I understand."

"We'll sweep up back here and make sure that your man is taken care of when the air ambulance shows up."

"You have no idea how grateful I am for that. Pat is one of the best."

"Oh, I know. We heard stories about him from some unit members when we were deployed to Afghanistan last year."

Deckard laughed. "I can only imagine."

* * *

The two platoons of mercenaries loaded into the ekranoplan, sitting on the bare metal floor. Since the craft was fitted for cargo transport, there were only a few seats for the pilots, Mann, and his entourage. The men of Samruk had to sit down with their rucksacks between their legs, skis pointing in every direction, and find something to hold on to.

As the turbines began to spin, Deckard's eyes swept across his men, who seemed quite small inside the hull of the massive ekranoplan. They looked exhausted, sleepy, and demoralized after suffering defeats, losing teammates, and being worn down by the Arctic itself. He knew exactly what they needed to get spirits up. With his Kalashnikov slung over his shoulder, he looked at the mercenaries and screamed.

"Judas was a buddy fucker!"

Eyeballs perked open and heads snapped up toward him.

"Fuck. That. Buddy fucker!" the men yelled back.

"Moses was a land nav no-go!"

"You can be one two o'lordy! Look away, beyond the blue hor-izon!" the mercenaries shouted in a handful of different accents.

"David was a small-arms expert!"

"You can be one two o'lordy! Look away, beyond the blue hor-izon!"

"Mary was a small-town whore!"

"You can be one two o'lordy! Look away, beyond the blue hor-izon!"

"Noah led a small boat movement!"

"You can be one two o'lordy! Look away, beyond the blue hor-izon!"

"Jesus had a wooden tripod!"

"You can be one two o'lordy! Look away, beyond the blue hor-izon!"

"Judas was a buddy fucker!"

"Fuck. That. Buddy fucker!"

David Mann sat in his comfortable suede seat, strapped in by the seat belt as his jaw hung open, his eyes widening like saucers. His aides looked at each other in horror as the loadie began closing the ramp.

"You can tell a Ranger by his boots!" Deckard yelled a new Ranger song.

"By his boots!"

"You can tell a Ranger by his boots!"

"By his boots!"

"Because they're shiny as glass and they're always kicking ass!"

"By his boots!"

"You can tell a Ranger by his room!"

"By his room!"

"You can tell a Ranger by his room!"

"By his room!"

"Because it smells like a shitter but you can always find a spitter!"

Now that their blood pressure was back up, Deckard walked the lines, stepping between the mercenaries sprawled out on the deck.

"You can tell a Ranger by his girlfriend!"

"By his girlfriend!"

"You can tell a Ranger by his girlfriend!"

"By his girlfriend!"

"Because she dances at Deja Vu, and she's been fucked by you, you, and you!" Deckard sang as he pointed to three of the young Kazakh troopers.

As the pilots guided the ekranoplan out into the open water, Deckard was forced to grab onto one of the metal ribs of the aircraft to support himself. The craft vibrated and shook, twisting like a 50-year-old tourist bus screaming down a mountain pass in Costa Rica. For a moment, it felt like it would come apart at the seams, washing the mercenaries out over the arctic waters. Suddenly, the craft leveled out and set down. Not on the ground, but on the air cushion the ekranoplan created.

They were riding the ground effects to Greenland.

Chapter 30
Off the coast of Greenland

The ekranoplan splashed down without incident and began making its way to the shore. They would deploy a small team to link up with Danish soldiers who had been dispatched to act as military liaisons. While in the air, Samruk International had gotten word that the Danish government had been unable to get calls through to the rare earth minerals mine that the NSA had pinpointed as a potential hotspot for enemy activity.

Deckard stepped into a small inflatable boat with Aghassi and Nikita, using the outboard electric motor to putter their way to shore. It was simply too steep and rocky for the ekranoplan to deliver them directly to land.

Although not on most people's radars, the sparsely populated country of Greenland was a Danish territory, one with immense political implications on the world stage. Greenland was strategically located in the Arctic, and was home to the Thule U.S. military base in the northwest, which provided maritime and air coverage as well as logistical support for NATO. Greenland also housed facilities for Five Eyes surveillance programs. Thule housed the Ballistic Missile Early Warning System or BMEWS. Since the Cold War, America had also harbored a fear that Greenland could be used as a staging ground by foreign powers to launch an invasion into the mainland United States.

In recent years, the Danes had aggressively ramped up defense spending on Greenland in order to deter and counter Russian military aggression in the Arctic as they expanded their sphere of influence in the region and engaged in strategic posturing.

This led to a new balance of power in the Arctic, and the Danish government had shrewdly leveraged access to the territory by the United States for various economic and political concessions over the years. As portions of the icepack continued to thaw, Danish mining consortiums were quickly setting up shop to harvest rare earth minerals which had been previously locked under the ice. Rare earth minerals were a critical component in the manufacturing of everything from computer hard drives to MRI machines to aircraft engines.

The rare earth mineral industry was once dominated by the United States, but today, China had pulled far ahead of any Western nation. Greenland, however, was rich in such elements, and that was not even mentioning the sizable hydrocarbon reserves offshore, but still inside Denmark's exclusive economic zone. Other claims of offshore reserves overlapped with claims made by the Russian government, leading to even more political friction.

It had been a short flight to Greenland, and it was still only midday as Deckard found a place to beach the rubber raft on shore. They had landed the ekranoplan well away from the rare earth minerals mine, but it would not take them long to get there. It was called an offset infiltration: getting close, but not so close that you tipped your hand before moving the last stretch as stealthily as possible.

Pulling the raft up on shore, the three mercenaries clawed their way up a small cliff and up onto the tundra. Unspoiled snow spread out in front of them leading up to the mountain ranges in the distance. White, blue, and black shadows fell between the ridges. The sun beat down on them, its power signaling the summer would arrive in the Arctic before much longer. Aghassi began scanning with his binoculars, but it was Nikita who first got eyes on with his 10-power sniper scope.

"Two dog sleds inbound."

"Dog sleds?" Deckard asked with a frown. "What the hell?"

"See for yourself."

Deckard grabbed the sniper's HK417 and looked through the scope.

"I'll be damned."

Sure enough, two sleds were on their way, each pulled by 11 dogs. The Danes rode on the back of their sleds, their supplies stowed in the front under canvas.

"Who the hell are these guys?"

"Tampa said something about a Danish military patrol that would rendezvous with us," Aghassi answered. "This must be them."

Five minutes later, the two sleds came to a halt in front of the trio, the dogs knee-deep in snow and clearly excited by the strangers they'd encountered. The Danes threw back their hoods and shook hands with the newcomers.

"I'm David, the patrol leader," the bigger of the two announced. "This is Evan, my apprentice."

"Hello," Evan said with a smile. He was a little older than the patrol leader and had graying hair peeking out from under his wool cap.

"Thanks for getting here so quickly," Aghassi said. "We didn't know what to expect."

"You're in luck," David replied. "We don't usually patrol out in this region."

"So who are you guys, exactly?" Deckard asked.

"Sirius Patrol," Evan said proudly.

"What do you guys patrol?" Deckard said, looking around the barren landscape.

"All of Greenland. We have to keep a security presence out here. Our unit has been at it for over sixty years."

"And how long have you two been out here?"

"You're the first people we've seen in four months."

"Holy hell!"

"Yes, so this distraction is quite welcome. We were instructed to be of assistance in any way we can."

"Right now we just need to get these two guys about six klicks south," Deckard said, motioning to Aghassi and Nikita, "to reconnoiter the mine."

"Ah, rare earth minerals, yeah? The ASX mine," David said knowingly. "What seems to be the problem?"

"Apparently the mine has been out of radio contact, and we have some intelligence leading us to believe that there is a bad actor in your area of operations."

"Bad actor?" Evan questioned. "Like whom?"

"Canadians?" David said with a laugh.

"I only wish. If that were the case, we could settle this over Canadian bacon. We've been trailing a group—a sort of syndicate—of Iranians, Russians, and Chinese paramilitary types."

The two Sirius Patrol members looked at each other, trying to figure out if Deckard was being serious or not.

"Listen, maybe it is nothing, but it is the only lead we have. This is an issue of grave national security concern to both our governments."

"Well, that explains why they rushed us out here."

Aghassi pulled out his map and pointed to the mine. Before he could even open his mouth, David spoke up.

"No problem. We can get you there within the hour."

289

"Good. I'll get the men ready to deploy," Deckard said. "Once you've got something, call it in. Especially if you can get eyes on the device we are looking for."

"Device?" David asked.

Deckard turned back toward the raft. "You can tell them, Aghassi. Sounds like you have a little road trip ahead of you."

* * *

Aghassi and Nikita rode on top of the sleds, watching the dogs race forward in the harnesses, shuttling them to the mine. David had been explaining Sirius Patrol to him on the way, which turned out to be a Danish special operations unit on par with the Jaeger Corps and the Frogman Corps. Established in 1950, Sirius Patrol was named after the brightest star in the Canis Major constellation. They patrolled the tundra, waters, and mountains of Greenland by dog sled, boat, and on skis, keeping a persistent presence on the ground for the Danish military. Fewer than a dozen Sirius Patrol members were present on Greenland at any given time.

"We spend a long time in training," David said, raising his voice to be heard over the wind created by their forward travel. "We have to go to Norway for winter warfare training, learn about weather patterns, survival techniques, radio communications, and everything else. They say that a Sirius man can do everything but give birth!"

"I don't doubt it," Aghassi replied. "Up here you have no one to rely on but yourself."

"We patrol in two-man teams, but yes, we're alone up here."

"That's a hard life."

"But worth it," the Sirius Patrol leader said. "I've been out here for eight months and I feel like it has changed my life forever. By the way, what is this device you guys are looking for?"

Aghassi hesitated a moment. The 11 dogs pulled the sled forward with almost fanatical devotion as they cruised through the arctic desolation.

"*Veenstre!*" David suddenly shouted to the dog team. Following his order, they began to veer to the left.

"Well, have you ever heard of the Aharonov-Bohm effect?"

"No."

"What about tectonic weapons?"

"Tectonic as in earthquakes?"

"Someone stole some kind of experimental super weapon from an underground Russian laboratory, and now we have to get it back."

"Very funny."

"I don't blame you for being skeptical. I wouldn't believe it either if I hadn't seen it for myself."

David was quiet for a moment. "You think this thing is in the ASX mine?"

"Not sure, but there are some weird indicators that the enemy is transmitting something from there, so we need to check it out."

"No worries. We'll get you close in and unobserved."

An hour later, a small ridge came into view that David pointed out as being the rare earth minerals mine. Then he directed the dogs down a shallow embankment to make sure they stayed out of the line of sight of the mine, lest they be detected. The dogs scrambled along without hesitation as the Sirius Patrol circled around the mine.

"*Hoole!*" the Danes called out, halting the dogs.

Aghassi and Nikita jumped off the sleds and began preparing their gear, pulling their skis from where they were tied down.

"This is as close as we can get without potentially being spotted," Evan said. "It is flat for about six or seven hundred meters up to the mine. I'm not sure how you plan on getting there over open ground if they have sentries on watch."

"We planned for this," Nikita announced. "We will make it."

"And we are just supposed to wait here?" David asked.

"I would love to take a few extra guns with us," Aghassi said. "You do have guns, right?"

David reached under the canvas covering of his sled and yanked free an M-10 rifle, basically the same as the Canadian C8.

"Give me your radio freq. We might need you guys if things go sideways. I really would like to take you, but it just isn't possible. You'll understand in a minute."

The mercenaries began stringing their skis together and then extended a series of stiff wires, which were then covered over with white cloth.

David just laughed. "I have a friend who is a Swedish sniper. He taught me that same technique."

"Does it work?" Aghassi asked in all seriousness.

"You've never tried before? You can't be serious."

"Well, it looked like it might work when we were training in Russia," Nikita said with a shrug.

* * *

Greenland

292

Jiahao pushed the two Persians out of the way and kicked open the door. It blasted inwards and slammed against the side wall with a metallic clang. The Assassin's Mace operative stepped inside, looked around the barren tunnel, and then waved the other Oculus members inside.

They filed in and spread out inside the tunnel, preparing the search the complex.

"There should be a six-man crew. I want them alive; we may need them to run some of the systems in here."

"Understood," one of the Iranian commandos replied.

Jiahao took off deeper into the tunnel, trailed by a dozen men. The others began hauling in the tectonic device on its sled.

"Find the geothermal power plant and get it connected," the Chinese commander ordered. "I want it energized and ready to fire as soon as possible."

"I'll oversee the installation myself," Shun volunteered.

"Come to me when It is done," Jiahao said.

Walking deeper into the tunnel, he smiled as he heard the Danish workers screaming when his gunmen confronted them, their cries echoing down the dark walls.

* * *

Infiltrating across the flat, open tundra seemed impossible at first glance, but Nikita had been perfecting the technique. Tying his skis together, the sniper lay on his belly, using the skis as a sled to slide across the snow. In front of the skis he had jury-rigged a wire mesh that had a piece of white fabric pulled tightly across it. Although it would never stop a bullet, it blended in perfectly with the snow, creating a camouflage screen between him and the suspected enemy position. Using the toes of his boots and hands to scoot forward, he pushed himself toward the mine.

Aghassi had a similar rig and was doing the same 10 meters off of his right flank. All they had to go off of was a picture he had pulled off of Google Earth back at the fiber optic station and a few stories that Evan and David had heard about the ASX mine, as neither of them had actually been there. The private sector had to provide their own internal security, so the men of Sirius Patrol were not going to hang around like mall cops.

"See anything yet?" Aghassi whispered over his radio to the Kazakh sniper.

"Da," he replied. Having cut a small hole in the white fabric, he was able to scout up ahead with his scope and, if need be, take a shot. "Five or six small buildings. It looks like there is a cable car system that runs up into the mines in the cliffs above."

As they scooted their way closer, Aghassi pulled out his binoculars and looked through a small slit he had cut in his own sniper blind. A cluster of squat one-story buildings formed near the base of a sheer cliff that rose about 900 feet up. The dark rocks looked as if they had been pushed from the earth's crust in primordial times, left standing as a memorial to a time before man.

"I've got someone," Nikita's voice whispered in Aghassi's earpiece.

This operation was starting to feel a lot like a previous recce mission they had done at a Mexican drug lord's villa.

"Two, no three," the sniper corrected himself. "Looks like a perimeter patrol. I don't see any communications platform or satellite dish though."

What did the NSA pick up, then? They had told him that it was a high-frequency system, and HF was usually very hard to track.

"We should hear generators as well," Aghassi said. "Otherwise, what is powering their commo system?"

"You want me to take these guys out?" Nikita asked eagerly.

Just as the transmission finished, Aghassi spotted another two Oculus men with Tavor assault rifles come out from one of the buildings.

"Hold your fire. We don't know how many there are and we are sitting ducks if they figure out where we are shooting from."

"No firefight? Then what's the plan?"

Aghassi looked up at the rectangular-shaped holes carved into the side of the cliff hundreds of feet above the ground. Perhaps it was just intuition speaking at this point, but they didn't have much else to go on.

"Same as always. You're on overwatch while I do something really stupid."

Chapter 31

Aghassi shifted his trajectory toward the shed that ran the cable cars up the side of the mountain, slowly kicking and pulling himself across the snow like a turtle. It was none too comforting to know that if he was spotted, there was only a thin piece of white cloth between him and a half dozen Tavor assault rifles.

Nikita radioed him several times, instructing him to remain still until a sentry passed and was no longer looking in his direction. Then he would continue forward, stealing a glance through the slit in the cloth to make sure he was still on azimuth to his intended destination. After half an hour, he arrived behind the shed and covered his skis and camo blind with snow. Inside, he could hear the gentle whirl of the cable being pulled along steel wheels.

"Let me know when I'm clear," Aghassi radioed to the sniper.

"Give it a minute. One of them is having a smoke about fifty meters from you."

"Any sign of the miners?"

"No, none."

Aghassi took a breath, knowing that he was about to take a huge gamble. Without any sign of a communications system outside, it was likely they had energized something else to turn it into an active antenna.

"OK," Nikita transmitted. "You're clear."

Aghassi broke from cover and snaked around the corner of the shed, into the wheelhouse, the cable running above his head as he disappeared into the shadows inside. When Oculus took over the compound, they had clearly not bothered to mess with the control panel and shut the cable cars down. Large rectangular boxes were running up and down from the mountain on a perpetual

296

loop. Most likely they were loaded with rare earth minerals that were now going for a merry-go-round ride since the miners had been killed or were tied up somewhere.

He watched pensively as one of the mineral boxes came down the cable from the mine toward him. Positioning himself on the opposite side of the giant iron wheel that turned the cable, he waited for it to approach. The metal box cranked down into the shed and flared outward from the bottom slightly as it went around the wheel. Aghassi pounced on it like a cat, his hands clawing for purchase as he was nearly thrown onto the concrete floor. Luckily, he found a metal rod sticking out of the back end of the box that the miners would use to position it when emptying minerals onto the nearby conveyer belt.

In seconds, he was being lifted skyward, quickly gaining elevation as the box was hoisted back up the side of the mountain. Looking down, he saw the mining camp, which looked like model railroad scenery from above. A sentry wearing his overwhites and carrying a spray-painted rifle patrolled below him, unaware of the Samruk mercenary's tactical gambit.

"That took some balls," Nikita's voice said inside the spy's earpiece.

Aghassi gritted his teeth and focused on not plummeting to his death. The dark entrance to the mine loomed ahead, slowly getting closer and closer. The cable car bounced, dropping a few inches and then righting itself as the cable strained. The mercenary held on with both hands, white knuckling it all the way up to the mine. Finally, the box slid into the cutout in the side of the cliff, passing with just inches to spare on either side.

Ensuring that he had solid ground beneath him first, Aghassi released and fell five feet, landing on the balls of his feet in a crouch. Taking a few steps out of the way so that he didn't get slammed by the next cable car, he unslung his Kalashnikov and took a knee. For a full minute he watched and listened for sounds of life. The first thing he noticed was the parallel set of rails for mining carts at his feet. He knew he had to be careful not to touch the rails. If his hunch was correct, making physical contact with the metal could kill him.

Slowly, he stepped forward, remaining as quiet as possible by setting down the heel of his boot with each step and then rolling it forward to his toes. A series of bare bulbs lit up the corridor that tunneled into the mountain, but they also left enough shadows for him to hide in. The sides of the tunnel were chipped black rock that had been drilled through, now coated in a thin sheet of slick ice. His breath hung in the air like a cloud. A few hundred meters in, Aghassi thought he spotted a distant glow that wasn't generated by one of the light bulbs. It seemed to be closer to the ground.

Tension filled his body with each step forward. If caught in an ambush, there was nowhere for him to run to. He would be gunned down in seconds. As the glowing rectangle grew clearer in his view, it became apparent that the glow was an open computer screen. He heard the shuffling of gravel under a booted foot, then some clicks coming from the computer terminal. It could have been one of the miners hiding in the tunnels, but Aghassi wasn't willing to take that bet.

Sticking to the side of the tunnel, he crept forward until he saw a silhouette passing in front of the computer screen. Just one person. Now he crouched down, careful not to cast a shadow from the light thrown off by one of the bulbs behind him. Finally, he found himself just a few meters away from the computer terminal and the lone figure crouched over it. A Tavor rifle lay propped against the wall of the mine next to him.

The Oculus commando had close-cropped hair and a medium build. He also wore overwhites like the rest of his teammates. As Aghassi neared, some sort of sixth sense must have told the Oculus member to turn around to face an imminent threat. He was a half second too late. Aghassi brought his buttstock down on his trapezius muscle. Aghassi didn't want to knock him unconscious as he needed to question him. Instead, he went for a muscle that would only incapacitate him. The butt stroke had the desired effect. The commando fell to the ground in a heap, clutching his shoulder.

The American put a boot down on his chest, pinning him to the ground as he trained his AK on the enemy.

"How many more of you guys are up here?"

The Oculus commando looked at him blankly. Maybe he was just playing dumb. The mercenary took a hard look at his face, noting the dark skin tone and thick eyebrows.

"You energized the minecart rails," Aghassi said in Persian Farsi.

Now the bushy eyebrows shot up his forehead in surprise.

"Yes, I know your language."

"Then you should know that I would never talk to the likes of you," the Iranian hissed.

"It's over," Aghassi said. "You played your cards well, but this is the end of the line for Oculus. Now you need to start thinking about an exit strategy for yourself. A bullet in a mineshaft, a lifetime sentence in a supermax prison, or a presidential pardon for defection and a nice house in Virginia. Your choice."

"I choose a fourth way."

"There is no—"

With that, the Iranian swung his hand and cupped it over his mouth, swallowing something.

Aghassi slammed his knee into the Iranian's chest and pried his hand away, but it was already too late. In seconds, the Iranian's eyes began to roll back into his skull and his body convulsed. As he shook, white foam formed at the corners of his mouth. The American shook his head, recognizing the smell of almonds. A cyanide pill.

"Death before dishonor," Aghassi whispered as he turned toward the computer terminal.

Sure enough, the computer was connected to a radio receiver, which was in turn wired to the minecart rails. Another line went deeper into the shaft, connecting to a generator with a transformer to modulate the electricity to the correct frequency. More than likely it was dialed in around 54.5 hertz to transmit on high frequency, which was harder to locate using direction-finding equipment. By energizing the rails, they had created a massive active antenna. Oculus had captured the mine to use as a massive radio relay station between their field team and their controllers. But where was the main body of the Oculus troops and the earthquake weapon?

The former ISA spy turned his attention to the computer and began working the keypad. Interestingly, the computer's operating system was set to English. Perhaps it was the common language that the multinational force communicated in. He could see that transmissions were going back and forth from the ASX mine as a relay station between the field team and the control team. Aghassi knew he had little hope of locating the controllers, as the signal would be rerouted dozens of times to protect their masters. The field team would not have that option, however.

Looking through the relay program, Aghassi was able to determine where the rest of Oculus was, but the grids were not making any sense.

"This can't be."

And yet, it was.

Turning back toward the entrance to the mine, Aghassi picked up a faster pace. He had to radio Nikita, who would in turn relay to Sirius Patrol, ultimately passing the information to Deckard. Something was seriously wrong.

* * *

"Deck," Kurt Jager called across the cargo hold of the ekranoplan. "They need you up in the cockpit. Sirius Patrol has something from Aghassi."

Deckard jogged toward the front of the craft and climbed a ladder into the cockpit.

"Just pick up that receiver," the pilot said from his seat, already knowing what he was there for.

"This is Six," he said picking up the hand mic.

"This is Sirius. Your men are on target. Stand by for a grid for the enemy location."

Deckard wrote down the numbers as they came in and referenced them on a map the pilot's navigator had.

"You're sure?" he radioed back. "That's in the middle of nowhere."

There was a long pause over the net.

"That is the grid that was relayed to us."

"But it is in the middle of fucking nowhere. What the hell would Oculus be doing in the middle of Greenland?"

Another long pause.

These fuckers are holding out on me, Deckard thought.

"Unknown at this time."

"Listen, your government instructed you to cooperate with us. Aghassi must have told you what the stakes are here."

"We are cooperating but...."

"But?"

"We need to clear it with higher."

"This is a state secret?"

"I cannot comment further," the Sirius Patrol leader said. "I apologize."

"Never mind. I'll clear it up on my end. Out."

Deckard set the radio down and looked to the pilot. His gray mustache bounced in anticipation as he looked back at the mercenary, a paper cup filled with instant coffee in his hand.

"Do you have a satellite phone? I need to call back to the States."

The pilot reached into a pouch on the back of his seat and tossed Deckard an Iridium phone.

"Want to pass that grid to my navigator so we can get moving?"

"Sure, but we can't leave until I get confirmation."

Deckard slid down the ladder and walked by the dozens of mercenaries who were sleeping and cleaning their weapons. A few were playing cards on top of a rucksack. Powering up the phone, Deckard waited for the screen to activate as he stood on the ramp, the ekranoplan gently rolling with the surf. He dialed the number. SCOPE picked up on the third ring.

"Hello?"

"It's me," Deckard said as he looked across the water and scanned the barren terrain in front of him. "We need to talk."

Jiahao strode into the radio room and stood behind one of the former Russian GRU operators who served as their commo tech. Sensing the presence of the Chinese commando, the Russian turned toward him.

"Is the relay site operational?" Jiahao asked.

"Up and running," he replied, handing over a note.

Jiahao took it from his hand but continued to stare straight through his commo man.

"From control," the Russian said uneasily.

Looking at the note, he read it with a smile.

"Perfect," he said as he flicked open a butane lighter and held it to the piece of paper.

Dropping the note as it finished burning, Jiahao left the radio room and walked down the icy corridors. The main drag was large enough to drive a tank through, or park a few dozen fighter jets if one was so inclined. Branching out from the corridor were other small tunnels that contained the various functions needed to keep the base operational: water, geothermal power, an armory, motor pool, chow hall, and even a club for recreation. As it stood, the compound was a ghost town, sitting empty and waiting for an Army Jiahao knew would never arrive.

Rounding a corner and ducking through another doorway, he entered the geothermal energy station. The previous custodians, three Danes who were now tied up in the corner of the room, had to drill deep to make geothermal energy possible in Greenland. It was to their benefit, as a large power source was exactly what he needed to make the device fully operational.

Chinese, Iranian, and Russian commandos surrounded the metal box that they had expended so much energy transporting across the Arctic from Russia. Of course, their original plan had been to load it on a submarine and operationalize it elsewhere, but plans change.

Deckard.

The Assassin's Mace soldier cursed his name. The American interloper was fighting windmills, unable to accept the fact that his country was going into a steep decline. Other powers would now rise, with China supplanting America as a global superpower. In the end, all Deckard had accomplished was to delay the inevitable.

"How much longer?" Jiahao demanded.

One of the Persians looked apprehensive. "A few more hours. We have to calibrate the energy intake—"

"You have an hour. We cannot delay any longer."

"Make it happen. I will not miss another opportunity. Control has authorized us to fire at will."

"We will get the weapon online."

"See that you do. And what about the fine-tuning of the standing waves?" he asked, turning to another Chinese member.

"We are almost there. At this point it is a matter of ensuring that the energy does not get lost as it travels through the Earth's core, or even worse, we overshoot and the energetics dissipate into the atmosphere."

"I want updates every ten minutes."

"Of course," the technician said, getting back to work.

Jiahao turned back to the corridor, searching for more of his men. They had their own work to do, preparing defenses and setting explosive charges at the entrances. At this stage of the game, he would leave nothing to chance.

* * *

The 60-some-odd mercenaries simultaneously rocked forward as the Ekranoplan set down, forcing them to desperately cling to any hard point before they somersaulted down the fuselage and did a faceplant on the ladder leading to the cockpit. Mann's Ekranoplan had the added benefit of being able to land on both water and snow, pontoons mechanically transforming into skis as needed.

It had been just a short skip to Thule Air Base from their location near the ASX mine. After retrieving the gear they needed for the final assault, it would then be a few hours to travel 400 kilometers to their target. Deckard still couldn't believe that the Danish government had been able to conceal such a secret from the world. Apparently, Russian military exercises has spooked the Danes far more than anyone had expected, leading them to take some fairly intense precautions.

As they came to a halt, the loadie dropped ramp.

The SCOPE think tank in Tampa had quickly coordinated with the Danish government, getting them to cave in and reveal what they had been hiding once they were made fully aware of the situation. Charlie was in the wire, and there wasn't much that Denmark's small military would be able to do about it. Letters of marque legitimized Deckard's pirate crew under the U.S. government, and so they were in like Flynn.

However, Deckard had been on enough suicide missions to know one when he saw one. First, he insisted on stopping by Thule Air Base, a U.S. military installation in a remote corner of Greenland. The facility was America's northernmost military base. It provided ballistic missile early warning systems and command-and-control systems for orbital surveillance platforms.

Since the ekranoplan needed much longer stretches to land and take off, they put down well outside the base, opting not to use their airstrip. In the distance, four snowmobiles left a wake of snow behind them as they sped toward the ekranoplan.

"Isn't it splendid!" Mann blurted out.

Deckard flinched, not expecting the billionaire to be right behind him.

"Gorgeous, just brilliant. You know this is the only place in the world where three active glaciers come together as one?"

"No, I had no idea," Deckard said.

"Well, I have you to thank. Short of an international security crisis, they never would have let me fly an experimental airplane like this over Danish territory."

"You're welcome. We'll just be loading the cargo and then we'll be on our way." Deckard excused himself.

As Deckard walked down the ramp to prepare to meet the American airmen en route, Kurt Jager strolled alongside him.

"Not a big fan of Mr. Mann, are you?" the former GSG-9 trooper asked.

"Call it a difference in motivations."

"I was thinking while we sat around waiting for Aghassi and Nikita to report back to us—"

"Please don't start waxing poetic on me. The last few days have been bad enough as it is."

"It's not that, it's just, I've realized what we all have in common."

"Yeah, fuck Hillary."

"No, besides that. I mean, all of us here in this group, from MARSOC, to SEALs, to the Italian 9th Regiment, to Delta Force, to the Norwegian FSK, to Germans like me, what we all have in common is that we have spent nearly our entire lives trying to hold Western civilization together, trying to maintain the current global order."

"I'm not sure we've done such a great job, then."

"No, we underestimated the importance of advanced communications networking and how this would lead to the erosion of the state, to the end of the Westphalian system that we have been trying to uphold all these years. Every deployment we have been on, from training African soldiers, to shooting al-Qaeda terrorists in Afghanistan, to low-visibility operations in Yemen, or Nigeria, or wherever, it has all had the same goal of maintaining the status quo."

"We were already on a decline; global order was bound to change and evolve," Deckard said. "A world where states are not so important freaks a lot of people out, but maybe it was inevitable."

"A non-state world with non-state actors may be yesterday's war. Now someone is challenging the global status quo. They don't want a non-state world, they want a world of one-state dominance, one where they are crowned the kings in a new type of world order."

Deckard squinted, his mind unsettled, then after a moment put his hand up on the hydraulic cylinder that opened the back ramp. "Damn Kurt, you should start charging parents to do kids' birthday parties. The youngsters would just have a gas of a time."

Kurt just shook his head, trying not to laugh.

Chapter 32
Greenland

"You're behind schedule!" Jiahao barked at his men.

The truth was, for all of his hyper-competency and supernatural abilities, Jiahao had little combat experience, and no real-world leadership experience. He had the skills, but not always the maturity that comes with hard-earned, real-world, life-or-death situations. Not that it mattered. The men feared him, and that was enough to motivate them.

His men were rapidly working to connect the weapon to the facility's geothermal power plant. They had enough juice in it for a small-scale local event when they were on the ice floe, but for what they had planned next, the geophysical weapon would need substantially more energy. Oculus was quickly approaching the end game, which would reduce America to a third-rate power and bring about a world dominated by the East rather than the West.

"Vladimir!" he called to another of his cell commanders.

"Sir?" The response came almost immediately.

"I see you walking around conducting inspections. Are the preparations already in place?"

"All the entrances, including emergency exits, have been booby trapped and barricaded. As we speak, the men are preparing for a defense in depth, setting up fortifications and anti-personnel mines inside the corridors. Nothing less than a battalion will be able to penetrate the facility, and even then it will take them hours and many casualties," the former Spetsnaz officer reported.

"How long until we are operational?" Jiahao asked the men setting up the geophysical weapon.

"We are about to start firing some test shots now to make sure our calibrations are correct. Another thirty minutes and we will be ready to trigger the event."

"Tell me when you are ready."

Jiahao paced back and forth inside the chamber, watching as the technicians worked, sending out invisible pulses of electromagnetic energy, firing them straight through the Earth's core. Soon, very soon, he would attain the status of a hero in the People's Republic.

Regardless of whether or not he ever lived to see his home country again, Jiahao would find immortality in a legacy that would live on for thousands of years.

* * *

The Ekranoplan lowered its ski wheels and landed on the tundra, skidding across the ice a few times before finally coming to a halt. Once the ramp dropped, the mercenaries disembarked, dragging plastic Skedco medical litters packed with the weapons and equipment they would need for one final assault.

There were only about 60 of the Samruk International mercenaries left after those who had been wounded or killed. All of them were well aware that they would be squaring off against a force that still outnumbered them and who occupied a dug-in, fortified position. They would have to rely on surprise, speed, and violence of action to level the playing field.

"Sergeant Major," Deckard said. Korgan turned toward him, the big Kazakh soldier's face in a permanent scowl. "Let's get 'em moving."

Deckard turned and watched as the Ekranoplan took off and flew back to Thule Air Base. The sun was getting low on the horizon now, and the mercenaries were running out of time before they would freeze to death on the barren ice field and before the enemy activated the stolen weapon one final time.

Getting their skis on, the mercs roped into the Skedco sleds and hauled them forward. Four hundred pounds of demo distributed between four plastic litters still made for a heavy load, but they had enough personnel to pull and rotate out as needed. Dag once again took the lead. With GPS not working and unreliable due to poor satellite coverage and probable enemy interference, Dag had to make some very careful calculations. Nate was backing him up, making his own separate calculations to cross reference with Dag's. This far north, magnetic compasses were also next to useless.

As the sun continued to sink beneath their field of view, it cast upon the snow brilliant shades of pink and orange, a deadly type of beauty in the world's most unforgiving environment.

The mercenaries pressed on, their legs burning, their arms numb from the straps of their rucksacks digging into them. The little rest they had gotten on the aircraft soon slipped away, replaced by the complete and utter exhaustion of pushing the human body beyond what it is supposed to be capable of over the course of their mission. Fedorchenko saw his men struggling and began stalking the lines, motivating them to press forward.

The offset infiltration had been necessary, as Samruk could not risk alerting the enemy by landing the airplane too close by. Too far away, and the movement would have killed the men, especially after nightfall. They just had to hope that the enemy had not put out seismic sensors that could give early warning.

Deckard simply focused on a fixed point in the distance, forcing his legs to keep moving and his arms to keep swinging as he dug his whippets into the snow. He had to admit that he had been shocked by what the Danes had told them when he finally got the full story. Recent Russian military aggression had inspired the Danish government to dust off a decades-old Cold War-era program that the U.S. Army had initiated back in the 1960s.

Called Camp Century, Army engineers had dug out an ice base under Greenland's ice sheet. It was a cut-and-fill type of construction that saw massive tractors digging out trenches that were then covered over with metal roofs. Then, the entire construct was buried under the snow. Officially, Camp Century was an Army experiment to try out new Arctic construction techniques and conduct scientific experiments. The reality was that it was just a cover for a highly secretive program called Project Iceworm.

All of this had been news to Deckard, who had only been told about it by the guys in Tampa while he was on the ekranoplan. It turns out that Uncle Sam had a plan to dig out 4,000 kilometers of tunnels under the ice and station 600 Minuteman nuclear missiles there, which could then be fired over the North Pole to strike the Soviet Union during a future nuclear war that never occurred.

Denmark had utilized the Cold War-era plan and built their own Arctic base in complete secrecy. The base was not to house nuclear weapons, since Denmark didn't have any, but would act as a perfectly camouflaged and secure military base in the event of a war with Russia. It would be a staging area for troops, and apparently they even planned on building an underground airstrip in the future. As he had witnessed firsthand, the Arctic was nearly impossible to run military operations in because of the tyranny of the long distances and harsh weather.

Denmark aimed to overcome some of those difficulties by situating a military base in the heart of

Greenland. The whole thing was surreal, but at this point Deckard was just rolling with the punches.

Up ahead, Dag raised a fist into the air, halting the patrol. He didn't use his radio, but simply waved Deckard forward in the last rays of sunlight poking out from behind the Norwegian mercenary. Face-to-face communication was better, as none of them were trusting their electronics not to be jammed, spoofed, or homed in on.

"It is time to put metal to matter and watch gray matter splatter," Deckard said as he skied up to the front of the patrol and took a look around.

Kurt ushered forward the mercs hauling the sleds. He was in charge of running the demo team and helped offload the 40-pound cratering charges that they had picked up at Thule Air Base. The Danes had advised that finding the entrances to the ice base would be almost impossible, and getting inside even more difficult. They were not going to take any chances. If the entrances were blocked, they would simply make a new one.

While the former GSG-9 operator got the charges arranged in an oval shape on the ice, another team led by Maurizio sank metal shanks into the ice 100 meters away to serve as their hard points. Fedorchenko and Shatayeva conducted a final inspection of men, weapons, and equipment. Everyone was going into the breach on this one: mortars, recce, every swinging dick who could carry a rifle and shoot in a generally straight direction.

* * *

Tampa, Florida

"It has begun," Joshua said, hanging up the phone.
"Seismic readings?" Craig asked.

"Small ones."

"They are test firing," Will said. "Getting ready for the real deal, making sure they kill us with the first shot."

"Which is exactly what will happen if the Yellowstone caldera cooks off."

"No, that is the thing," Joshua said. "It isn't Yellowstone. These odd readings are being reported by seismic stations in Europe. They are being detected near the Canary Islands."

"That doesn't make any sense," Craig said, shaking his head.

"Get the seismologist on the phone again," Will whispered.

Joshua picked up the phone and dialed.

"What do you think this means?" Joshua asked as the phone rang.

"I think it means we are fucked."

Joshua blew out his cheeks impatiently until someone picked up on the other end of the line.

"Uh, yeah, hello. This is Joshua again. Yes. We need a threat assessment on an earthquake on or near the Canary Islands." Joshua set the phone down and hit a button on the console. "Dr. Flynn, you are now on speaker."

"OK, well without knowing the specifics, I can project some scenarios," the seismologist told the think tank.

"We already know that the opposition has put an unprecedented amount of resources into making this attack happen in a way that cannot be attributed to the sponsor," Will said. "Give us the worst-case scenario, which is exactly what we have to expect."

"Worst case is that the earthquake triggers a mega-tsunami, which happens when a large mass displaces a significant amount of ocean water. They are far more dangerous than a tsunami created by seismic activity along the tectonic plates on the seabed. The initial wave could reach hundreds of meters high, if not more."

"I'm not sure I'm tracking here, Doc," Will said.

"In the worst case, the seismic activity would trigger the Cumbre Vieja volcano on the Canary Islands, causing the entire flank of the island to collapse into the ocean. This would displace enough water to create an initial wave over a thousand meters high. Eight or nine hours later, the resulting tidal wave would hit America's Eastern Seaboard. That wave would be somewhere between fifty to a hundred meters high."

"My god," Craig said, his eyes getting wide.

"Yes, it would take out a good portion of southern England as well," Dr. Flynn informed them.

"An earthquake that triggers a volcano that triggers a tidal wave," Will said to himself. "And none of it can be traced back to those responsible because of all of the human and geological cutouts used."

"What kind of damage are we looking at?" Joshua asked.

"Tens of millions dead in the United States alone. Then you have significant damage to South America, Africa, and Europe as well."

"Those are the desired second- and third-order effects. China and their partners get to swoop in with economic recovery packages, supplanting the economic balance of power that America has had for the last seventy years," Will extrapolated. "Maybe even sending armed troops into these areas in the name of humanitarian aid."

"But once they are there, they won't be leaving," Craig said, continuing his line of thought.

314

"The tsunami that hit southeast Asia in 2004 was only thirty meters high," Flynn said. "If the flank of this island cleaves off during the eruption and slides into the ocean, the amount of devastation this tidal wave causes will be unlike anything we have seen before."

* * *

"Standby, I have control," Kurt said.

He stood behind the front line of mercs going into the breach. He held the fuse ignitor in his hand, which was connected to the detonation system wired into a cluster of cratering charges. Arranged in a circle out on the ice, the explosives were designed to create massive craters in roads and airfields, preventing the advance of enemy troops.

"Five."

The Samruk mercenaries were strung into four separate lines, dynamic climbing rope running through carabiners attached to their harnesses. The ends of the ropes had been secured to the steel shanks they had driven into the snow.

"Four."

The cratering charges were aligned directly above what would be the main chamber of the Danish ice base, now occupied by Oculus. According the Aghassi, this was where the radio transmissions were emanating from, and there sure as hell wasn't anything else in the middle of Greenland.

"Three."

The mercenaries tensed, like Olympic runners ready to sprint the second the pistol fired. Everything came down to a very exacting sequence of events. Fuck it up in any way, and they were all dead.

315

"Two."

The mercenaries ran toward the charges. "Go, go, go!" someone yelled. They had to get there, pushing the minimum safe distance so they were ready to take advantage of the chaos and confusion caused by the explosive breach. Kurt yanked the safety pin out of the ignitor.

"One."

Kurt put his finger through the metal loop at the end of the ignitor, twisted it, and then pulled it straight out. The cratering charges blew, shooting white shrapnel high into the air. The mercenaries buckled as the concussion of the blast washed over them, but continued running straight forward toward the gaping hole in the ice as the smoke was cleared away by the wind.

Chapter 33

Deckard hurled the coiled rope into the dark chasm, where it spiraled out as it descended down into the breach. He threw himself over the ledge, chasing it into the darkness. He was suddenly weightless, gravity sucking him into a black hole. Gripping the leading edge of the rope, Deckard brought it behind his back, slowing his fall as the line was routed through the carabiner on his climbing harness. He had to get to the bottom fast, before the shooting started, but too fast and he would end up a greasy stain on the ice.

His boots came down hard on the floor and he spilled onto the ground, his Kalashnikov clattering on the ice. In the haze created by the cratering charges and falling ice, he could not see what was going on, but knew he needed to get out of the way before the next mercenary came down behind him. Unclipping the rope from his carabiner, gunshots nearly deafened him inside the chamber.

Rolling left, Deckard brought the butt of the AK into his shoulder and scanned for muzzle flashes. Staccato bursts of fire echoed off the chamber walls, coming from everywhere and nowhere. Seeing a muzzle flash in the corner of one eye and a stack of wooden crates in the corner of the other, he dashed for cover. His men came pouring down through the smoke behind him, landing in the chamber and detaching from the ropes.

Taking a knee, Deckard aimed at the location of a muzzle blast and fired beneath it. Hot brass bounced off the crates and ricocheted back at him, one of them burning his neck.

Voices screamed in Russian, some of them belonging to Oculus. Others were his own men. It was impossible to tell who was who. Deckard palmed a frag grenade, pulled the pin, and overhanded it through the haze toward another two muzzle blasts he had spotted.

"Frag out!"

The resulting explosion collapsed a large chunk of ice, which fell from the ceiling and shattered into a million pieces. Samruk troopers moved to Deckard, taking cover with him behind the crates as they returned fire, snuffing out the enemy even as the smoke cleared.

"On me, let's go!" Deckard ordered.

"Go where?" one of the Kazakhs asked.

"Doesn't matter. We can't lose the initiative."

Deckard broke cover and dove into the haze, running toward where the frag had gone off in hopes that the immediate area had been cleared by the explosion. A half-dozen Kazakhs followed after him. They found themselves at a T-intersection, the white walls that had been cut into the snow rising up around them. It was the most dangerous place they could possibly be because of the multiple angles of fire they were exposed to.

Grabbing the nearest Kazakh, Deckard pushed him forward into the adjacent corridor. Now it was apparent that they had breached right into the main corridor. Wide enough to drive a couple tanks through side by side, it probably ran the length of the ice base. Off of that main artery, it appeared that a series of smaller corridors broke off to the sides. Whatever the case, they needed to flood the compound with men as quickly as possible to clear it and locate the weapon before it could be used.

Several more mercenaries joined them, catching up with the lead element as Deckard pushed deeper into the facility. Two white-clad gunmen spilled out through a doorway toward the end of the corridor. Deckard got his front sight post lined up center mass on the first and stroked the trigger. The gunman squeezed the trigger as well, even as he dropped to the ground. The Israeli bullpup coughed yellow, and chunks of ice were blasted off of the wall. The second gunman met a similar fate as the mercenary next to Deckard put a double tap in his chest.

Priming another frag, Deckard pitched it through the doorway and counted off the seconds as it cooked off. The air went thick, washing over the mercenaries as the explosion increased the air pressure, burping out a gust of wind from the door. Flowing inside, the men cleared their corners and searched for targets. An Iranian-looking dude lay on the ground filled with shrapnel. He only had one boot on, and had probably been in the process of putting on the other. Deckard put a round through his forehead just to make sure.

Becoming more aware of the details of his surrounding, the American looked around in confusion.

"What the hell?"

The walls were hardwood and the floor was covered in carpet. Tables and chairs were spread around the room between couches and overstuffed chairs. Fake windows displayed typical countryside outdoor scenes. There was even a billiards table. It was a recreation room for Danish soldiers who might be stationed underground for long periods of time.

"Dead end. We need to get back out there."

In the side corridor, the mercenaries could hear a raging firefight in the main chamber. Three Samruk mercenaries were at the corner of the side corridor and the chamber, using the angle for cover as they returned fire. Deckard could see some of the boys taking cover around the chamber, but others looked like they had already moved on to clear the rest of the base.

319

Worse, three or four snow-camouflaged bodies lay face-down on the ice. Another was motionless, hanging above them, tangled up in one of the rappel ropes.

* * *

"Now!" Jiahao ordered. "Fire!"

The walls shook as another explosion reverberated from deeper in the ice base. They were under attack.

"I can't! It doesn't have enough of a charge since the last test shot," the technician's voice sounded like nails on a chalkboard as he lost his composure and shrieked like a schoolgirl.

Jiahao picked up his assault rifle, then turned and drop-kicked the Russian. The Chinese commando could have caved in his chest, but frankly, he needed a moderately useful pawn to finish the job. Looking at the touchscreen that controlled the device, he could see the power bar recharging quickly, but not fast enough for his liking.

"I'll deal with the American myself. If you don't cause the Canary Island collapse before they get here, you'd better surrender to the mercenaries before I get back, because it will be your only chance at surviving," he warned, even as the last words were drowned out by the sound of gunfire.

* * *

Rochenoire ducked as a trio of rounds chiseled into the ice above his head.

A group of Oculus shooters had retreated to another chamber, taking cover as Samruk quickly gained the tactical inertia. Now they had found refuge inside the

320

ice base motor pool, taking cover behind the massive tractors and sleds that served as the base's logistical line of resupply.

The former SEAL sent a return volley from his Kalashnikov, which sent a shower of orange sparks washing over the enemy soldiers behind the tractors. One of the Kazakhs came up behind him with a PKM and began firing rapid bursts of suppressive fire. Now Fedorchenko and Sergeant Major Korgan were on the scene, directing the troops and shaking them out into a haphazard assault line.

Firing on an empty chamber, Rochenoire pulled a fresh magazine from his kit. Using the loaded magazine, he pressed it against the magazine-release lever on his AK. When the empty mag dropped, he quickly rocked the loaded one into position and racked the bolt. Suddenly, his head felt like it had exploded inside. He slammed his eyes shut trying to shake the debilitating burning he felt.

"It's the damn lasers," he heard an Italian-accented voice say. "They are bouncing the lasers right off the ice on the walls."

The PKM machine gun fell silent as the enemy gunfire picked up. Slightly opening one eye, Rochenoire saw that the gunner was face-down on the floor. It was unclear if he was blinded by the lasers or had been shot.

"This is motherfuckin' bullshit, man."

Reaching down, he grabbed the machine gun, pointed it toward the enemy, and depressed the trigger. The metal-link belt cycled through the feeding mechanism, dropping hot brass at his feet. At least it kept the enemy's heads down for a few seconds.

To his flank, a half-dozen Samruk mercenaries collapsed to the ground as something flashed at their feet. They were going into convulsions, shaking as if they were having some kind of epileptic fit. Another one of those damn seizure grenades like the one they had encountered in Alaska.

Amidst all of the gunfire, he could hear one of the enemy commanding his men in English.

"Advance! Get up!"

For a split second, Rochenoire saw him as he walked behind one of the giant sleds. It was one of the big Chinese dudes. Maybe the one who had killed some of his men in their sleep. Maybe the one who took down Pat in Canada.

Another flash.

Rochenoire shuffled back behind cover, slamming his eyes shut once more. He had been looking in the wrong direction, but upon hearing bodies around him crumpling to the ground, he knew they had nailed the mercs with another seizure grenade. The non-lethals were the perfect weapon to cut their balls off. Incapacitate the mercenaries, and then Oculus could just casually stroll around, putting a bullet between their eyes.

Opening his eyes, he ignored the fact that Fedorchenko was doing the clucking chicken right next to him and reloaded the PKM with another belt of ammo from the dead or unconscious machine gunner. It was a last-ditch effort, but Rochenoire knew that he had to at least keep the enemy preoccupied in the motor pool so they would be unable to mount a counterattack against Deckard and the other men as they attempted to take control of the weapon.

He was about the open fire as the enemy advanced toward him when he noticed something on the ceiling of the chamber. The black giant took a few steps away from his cover while making sure he remained unexposed to the Oculus commandos. It was time for some indirect fire.

Shooting from the ,hip, he raked 7.62x54R autofire across the stalactites, some of them four or six feet long and hanging above the motor pool like massive daggers. One by the one, the giant icicles broke away from the ceiling and fell free toward the Oculus troops below. Then, they all came tumbling down like a Jacob's Ladder, landing with a crash.

Rochenoire dropped the smoking PKM and transitioned back to his Kalashnikov. The Samruk men were groaning and trying to stagger to their feet. Several of them had vomited on themselves. They had their bell rung, but they were alive.

The same could not be said for the Oculus troops. They lay sprawled out in the empty space between the line of sleds and tractors they had broken cover from, assaulting toward the other line of vehicles that Samruk hid behind. Their broken bodies were heaped around shattered shards of white and blue ice. Rochenoire walked between the still bodies, plugging them with insurance rounds.

That was when he came across the big Chinese one. A stalactite had caught him on the shoulder, nearly taking his arm off. His breaths were rapid, his eyes searching. He was scared. Rochenoire placed a boot on his chest and smiled.

"Welcome to the Thunderdome, bitch."

* * *

Deckard moved with Shatayeva's platoon, Nate and Dag backing up his play as they drove deeper into the compound. The volume of enemy gunfire was increasing, leading him to believe they were closing in on the earthquake weapon. Now they were back under the

323

breach, the interior illuminated only by the florescent bulbs that hadn't been blown out in the explosion. From the main chamber, the enemy had barricaded themselves down a side corridor in a prepared position constructed from refuse and packed snow.

Two of the Kazakhs lobbed grenades, which detonated ineffectively in front of the barricade. Deckard reached into his parka and gripped a party favor he had been saving. Clicking a button on the metallic egg, he threw it as far and as high as he could, rocketing it like a baseball pitcher down the corridor. It gained both depth and height before cutting loose a flash of light. The seizure grenade that had taken down Deckard in Alaska worked just as well against the enemy. Their limp bodies hit the ground, their guns falling silent.

The mercenaries ran down the corridor, firing bursts of gunfire into the barricade. Clearing around it, they hosed the Oculus commandos down with lead as they kicked and twitched in the throes of their collective seizure.

Deeper down the corridor, a few shots rang toward the mercenaries. The mercs returned fire toward doorways and muzzle flashes. Deckard leveled his rifle. Suddenly, he felt like he'd hit a brick wall. Stumbling forward, his vision exploded, whiting out. Oculus was lazing them again, the beams bouncing all around the corridor of ice.

Attempting to keep his rifle pointed ahead, he squeezed off a couple of rounds before the world spun so much around him that he fell to his knees. Around him, the Kazakhs were cursing in Russian. Nate was down beside Deckard, his fingers limply gripping his rifle, his dexterity deteriorated.

Oculus gunmen burst out into the corridor from one of the doorways, their shifting forms dancing in front of what was left of Deckard's vision.

They had him dead to rights.

Chapter 34

At the ASX mine, Nikita's HK417 cracked, the shot taking the farthest gunman down with a round that carved through his lungs at an oblique angle.

Upon hearing Nikita's shot initiating the attack, David and Evan opened fire on a second Oculus member who had been patrolling down a small embankment, out of the sniper's view. The two Sirius Patrol men took him down with precision fire, and the Tavor rifle slipped from his grasp as he collapsed to the ground.

The Danes entered and cleared the first structure, barreling their way through the door. A Chinese man wearing overwhites hunched over a small stove. He looked up at them. He had been warming a flask of tea. Evan stared slack-jawed at the bloodied bodies of two of the mine's engineers who lay in a bloody mess off to the side of the shack. The Oculus commando saw a small opening as they were momentarily distracted and reached for a pistol on his hip. David swung his M-10 rifle toward the interloper and fired, the round coring a hole through the would-be killer's skull. The exit wound splattered the walls red with brain matter.

"Holy shit," Evan gasped.

Sirius Patrol had been in existence for over 50 years, but this was the first time the unit had ever killed anyone in the line of duty.

"Come on," David said. Opening the door, he instantly rocked back and fell over as bullets slammed into the side of the hut and punctured holes through the door. The Danes instinctive reaction saved his life. Outside, another gun joined the barrage, quickly turning the small structure into a sieve.

* * *

Kurt Jager ducked as one of the Chinese commandos picked up and hurled Ivan, their mortar sergeant, toward him. The Kazakh spun through the air and crashed into a wall. After clearing the armory inside the ice base, Kurt and a dozen other men who had rapelled into the icy depths found themselves in another open room. The Chinese super soldier had fled here after his men had been killed. Cornered, he had attacked with superhuman strength, the likes of which the German had never seen before.

Out of ammunition, the commando had ambushed the mercs, taking several down with a knife before it got stuck in a collarbone. That didn't slow him down much, as he simply took the fight hand to hand. Kurt leveled his AK, only to have the barrel swatted away with a kind of speed that no one should possess.

Next, the commando yanked the barrel, making Kurt lose his footing. Grabbing him by the neck, the Oculus killer yanked Kurt right off his feet as the other mercenaries surrounded him.

"Back away or I will kill him," the genetically modified assassin said, his words spoken in near-perfect english.

The Kazakhs held their ground, rifles trained on the enemy as he backed away with his hostage.

Kurt looked out of the corner of his eyes, spotting the reason why this particular chamber existed. There was a well in the center of the room with a black cable running down inside it. He understood at once that this was the base's aquifer. The Danes had run an electrical heating component down into the well they had drilled out. Once

327

heated, the ice would melt and become their source of drinking water.

"Lay your arms down. This fight is already over. You are too late."

The Kazakhs held their ground. Dropping their weapons was just a bridge too far, hostage or no hostage. Kurt couldn't say he blamed them. This man was clearly hard to kill. He knew he would have to time his move carefully, because he was only going to have one shot. The hand around his throat was like a vise. The Chinese commando wasn't actually trying to choke him to death though, not yet.

Reaching down, Kurt grabbed the hilt of his Randall fighting knife. In one smooth motion, he drew the knife from its sheath, twisted his abdomen away, and plunged the eight-inch steel blade into his attacker's stomach.

The commando howled, releasing Kurt from his grip. Just as he reached for the knife stuck in his midsection, Kurt body checked him as hard as he could, putting every ounce of his weight into it. With his hands still around the hilt of the blade, the commando bucked backwards and toppled over, going head-first down the well.

His screams were cut off as he splashed into the ice-cold water below.

The Kazakhs rushed up, ready to empty their magazines down the well.

"Hold on," Kurt said. "I've got this one."

Pulling the pin on a fragmentation grenade, he let the spoon fly and dropped it down the well.

"*Gwai lo!*" a shout came from the bottom of the well.

The mercenaries backed away as the grenade blew and collapsed the well in a gust of freezing air.

328

"I don't have them!" Nikita said over the radio, unable to acquire the two Oculus troops firing on the Sirius Patrol.

But Aghassi did. The two gunmen were walking toward the hut the Sirius Patrol currently occupied, firing on automatic as their streams of autofire crisscrossed each other. From his vantage point high up in the opening of the mine, Aghassi looked down the iron sights of his Kalashnikov and aimed center mass. One Oculus member flinched as he was hit, Aghassi following up with another two quick shots that put him down for good.

The second gunman spun around, not knowing where the shots were coming from. Aghassi helped him out with a burst of fire that stitched him up from groin to chest.

With the shooting over, the two Danes came walking outside in a daze, both holding their weapons at the low ready.

"Nice job!" Aghassi called down to them, giving the team a thumbs-up.

* * *

Two dark forms fell in front of Deckard.

He never heard the gunshots, his ears ringing, his brain feeling like it was exploding behind his eyes. He came up on all fours, gunfire raging around him. Then the single shots could be faintly heard above everything else. It had to be Aslan, Nikita's sniper partner, down at the end of the corridor, firing over the prostrate forms of his teammates.

Deckard forced himself up, holding his AK loosely in his hands as he tried to force his body to function.

Tripping, he stumbled up against the wall and cut loose with a burst from the hip, spraying fire downrange. Next to him, he felt Nate grabbing his parka, the former MARSOC Marine also trying to pull himself up and get back into the game.

"We can do this," Deckard said, although he couldn't hear his own voice.

Walking on wobbly feet, he helped Nate up and then ran to the nearest Kazakh, pulling him off the ground. The dead bodies of Oculus soldiers and a few of their own men littered the ground. Deckard pushed himself deeper into the corridor. Seeing their commander stagger forward, the others had no choice but to will themselves on to the completion of their mission.

Large steel doors hung ajar where the Oculus commandos had emerged. Deckard glanced inside and was greeted with the popping of several more shots. Sidearming his last frag grenade through the door, he held back one of the Kazakhs who, in a moment of disorientation, tried to chase the grenade through the door. It went off with a *whoosh*. The mercenaries followed the explosion inside, where they found another large chamber filled with dead or dying enemies.

There was only one way forward, and Deckard charged, just as the ground began to shake beneath their feet.

* * *

Jiahao fired a burst from his Tavor rifle, the shots peeling back the Russian's scalp. He flew backwards with arms stretched into the air before sprawling across the floor.

330

Driven back by the mercenaries, the Oculus leader was not leaving any room for further discussion from his men. An Iranian backed away from the device as Jiahao moved to it and began keying in the destruct sequence. They were out of time to execute their planned attack, so he would bring the house down on top of them before he let the imperialist killers-for-hire take control of the geophysical weapon.

Shun strode into the chamber, covered in someone else's blood, which had drenched his overwhites in crimson. A light vibration was already thrumming under the soles of their boots.

"Orders?" Shun asked.

"This battle is over, but the war continues," Jiahao said.

"We fight to the death."

"Not here. Take whatever men you can and make your way to the garage. Blow the charges and save yourselves if you can."

"It was an honor, Jiahao."

"And you, Shun. You have been a good soldier."

Shun offered a small bow and then disappeared into a side tunnel. The Iranian looked over at Jiahao, wondering if he was to receive a pardon as well. Jiahao nodded toward the tunnel that Shun had escaped into.

"Go."

The Oculus commando did not need to be told twice.

Jiahao unslung his rifle, gripped it by the stock and barrel, then smashed it down on the control pad several times, destroying the keypad and touchscreen. The weapon would destroy itself and everyone around it in minutes.

* * *

Deckard recoiled as shards of glass-like ice came crashing down in front of the entrance to the geothermal power chamber, where the device was located. The entire ice base was beginning to vibrate and become unstable. The roof was already deteriorating, the entire entrance to the antechamber collapsed and blocked off.

"There has to be away around," Nate said. "Let's skirt around the edge and look for another tunnel leading in."

Deckard nodded. As they backtracked looking for another way into the chamber, he saw that Nate, Aslan, and two other Samruk mercenaries were still on his back. The others had become separated, engaged in other firefights, or killed.

"Look, I'm calling landslide on this objective. This place is toast. It's over," Deckard said loud enough so the men could hear him over the cracking ice above their heads and under their feet.

"Is there a *but* in there somewhere?" the former Marine asked.

Everyone was looking for a pardon at this point.

"I need a confirmation on the super soldiers' and the weapon's destruction. They might be the only thread that can lead us back to their masters. You can roll; I don't have the heart to order any more men to their deaths today."

Aslan said something in Russian.

"What was that?" Nate asked.

"He said, 'Fuck that,'" Deckard replied, rolling his eyes.

"Let's go, the enemy is probably heading for an escape hatch anyway. We'll get out that way."

332

"Sure about that?" Deckard asked with a frown. Clicking his hand mic, he then spoke into his radio. "Landslide, I say again, landslide!"

It was the code word to evacuate everyone off of the objective immediately.

"Landslide, landslide!" other voices shouted over the assault net, making sure everyone heard the order. Just then, a large chunk of ice broke free from the ceiling and crashed just behind Aslan. The walls on both flanks were also starting to shake violently. The mercenaries looked around them with some hesitation as snow shook from the ceiling like massive flakes of dandruff.

Their distraction was broken by a single gunshot that cracked through the corridor.

Smoke wisped from the barrel of Deckard's Kalashnikov, his single shot having felled an Oculus commando dashing across the corridor up ahead from one tunnel to another. Several shots greeted the mercenaries in return as more of them quickly crossed the corridor. Taking a knee, Deckard let loose a burst just in front of the feet of another Oculus shooter, driving him backwards into the passageway he had just been in.

"You three go after the others who got away, I'll take on the straggler," Deckard ordered. The one he had forced back looked like a bigger guy. It was just a hunch, but one he wanted to follow. They were all in at this point anyway.

"Got it," Nate said, and took the three men down the side passage in pursuit, each of them hopping over the dead body Deckard had made.

Deckard edged around the corner and into the tunnel on the other side of the wider corridor. His rifle was shaking in his hands, reciprocating the vibrations that ran up the length of his body. The device had obviously been put into the geophysical version of a Chernobyl meltdown. Oculus was going for a last-ditch effort, knowing that the mercenaries were closing in. In the distance, a shadow shuffled through the dark.

Firing a snapshot off, a burst instantly responded back to Deckard, cutting through the air inches for his side. He was staring down his sights, looking for a second sight picture, when the tunnel suddenly collapsed behind him. Deckard scrambled forward, chancing the gunfire as snow and ice came splashing down behind him. Nearly losing his footing, the floor gave out and Deckard found himself momentarily in free fall before landing hard on his back. The ice was cracked apart beneath him.

The ceiling opened up above him, letting in the last light of dusk as he slid down into the abyss. Sliding into the darkness, Deckard skidded around the ice, momentarily going upside down before he kicked his boots a few times and managed to right himself. In front of him, he caught the vague outline of another human being on the same trajectory with him.

Determined to at least go out with a fight, Deckard sat up and blasted off rounds at his target as fast as he could pull the trigger. Realizing someone was above him, the Oculus member sprayed fire behind him, the shots disappearing into the collapsing ice walls. The floor continued to cant downwards, terminating in what looked like a bottomless drop. Sensing his impending doom, the Oculus super soldier managed to get up on one knee as he slid down. At the last moment, he vaulted into the air like a gymnast and flew right over the pit. He grabbed the ice with his bare hands and scrambled up to safety.

Deckard knew his hunch had been right, that he was tracking one of the Chinese test-tube experiments, but he didn't have time to dwell on that. All he had time for was to free his ice axe and execute an extremely weak attempt at jumping up and over the chasm. The American hurtled through the air like a retarded puppy and slammed the ice axe in just as he hit the wall in front of him. Every joint and muscle in Deckard's body screamed in pain.

Somewhere below, his Kalashnikov fell into the pit.

Forcing himself to ignore his body's protests, he grabbed for the ice tool on his belt and swung it into the ice. Using only his upper-body strength, he muscled his way up the ice wall, even as everything collapsed down around him. A fissure erupted right up the middle of the ice he was climbing, causing him to lose his grip on both tools at the same time. For a second, he dangled in the air, hanging by the lanyard he had managed to get around his wrist on the handle of the ice tool. Reaching out, he grabbed both and pushed himself, swinging arm over arm.

Grunting in pain and exhaustion, he reaching the lip of the wall. Just as he got the ice tool up over the edge and began to pull himself up, a hand came over the edge straight at him and grabbed his parka, dragging him up.

Chapter 35
Greenland

The charges detonated in sequence, multiple puffs of smoke going off and forming an explosive ring around the garage entrance. A plume of gray smoke floated over the vehicles, the hatch to the chamber blown open. Turning over the engine, Oculus commandos in the hulking treaded tractor guided the light swing out of the facility. Hauling six sleds packed with military equipment, the tractor's snow treads dug in. Just as the caterpillar-looking monstrosity was pulling out, Shun and two more Oculus members materialized from the connecting tunnel and jumped up onto the last sled.

Nate, Aslan, and two other mercenaries spilled out into the garage, their rifle barrels sweeping across its breadth in search of targets. They were just in time to see the ass end of the light swing pull out of the garage and disappear onto the tundra.

"We need to get the hell out of here," Nate said, yelling above the sound of the ice base shaking itself apart. One of the buttresses holding up a wall broke, causing snow to flow into the garage in a miniature avalanche.

Aslan slung his sniper rifle and ran to the side of the garage where some gear was stacked. Reaching down, he yanked a green tarp off a pallet.

The smile on his face seemed oddly out of place given the fact that the roof was about to collapse at any moment, but the other mercenaries could not help but smile back.

* * *

Deckard landed on his back and immediately swung his ice axe toward where he thought the enemy soldier was. The Chinese commando easily swatted the axe away and clamped down on Deckard's wrist, squeezing it in his hand with an iron grip.

"It is about time that we met face to face, Deckard."

Deckard looked up at him, his opponent's brown eyes piercing him with their gaze.

"I'm called Jiahao, and I have waited a long time for this."

"I'm called go fuck yourself," Deckard replied, just as the platform of ice suddenly crumbled again. Deckard's vision was obscured by the crashing ice, but he knew he was falling. Sliding down the fissure that had opened up under him, he grasped for the ice axe hanging from his wrist while swinging the ice tool wildly, hoping to stick it in something, anything, to break his fall. Once he had both tools in his hands, he frantically tried to shove them into the ice and slow himself down. One stuck, but then broke free from the ice.

The best he could do at that point was keep both feet together when he slammed into the bottom. He came down hard, landing in a shallow pool of water, and had the wind knocked out of him. With a groan, he rolled over onto his side, the freezing water seeping through his jacket and startling him back to his senses.

It was never enough to kill him, just enough to hurt really, really badly.

The fissure had grown above him, the last light of the day streaming inside what appeared to be a naturally made ice tunnel. Whether it was entirely natural or formed by warm water exiting the ice base from their shower and chow hall facilities was impossible to guess at the moment. The ground still shook beneath his feet, the scary part being that it wasn't really ground, but more ice that could come apart at any second.

Deckard staggered to his feet and tried to get some feeling into his hands, messing around with several failed attempts before he finally tethered his axe and ice tool to his belt. With his Kalashnikov long gone, he drew the Glock 19 from its holster. Jiahao was somewhere down here, and having seen his abilities firsthand, he didn't believe for a moment that the Oculus leader had died in the fall.

Water gushed around his boots as he looked up at the pockmarked ice at the top of the tunnel, then back down in search of Jiahao. A chunk of ice broke free and splashed into the water next to Deckard, the entire cavern groaning as the elasticity of the ice was strained by invisible electromagnetic energy from the device, most likely buried in the ruins of the ice base at this point.

"Deckard," a voice echoed from the darkness of the tunnel, "how does it feel to know that your country is in decline? To have your power challenged?"

Holding his pistol in both hands, Deckard cautiously moved forward.

"China suffered decades of humiliation at America's hands, but now it is our time. It is our right to take what belongs to us!"

The tunnel shook again, Deckard's boots sliding on the slick ice. Half soaked, he was beginning to shiver already.

"We have suffered your spiritual pollution long enough," Jiahao wailed like a child.

Deckard squinted to see through the dark, searching for his quarry. The Chinese soldier sounded like a full-blown fanatic, a frustrated young man pumped full of communist propaganda. Frustrated or not, the kid was clearly one of the vat-grown super soldiers Will had described. Reaching into his pocket, Deckard pulled the elastic band of a headlamp over his head, but did not dare to turn it on yet. Activating a "shoot-me" light in the confines of a dark cave would be the quickest way for him to receive a tight burst from Jiahao's Tavor rifle.

"You met the mage, Deckard. I know he told you these things."

The voice came as a hiss, over Deckard's shoulder, behind him, in front of him, it was impossible to tell where he was. Everywhere and nowhere all at the same time.

The American flinched as the roof of the tunnel collapsed behind him, plunging him into the darkness. The rumbling continued as ice crumbled and fell around him, the vibrations under his feet rattling the tunnel to pieces. Hearing another section of the tunnel collapse, Deckard turned and ran.

Now he reached up and turned on his head lamp. The pillar of light cut through the darkness, reflecting off the ice and the stream of water as he splashed through it, slipping every few steps. The tunnel continued to collapse behind him, falling in one massive chunk after the other.

In front of him he could see glimpses of Jiahao running for his life as well. The Chinese commander was sprinting at full tilt, striding like a marathon runner. Deckard was lagging behind, battered, beaten, and unable to get any traction on the ice as he ran. The thuds got louder and louder in his ears as the tunnel imploded, nipping right at his heels. Deckard skidded to a stop as a car-sized piece of ice dropped down right in front of him.

For a second, claustrophobia set in, Deckard's heart racing as he feared being entombed alive. Images of Jacob, buried underneath an avalanche, fluttered in front of his eyes for a split second. Feeling his way around the block of ice, Deckard pushed the fatalistic thoughts from his mind and forced his legs to carry him forward.

Dodging several more ice blocks, Deckard again caught sight of Jiahao just as the Chinese commando lost his footing and went face-first into the stream. The Oculus commander quickly recovered and got back to his feet. Up ahead he could now see a way out, the tunnel terminating in another 100 meters. Moonlight formed a glow around the exit, summoning them.

Stumbling forward, Deckard's felt his quadriceps seizing up, the cramping slowing him down. He gritted his teeth and fell forward more than running forward. The tunnel was coming down in sections behind him, each one sounding with a boom.

Now Jiahao was showing his own weakness as he fell on his face and split his head open on the ice. Deckard was actually catching up with him in the final 25-meter dash of their lives. Jiahao looked back at him with a snarl, bright red blood running down his face.

Deckard slammed into him as the final section of the tunnel collapsed. A sneeze of snow and ice pushed them both the rest of the way out, flinging them through the air and back out onto the tundra.

* * *

Nate steered his snowmobile toward the light swing, kicking up a spray of snow in their wake. One of the Kazakhs held on to the seat behind him, pointing toward the tractor and sleds up ahead. Aslan and another Kazakh came up on their flank, riding their own snowmobile. The former Marine had to admit, this had been the most batshit crazy deployment he had ever been on, and that was saying a lot.

The twin snowmobiles raced up alongside the rear end of the light swing. The industrial-grade treaded tractor effortlessly hauled the six connected sleds behind it like the Arctic locomotive it was. Nate hit the throttle and took them right alongside the trail sled, just as a shot rang in his left ear. The Kazakh trooper took down a white-clad Oculus member who had spotted them. The corpse slid off the side of the sled, forcing Nate to react abruptly, nearly flinging the Kazakh off his seat as he swerved around the body.

The Samruk trooper didn't waste any time once Nate got them realigned, jumping up onto the platform. Standing up on the seat, Nate guided himself as closely as possible to the sled and then vaulted off. The Kazakh caught his wrist and pulled him up. Aslan and the other Kazakh were repeating the maneuver, but the staccato bursts of gunfire coming from up ahead made it clear that they had been compromised.

The sled was packed full of pallets, giving something for the Samruk mercenaries to take cover behind. Taking a knee behind a pallet strapped down to the bed of the sled, they returned fire on several muzzle flashes coming from the three Oculus members who had escaped them earlier. Nate gained target acquisition and gently stroked the trigger as he transitioned from target to target until the guns fell silent. By the time he finished, their two Samruk comrades had joined them behind the pallet.

Then the second wave hit them hard. The pallet began disintegrating under the onslaught of incoming fire, the four mercenaries crowding behind what little cover they had. The two Kazakhs reached for fragmentation grenades, primed them, and made ready to overhand toss both of them farther up onto one of the forward sleds.

When they stood up to throw, one chucked his toward the target. The other immediately collapsed with a gunshot wound to the head. Nate flung himself forward toward the frag grenade as it bounced across the sled. With no desire to be a martyr, he quickly picked it up and threw it before the fuse burned down. The grenade went off in mid-air, just a split second after the first. Severed arms flew up in the air. The grenades had successfully killed at least a couple of Oculus shooters.

Between their cover and the enemy were two nearly empty sleds, resulting in an up-close-and-personal free-fire zone, both forces beating back against each other as they moved across the tundra. Aslan took advantage of the chaos caused by the grenade blast and began returning fire with his HK417. One, two, three, the enemy began dropping like flies under the sniper's precision fire. Identifying where their cover was weak, Aslan effectively put shots through pallets of dry goods and other sundries. It was an effective tactic until he took a round through the shoulder.

The Kazakh sniper howled. The parasympathetic reaction of his body upon being struck by a 5.56mm round was to pitch backwards. Nate watched as the sniper fell right off the back of the sled, dropping into a heap in the snow behind them.

"Fuck my life," he said to himself, the words lost amidst all the gunfire.

Turning his attention back to the firefight, he saw one of the Chinese soldiers sprinting straight across the open sleds toward their position. It was a suicidal maneuver at best. The former Marine leveled his weapon, his trigger finger applying pressure a nanosecond too late. The Chinese commando bent at the knees as he approached and launched himself into the air. Spiraling through the open space in some kind of Olympic backflip, Nate struggled to get his sights on target, hopelessly squeezing off round after round from his Kalashnikov.

Shun landed behind the pallet with a thud, a side kick instantly delivered to Nate's midsection. His ribs exploded in pain, doubling him over. The Kazakh mercenary nearby was not so lucky. He didn't even have the chance to move his rifle barrel from downrange toward his new target, the sprint and jump had been nothing short of a display of inhuman abilities.

The genetically enhanced commando swung both of his firsts toward either side of the Kazakh's head, slamming into his skull like twin pistons, which effectively pulped his brain. The Kazakh fell dead instantly. Unable to catch his breath, Nate had done his best to crawl away, dragging his rifle behind him. Shun snorted in disgust at the sight of the Marine trying to keep himself in the fight. Kicking the Kalashnikov away, he then lifted Nate with one hand and threw him forward onto the empty sled.

"Leave him to me!" Shun yelled to his comrades.

Two remaining Oculus gunmen lowered their weapons. By now it was dark and the only light came from those on the tractor. The shadows played across the Oculus commando's face as he looked toward Nate.

"Yankee garbage," he sneered at the American.

Shun strode over to Nate and crouched down.

"How does it feel to know that you are about to die, just as your country is? How does it feel to realize that you are utterly helpless and impotent in the face—"

Shun froze in mid-sentence, his face turning the color of ash. Seven inches of ice axe were sticking out of the side of his neck. Nate pulled backwards, yanking the serrations of the axe through Shun's throat, casting a spray of blood.

"Semper Fi, you motarded motherfucker."

Shun grasped his neck, his hands slick with the liquid as he made one last futile effort to stop his life from draining from his body. With a gurgle of blood bubbling from his lips, Shun's hands fell away and he lay still.

Nate reached inside his jacket and pulled free his Glock 19 pistol.

The two Oculus commandos who had been watching, expecting Shun to brutally mutilate Nate with his bare hands, now looked at each other.

In unison, they both dived off the edge of the sled into the snow.

* * *

Deckard rolled through the snow with Jiahao. The two tumbled over one another, wrestling for control. The American pushed his Glock into Jiahao's chest and pulled the trigger, but somehow his adversary managed to slap the pistol to the side at the very last moment. Rolling to the bottom of the embankment, Jiahao planted a foot on Deckard's stomach and launched him into the air, flinging him into the snow. His Glock went spinning away into a snow drift.

Having escaped the collapsing tunnel, the two now found themselves outside in the darkness of night. The moon cast the snow in surreal, muted colors, gusts of wind blowing snow around the two men. Winded, but not out of the fight, Deckard rolled over and drew his ice tool and axe, holding one in each hand.

Jiahao stood and dusted the snow off his parka with a laugh.

"You are a funny one, Deckard," the Chinese commando mocked him. "But sure, OK."

344

Deckard assumed a fighter's stance, readying himself for combat. Jiahao bounded forward, parrying left, then right, easily avoiding Deckard as he flailed with both weapons. With one of Deckard's arms out at full extension at the bottom of a swing, Jiahao reached over and wrenched his opponent's wrist, snapping it like a twig. The Chinese commando tore the axe away and cast it into the snow, then snatched away the ice tool as Deckard tried to backpedal.

The Samruk mercenary instantly knew that this was how Pat had felt. He was simply outclassed. It wasn't that he was outmatched by a margin, like when Delta Force operators went head to head in a shooting competition, or when Rangers competed to see who could run a faster two miles in full kit. No, Deckard was inferior by a landslide, an avalanche that was cascading down on top of him.

Knowing his right hand was broken, Deckard reached around with his left and unsheathed his Company Knife, searching for an opening in Jiahao's defenses. The truth was that the commando did not have any defense; he was pure offense, moving so fast that Deckard could not even touch him. Jiahao reached out and did something too quickly for Deckard to recognize. All he knew was that the knife had been torn from his grasp. Jiahao smiled as he tossed the blade over his shoulder.

Jiahao then shook his head before launching into a crescent kick. Deckard bucked backwards, avoiding the brunt of it, but the glancing blow off of his head was nearly enough to knock him unconscious. Falling to his knees, Deckard propped himself up with one hand in the snow.

"Shall we end this charade?" Jiahao said, sounding almost bored.

Beneath him, Deckard could feel the gentle vibrations of the device, still humming away in some

345

collapsed chamber under the ice. He was only going to get one more chance at this. Deckard knew that it would only take one more solid hit from the Oculus leader to kill him.

Jiahao reached down and grabbed Deckard by the hood of his jacket, pulling him up. On his way, Deckard reached out with a gloved hand, going right up into Jiahao's groin. His fingers clasped around a smooth egg under Jiahao's trousers. The Chinese commando drew a sharp breath as Deckard crushed one of his nuts with all of the strength he had left. The testicle exploded in his hand like an overripe tomato.

Dropping to the ground, Jiahao clutched his beanbag in agony, his howls and cries carrying in the wind. Meanwhile, Deckard felt like he had been run over by a tank from the beating he had taken. His body had red-lined a long time ago, and now it was simply running on some kind of muscle memory developed through years of military training and combat experience.

"Damn, you talk too much," Deckard mumbled as he stumbled off, leaving Jiahao to mourn his manhood. "All this bullshit about Red China and the end of the world. Don't you ever shut up?"

Jiahao rolled back and forth sobbing. Not even the Chinese version of Captain America had steel balls, apparently. Deckard groaned as he got down on a knee and started pawing through the snow. His knees ached, his elbows ached, every muscle in his body felt like a frozen T-bone steak. His hand hung limply as he held it against his chest. It didn't phase him much, but he knew the pain would come soon.

Batting the snow around with his good hand, he continued his search.

The Chinese super soldier whimpered as he tried to breath.

"OK, dammit," Deckard cursed. "I'll have some of that General Tso's chicken."

The mercenary looked up at the dark horizon for a second, realizing that the ground had ceased to shake under his feet. With a smirk, he went back to digging around. The device had finally burned itself out or run out of power. Now it was buried under tons of ice and going nowhere fast, if ever.

"Ah, here we go," Deckard said as he reached into the snow. *"Shall we end this charade?"* he said in a whiny, high-pitched voice.

He winced as he stood, taking a deep breath as he righted himself. Jiahao was coughing like he had the dry heaves, his face having turned bright red. Standing above him, Deckard angled the muzzle of his Glock toward Jiahao's head.

Jiahao looked up at him, a flash of fury crossing his eyes once more.

The Glock spat five bullets, making another patch of white snow turn red.

Chapter 36
China

Crickets chirped and a stream gently gushed alongside the finely manicured lawns of the imperial garden. Zhongnanhai was a place of peace and tranquility, a place of culture and tradition, where communist party officials carried out their administrative tasks. Inside one of the many pavilions on the compound, the stillness was suddenly broken.

Black and white pieces of a game board flew through the air, a door slammed, and a communist party leader disappeared into an adjacent room as he attempted to regain control over his emotions. The pieces of the board game lay scattered between two men who sat on antique chairs crafted during a past dynasty. The monochromatic game pieces belonged to an encirclement board called *wei bo*. It was a game of both encirclement and counter-encirclement.

"He did not take that well," the Iranian said.

"Would you?" the Russian countered.

The Iranian's brow furrowed, his short white beard shifting beneath his jowls. Well into his middle years, the Iranian was the leader of the Iranian Revolutionary Guard's covert action branch—Quds Force. Like the Russian, he had been summoned to Beijing to oversee the final stages of a plan that had been years in the making. Now that plan lay in ruin, scattered across the game board in chaos.

"Perhaps not. Do you know the relation?"

"His grandson," the Russian answered, his expression flat and unreadable.

"They both knew the risks."

"My people will not be pleased by this development. The Kremlin may very well have me liquidated for this."

"They have no exposure. The Americans are already ramping up to strike ISIS in the Middle East. The misdirection was a master stroke by the old man," the Quds Force leader said, nodding toward the door the Chinese official had just exited. "You know what the Chinese say about a win-win situation?"

"I imagine there is some clever proverb."

"Indeed. In a win-win situation, China wins twice. Even if we lose, we still win. America sinks itself back into another protracted, unwinnable conflict in the Middle East, giving us increased freedom of movement to pursue our own objectives."

"We will see."

The Iranian shook a cigarette out of his pack and lit it up, seemingly unconcerned by the massive operational failure they had been dealt by the American mercenaries.

"At the most, this will be attributed to terrorists from Chechnya, Iraq, and Xiangyang. The back-up plan for the back-up plan," the Iranian said, leaning over and picking up the encirclement board. Setting it down on the table, he took another drag on his cigarette and looked over at the Russian.

"Why don't we play another game?"

* * *

Will walked out of the office building in Tampa, muttering something to the security guard on the way out. Having worked through the entire crisis, Will was now in desperate need of a shower, a shave, and a solid eight hours of sleep. Instead, he was planning to visit his favorite titty bar downtown.

"Fuck me," he said, popping a cigarette between his lips as he thought over recent events. "Chalk up a win for the good guys."

He lit up with his stainless-steel lighter, on the side of which was engraved an anchor, trident, and eagle. Images from a past life.

Deckard had managed to pull off the impossible, all while the American government and people were distracted by a dozen other emergencies at home and abroad. Whatever had happened, they would now have to convince their own bureaucracy that America was under attack by Iran, Russia, and China. For the first time, Will had the proof. But would anybody listen?

Reaching into his pocket, Will thumbed the automatic lock remote for his car, opened the door, and sat down in the driver's seat. Exhaustion was washing over him as his body dumped the adrenaline he had been running on for days.

Looking down at his wrist, Will eyed the red metal bracelet he had worn for decades. Many intelligence analysts wore black KIA bracelets for fallen soldiers, a reminder of who they are supporting, and of the life-and-death consequences of their work. Will's was for a former soldier who was officially listed as missing in action in some Third World shithole. As hard as he tried, he could never get the full story out of anyone, maybe because no one knew the truth.

Starting the car, he pulled out of the parking lot, through the security checkpoint, and out onto the highway. Staring out at the road in front of him, Will shook his head. Suddenly, he broke out laughing.

"Something wrong with that family," he said under his breath between laughs. "His father was a piece of work too."

The red MIA bracelet slipped out from his shirt sleeve as he spun the wheel. It read, *Sergeant Sean Deckard. Missing in action. 20JUL88.*

* * *

Twin lines ran through the snow, a trail made by two feet dragging their way forward. Fresh snow crunched as it compacted under each footstep. The lone figure limped across Greenland's expanse, hugging himself with both arms to try to contain the pain as well as to stay warm. He was broken, bruised, and expended, but still alive.

Deckard tripped, stumbled, but regained his footing —before continuing to stagger some more. He had been sleeping on his feet. Cresting the top of a gentle slope, he looked down and breathed a sigh of relief as he saw his men. Two platoons of mercenaries stood assembled below, having evacuated the ice base before it collapsed. Fedorchenko and Shatayeva were organizing the men, but there were no high fives or celebrations. A lot of good soldiers had died on this mission. Too many.

In the skies above, the Northern Lights flared. The fluttering green streaks were created by light bouncing off the gases of the upper atmosphere. Deckard stood and watched the lights, cast in the ethereal awe of reality. The Arctic was beautiful and deadly in some of the same ways as other parts of the world he had visited, but none of those places combined beauty and desolation the way the Arctic Circle did.

It was the emptiness, the lack of human presence that made the Arctic so different. It was so quiet, just the sound of wind in his ears. Without any artificial light sources, the stars in the sky were brilliant, bold in a way that could never be observed in most parts of the world. Craning his neck, Deckard looked straight up into the sky. Above the Northern Lights, the Milky Way could be seen bubbling amongst the stars.

Deckard smiled.

It was a good night to be alive.

Epilogue
Three days later

In a faraway land, a dark castle sat at the summit of a mountain. Circular clouds the color of coal slowly spun in concentric circles above, the occasional burst of lightning making the heavens glow. Inside the castle, long halls made of fieldstone stretched into the darkness, only illuminated by a few flickering torches.

The mage waited in one of the antechambers, breathing slowly, waiting with his back turned toward the door. Soft footsteps approached, only audible once they grew near, just inside the chamber itself.

"I have been waiting for you," the mage said.

"And I you," the blade master replied.

The mage turned to face the blade master. The intruder stood before him, bristling with weapons, blades, swords, knives, and projectile weapons stashed in pouches and sheaths spread across his entire body.

"You asked the weight of the cauldrons," the mage said. "You have my respect."

"Did you really expect otherwise?"

The mage considered this for a moment.

"No, I did not."

The blade master circled around the portal in the center of the room.

"Jiahao mentioned you."

The mage paused. "You faced him in combat?"

"Yes. You were close to Jiahao?" the blade master asked, noting the mage's hesitation.

"Yes."

"Your son?"

"My grandson."

"If it means anything to you, we fought in hand-to-hand combat."

The mage's eyes burned.

"Impossible."

"It is true. He died a warrior's death."

The mage began to say something but stopped himself, forcing restraint upon his words.

"Thank you."

The blade master nodded his head slightly. "And now?" he asked the mage.

"Now I must rearrange the pieces on the game board, reposition my assets and judge their credibility against your own."

"The game is the game."

The mage smiled. "Then we play another round." The mage opened his mouth to speak, but the blade master dropped something on the floor. It exploded into a cloud of smoke that filled the chamber for an instant. By the time it cleared, the mage stood in his antechamber alone. "So be it."

Casting a spell, fog rose from the stone floor, quickly engulfing the mage. Just as soon as the fog appeared, it dissipated, and the stone chamber in the dark castle at the top of the mountain sat empty and hollow.

There the castle remained quiet, waiting for another game.

Acknowledgements

Gray Matter Splatter probably involved more research than the past three Deckard novels combined. In the past I was able to rely on a lot of personal experience, do some brushing up on certain subjects, and make the plot work. In other cases, I was carrying out other investigations that fed into the plot. But for this book, I had to hit the books and ask a lot of friends for their help because of the simple fact that I have never been to the Arctic and have no experience in winter warfare.

I want to thank Dan and Matthew for their advice and guidance in tightening up the tactics and equipment featured in *Gray Matter Splatter*. I also want to thank my Ranger buddy, Isaiah Burkhart, who helped me select the right types of skis, ice axes, and other kit. Kevin Doherty's advice was also immensely valuable on Arctic and maritime matters. The great Chuck Rogers had some terrific advice for me in regards to the plot and pacing of the novel—no easy task for a book set in the high Arctic. I also owe a special thanks to Jussi for sending me a handful of Finnish Arctic warfare manuals and helping me translate parts of them.

Once again, Marc Lee came through with a bang-up amazing job on the cover artwork and design. Marc's talents go a long way to making each of these books something different and special, at least in my eyes. Thanks to Nate Granzow for his copy-editing skills, something I'm much in need of. This book would be a shell of what it is without his help.

Last, but certainly not least, I want to thank Benni for supporting my work as a writer, tolerating me chipping away at this book, even on weekends and so-called vacations.

Glossary

ACE: ammunition, casualties, equipment

ADM: Anti-personnel round for the 84mm Carl Gustav recoilless rifle. The round expels 1,100 flechettes via gas pressure when fired.

AGS30: Russian 30mm automatic grenade launcher

AIS: Automatic Identification System

AK: Kalashnikov

AK-103: An updated form of the AK-47 rifle that can be fitted with a variety of different optics

AK-47: Avtomat Kalashnikova-1947, following the standard Soviet weapons naming convention. Avtomat means the type of rifle: automatic. Kalashnikov comes from the last name of the inventor, Mikhail Kalashnikov, and the year, 1947, is when the rifle went into production. The AK-47 is the world's most ubiquitous battle rifle, having been used in virtually every conflict since the Cold War.

An-125: Large Russian-made cargo airplane

AO: area of operations

AT: anti-tank

BMEWS: the Ballistic Missile Early Warning System

C17: the C130's big brother, can carry more equipment and personnel

C27J: a smaller version of the C-130 transport aircraft

CANSOF: Canadian Special Operations Forces

CANSOFCOM: Canadian Special Operations Forces Command

CIA: Central Intelligence Agency

CIF: Commander's In-Extremis Force

CNO: computer network operations

CONUS: continental United States

CP: control point

D&D: Dungeons and Dragons

Derna Bridge: MARSOC's answer to Robin Sage, final cumulative exercise

DOD: Department of Defense

DOE: Department of Energy

DShK: Soviet-era 12.7mm machine gun

EENT: End of Evening Nautical Twilight

ETA: estimated time of arrival

FBI: Federal Bureau of Investigation

FSB: Russian intelligence service

FSK: Norwegian special operations unit

GPS: Global Positioning System

GRU: Russian military intelligence

GSG-9: German police anti-terrorism unit

HE: high explosive

HF: high frequency

IED: improvised explosive device

IRGC: Islamic Revolutionary Guard Corps, elite unit of Iran

ISA: Intelligence Support Activity

ISIS: Islamic State of Iraq and the Levant

ISR: intelligence, surveillance, reconnaissance

JDAM: Joint Direct Attack Munition

JSOC: Joint Special Operations Command

JTF2: Joint Task Force 2, Canadian special operations unit

JWICS: The Joint Worldwide Intelligence Communications System

KIA: killed in action

KSK: German Army special operations unit

LMV: Light Multi-role Vehicle

MARSOC: Marine Corps Special Operations Command

MBITR: Multiband Inter/Intra Team Radio

MIA: missing in action

Mk14: Six-shot 40mm grenade launcher

MMORPG: massive multiplayer online role-playing game

MRE: Meal Ready to Eat

MSS: Ministry of State Security, primary intelligence service of China

MTSC: Marine Technical Surveillance Course

NATO: North Atlantic Treaty Organization

NORTHCOM: Northern Command

NRO: National Reconnaissance Office

NSA: National Security Agency

NVG: night vision goggles

OD: olive drab

PKM: Russian light machine gun

PMC: private military company

PT: physical training

PvP: player versus player

PVS-14: night vision monocular

Quds Force: a covert action unit within Iran's Revolutionary Guard Corps

RPG: rocket-propelled grenade

SCOPE: JSOC think tank

SEAL: SEa, Air, and Land. U.S. naval commandos.

SEAL Team Six: The U.S. Navy's elite counterterrorism unit

SITREP: situation report

SLLS: stop, look, listen, smell

SMVIED: suicide merchant vessel improvised explosive device.

SOG: Swedish Special Operations Task Group

SPG-9: 73mm recoilless rifle

SSE: sensitive site exploitation

Task Force 45: Italian special operations task force in Afghanistan

UAV: unmanned aerial vehicle

UNS: universal night sight

VTC: video teleconference

XO: executive officer

Jack Murphy is an eight-year Army special operations veteran who served as a sniper and team leader in 3rd Ranger Battalion, and as a senior weapons sergeant on a military free fall team in 5th Special Forces Group. Having left the military in 2010, he graduated from Columbia with a BA in political science. Murphy is the author of *Reflexive Fire*, *Target Deck*, *Direct Action*, and numerous non-fiction articles about weapons, tactics, special operations, terrorism, and counterterrorism. He has appeared in documentaries, national television, and syndicated radio.

Follow Jack Murphy:

Website: Reflexivefire.com
Twitter: @JackMurphyRGR
Instagram: JackMcMurph
Facebook: facebook.com/JackMurphyAuthor

Join the author and fellow readers at the Samruk International Facebook group for exclusive first looks at future works and live question and answer sessions: https://www.facebook.com/groups/SamrukInternational/

Made in the USA
Lexington, KY
26 August 2016